D0959515

THE LEGEND OF GRIMM'S WOODS

MANURO
GOROBEI

QUIRK BOOKS
PHILADELPHIA

Originally published in France as Hocus & Pocus:
L'épreuve des fabulins in 2016 by Makaka Éditions.

Story by Manuro
Drawings by Gorobei

First published in the United States
in 2018 by Quirk Productions, Inc.

Library of Congress Cataloging
in Publication Number: 2018933925

ISBN: 978-1-68369-057-3

Printed in China
Translated by Mélanie Strang-Hardy
Typeset in Sketchnote
Cover design by Andie Reid
Production management by John J. McGurk

Quirk Books
215 Church Street
Philadelphia, PA 19106
quirkbooks.com

10 9 8 7 6 5 4 3 2 1

STOP!
THIS ISN'T A REGULAR COMIC BOOK!

In this comic book, you don't read straight through from first page to last. Instead, you'll begin at the beginning, and soon be off on a quest where you choose which panel to read next. On your adventure, you will solve puzzles, encounter friends and foes, and collect magical objects—because YOU are the main character!

It's easy to get the hang of once you see it in action. Turn the page for an example of how it works!

POCUS

HOCUS

HOW TO PLAY COMIC QUESTS

1 First, pick where you want to go in the panel——doors, paths, signs, and objects can all have numbers.

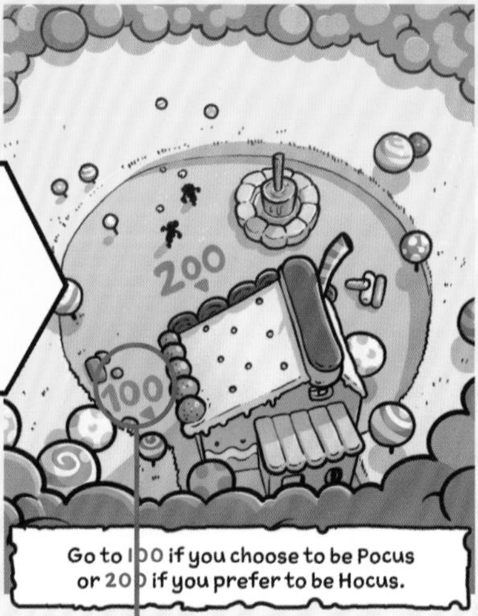
200
100
Go to 100 if you choose to be Pocus or 200 if you prefer to be Hocus.

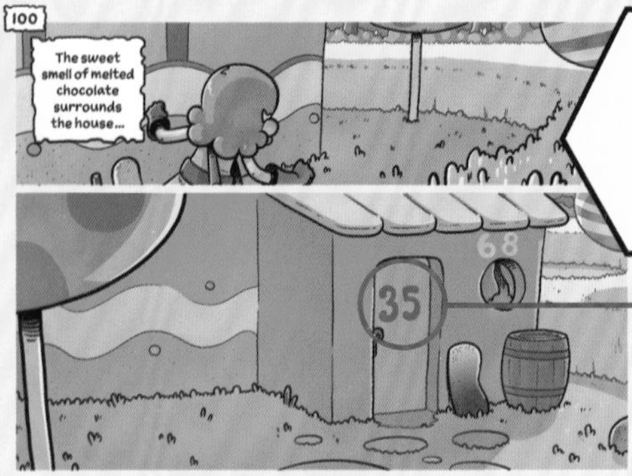
100
The sweet smell of melted chocolate surrounds the house...
68
35

2 Flip to the panel with the matching number.

3 Continue reading from there, making more choices as you go to complete the quest!

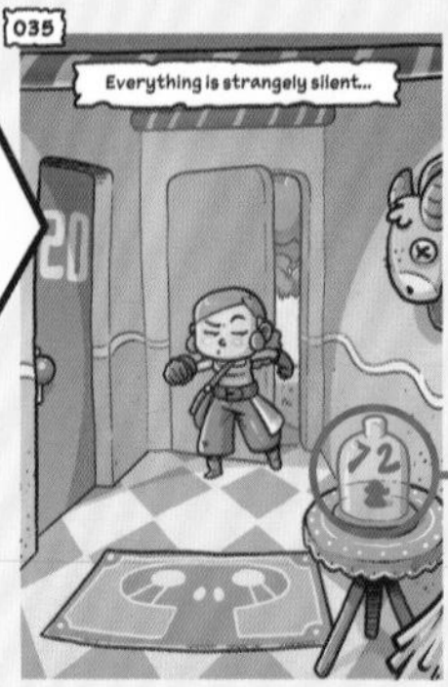
035
Everything is strangely silent...
20
72

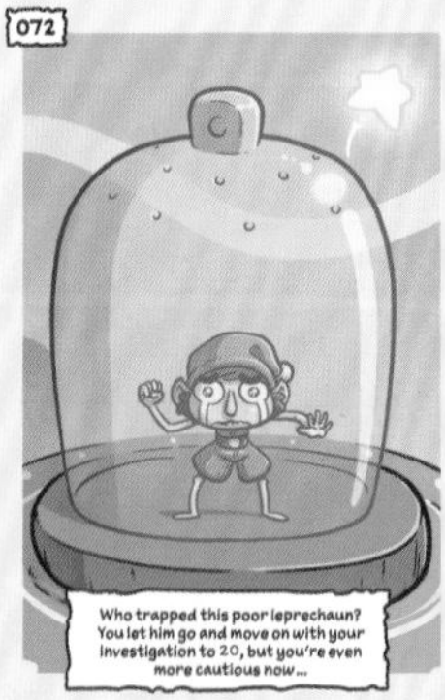
072
Who trapped this poor leprechaun? You let him go and move on with your investigation to 20, but you're even more cautious now...

HOW TO PLAY COMIC QUESTS

As you go, use the handy Quest Tracker sheets on the next few pages to log your progress. Use a pencil so you can erase. (You can also use a notebook and pencil, or download extra sheets at comicquests.com).

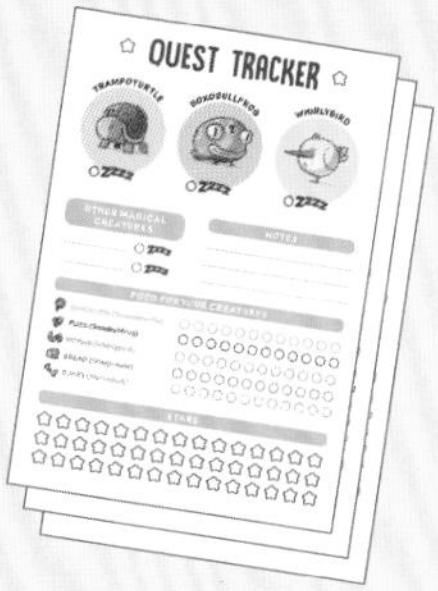
QUEST TRACKER

Here are some of the things to look out for as you go!

THE MAGICAL CREATURES

Choose your magical creature by checking the corresponding box on the Quest Tracker.

AWAKE OR ASLEEP?

- At the beginning of your adventure, your creature is awake.
- Each time you call upon it, it will help you, but then it will fall asleep from exhaustion. To remember when your creature is asleep, check the **Zzzz** box on your Quest Tracker.
- If your creature is sleeping and you need its help, you will have to feed it. (See "Food for Your Creatures," below.) Once your creature has eaten, it will wake up. Erase the checkmark in the **Zzzz** box on your Quest Tracker to remember that it's awake.

FOOD FOR YOUR CREATURES

- At the beginning of your trip, you will need to build up your reserves of food. Each creature eats something different. For example, if you have Trampoturtle, you will need dandelions. Whirlybird eats worms. Look on your Quest Tracker to see which food your creature eats.
- Look closely in each drawing to find your creature's food. When you find it, check a box beside that food on your Quest Tracker.
- If your creature needs energy to wake up, feed it **two units** of its food and uncheck two boxes on your Quest Tracker. You just used up those units.

THE STARS

During your trip, you will often see stars. These appear when you do a good deed or when you are very wise. Pick them up along the way and check the right boxes on your Quest Tracker to show off to your teachers when you get home.

PUZZLE-SOLVING SYMBOLS

When you solve a puzzle, you will see a small symbol next to your current panel's number. If you answer correctly, you'll go to a panel that shows the same symbol. If it does not match or there is no symbol, it means you answered incorrectly. Go back to the puzzle and try again.

HOW TO BEGIN

Start the adventure at page number 1, but you won't read the pages in order. You will follow the instructions and turn to the page indicated by the choices you make.

- Either the narrator will tell you where to go
- Or you will be able to pick a number hidden in the picture. Look closely! Sometimes the numbers are small and well hidden.

GOOD LUCK! LET THE ADVENTURE BEGIN . . .

QUEST TRACKER

TRAMPOTURTLE

○ **ZZZZ**

BOXOBULLFROG

○ **ZZZZ**

WHIRLYBIRD

○ **ZZZZ**

OTHER MAGICAL CREATURES

.... ○ **ZZZZ**

.... ○ **ZZZZ**

NOTES

....

....

....

FOOD FOR YOUR CREATURES

 DANDELION (Trampoturtle) ○ ○ ○ ○ ○ ○ ○ ○ ○ ○ ○ ○

 FLIES (Boxobullfrog)

 WORMS (Whirlybird)

 BREAD (Gluey-Ewie) ○ ○ ○ ○ ○ ○ ○ ○ ○ ○ ○ ○

BONES (Wolfoclock) ○ ○ ○ ○ ○ ○ ○ ○ ○ ○ ○ ○

STARS

☆ ☆ ☆ ☆ ☆ ☆ ☆ ☆ ☆ ☆ ☆ ☆ ☆ ☆
☆ ☆ ☆ ☆ ☆ ☆ ☆ ☆ ☆ ☆ ☆ ☆ ☆ ☆
☆ ☆ ☆ ☆ ☆ ☆ ☆ ☆ ☆ ☆ ☆ ☆ ☆ ☆

QUEST TRACKER

TRAMPOTURTLE

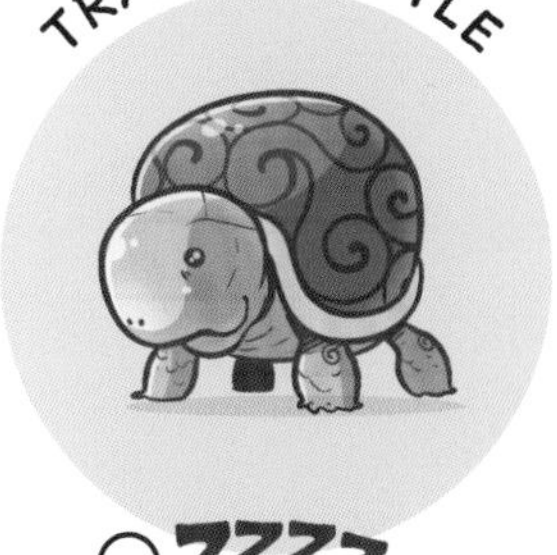

○ Zzzz

BOXOBULLFROG

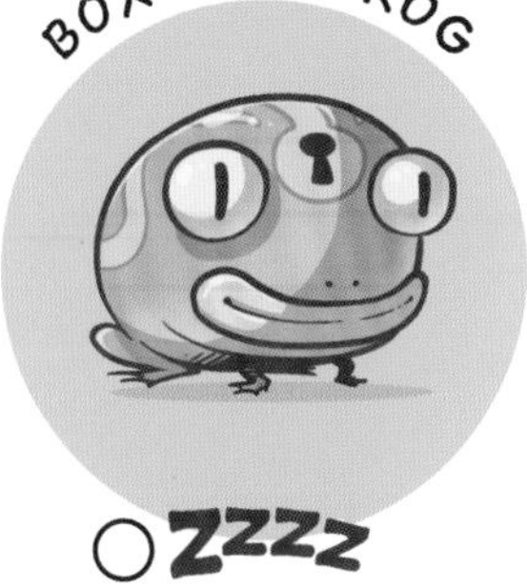

○ Zzzz

WHIRLYBIRD

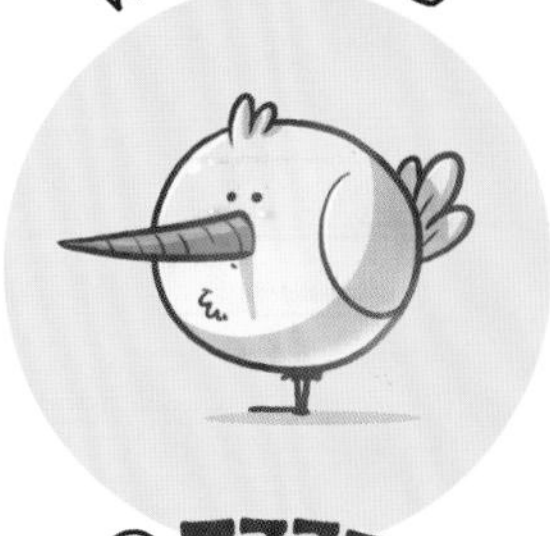

○ Zzzz

OTHER MAGICAL CREATURES

.... ○ Zzzz

.... ○ Zzzz

NOTES

....

....

....

FOOD FOR YOUR CREATURES

- DANDELION (Trampoturtle)
- FLIES (Boxobullfrog)
- WORMS (Whirlybird)
- BREAD (Gluey-Ewie)
- BONES (Wolfoclock)

STARS

QUEST TRACKER

TRAMPOTURTLE

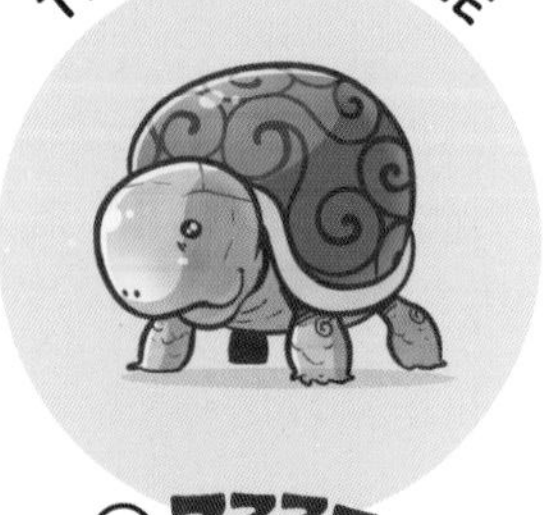

○ ZZZZ

BOXOBULLFROG

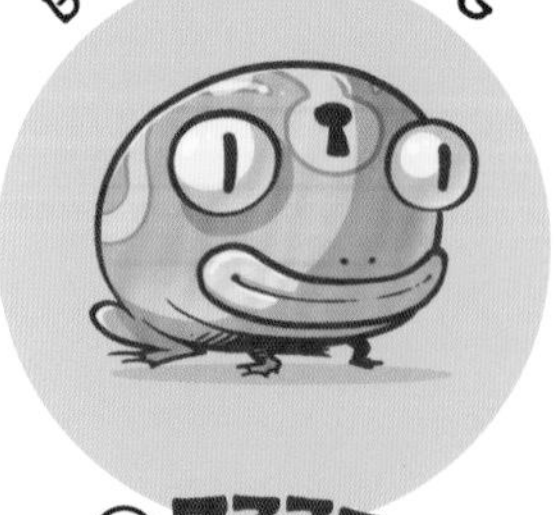

○ ZZZZ

WHIRLYBIRD

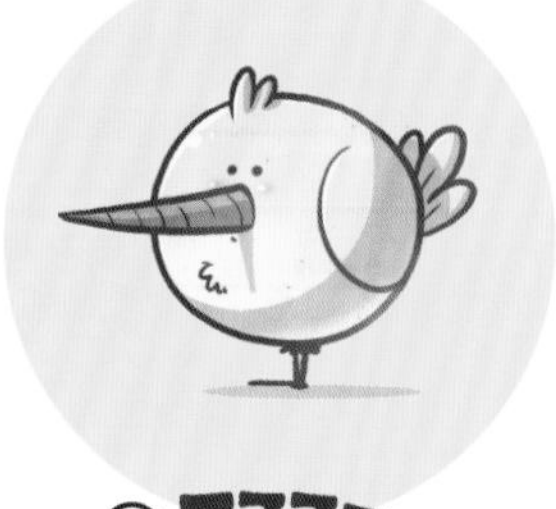

○ ZZZZ

OTHER MAGICAL CREATURES

.... ○ ZZZZ

.... ○ ZZZZ

NOTES

....

....

....

FOOD FOR YOUR CREATURES

DANDELION (Trampoturtle) ○ ○ ○ ○ ○ ○ ○ ○ ○ ○ ○ ○

FLIES (Boxobullfrog) ○ ○ ○ ○ ○ ○ ○ ○ ○ ○ ○ ○

WORMS (Whirlybird) ○ ○ ○ ○ ○ ○ ○ ○ ○ ○ ○ ○

BREAD (Gluey-Ewie) ○ ○ ○ ○ ○ ○ ○ ○ ○ ○ ○ ○

BONES (Wolfoclock) ○ ○ ○ ○ ○ ○ ○ ○ ○ ○ ○ ○

STARS

⭐ QUEST TRACKER ⭐

TRAMPOTURTLE

◯ ZZZZ

BOXOBULLFROG

◯ ZZZZ

WHIRLYBIRD

◯ ZZZZ

OTHER MAGICAL CREATURES

.... ◯ ZZZZ

.... ◯ ZZZZ

NOTES

....
....
....
....

FOOD FOR YOUR CREATURES

 DANDELION (Trampoturtle) ◯◯◯◯◯◯◯◯◯◯◯◯

 FLIES (Boxobullfrog) ◯◯◯◯◯◯◯◯◯◯◯◯◯

 WORMS (Whirlybird) ◯◯◯◯◯◯◯◯◯◯◯◯

 BREAD (Gluey-Ewie) ◯◯◯◯◯◯◯◯◯◯◯◯◯

 BONES (Wolfoclock) ◯◯◯◯◯◯◯◯◯◯◯◯

STARS

☆☆☆☆☆☆☆☆☆☆☆☆☆☆
☆☆☆☆☆☆☆☆☆☆☆☆☆☆
☆☆☆☆☆☆☆☆☆☆☆☆☆☆

QUEST TRACKER

TRAMPOTURTLE

◯ ZZZZ

BOXOBULLFROG

◯ ZZZZ

WHIRLYBIRD

◯ ZZZZ

OTHER MAGICAL CREATURES

.... ◯ ZZZZ

.... ◯ ZZZZ

NOTES

....

....

....

FOOD FOR YOUR CREATURES

 DANDELION (Trampoturtle)   ◯◯◯◯◯◯◯◯◯◯◯◯

 FLIES (Boxobullfrog)   ◯◯◯◯◯◯◯◯◯◯◯◯

 WORMS (Whirlybird)   ◯◯◯◯◯◯◯◯◯◯◯◯

 BREAD (Gluey-Ewie)   ◯◯◯◯◯◯◯◯◯◯◯◯

 BONES (Wolfoclock)   ◯◯◯◯◯◯◯◯◯◯◯◯

STARS

☆☆☆☆☆☆☆☆☆☆☆☆☆☆
☆☆☆☆☆☆☆☆☆☆☆☆☆☆
☆☆☆☆☆☆☆☆☆☆☆☆☆☆

QUEST TRACKER

TRAMPOTURTLE

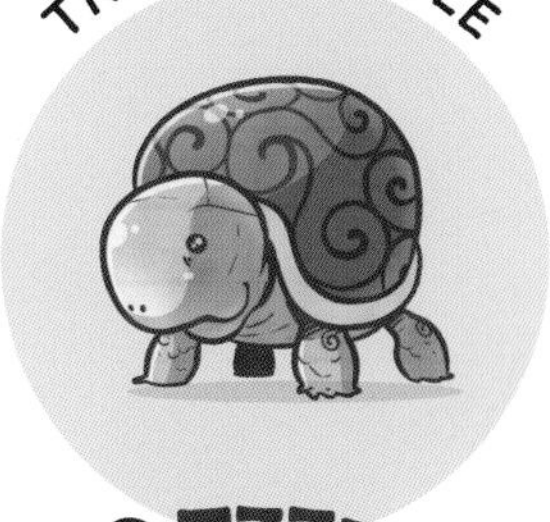

○ ZZZZ

BOXOBULLFROG

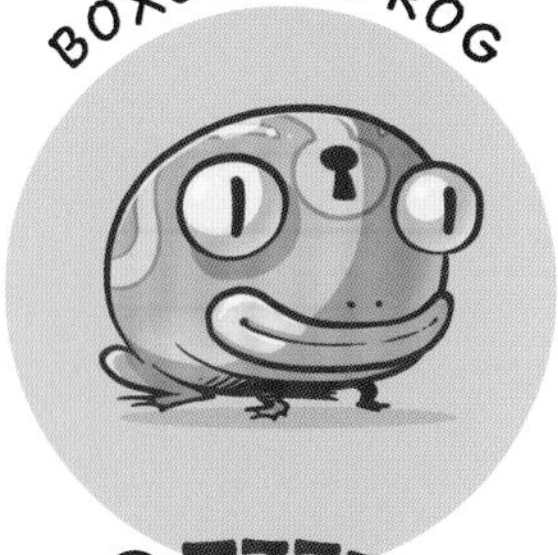

○ ZZZZ

WHIRLYBIRD

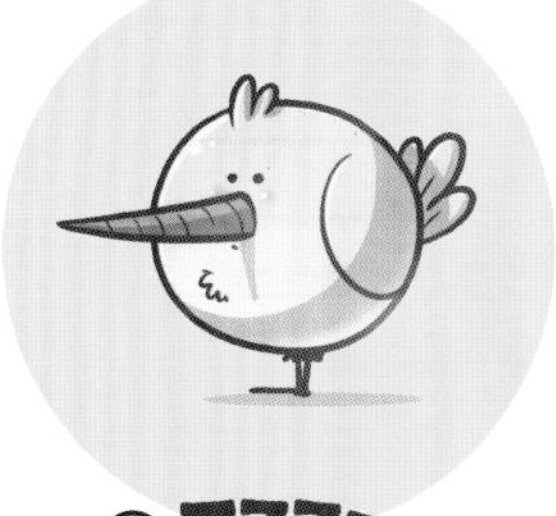

○ ZZZZ

OTHER MAGICAL CREATURES

.... ○ ZZZZ

.... ○ ZZZZ

NOTES

....

....

....

FOOD FOR YOUR CREATURES

DANDELION (Trampoturtle)	○ ○ ○ ○ ○ ○ ○ ○ ○ ○ ○ ○
FLIES (Boxobullfrog)	○ ○ ○ ○ ○ ○ ○ ○ ○ ○ ○ ○
WORMS (Whirlybird)	○ ○ ○ ○ ○ ○ ○ ○ ○ ○ ○ ○
BREAD (Gluey-Ewie)	○ ○ ○ ○ ○ ○ ○ ○ ○ ○ ○ ○
BONES (Wolfoclock)	○ ○ ○ ○ ○ ○ ○ ○ ○ ○ ○ ○

STARS

☆☆☆☆☆☆☆☆☆☆☆☆☆☆☆

☆☆☆☆☆☆☆☆☆☆☆☆☆☆☆

☆☆☆☆☆☆☆☆☆☆☆☆☆☆☆

BEGIN YOUR QUEST!

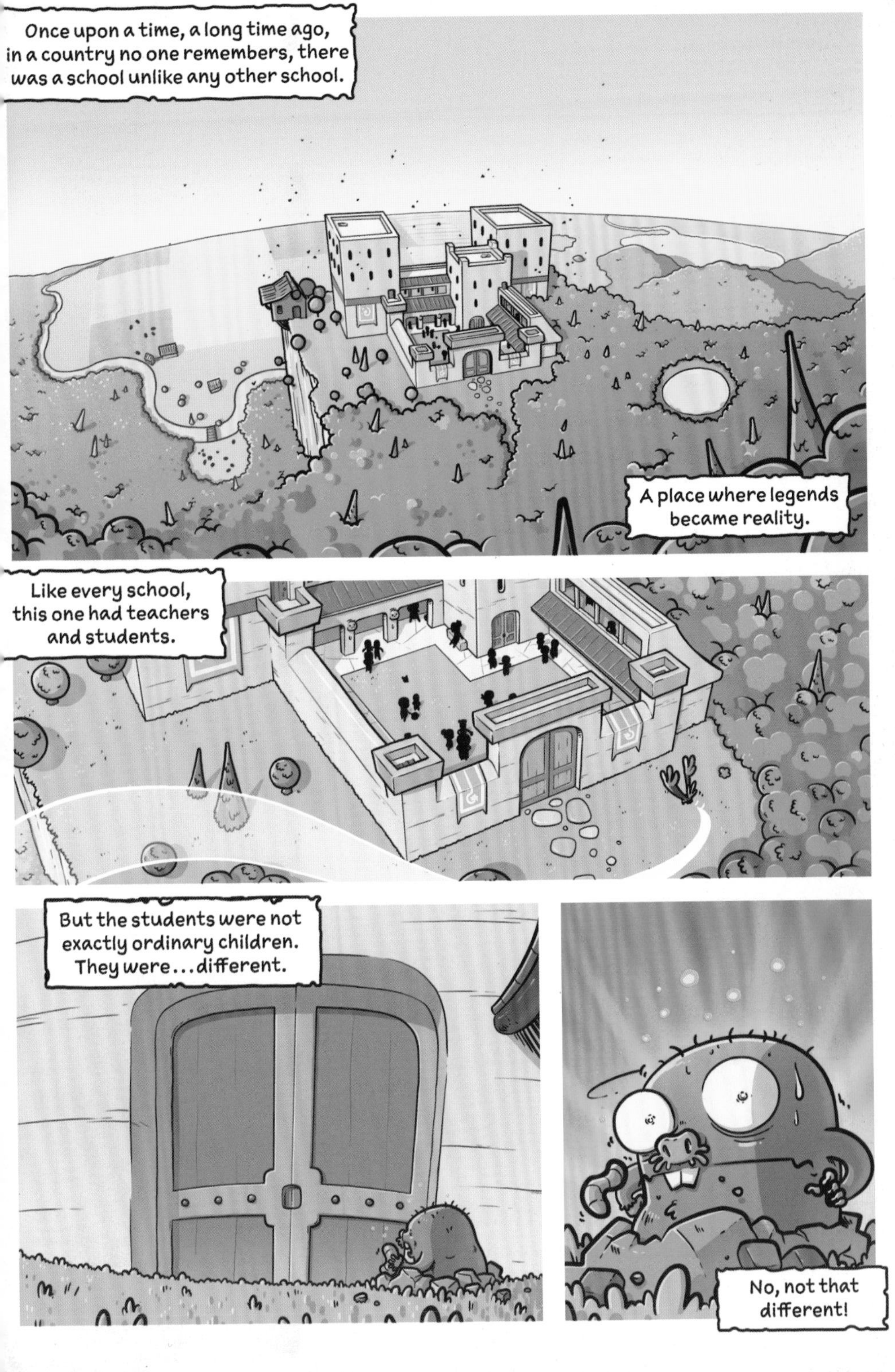
Once upon a time, a long time ago, in a country no one remembers, there was a school unlike any other school.
A place where legends became reality.
Like every school, this one had teachers and students.
But the students were not exactly ordinary children. They were... different.
No, not that different!

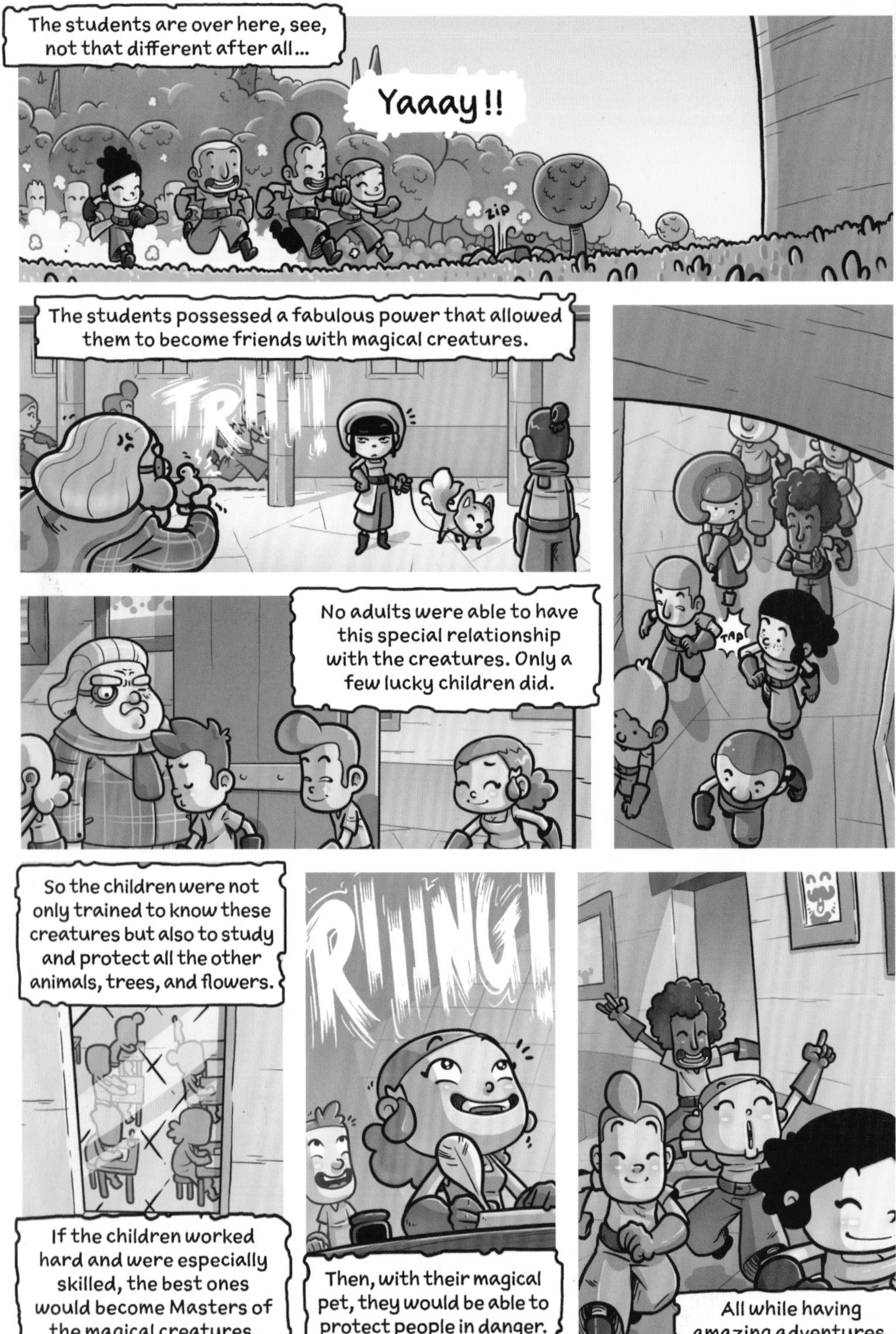
The students are over here, see, not that different after all...
Yaaay!!
ZIP
The students possessed a fabulous power that allowed them to become friends with magical creatures.
TRIIII
No adults were able to have this special relationship with the creatures. Only a few lucky children did.
TAP
So the children were not only trained to know these creatures but also to study and protect all the other animals, trees, and flowers.
If the children worked hard and were especially skilled, the best ones would become Masters of the magical creatures.
RIIING!
Then, with their magical pet, they would be able to protect people in danger.
All while having amazing adventures.

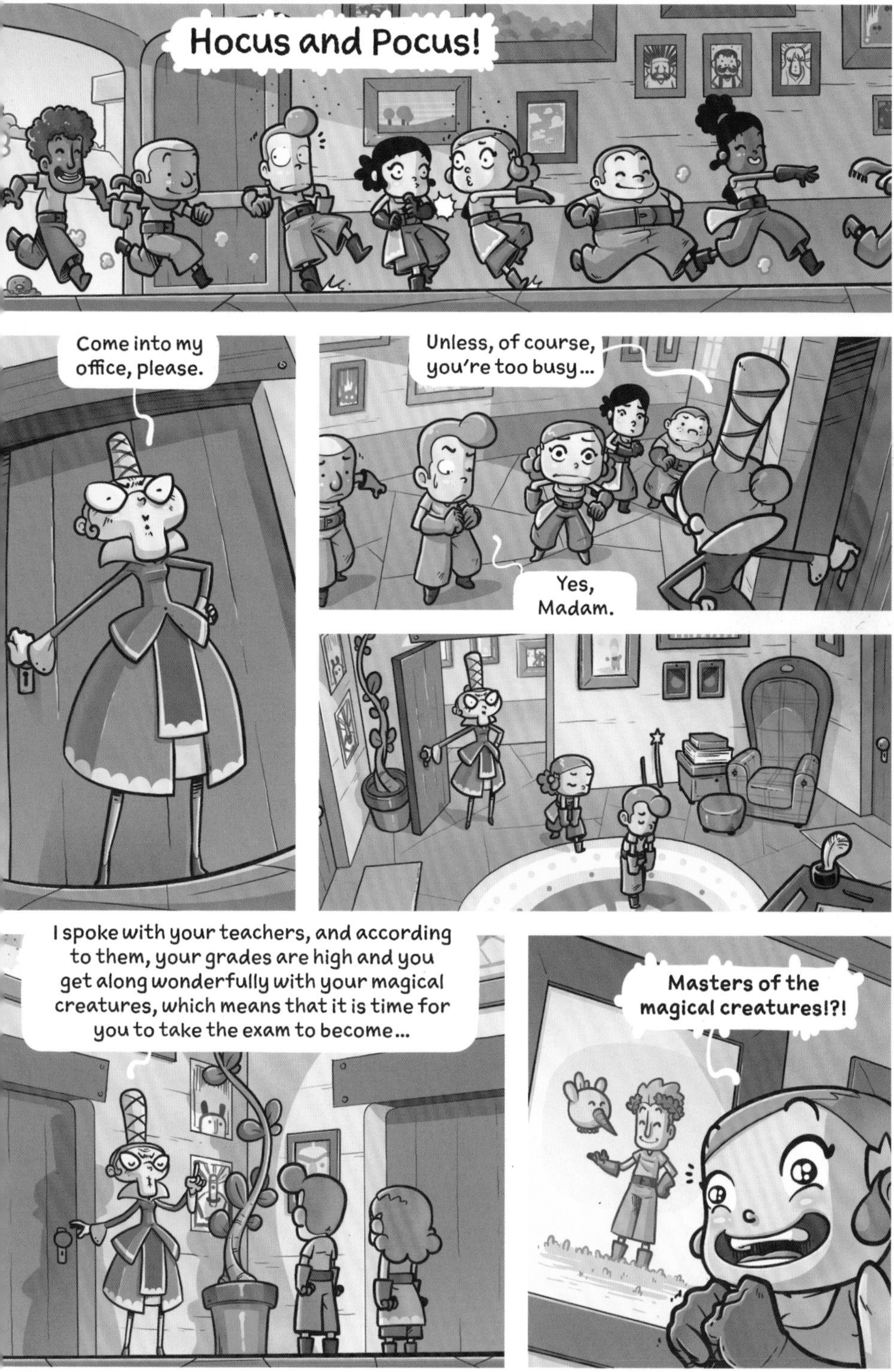
Hocus and Pocus!
Come into my office, please.
Unless, of course, you're too busy...
Yes, Madam.
I spoke with your teachers, and according to them, your grades are high and you get along wonderfully with your magical creatures, which means that it is time for you to take the exam to become...
Masters of the magical creatures!?!

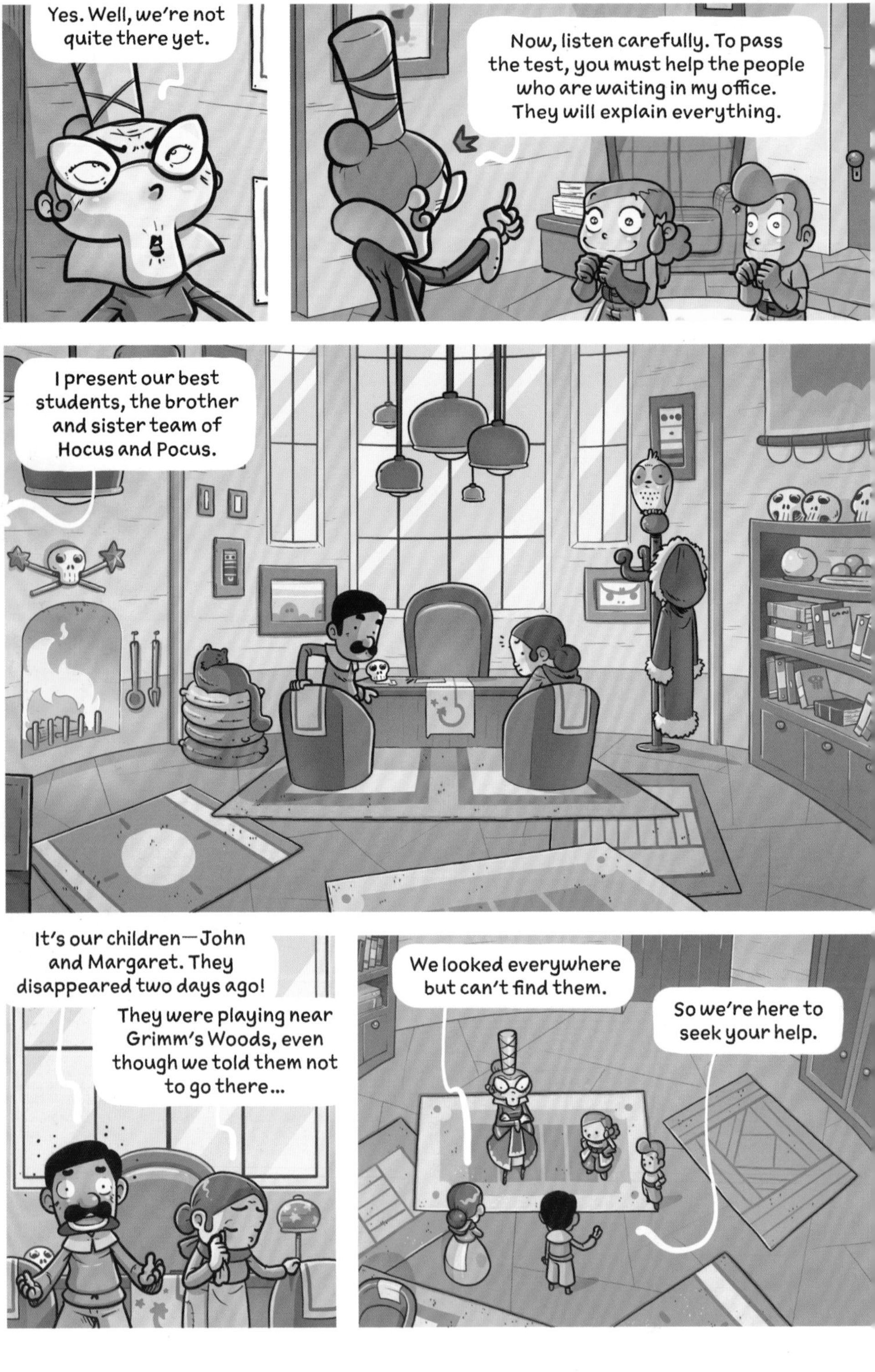
Yes. Well, we're not quite there yet.
Now, listen carefully. To pass the test, you must help the people who are waiting in my office. They will explain everything.
I present our best students, the brother and sister team of Hocus and Pocus.
It's our children—John and Margaret. They disappeared two days ago!
They were playing near Grimm's Woods, even though we told them not to go there...
We looked everywhere but can't find them.
So we're here to seek your help.

You were wise to come to us. Rest assured, I am putting this rescue mission in very good hands.

Don't worry, sir. The magical creatures are the best trackers in the world. They will find your children in a flash!

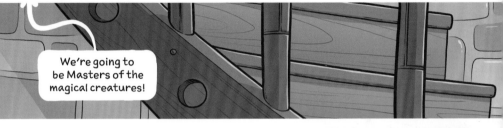

We're going to be Masters of the magical creatures!

I hope the kids are okay. We should hurry.

Don't worry. Margaret's mother gave me her doll. Her scent will lead our creatures straight to her.

Let's just hope that Baldar fed them recently. Otherwise they'll be asleep.

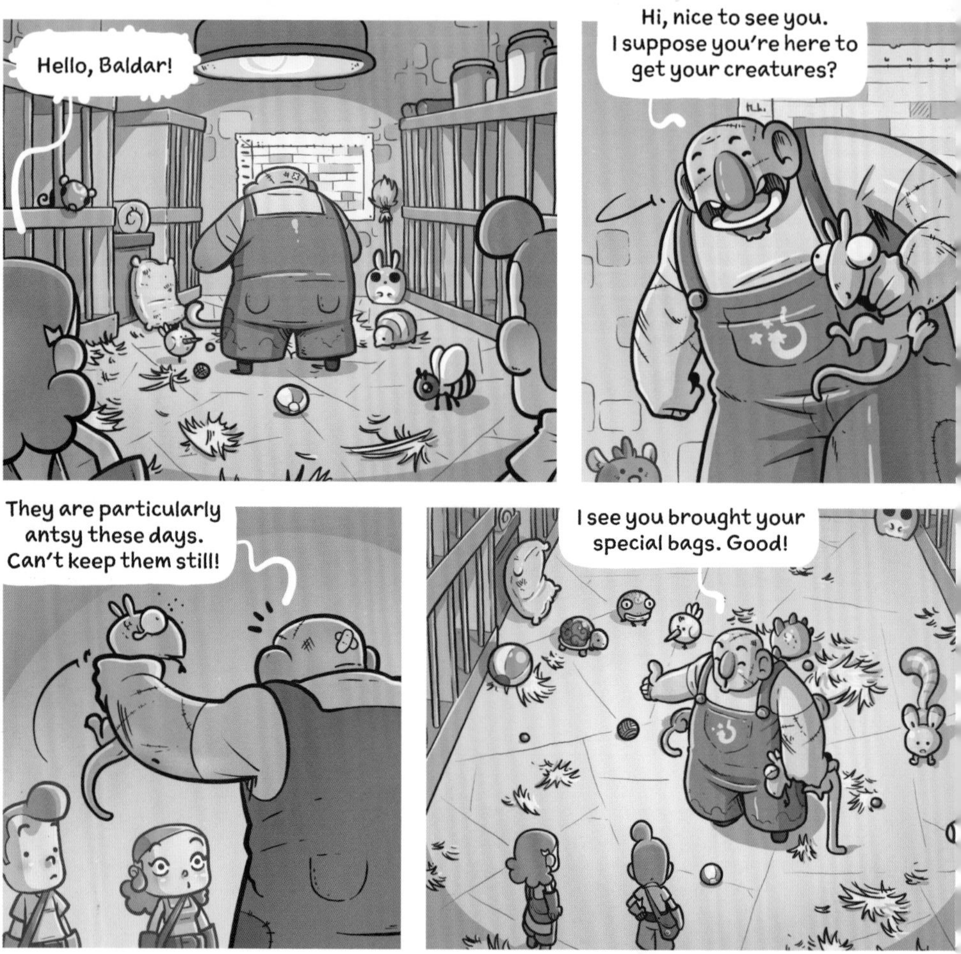
Hello, Baldar!
Hi, nice to see you. I suppose you're here to get your creatures?
They are particularly antsy these days. Can't keep them still!
I see you brought your special bags. Good!

Students usually carry their magical companions in a special pouch. If they didn't, the creatures would quickly tire and fall asleep just when their powers are needed! Now it's time to choose your own magical creature. Which one will it be:

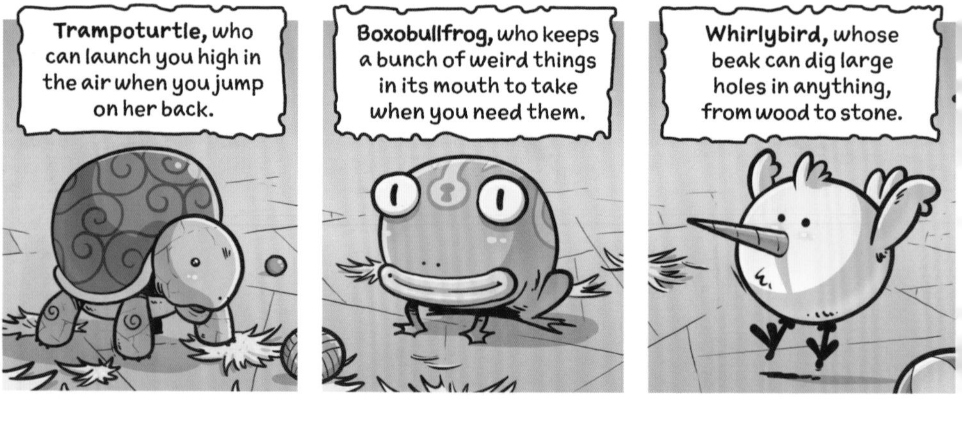
Trampoturtle, who can launch you high in the air when you jump on her back.
Boxobullfrog, who keeps a bunch of weird things in its mouth to take when you need them.
Whirlybird, whose beak can dig large holes in anything, from wood to stone.

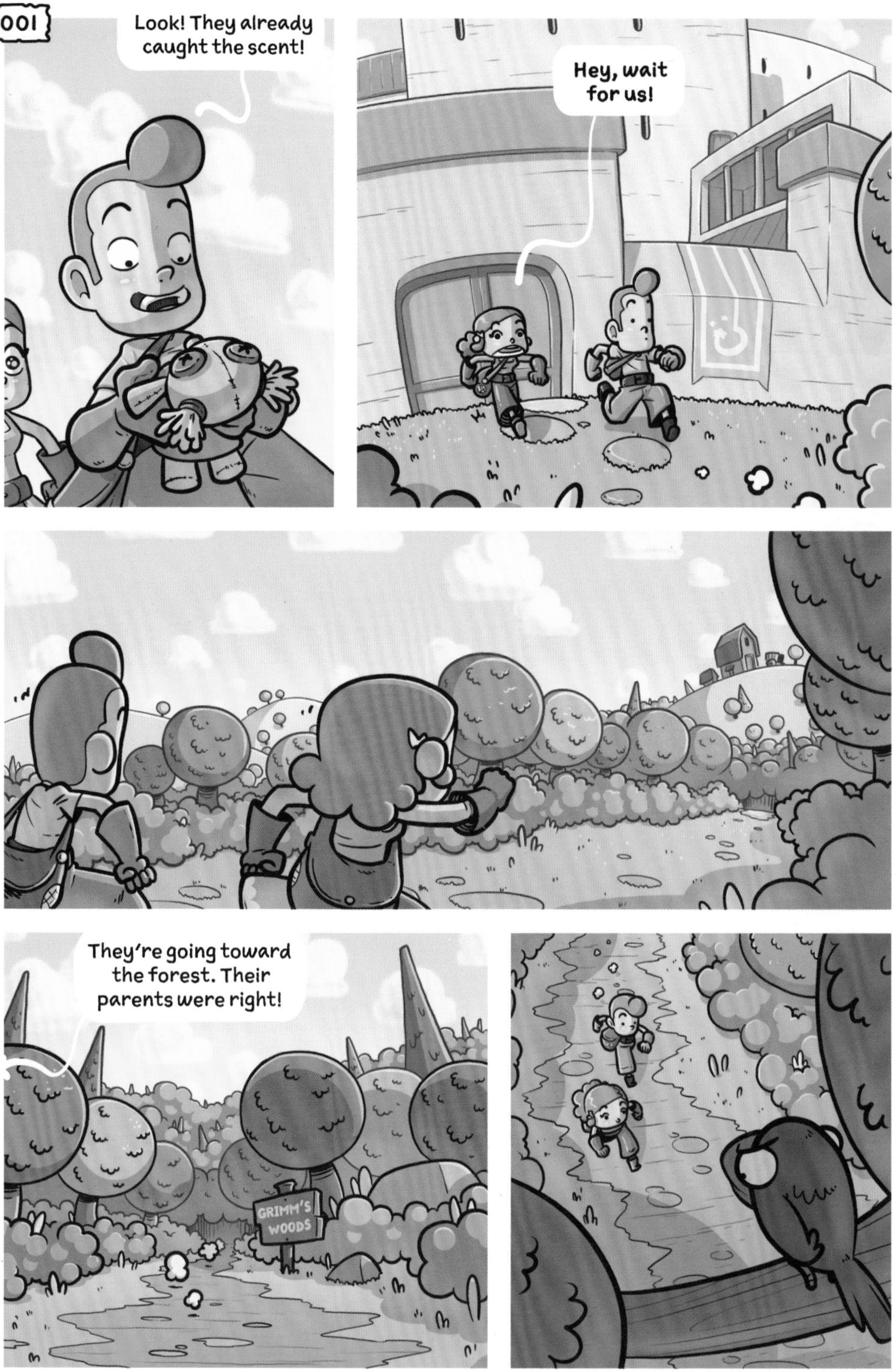
Look! They already caught the scent!
Hey, wait for us!
They're going toward the forest. Their parents were right!
GRIMM'S WOODS

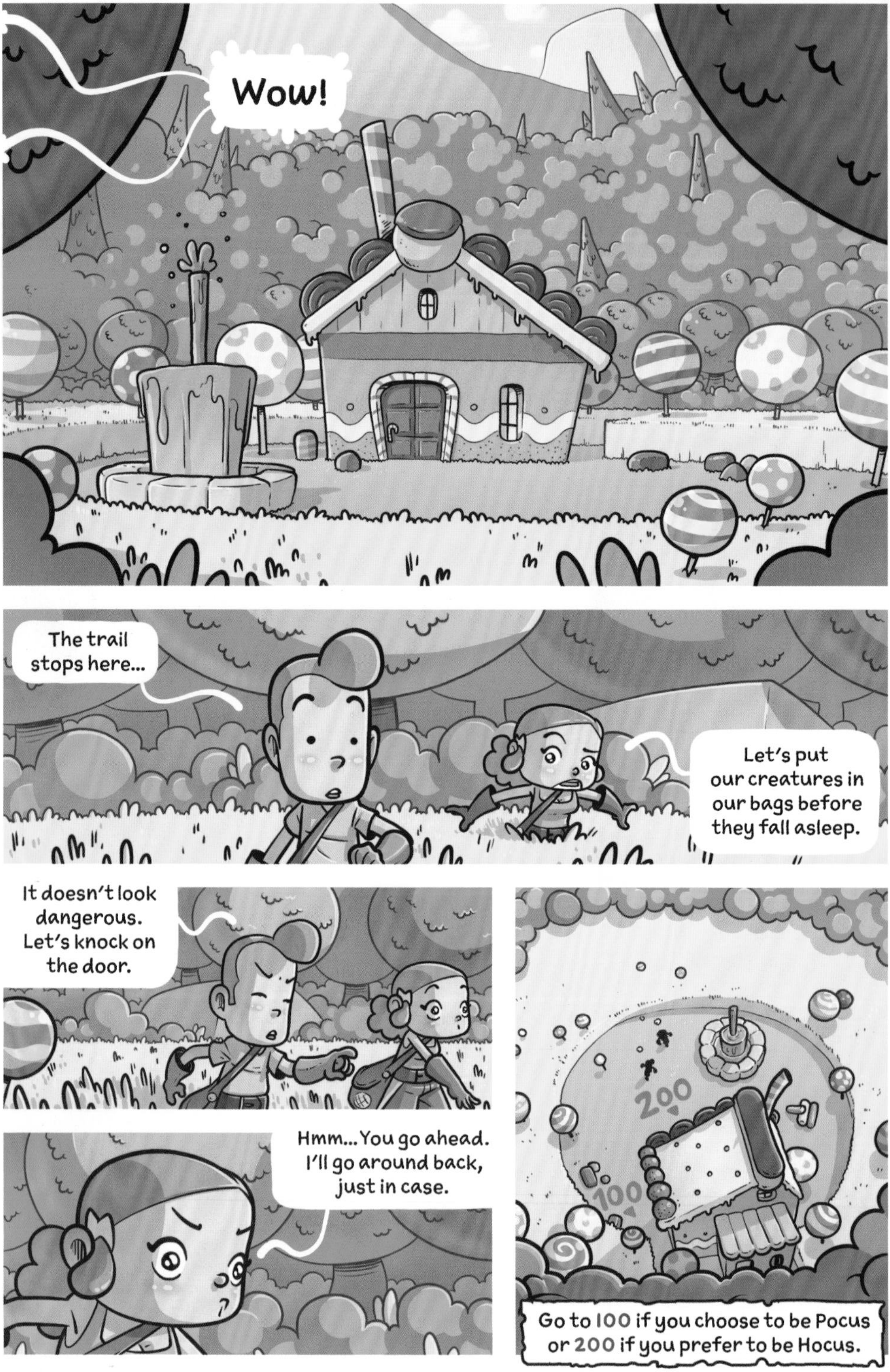
Wow!
The trail stops here...
Let's put our creatures in our bags before they fall asleep.
It doesn't look dangerous. Let's knock on the door.
Hmm... You go ahead. I'll go around back, just in case.
200
100
Go to 100 if you choose to be Pocus or 200 if you prefer to be Hocus.

002

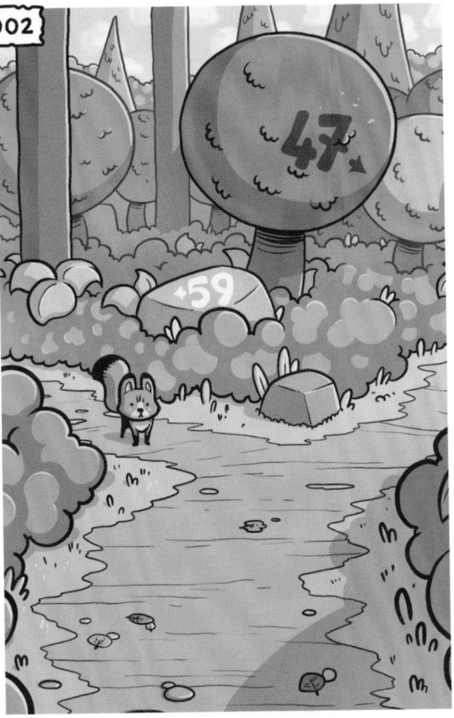
47
+59

003

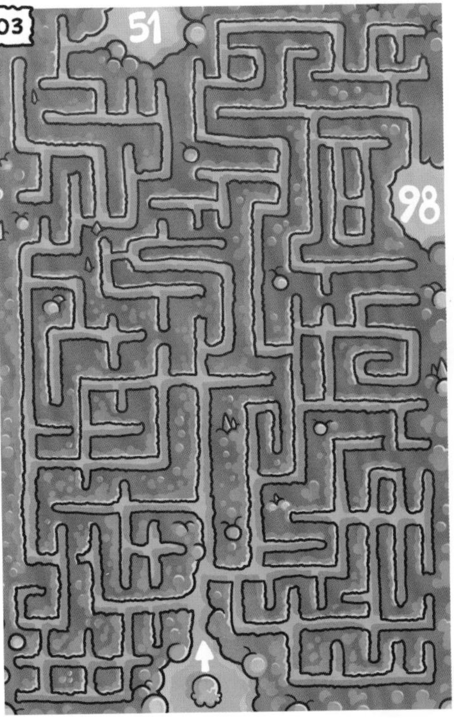
51
98

004

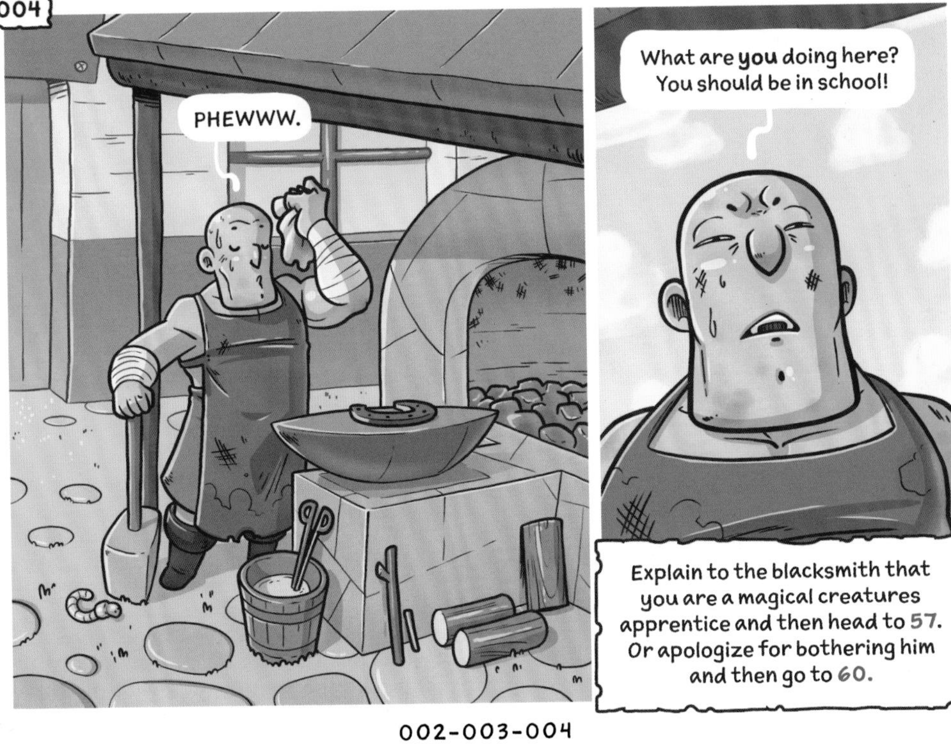
PHEWWW.
What are you doing here? You should be in school!
Explain to the blacksmith that you are a magical creatures apprentice and then head to 57. Or apologize for bothering him and then go to 60.

005

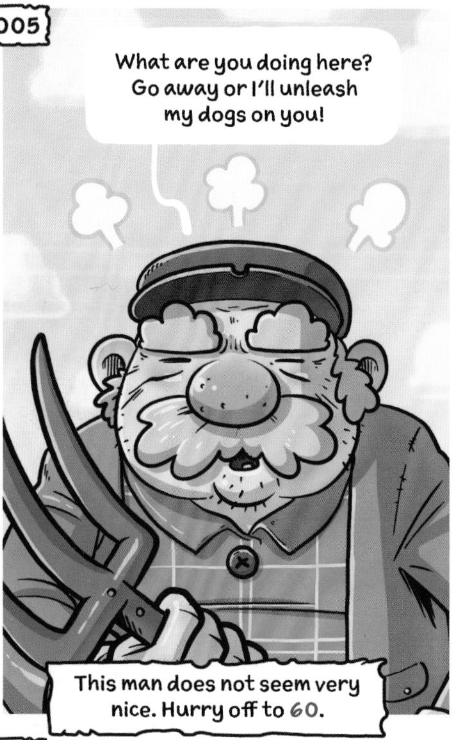
What are you doing here? Go away or I'll unleash my dogs on you!
This man does not seem very nice. Hurry off to 60.

006

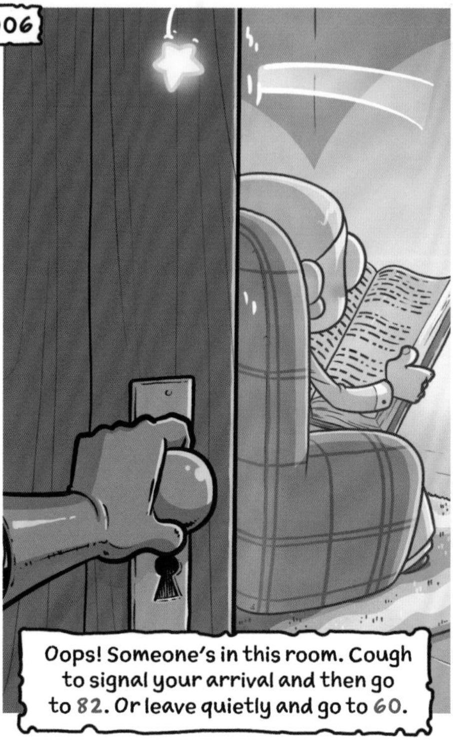
Oops! Someone's in this room. Cough to signal your arrival and then go to 82. Or leave quietly and go to 60.

007

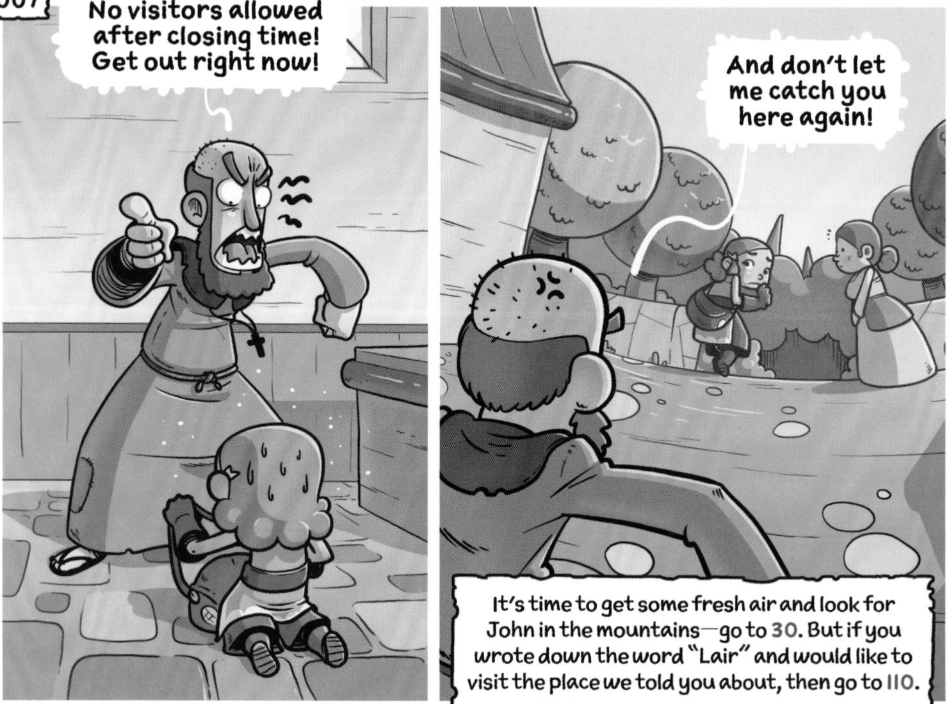
No visitors allowed after closing time! Get out right now!
And don't let me catch you here again!
It's time to get some fresh air and look for John in the mountains—go to 30. But if you wrote down the word "Lair" and would like to visit the place we told you about, then go to 110.

008

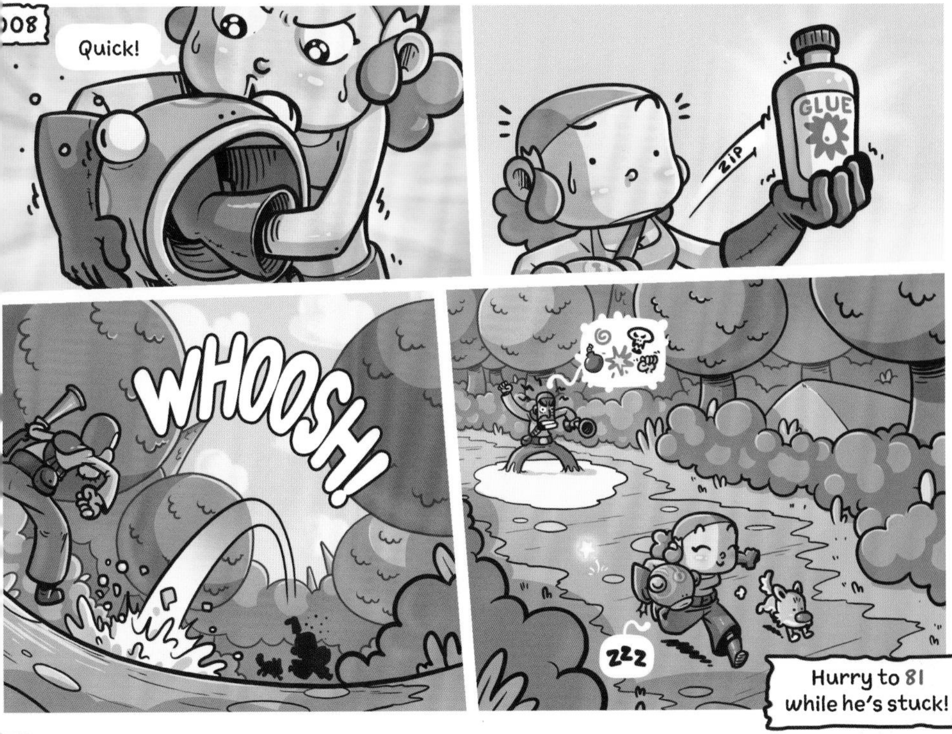
Quick!
GLUE
ZIP
WHOOSH!
ZZZ
Hurry to 81 while he's stuck!

009

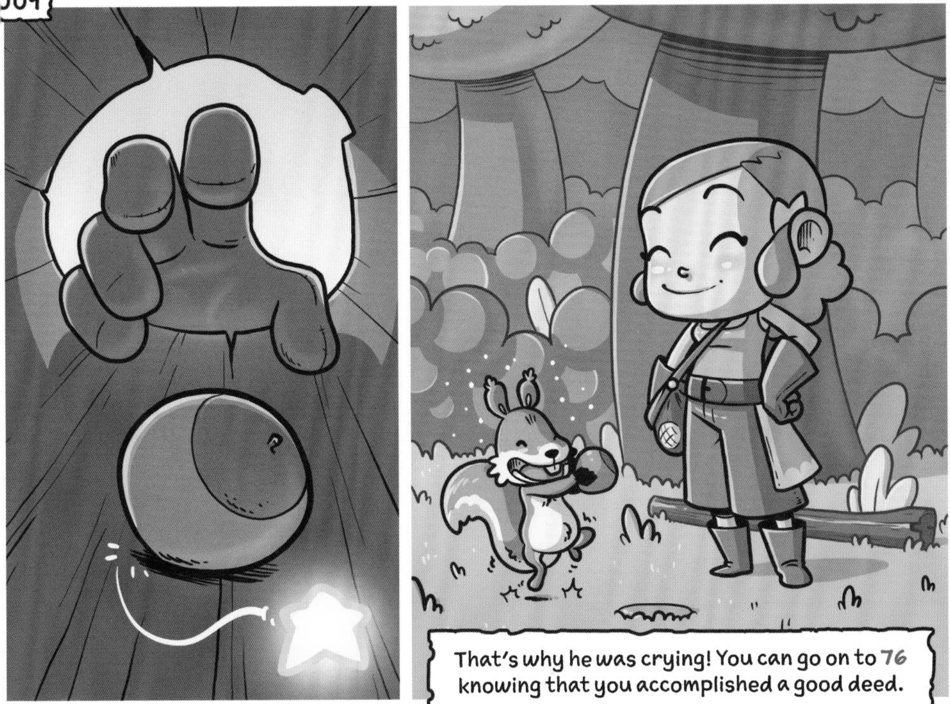
That's why he was crying! You can go on to 76 knowing that you accomplished a good deed.

010

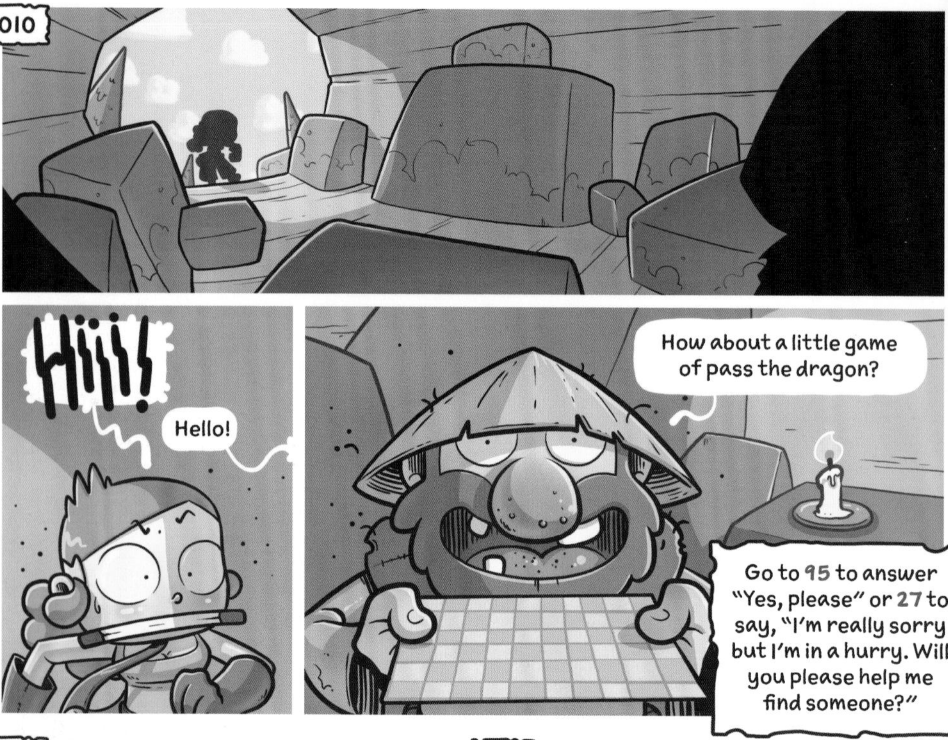

Hello!
How about a little game of pass the dragon?
Go to 95 to answer "Yes, please" or 27 to say, "I'm really sorry but I'm in a hurry. Will you please help me find someone?"

011

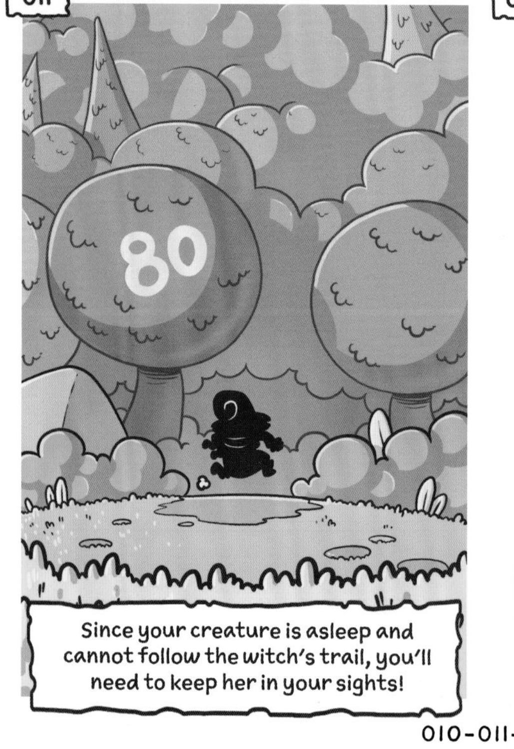

80
Since your creature is asleep and cannot follow the witch's trail, you'll need to keep her in your sights!

012

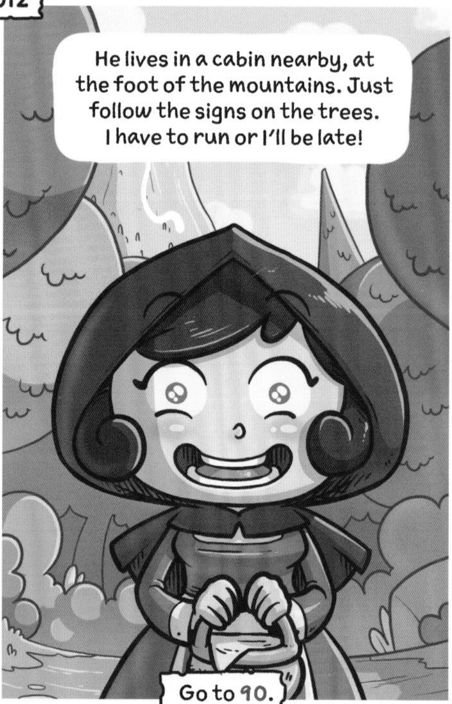

He lives in a cabin nearby, at the foot of the mountains. Just follow the signs on the trees. I have to run or I'll be late!
Go to 90.

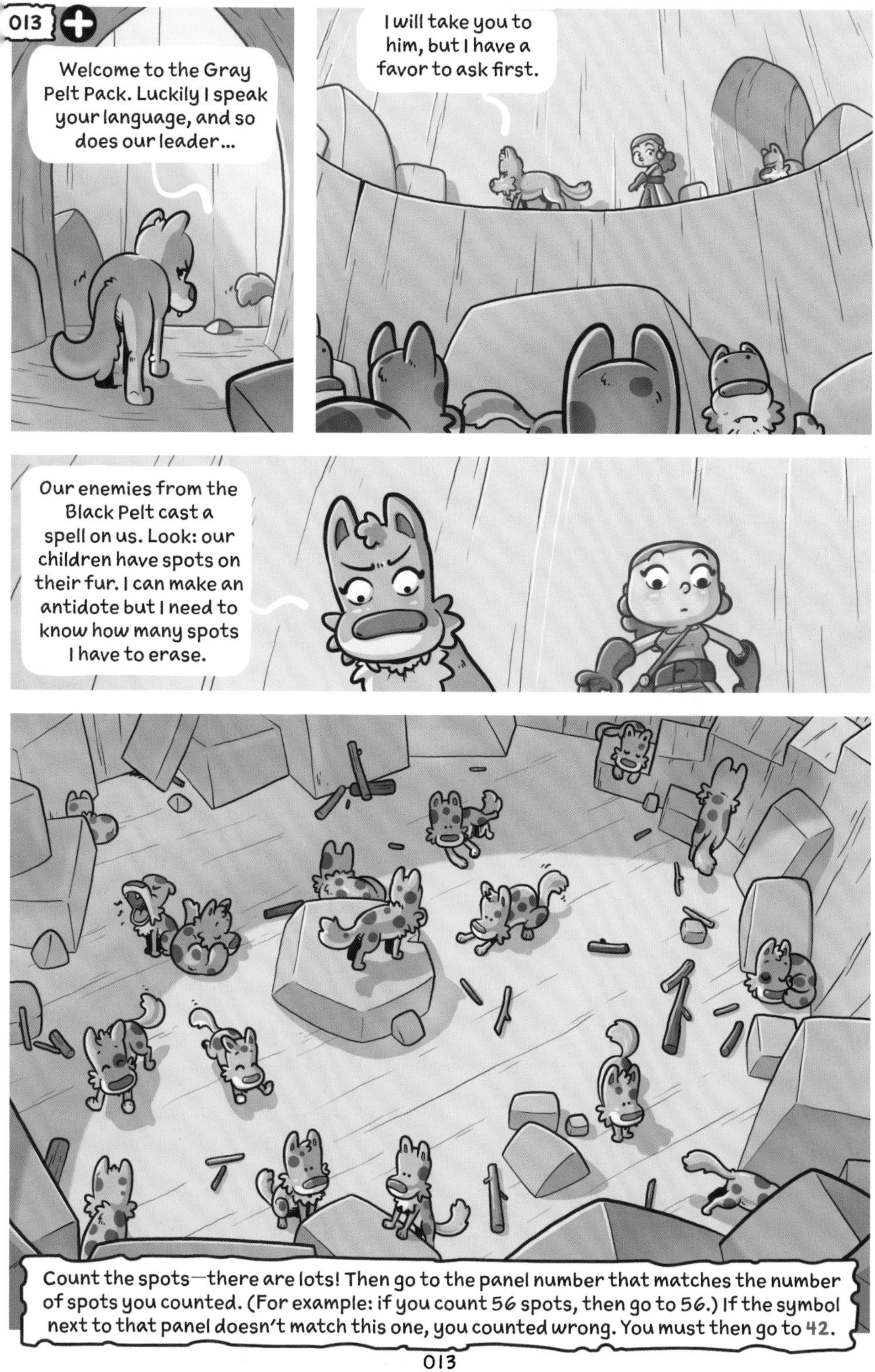
013
Welcome to the Gray Pelt Pack. Luckily I speak your language, and so does our leader...
I will take you to him, but I have a favor to ask first.
Our enemies from the Black Pelt cast a spell on us. Look: our children have spots on their fur. I can make an antidote but I need to know how many spots I have to erase.
Count the spots—there are lots! Then go to the panel number that matches the number of spots you counted. (For example: if you count 56 spots, then go to 56.) If the symbol next to that panel doesn't match this one, you counted wrong. You must then go to 42.

014

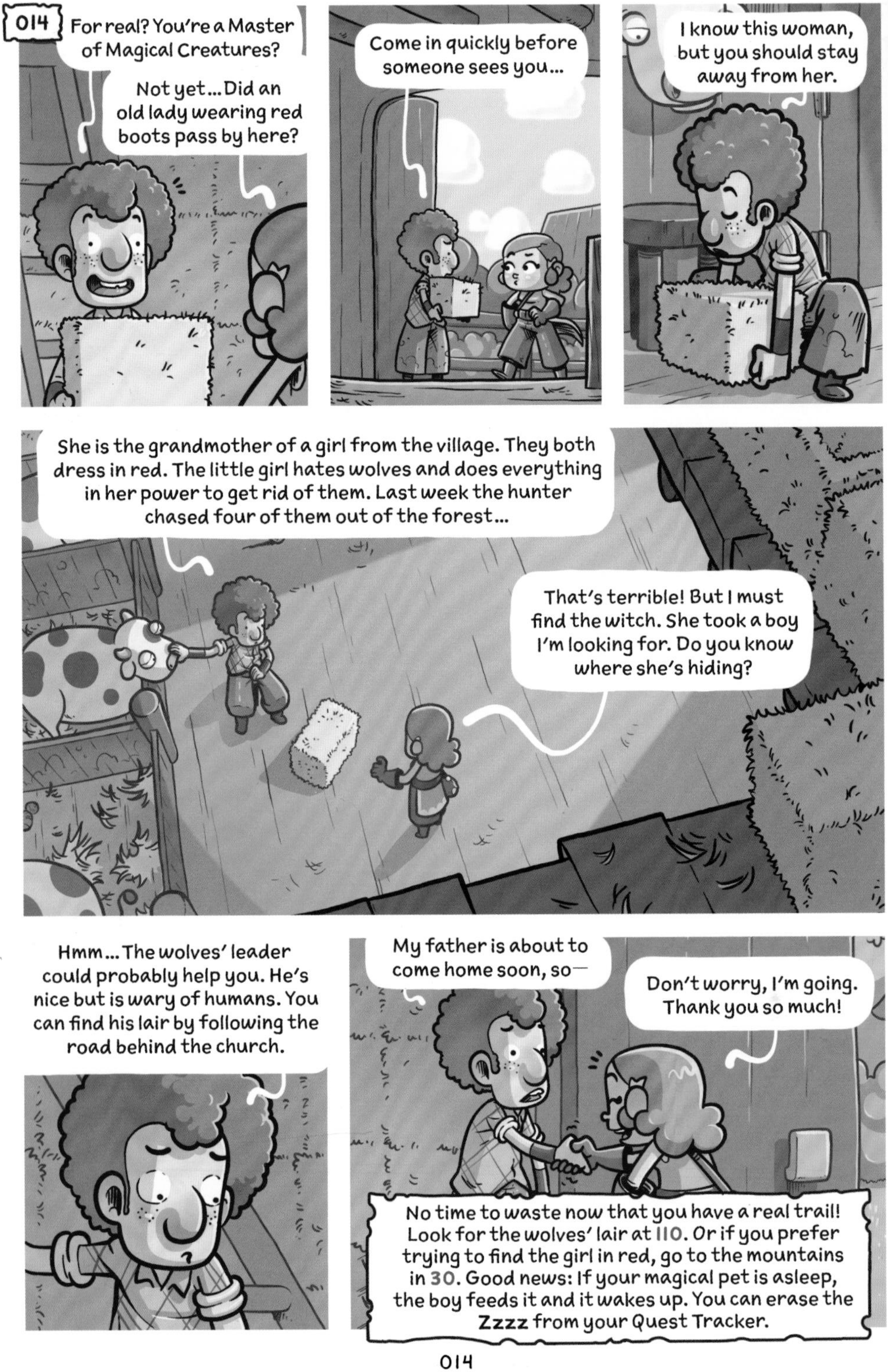
For real? You're a Master of Magical Creatures?
Not yet... Did an old lady wearing red boots pass by here?
Come in quickly before someone sees you...
I know this woman, but you should stay away from her.
She is the grandmother of a girl from the village. They both dress in red. The little girl hates wolves and does everything in her power to get rid of them. Last week the hunter chased four of them out of the forest...
That's terrible! But I must find the witch. She took a boy I'm looking for. Do you know where she's hiding?
Hmm... The wolves' leader could probably help you. He's nice but is wary of humans. You can find his lair by following the road behind the church.
My father is about to come home soon, so—
Don't worry, I'm going. Thank you so much!
No time to waste now that you have a real trail! Look for the wolves' lair at 110. Or if you prefer trying to find the girl in red, go to the mountains in 30. Good news: If your magical pet is asleep, the boy feeds it and it wakes up. You can erase the Zzzz from your Quest Tracker.

015

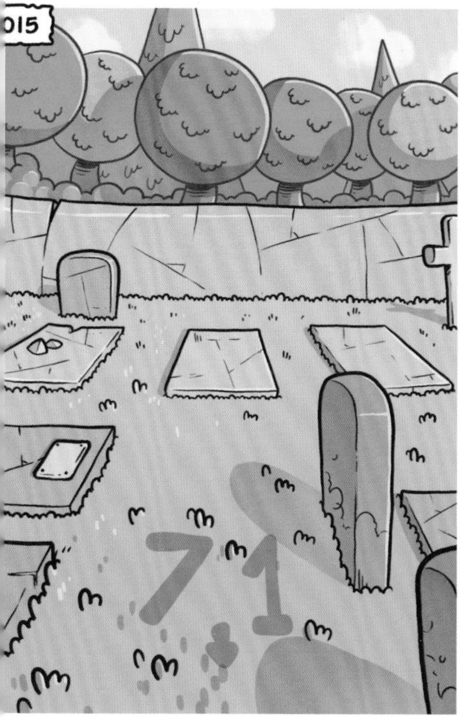
71

016

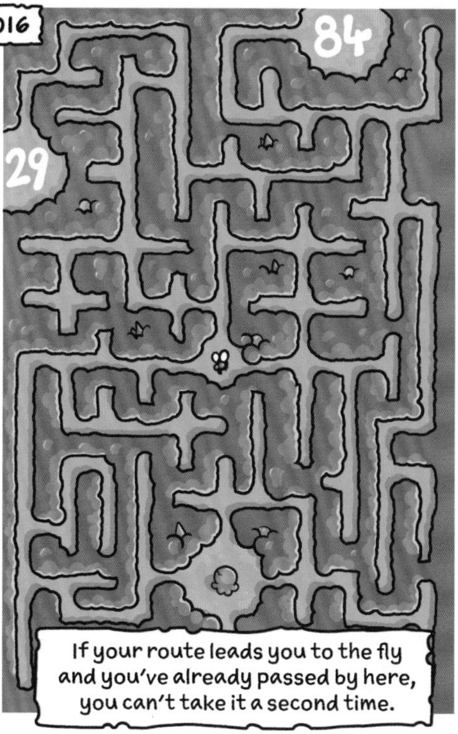
84
29
If your route leads you to the fly and you've already passed by here, you can't take it a second time.

017

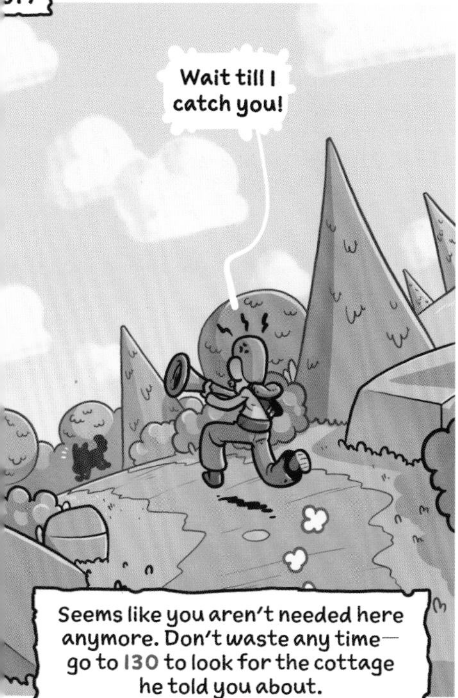
Wait till I catch you!
Seems like you aren't needed here anymore. Don't waste any time—go to 130 to look for the cottage he told you about.

018

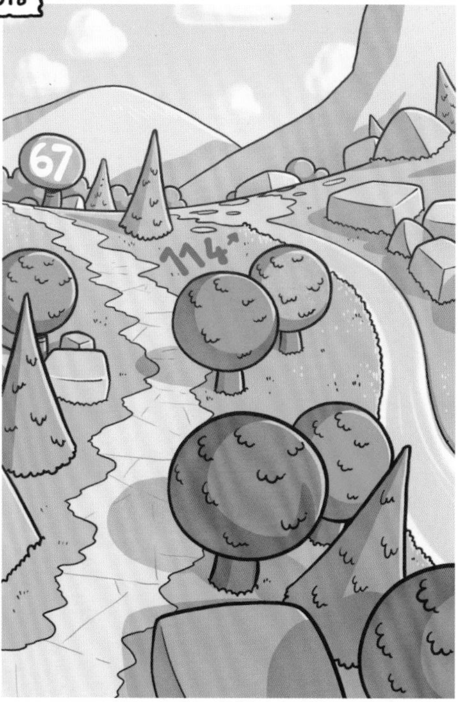
67
114

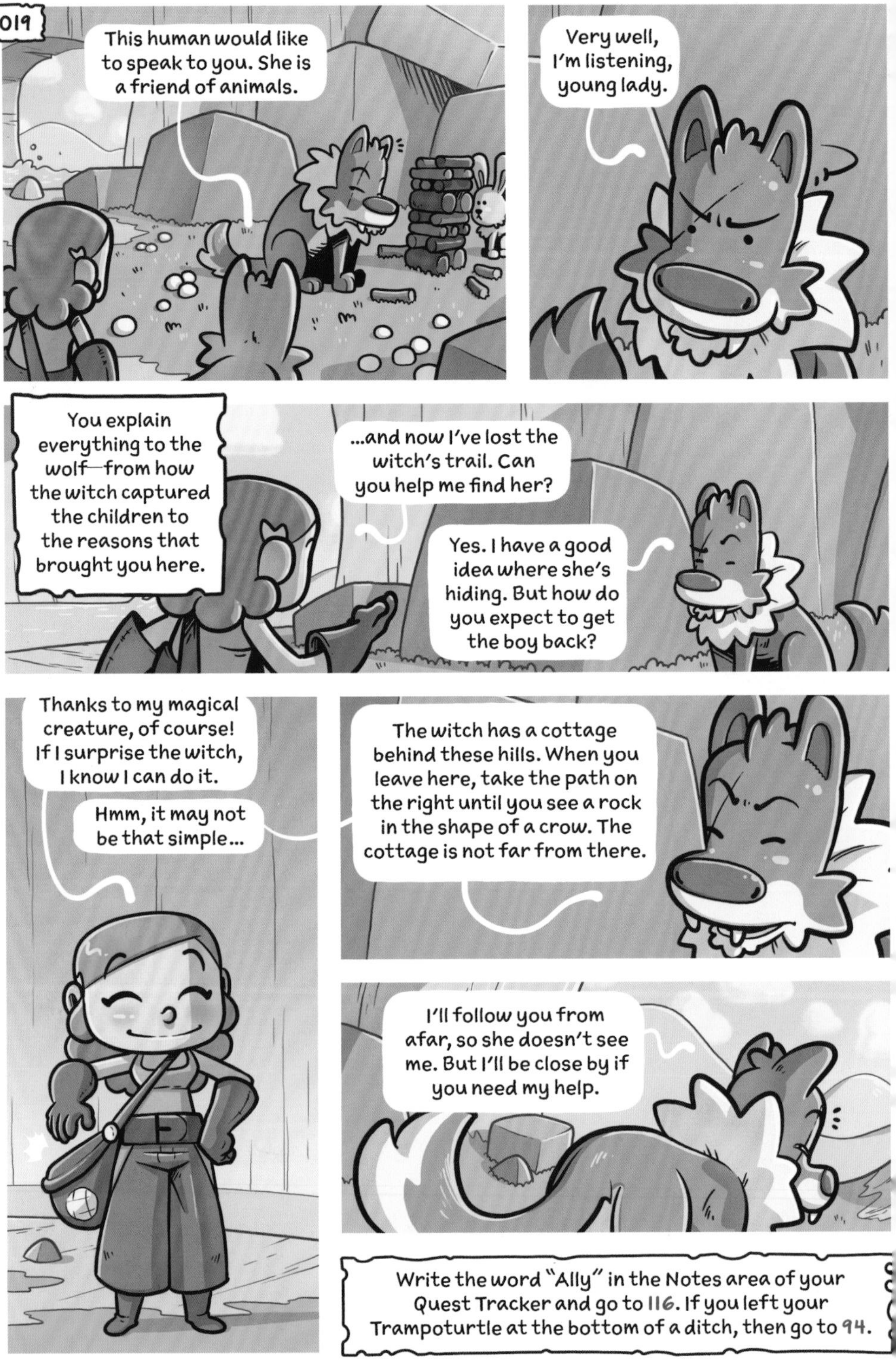
This human would like to speak to you. She is a friend of animals.
Very well, I'm listening, young lady.
You explain everything to the wolf—from how the witch captured the children to the reasons that brought you here.
...and now I've lost the witch's trail. Can you help me find her?
Yes. I have a good idea where she's hiding. But how do you expect to get the boy back?
Thanks to my magical creature, of course! If I surprise the witch, I know I can do it.
Hmm, it may not be that simple...
The witch has a cottage behind these hills. When you leave here, take the path on the right until you see a rock in the shape of a crow. The cottage is not far from there.
I'll follow you from afar, so she doesn't see me. But I'll be close by if you need my help.

Write the word "Ally" in the Notes area of your Quest Tracker and go to 116. If you left your Trampoturtle at the bottom of a ditch, then go to 94.

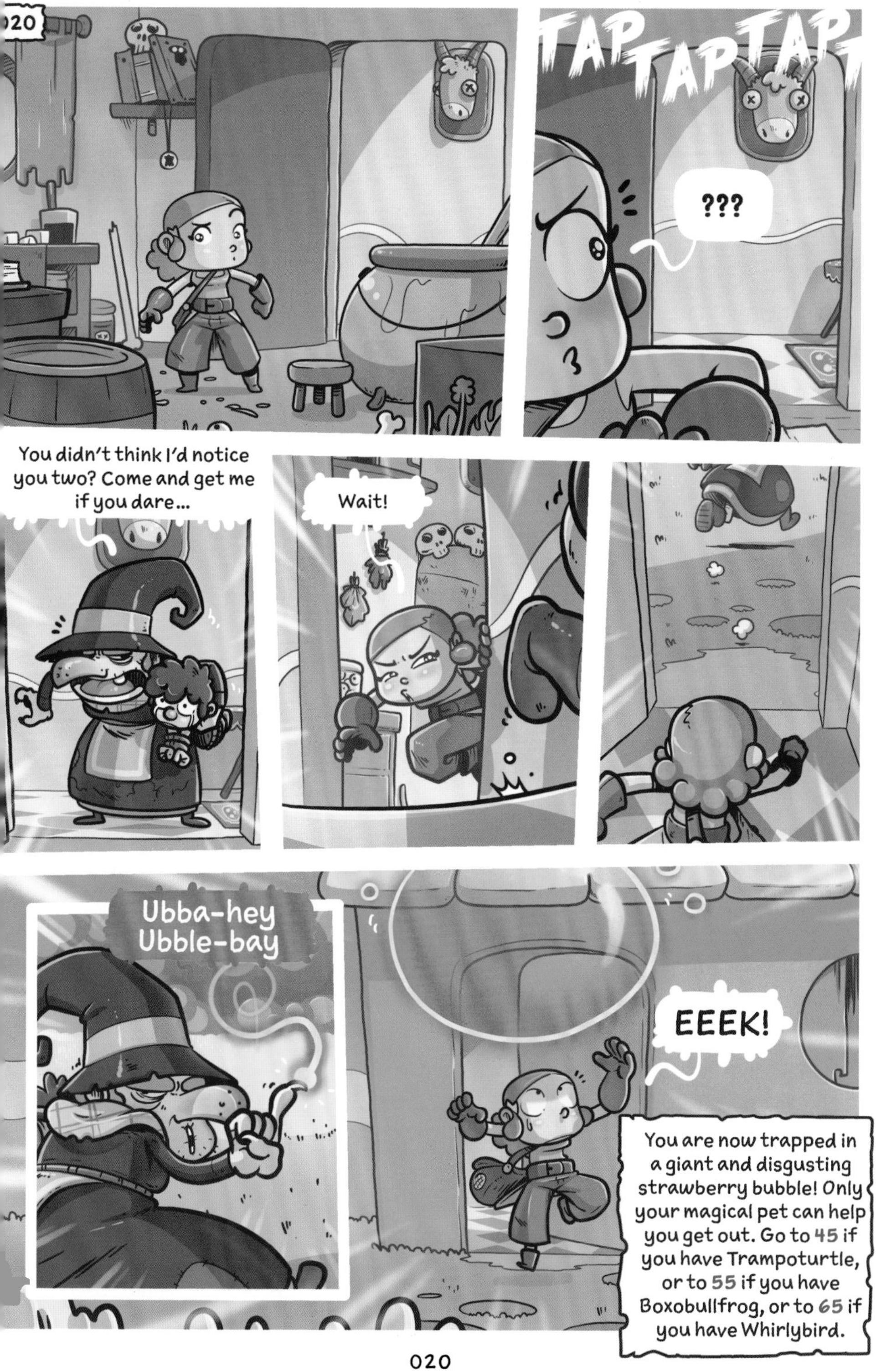
TAP TAP TAP TAP
???
You didn't think I'd notice you two? Come and get me if you dare...
Wait!
Ubba-hey Ubble-bay
EEEK!
You are now trapped in a giant and disgusting strawberry bubble! Only your magical pet can help you get out. Go to 45 if you have Trampoturtle, or to 55 if you have Boxobullfrog, or to 65 if you have Whirlybird.

021

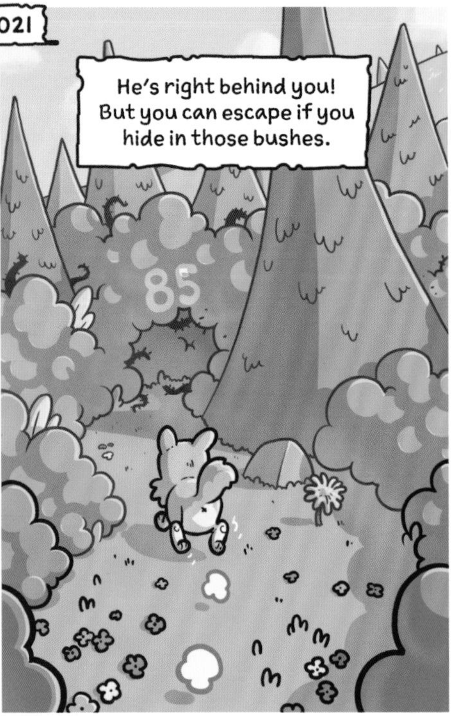
He's right behind you! But you can escape if you hide in those bushes.
85

022

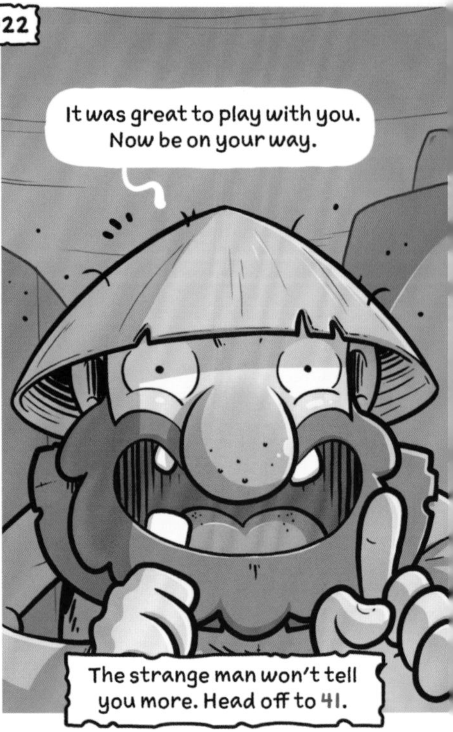
It was great to play with you. Now be on your way.
The strange man won't tell you more. Head off to 41.

023

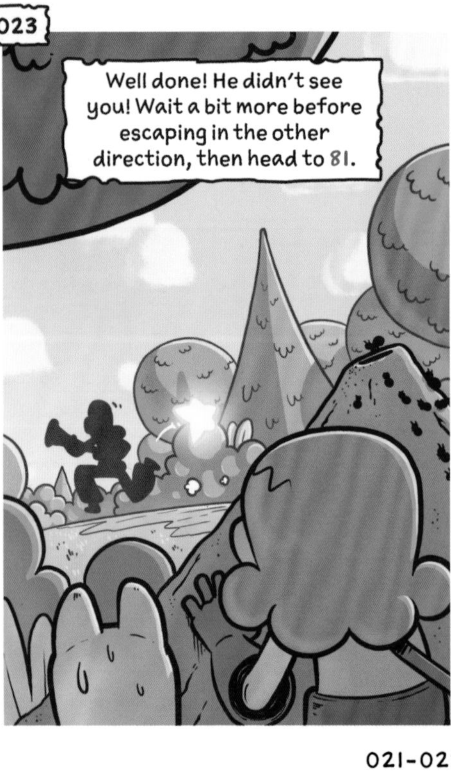
Well done! He didn't see you! Wait a bit more before escaping in the other direction, then head to 81.

024

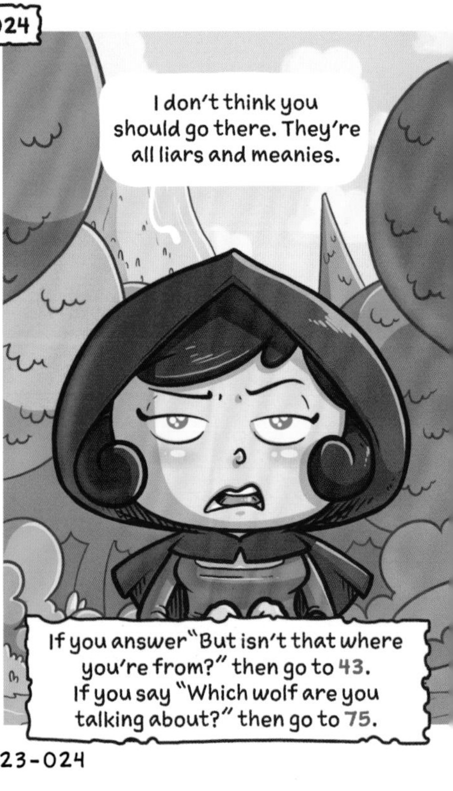
I don't think you should go there. They're all liars and meanies.
If you answer "But isn't that where you're from?" then go to 43.
If you say "Which wolf are you talking about?" then go to 75.

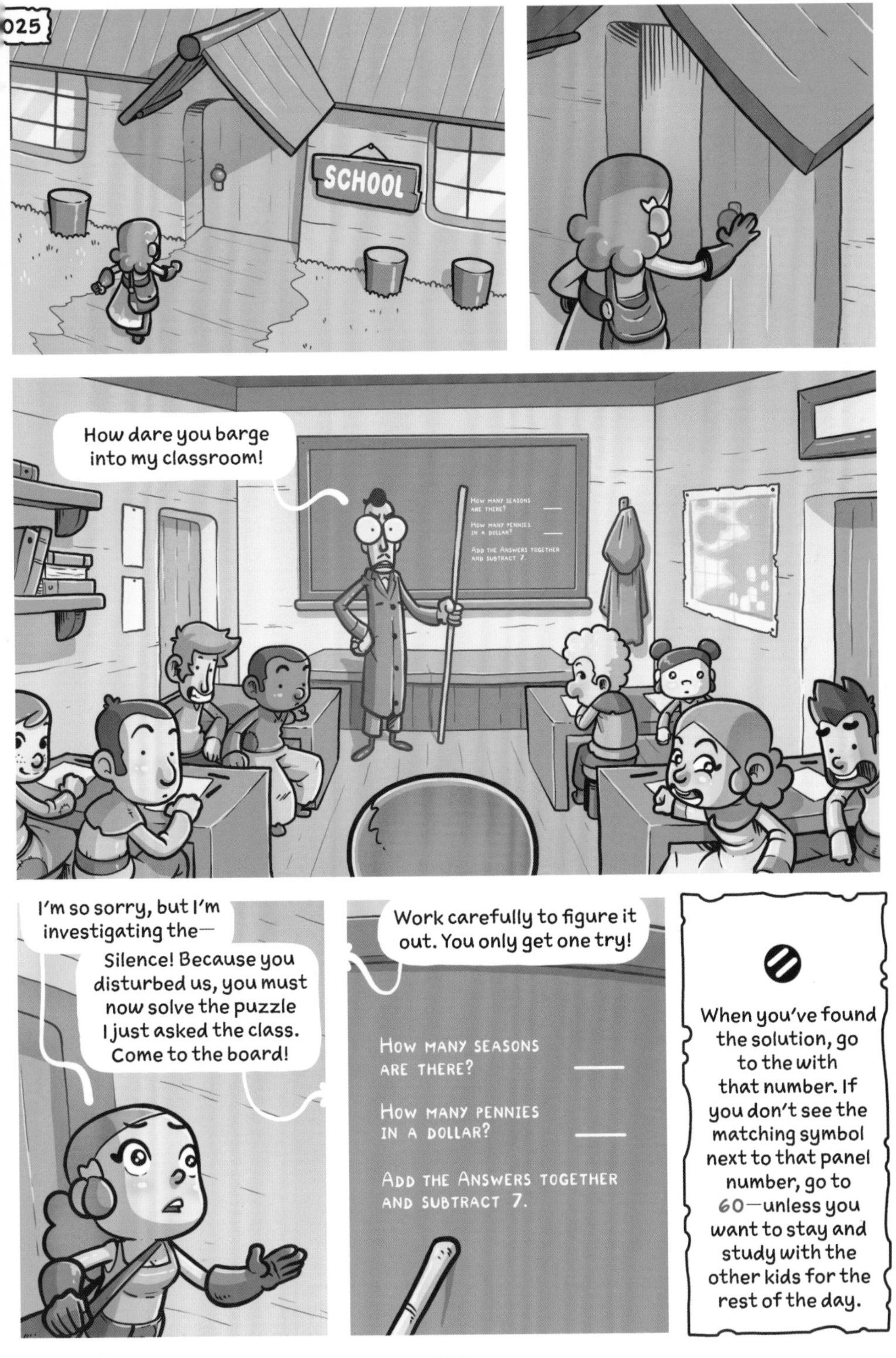
025
SCHOOL
How dare you barge into my classroom!
I'm so sorry, but I'm investigating the—
Silence! Because you disturbed us, you must now solve the puzzle I just asked the class. Come to the board!
Work carefully to figure it out. You only get one try!
HOW MANY SEASONS ARE THERE? ____
HOW MANY PENNIES IN A DOLLAR? ____
ADD THE ANSWERS TOGETHER AND SUBTRACT 7.
When you've found the solution, go to the with that number. If you don't see the matching symbol next to that panel number, go to 60—unless you want to stay and study with the other kids for the rest of the day.

026

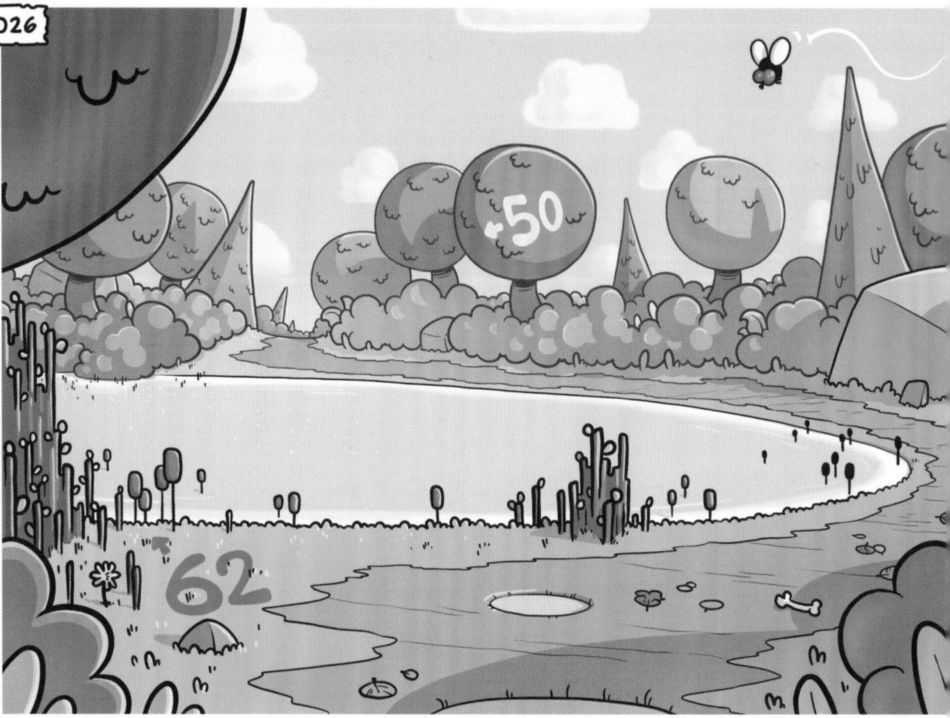
+50
62

027

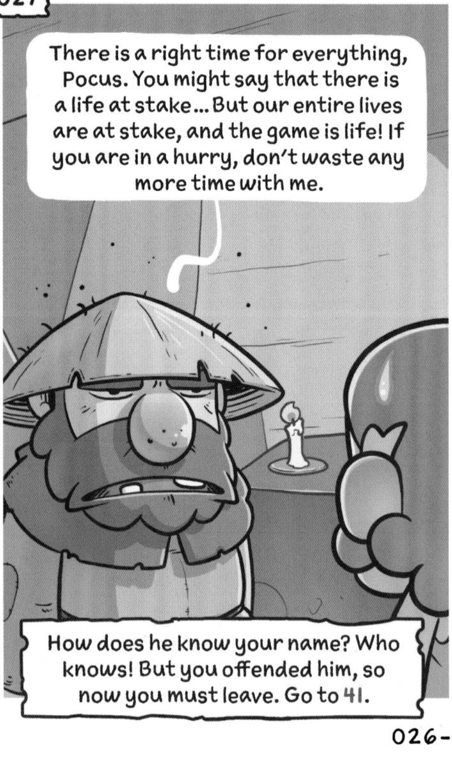
There is a right time for everything, Pocus. You might say that there is a life at stake... But our entire lives are at stake, and the game is life! If you are in a hurry, don't waste any more time with me.
How does he know your name? Who knows! But you offended him, so now you must leave. Go to 41.

028

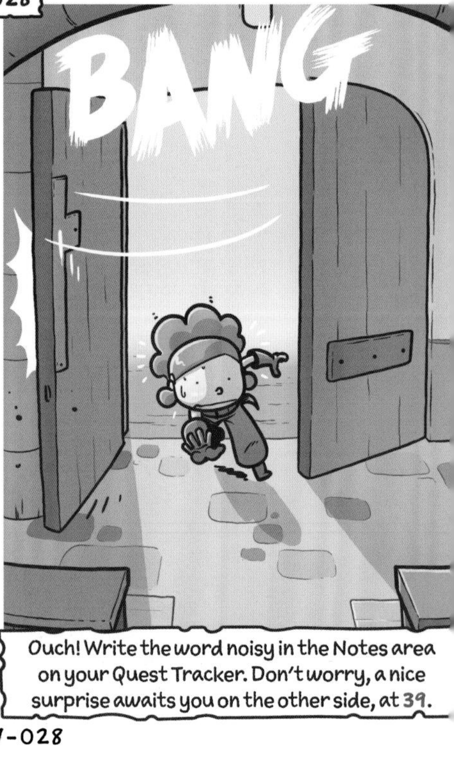
BANG
Ouch! Write the word noisy in the Notes area on your Quest Tracker. Don't worry, a nice surprise awaits you on the other side, at 39.

029

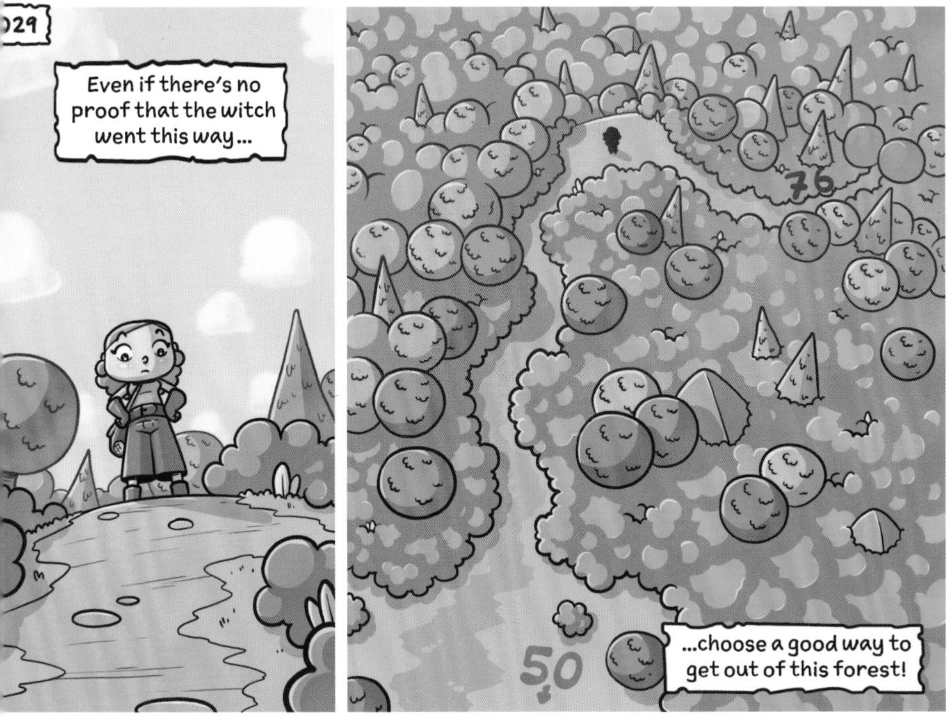

Even if there's no proof that the witch went this way...
76
50
...choose a good way to get out of this forest!

030

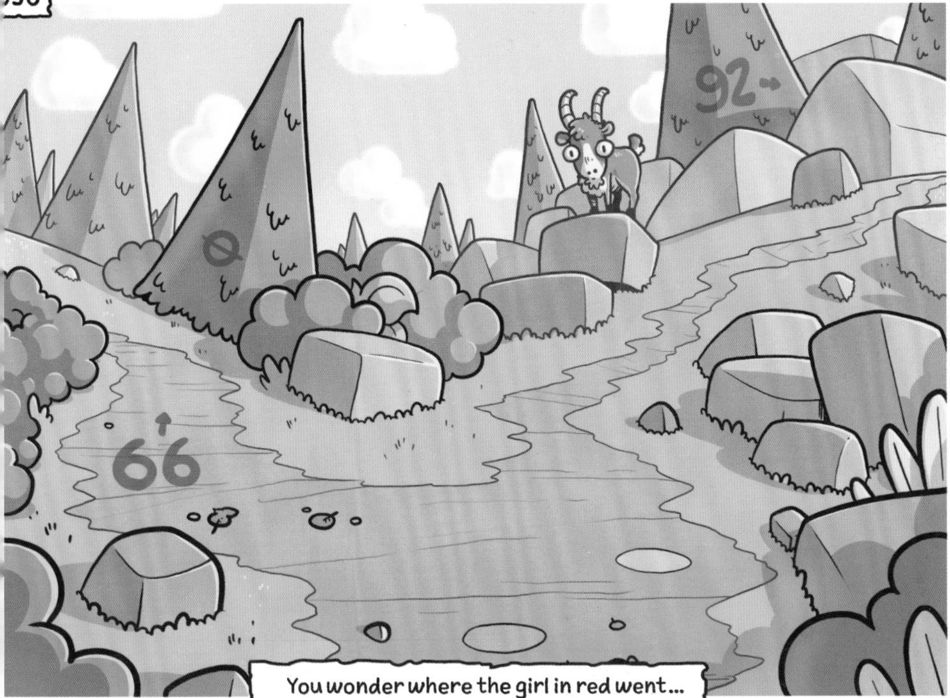

92
0
66
You wonder where the girl in red went...

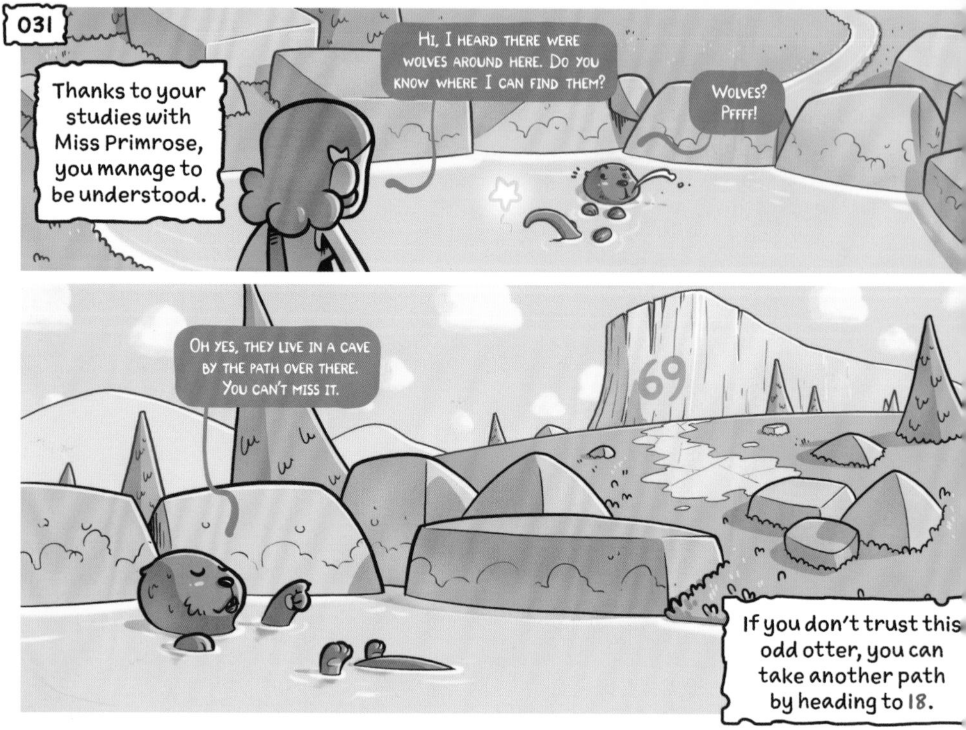
031
Thanks to your studies with Miss Primrose, you manage to be understood.
Hi, I heard there were wolves around here. Do you know where I can find them?
Wolves? Pffff!
Oh yes, they live in a cave by the path over there. You can't miss it.
69
If you don't trust this odd otter, you can take another path by heading to 18.

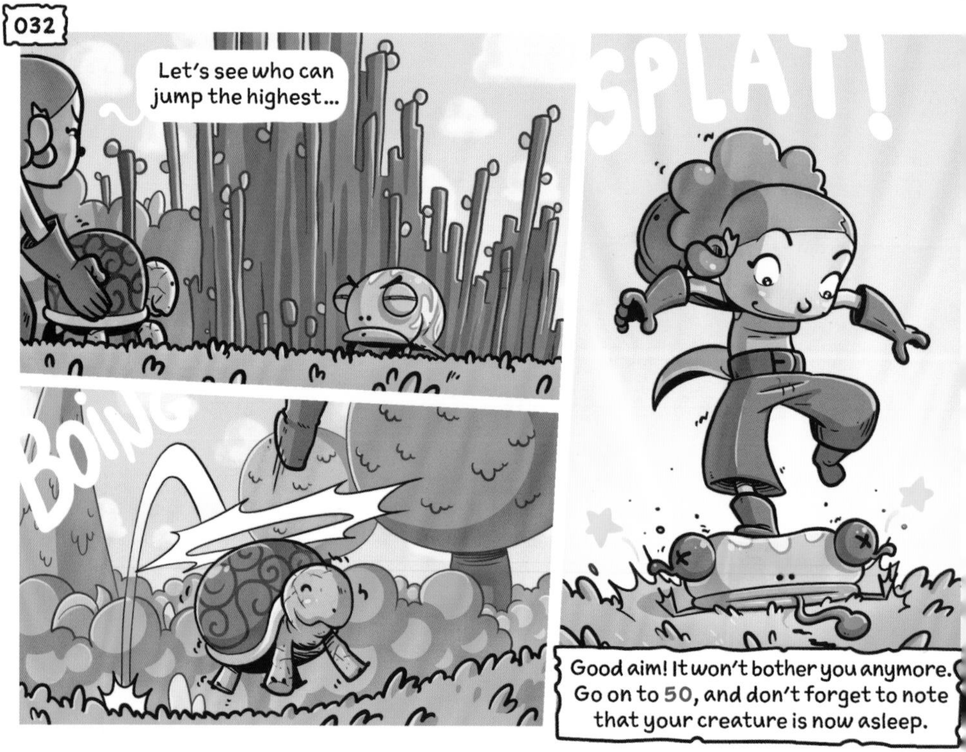
032
Let's see who can jump the highest...
BOING
SPLAT!
Good aim! It won't bother you anymore. Go on to 50, and don't forget to note that your creature is now asleep.

033

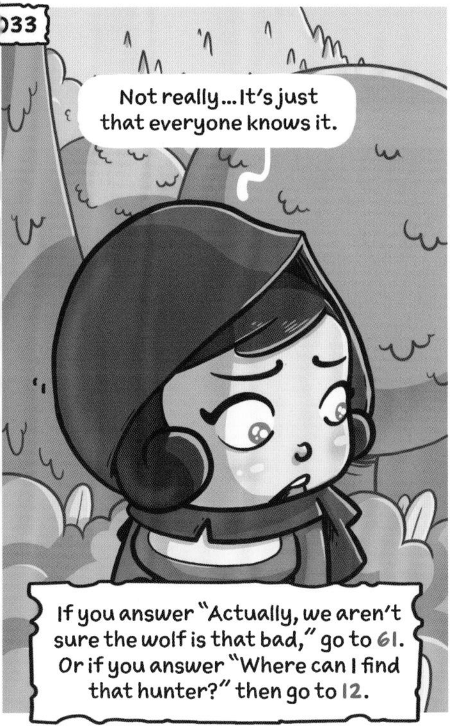
Not really... It's just that everyone knows it.
If you answer "Actually, we aren't sure the wolf is that bad," go to 61. Or if you answer "Where can I find that hunter?" then go to 12.

034

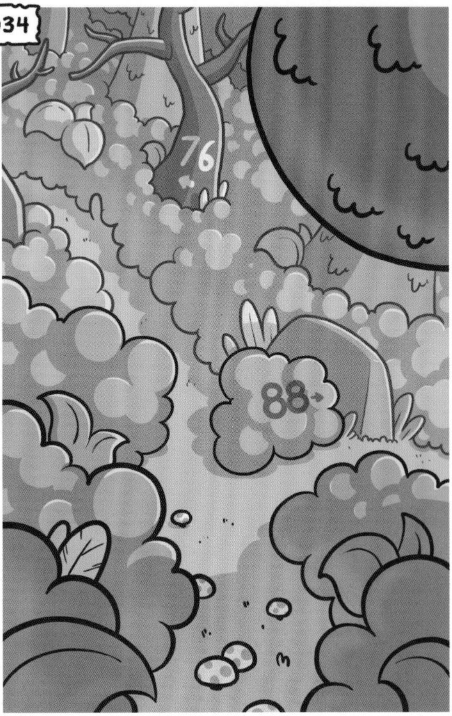
76
88

035

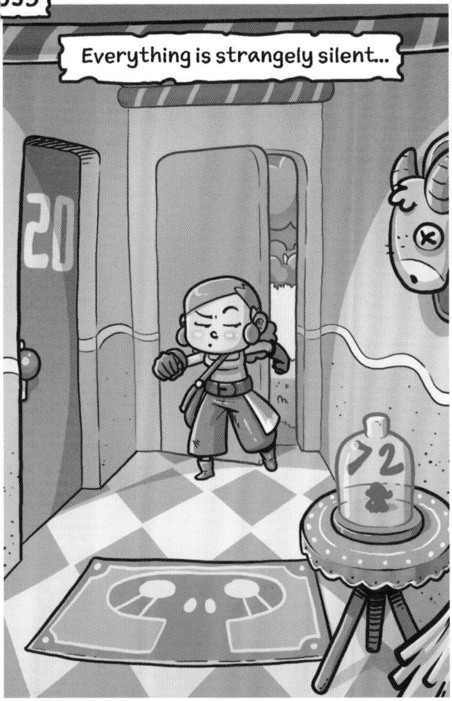
Everything is strangely silent...
20
72

036

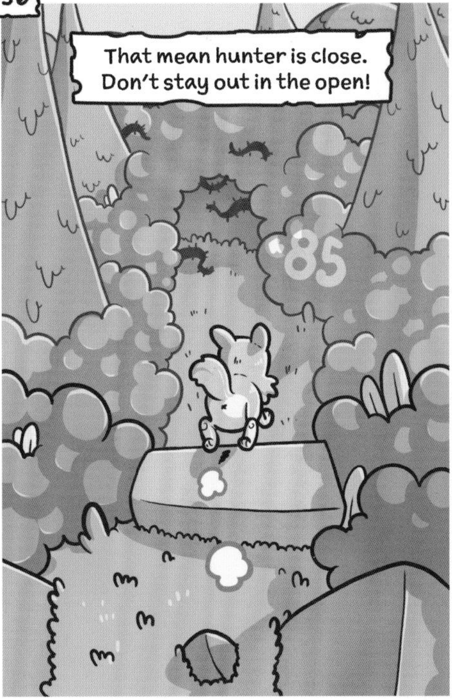
That mean hunter is close. Don't stay out in the open!
85

037

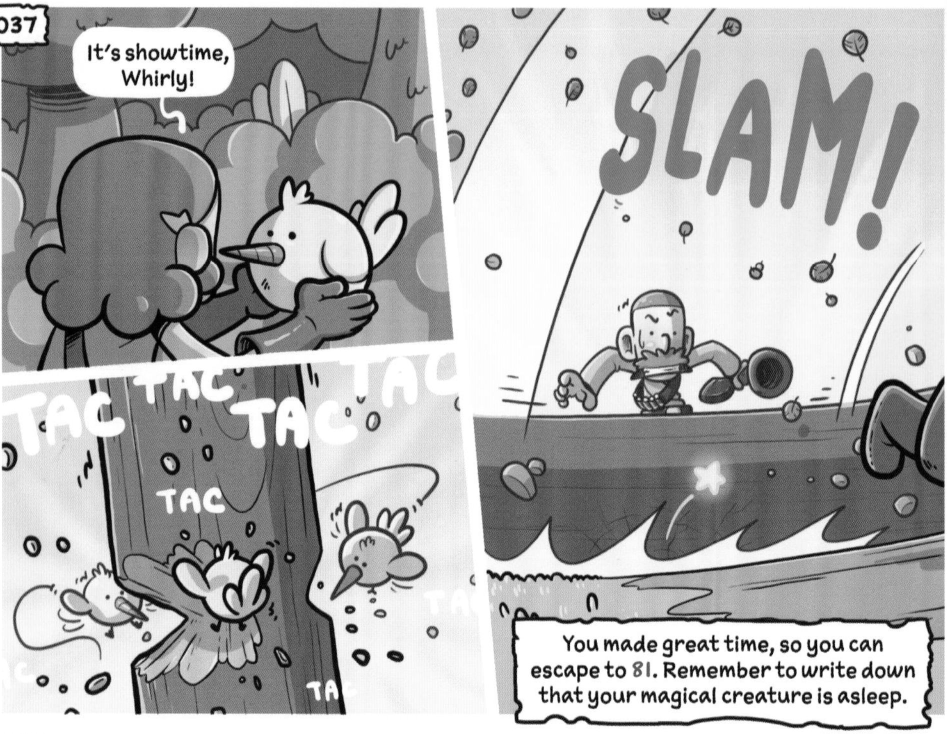
It's showtime, Whirly!
SLAM!
TAC
TAC
TAC
TAC
TAC
TAC
You made great time, so you can escape to 81. Remember to write down that your magical creature is asleep.

038

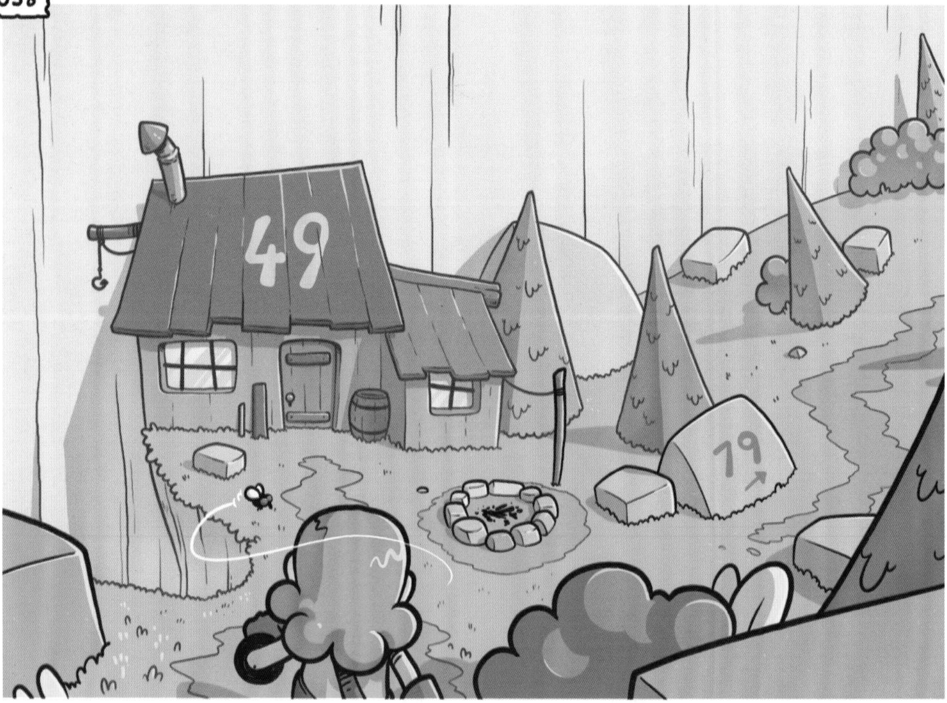
49
79

039

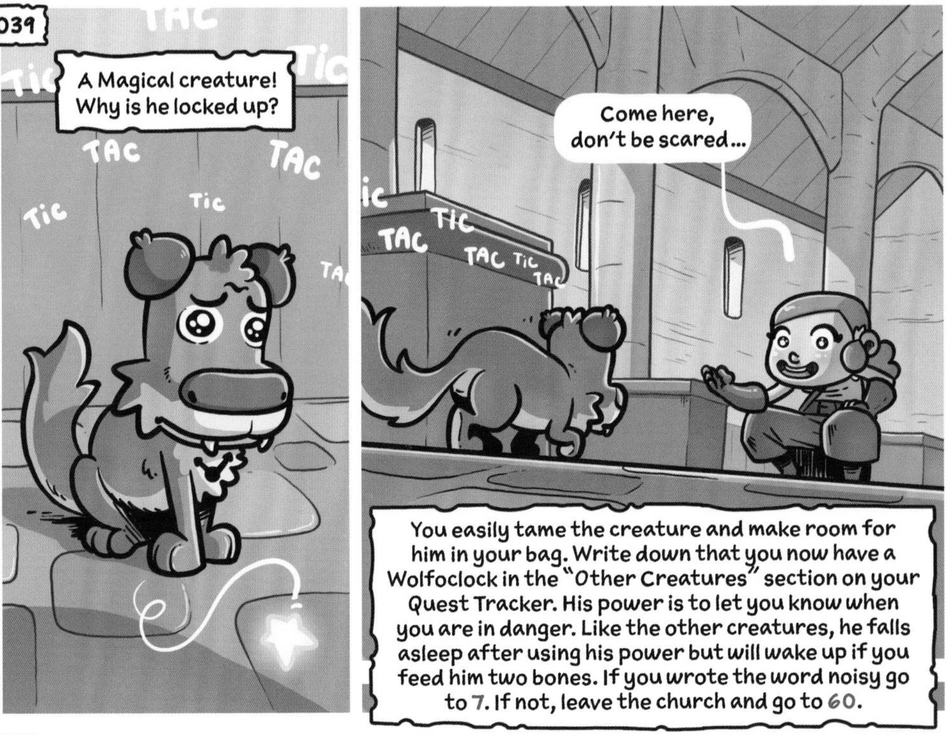
TAC
TIC
A Magical creature! Why is he locked up?
TAC
TAC
TIC
TIC
Come here, don't be scared...
TAC
TIC
TAC
TIC
You easily tame the creature and make room for him in your bag. Write down that you now have a Wolfoclock in the "Other Creatures" section on your Quest Tracker. His power is to let you know when you are in danger. Like the other creatures, he falls asleep after using his power but will wake up if you feed him two bones. If you wrote the word noisy go to 7. If not, leave the church and go to 60.

040

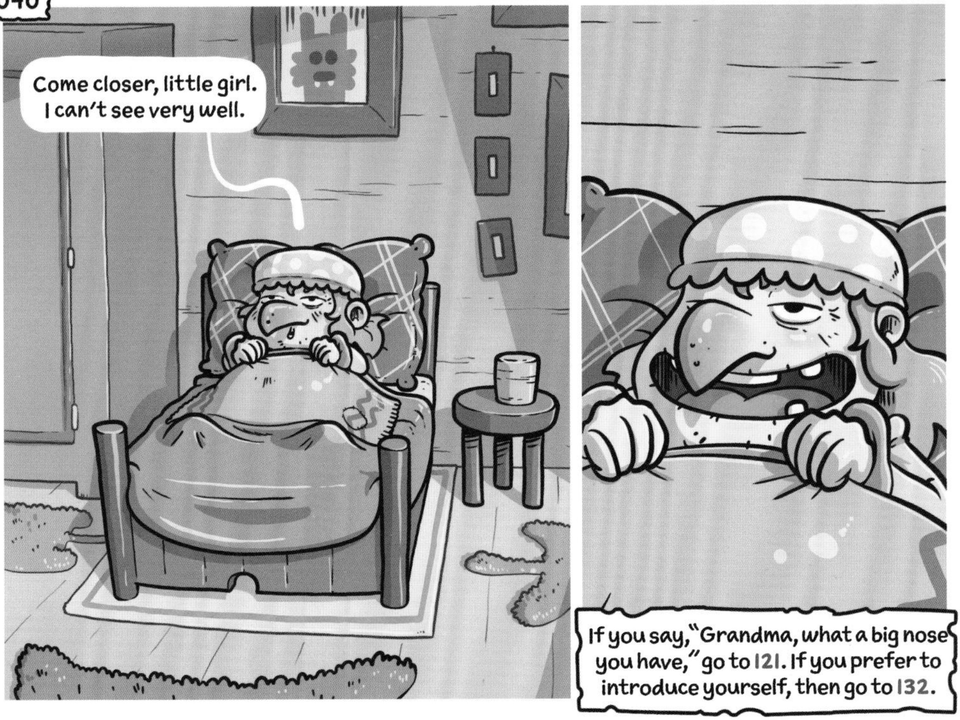
Come closer, little girl. I can't see very well.
If you say, "Grandma, what a big nose you have," go to 121. If you prefer to introduce yourself, then go to 132.

041

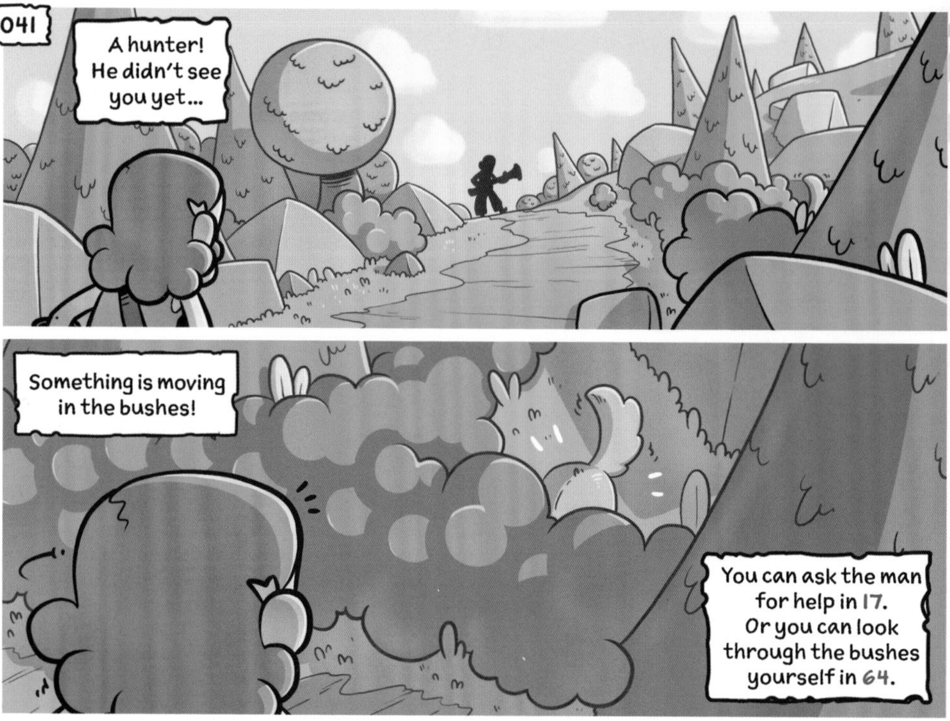

A hunter! He didn't see you yet...
Something is moving in the bushes!
You can ask the man for help in 17. Or you can look through the bushes yourself in 64.

042

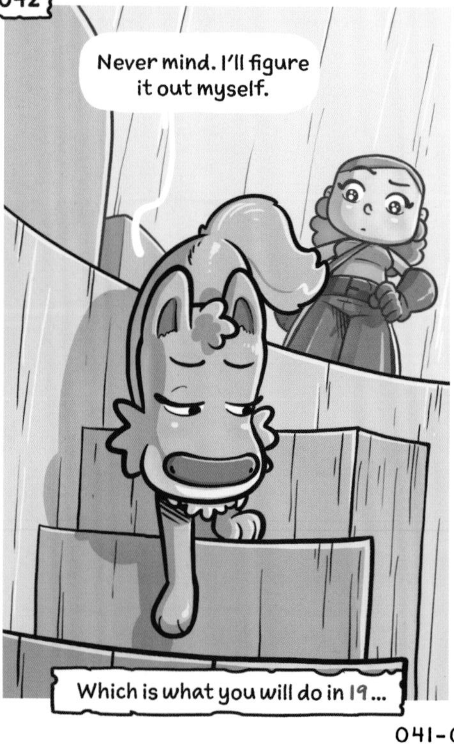

Never mind. I'll figure it out myself.
Which is what you will do in 19...

043

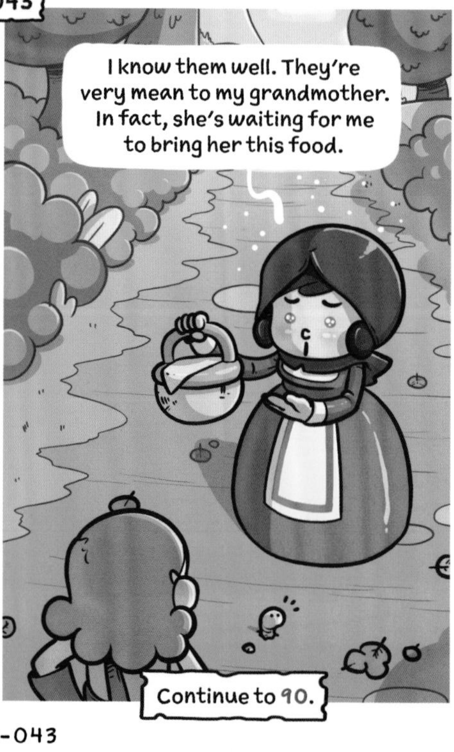

I know them well. They're very mean to my grandmother. In fact, she's waiting for me to bring her this food.
Continue to 90.

044

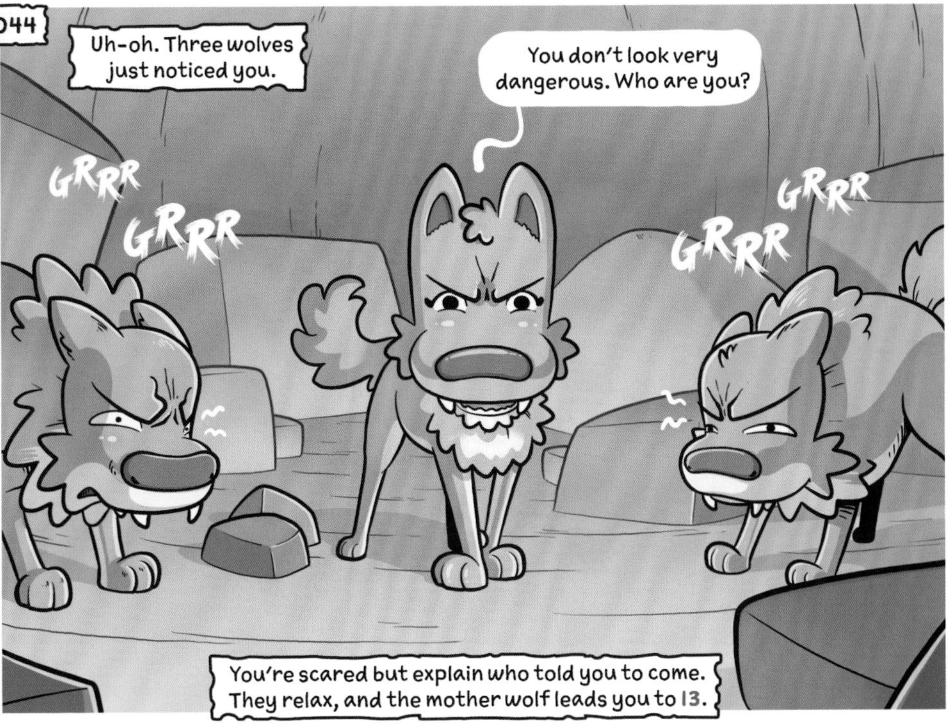
Uh-oh. Three wolves just noticed you.
You don't look very dangerous. Who are you?
GRRR
GRRR
GRRR
GRRR
You're scared but explain who told you to come. They relax, and the mother wolf leads you to 13.

045

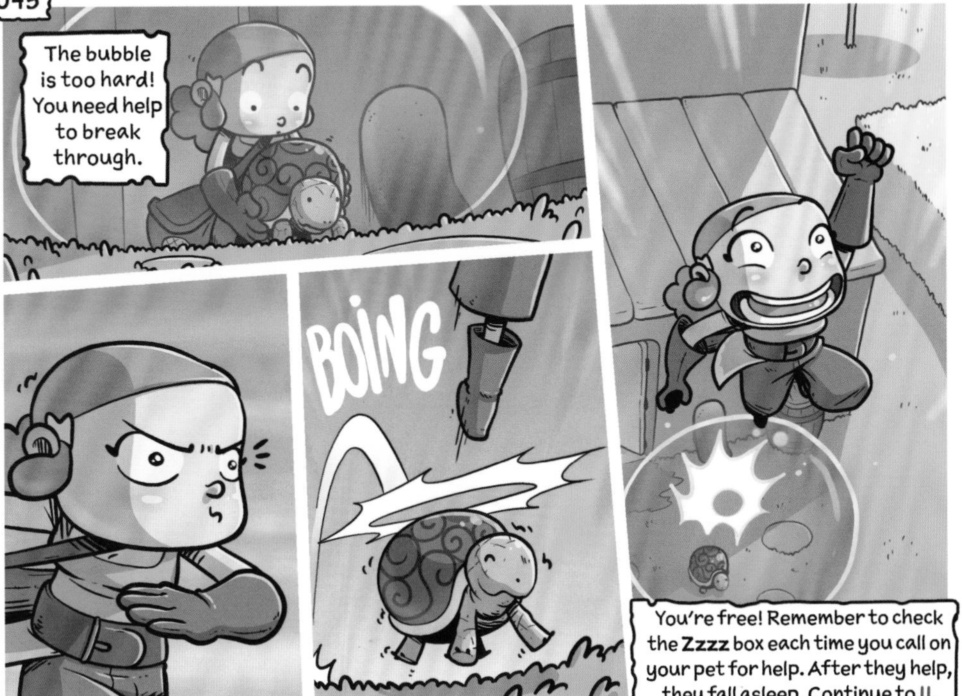
The bubble is too hard! You need help to break through.
BOING
You're free! Remember to check the **Zzzz** box each time you call on your pet for help. After they help, they fall asleep. Continue to 11.

046

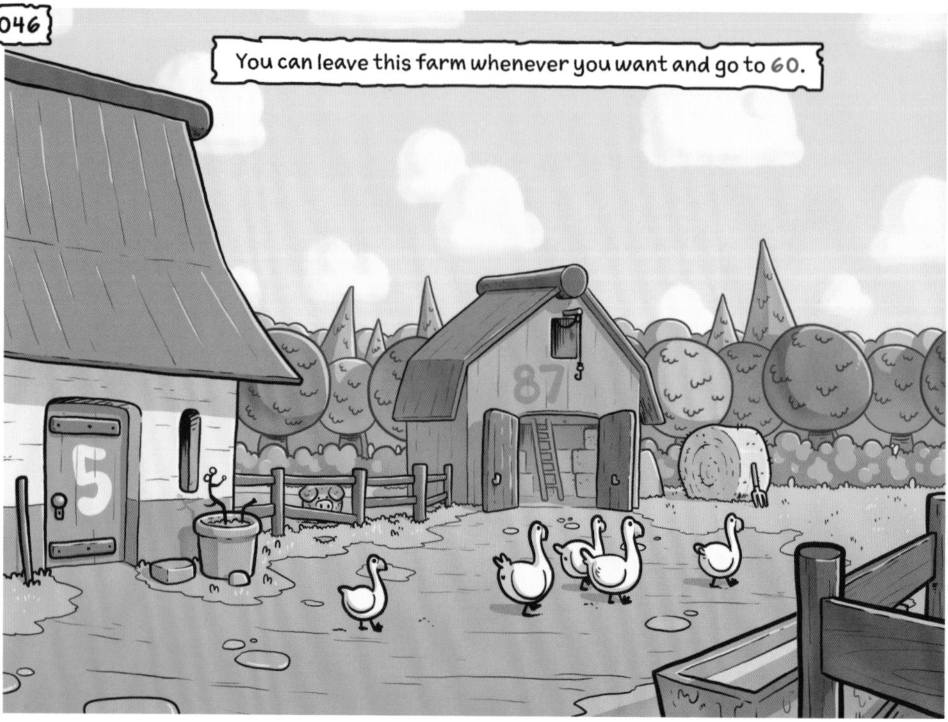
You can leave this farm whenever you want and go to 60.
87
5

047

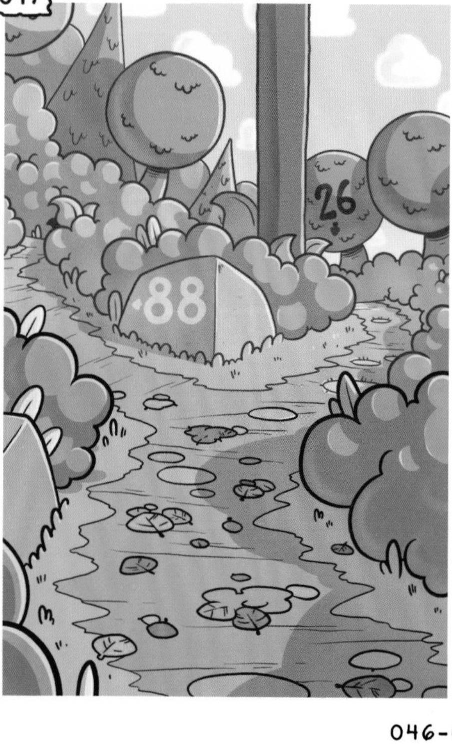
26
88

048

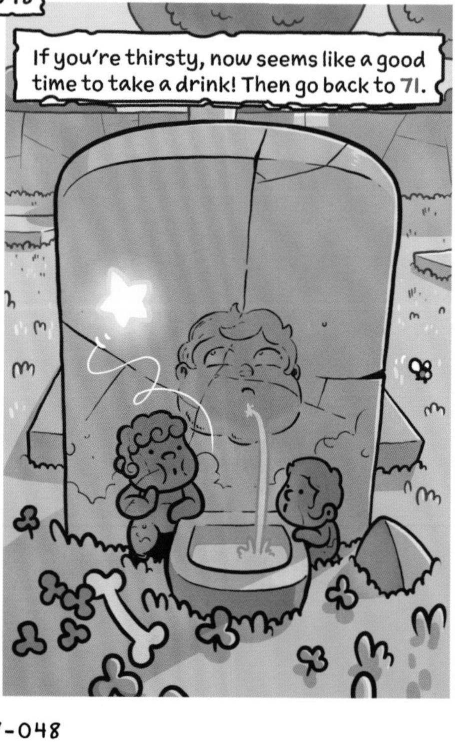
If you're thirsty, now seems like a good time to take a drink! Then go back to 71.

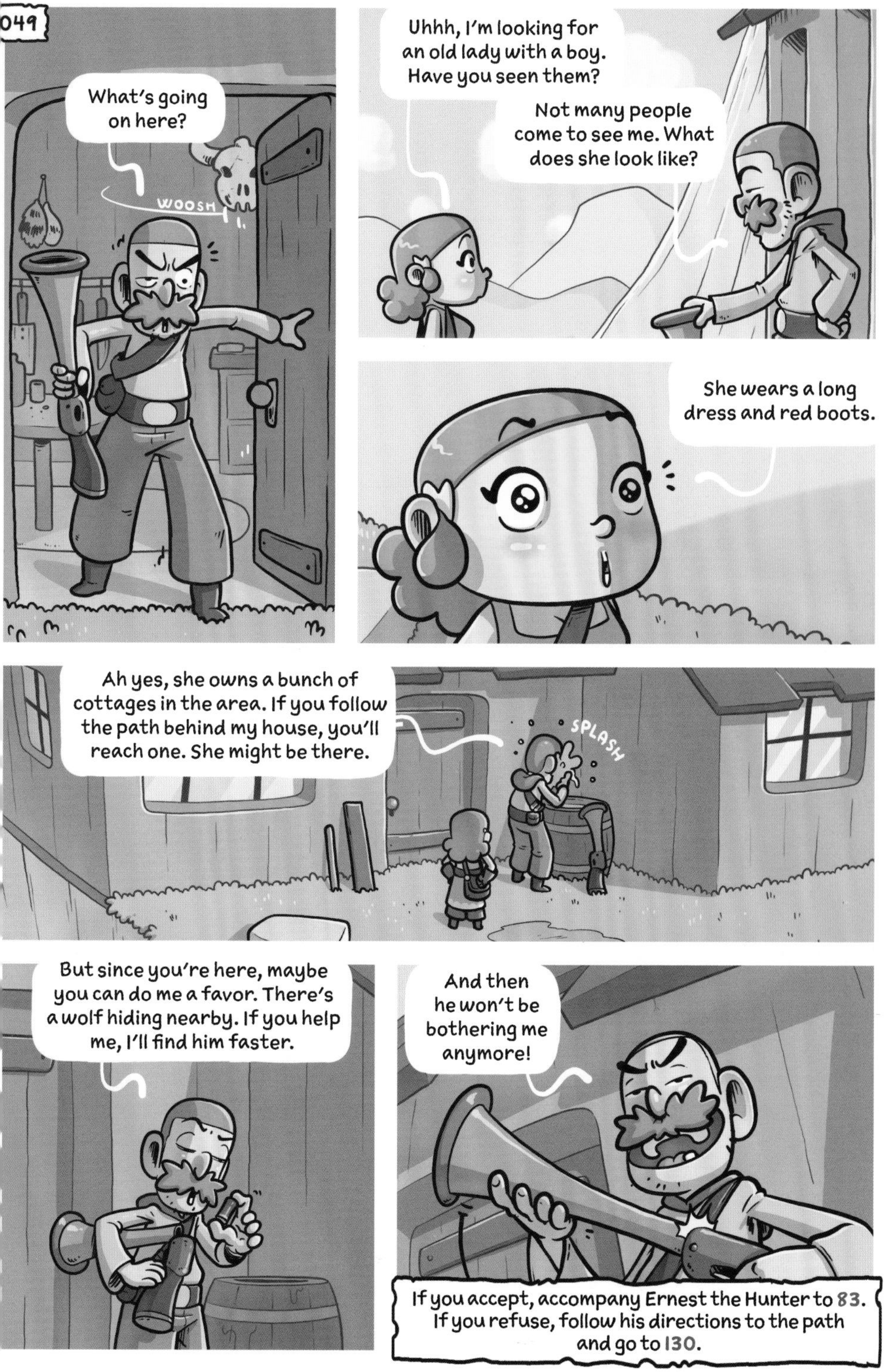

What's going on here?
WOOSH
Uhhh, I'm looking for an old lady with a boy. Have you seen them?
Not many people come to see me. What does she look like?
She wears a long dress and red boots.
Ah yes, she owns a bunch of cottages in the area. If you follow the path behind my house, you'll reach one. She might be there.
SPLASH
But since you're here, maybe you can do me a favor. There's a wolf hiding nearby. If you help me, I'll find him faster.
And then he won't be bothering me anymore!
If you accept, accompany Ernest the Hunter to 83. If you refuse, follow his directions to the path and go to 130.

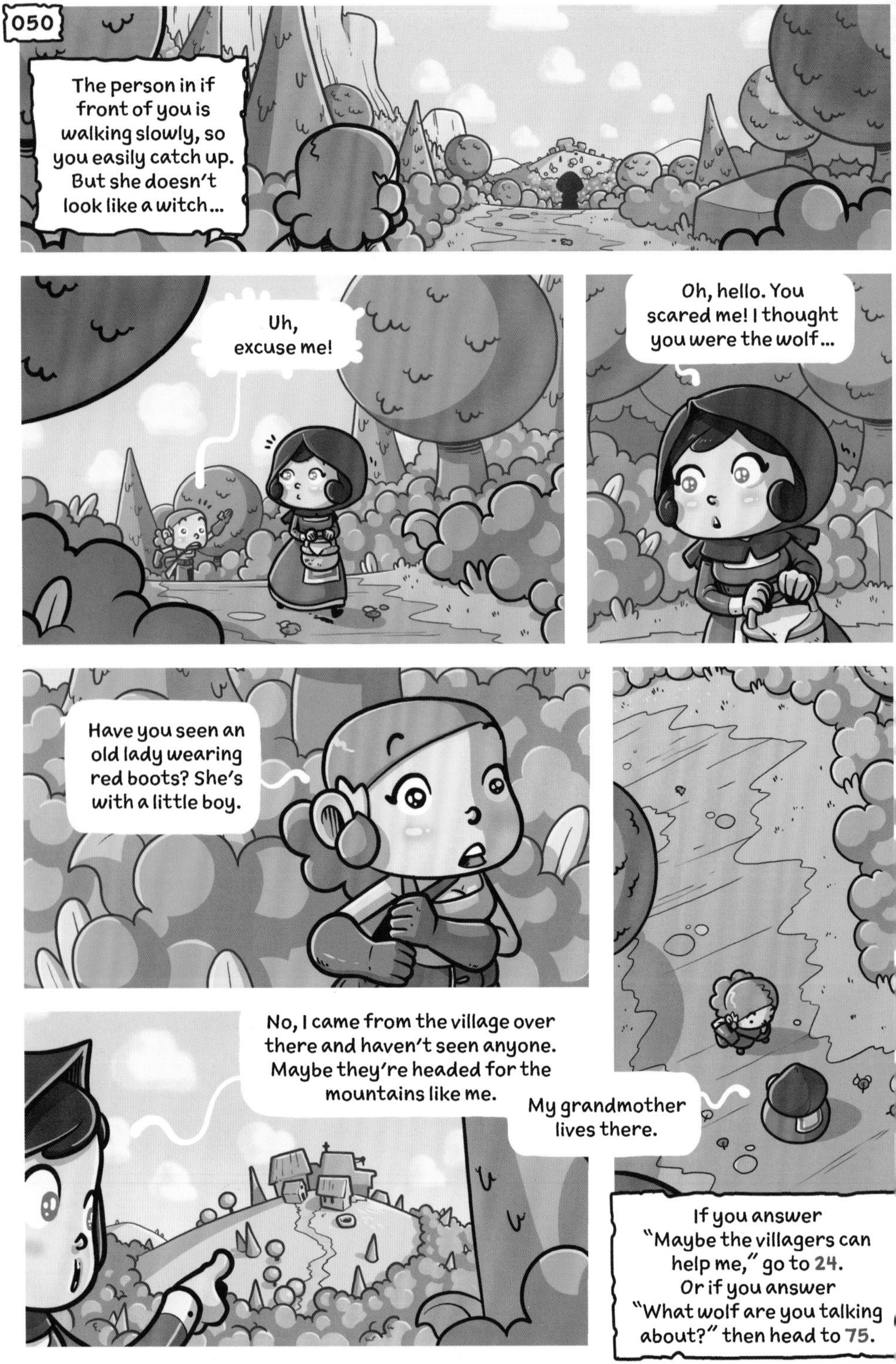

The person in if front of you is walking slowly, so you easily catch up. But she doesn't look like a witch...
Uh, excuse me!
Oh, hello. You scared me! I thought you were the wolf...
Have you seen an old lady wearing red boots? She's with a little boy.
No, I came from the village over there and haven't seen anyone. Maybe they're headed for the mountains like me.
My grandmother lives there.
If you answer "Maybe the villagers can help me," go to 24.
Or if you answer "What wolf are you talking about?" then head to 75.

051

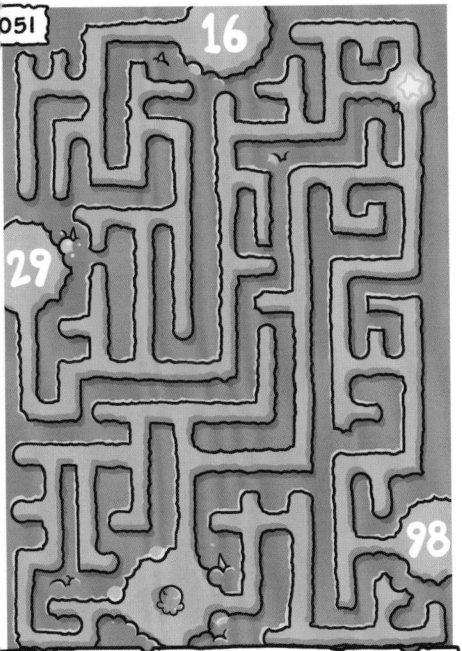
16
29
98

If you get to the star but already picked one up earlier, you cannot take it again.

052

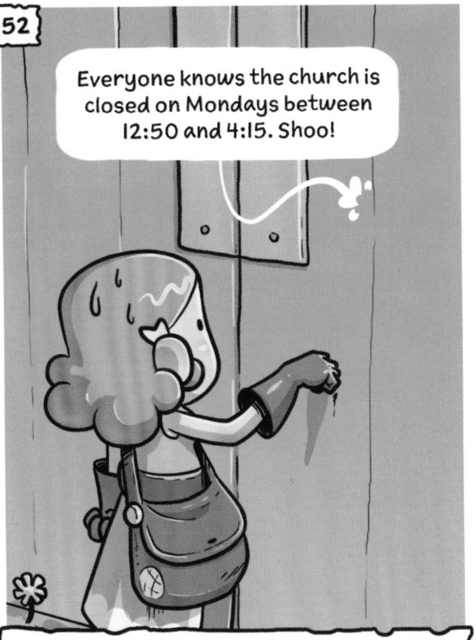
Everyone knows the church is closed on Mondays between 12:50 and 4:15. Shoo!

You can visit another spot in 60 or wait a little while and come back with a different approach in 89.

053

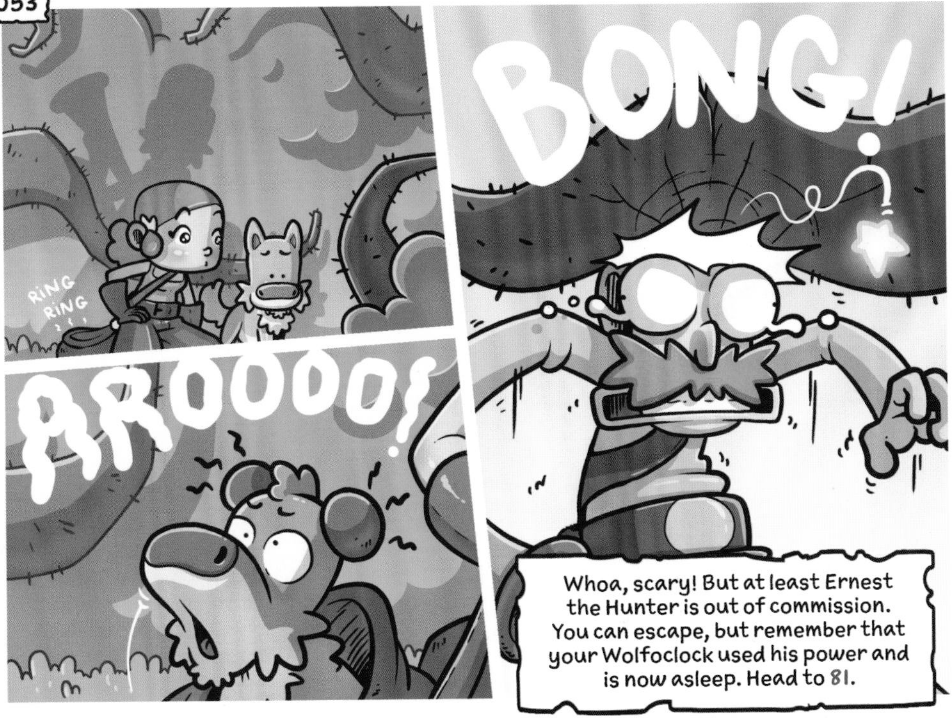
RING RING
BONG!
AROOOO!

Whoa, scary! But at least Ernest the Hunter is out of commission. You can escape, but remember that your Wolfoclock used his power and is now asleep. Head to 81.

054

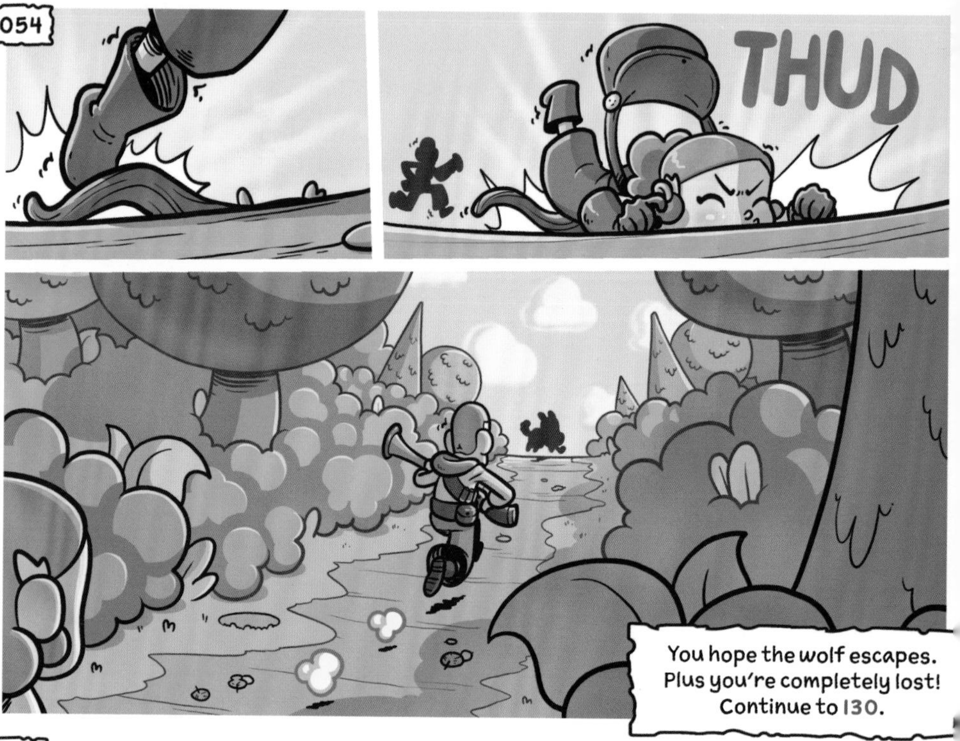
THUD
You hope the wolf escapes. Plus you're completely lost! Continue to 130.

055

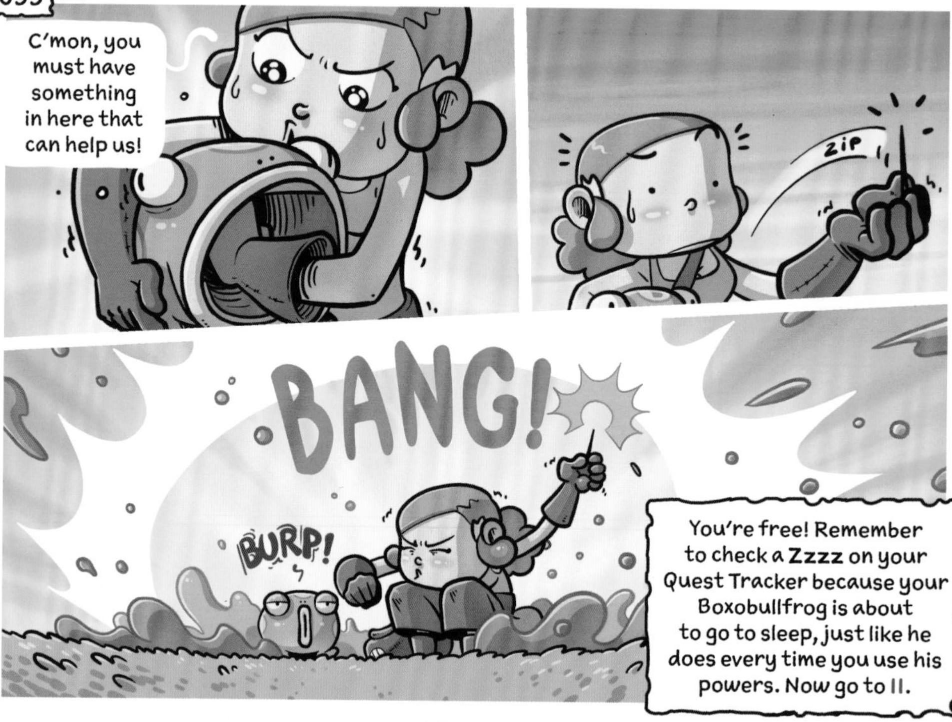
C'mon, you must have something in here that can help us!
ZIP
BANG!
BURP!
You're free! Remember to check a **Zzzz** on your Quest Tracker because your Boxobullfrog is about to go to sleep, just like he does every time you use his powers. Now go to 11.

056

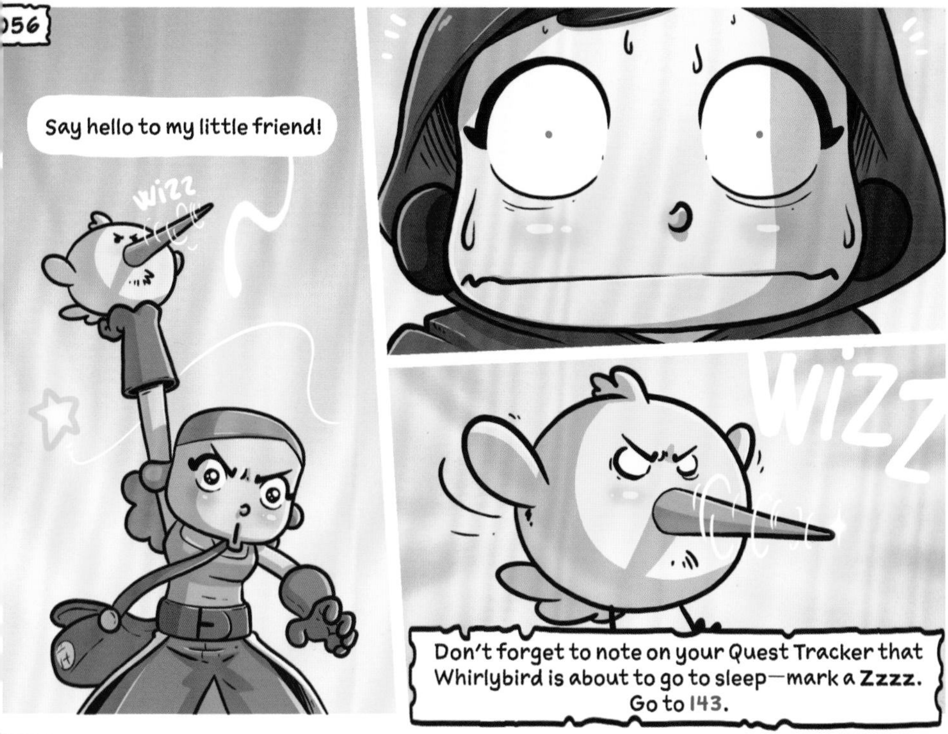

Say hello to my little friend!
WIZZ
WIZZ
Don't forget to note on your Quest Tracker that Whirlybird is about to go to sleep—mark a **Zzzz**.
Go to 143.

057

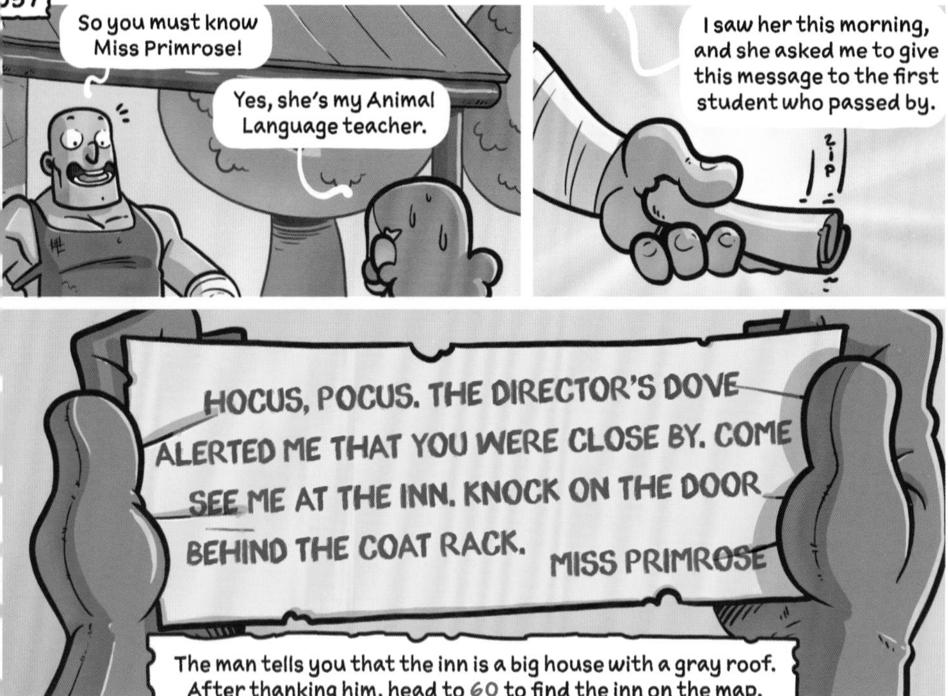

So you must know Miss Primrose!
Yes, she's my Animal Language teacher.
I saw her this morning, and she asked me to give this message to the first student who passed by.
ZIP
HOCUS, POCUS. THE DIRECTOR'S DOVE ALERTED ME THAT YOU WERE CLOSE BY. COME SEE ME AT THE INN. KNOCK ON THE DOOR BEHIND THE COAT RACK.
MISS PRIMROSE
The man tells you that the inn is a big house with a gray roof. After thanking him, head to 60 to find the inn on the map.

058

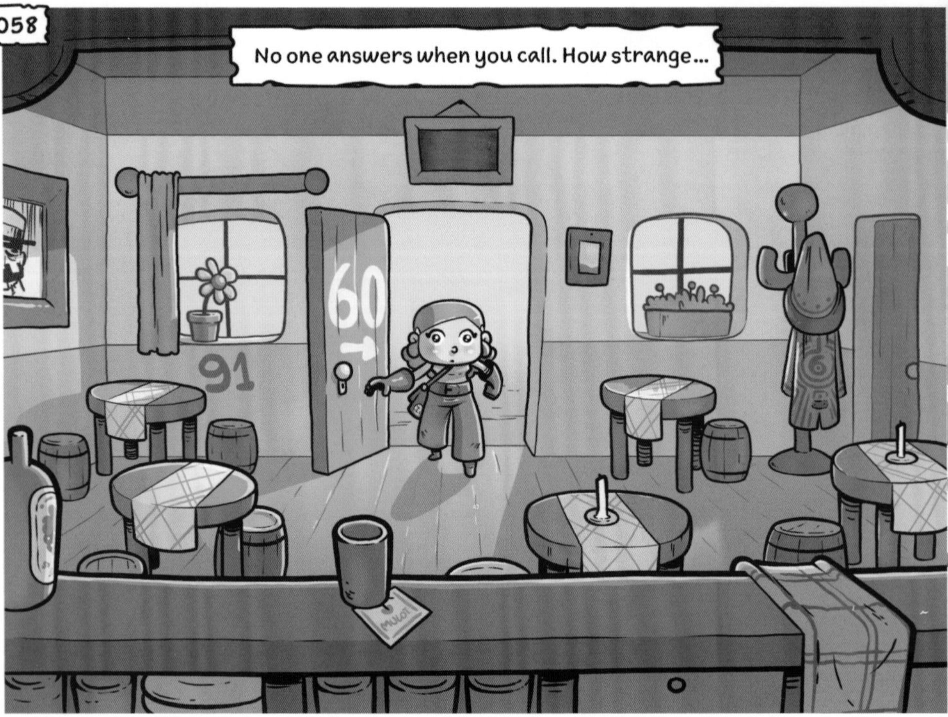
No one answers when you call. How strange...
60
91

059

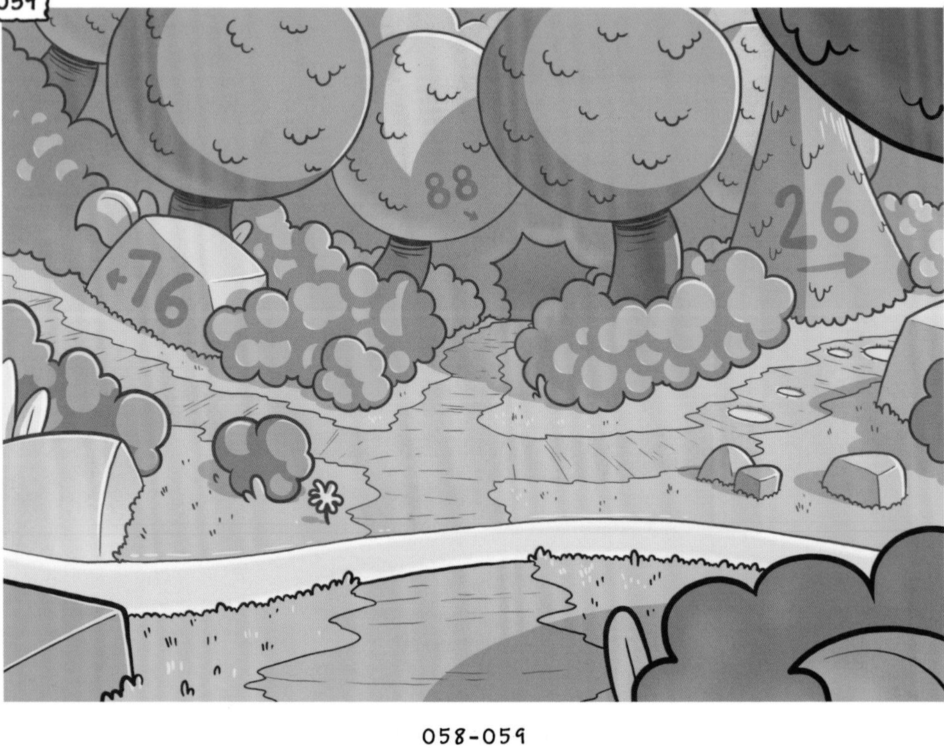
88
26
76

060

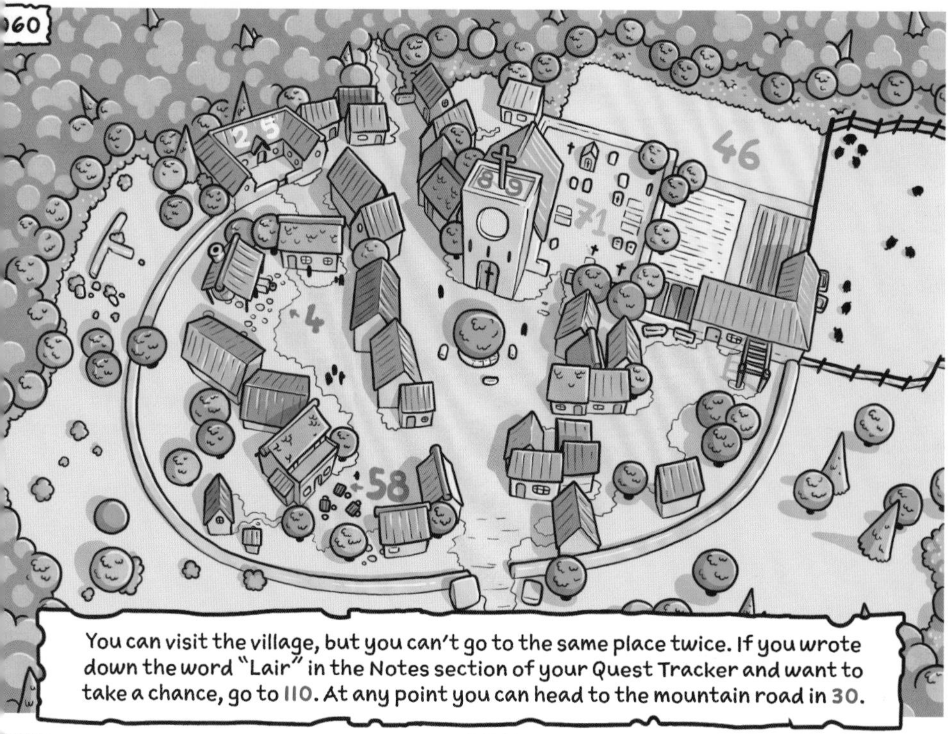
25
89
71
46
4
58
You can visit the village, but you can't go to the same place twice. If you wrote down the word "Lair" in the Notes section of your Quest Tracker and want to take a chance, go to 110. At any point you can head to the mountain road in 30.

061

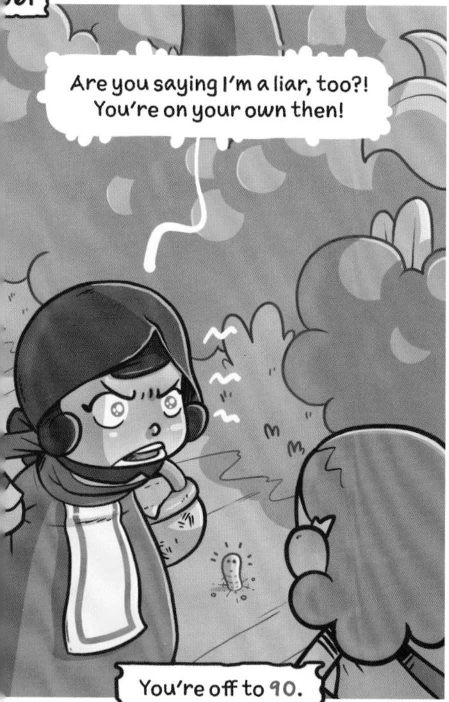
Are you saying I'm a liar, too?! You're on your own then!
You're off to 90.

062

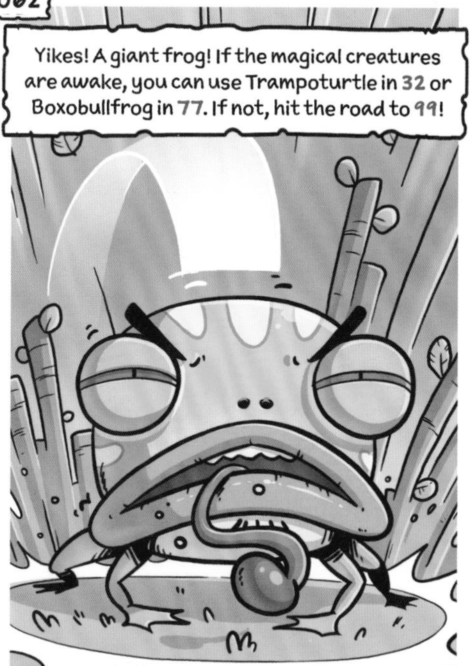
Yikes! A giant frog! If the magical creatures are awake, you can use Trampoturtle in 32 or Boxobullfrog in 77. If not, hit the road to 99!

063

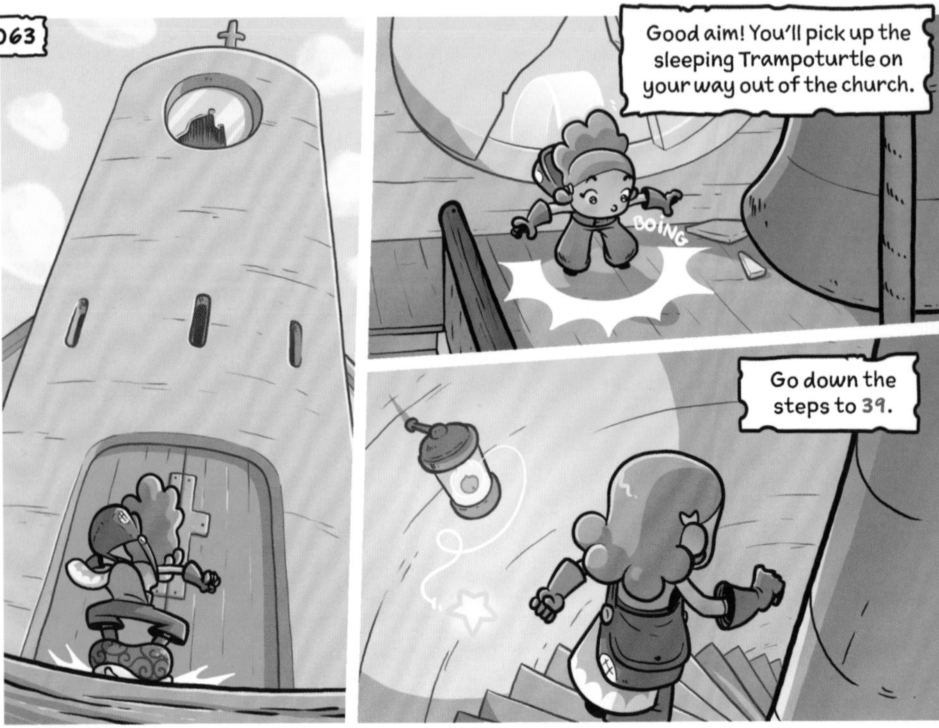
Good aim! You'll pick up the sleeping Trampoturtle on your way out of the church.
BOING
Go down the steps to 39.

064

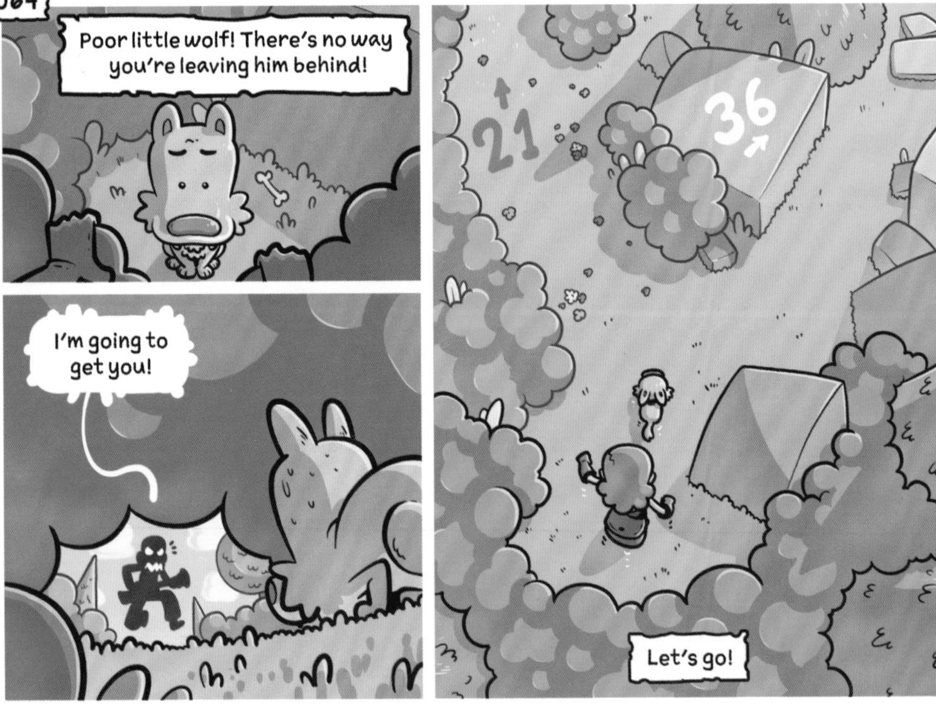
Poor little wolf! There's no way you're leaving him behind!
I'm going to get you!
21
36
Let's go!

65

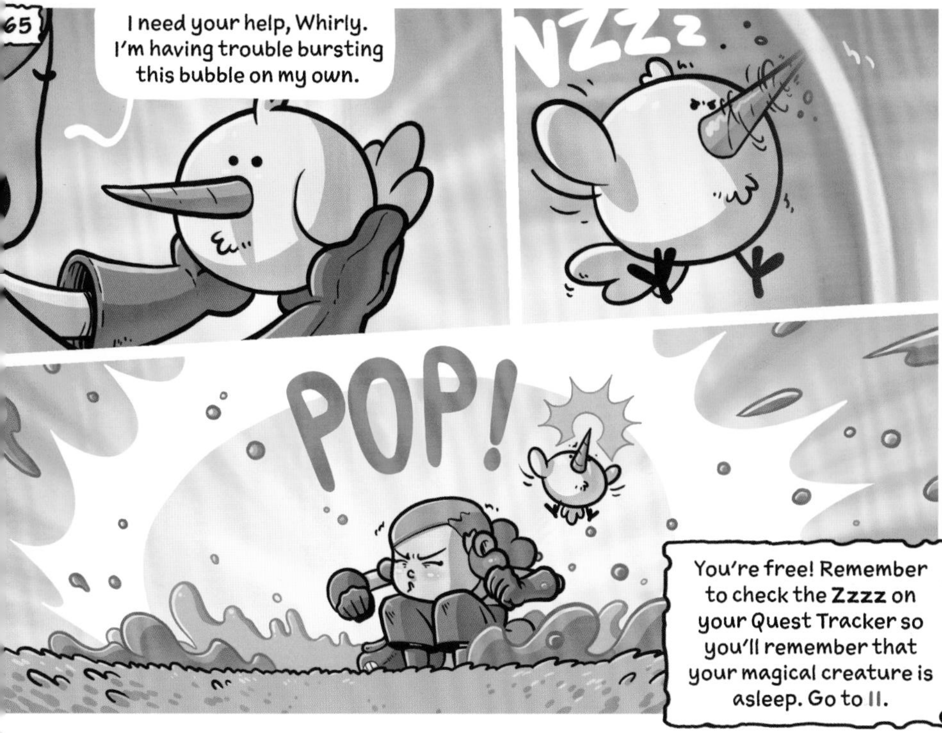
I need your help, Whirly. I'm having trouble bursting this bubble on my own.
POP!
You're free! Remember to check the **Zzzz** on your Quest Tracker so you'll remember that your magical creature is asleep. Go to 11.

66

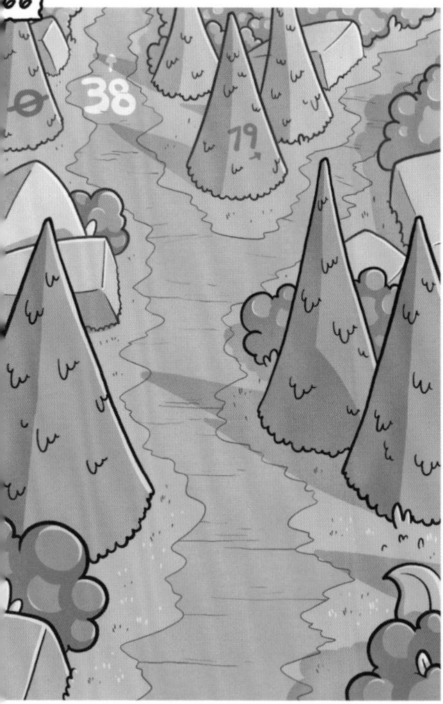
38
79

067

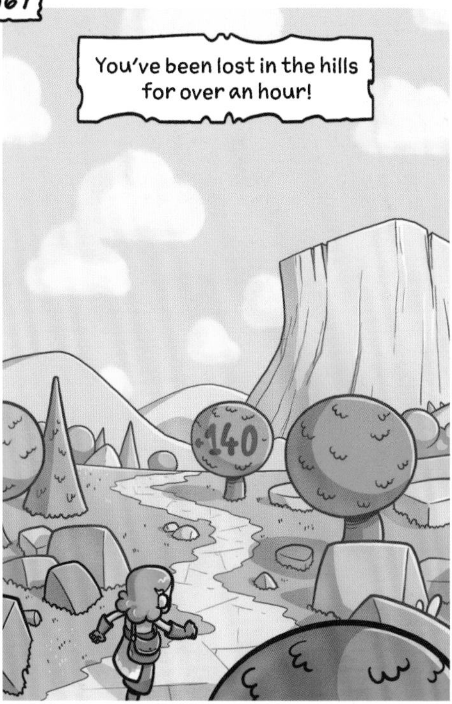
You've been lost in the hills for over an hour!
140

068

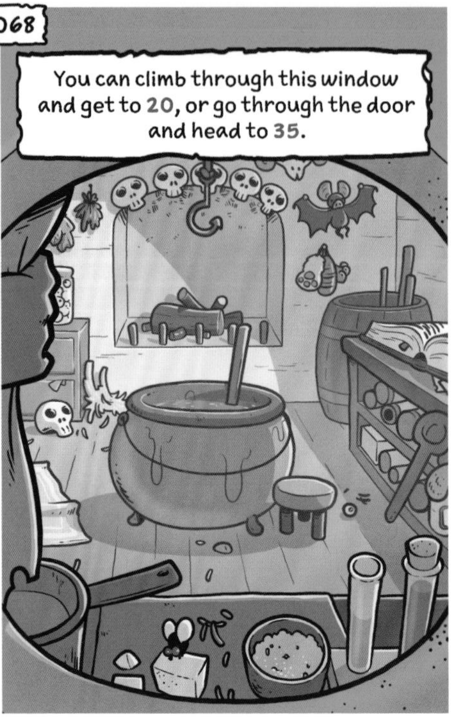
You can climb through this window and get to 20, or go through the door and head to 35.

069

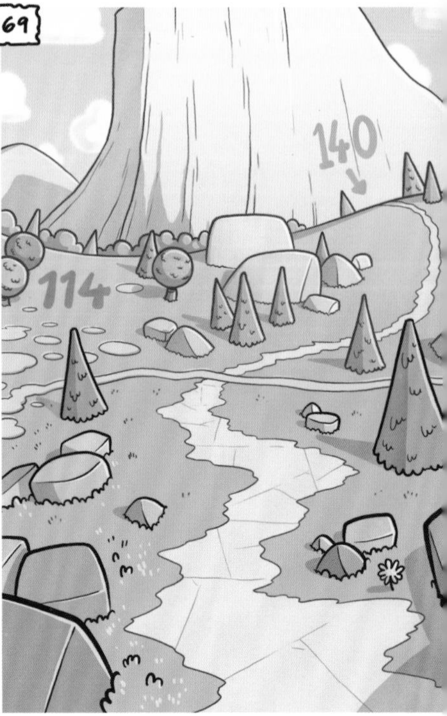
140
114

070

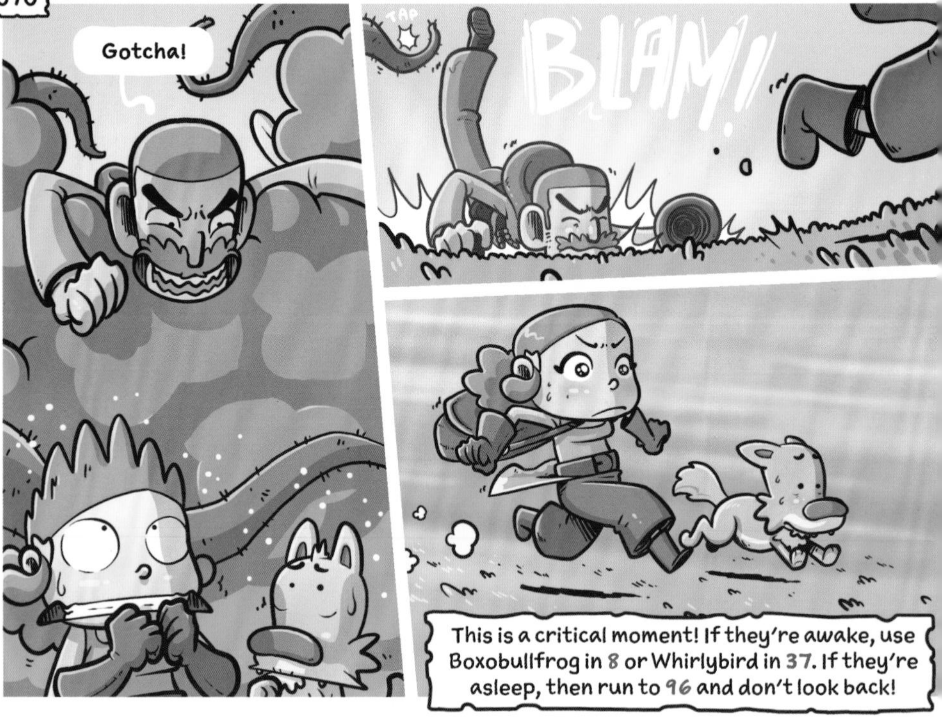
Gotcha!
TAP
BLAM!
This is a critical moment! If they're awake, use Boxobullfrog in 8 or Whirlybird in 37. If they're asleep, then run to 96 and don't look back!

071

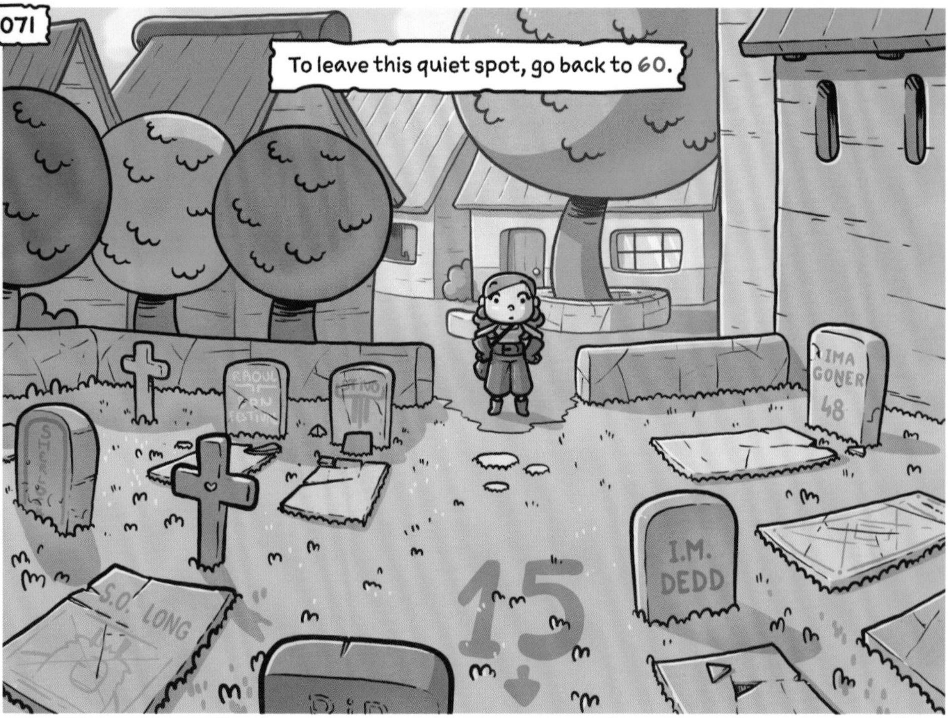
To leave this quiet spot, go back to 60.
IMA GONER 48
I.M. DEDD
S.O. LONG
15

072

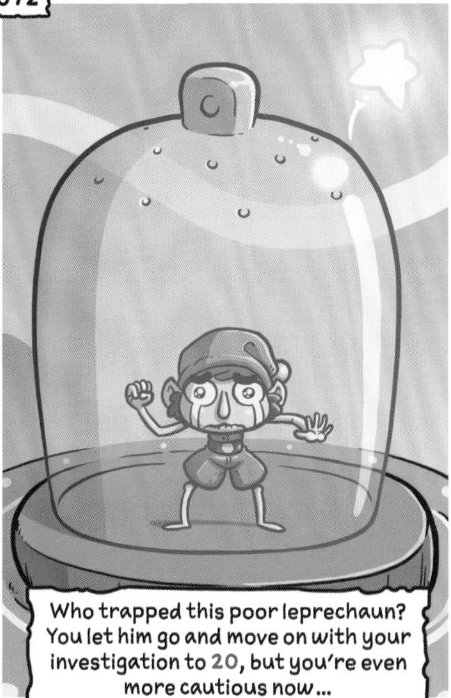
Who trapped this poor leprechaun? You let him go and move on with your investigation to 20, but you're even more cautious now...

073

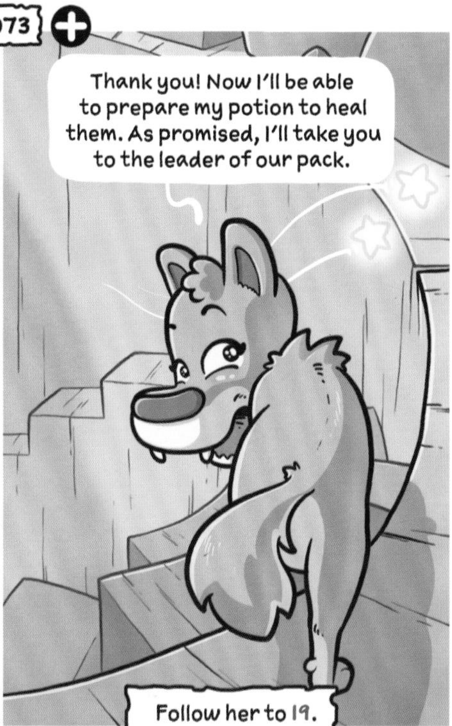
Thank you! Now I'll be able to prepare my potion to heal them. As promised, I'll take you to the leader of our pack.
Follow her to 19.

074

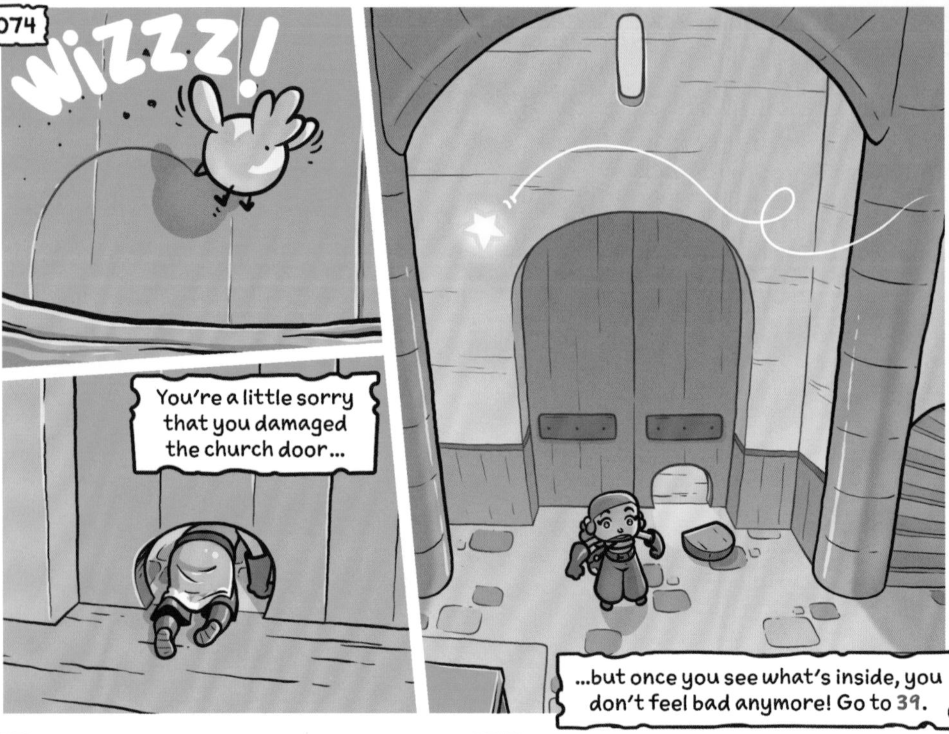
WiZZZ!
You're a little sorry that you damaged the church door...
...but once you see what's inside, you don't feel bad anymore! Go to 39.

075

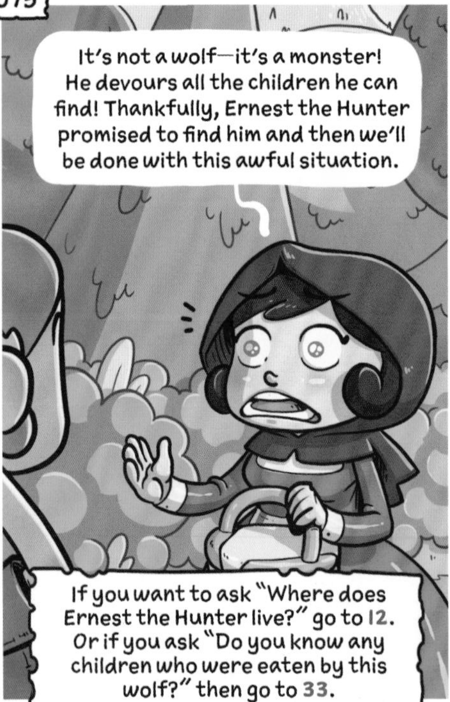
It's not a wolf—it's a monster! He devours all the children he can find! Thankfully, Ernest the Hunter promised to find him and then we'll be done with this awful situation.
If you want to ask "Where does Ernest the Hunter live?" go to 12. Or if you ask "Do you know any children who were eaten by this wolf?" then go to 33.

076

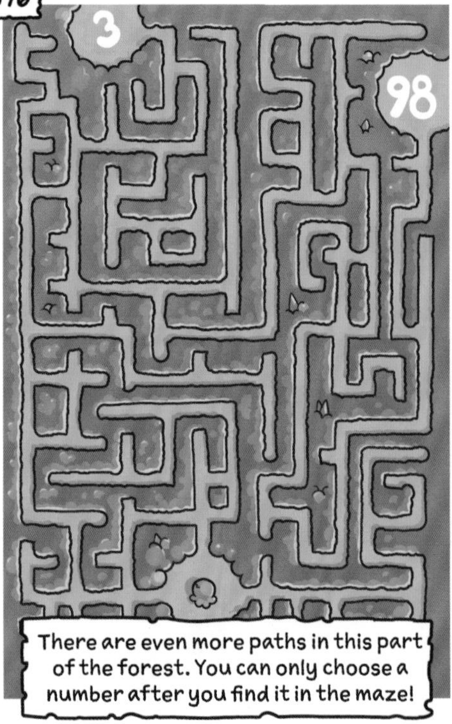
3
98
There are even more paths in this part of the forest. You can only choose a number after you find it in the maze!

077

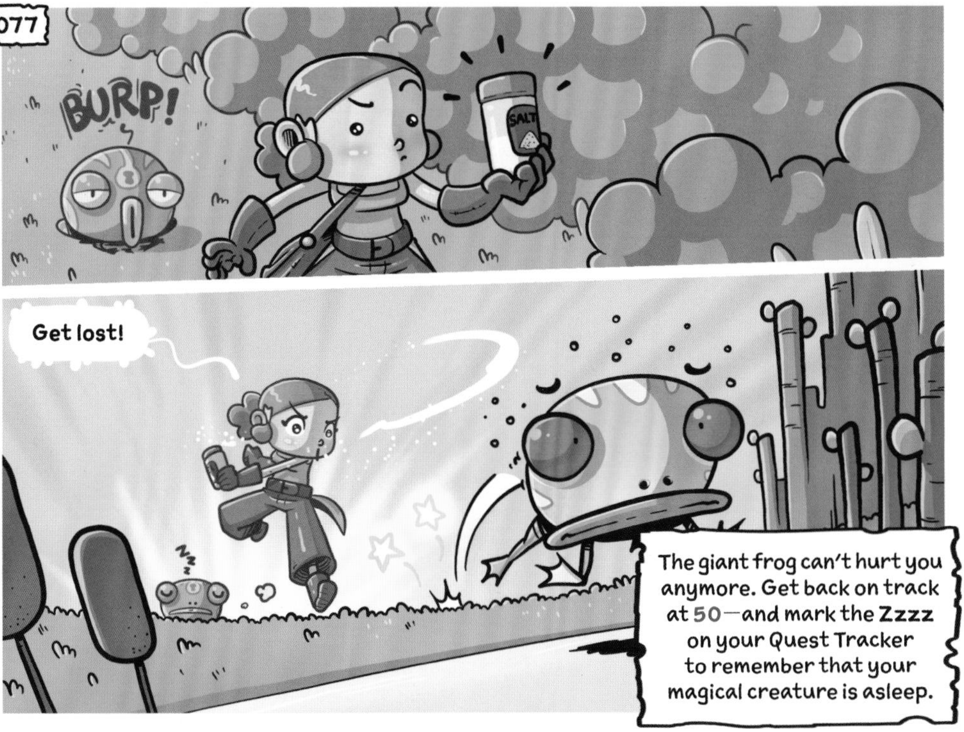
BURP!
SALT
Get lost!
The giant frog can't hurt you anymore. Get back on track at 50—and mark the Zzzz on your Quest Tracker to remember that your magical creature is asleep.

078

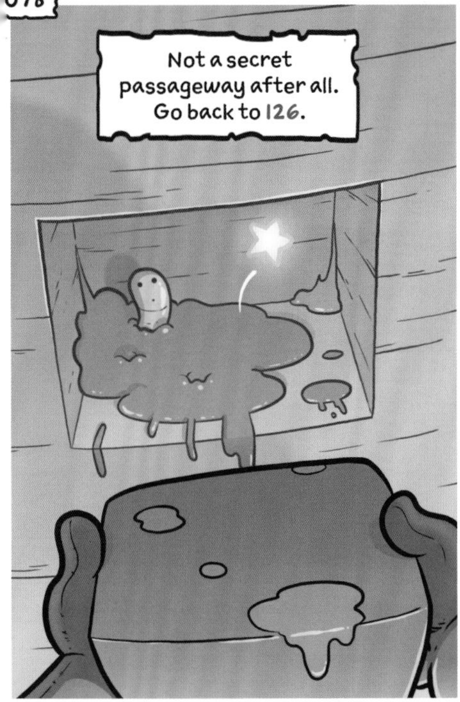
Not a secret passageway after all. Go back to 126.

079

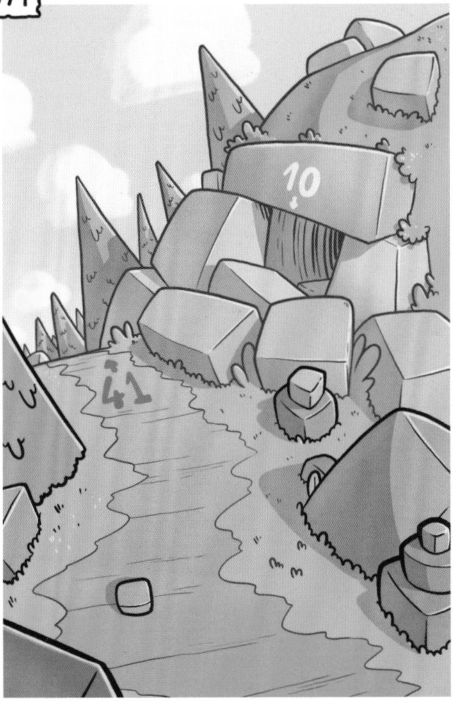
10
41

080

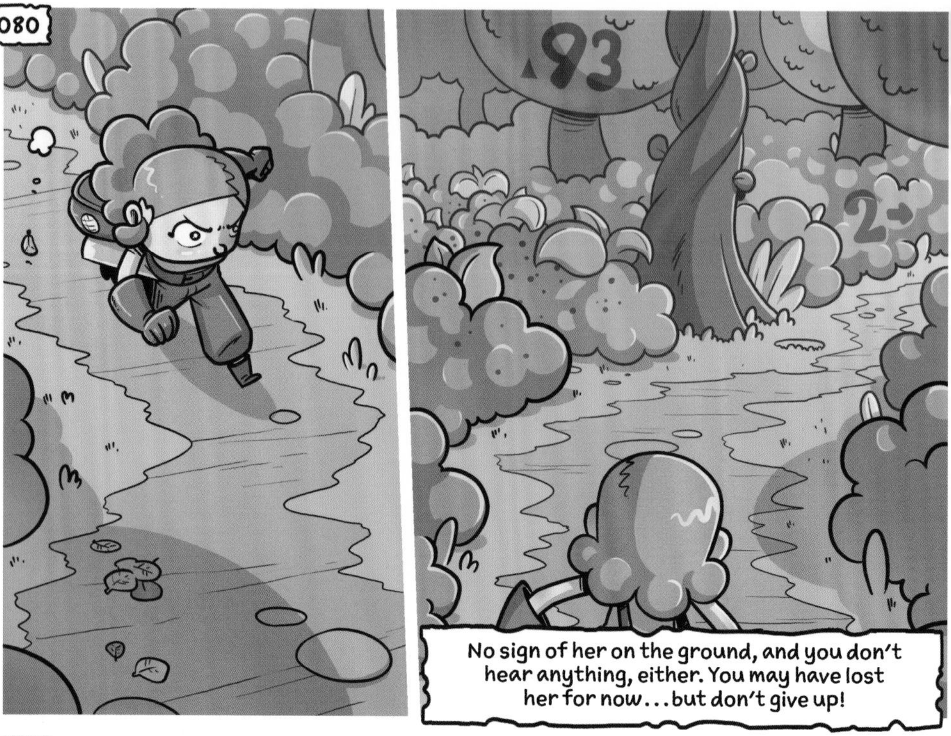

93
2
No sign of her on the ground, and you don't hear anything, either. You may have lost her for now... but don't give up!

081

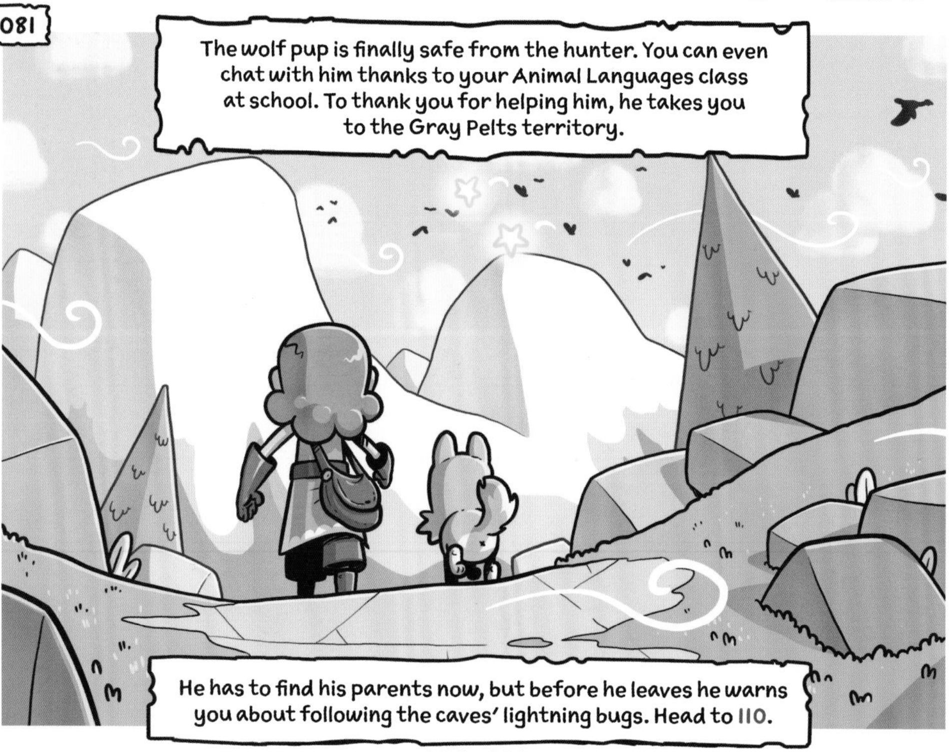

The wolf pup is finally safe from the hunter. You can even chat with him thanks to your Animal Languages class at school. To thank you for helping him, he takes you to the Gray Pelts territory.
He has to find his parents now, but before he leaves he warns you about following the caves' lightning bugs. Head to 110.

Miss Primrose, your Animal Languages teacher.

Pocus! Come in. Your brother isn't with you?

I left him near a cabin made of candy in Grimm's Woods.

Hmm... The witch's house! My little bird friends told me she had trapped two children. Please, sit down.

So you know?

Of course! This is where I live when I'm not at school. Even though this witch is dangerous, I can't help you and Hocus—this is **your** test, after all. But I will tell you where you can find an ally.

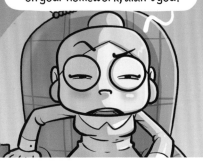

You must find the wolf who can talk. But you'll need to communicate with the other wolves in their own language, too. You got a good grade on your homework, didn't you?

Uhhmm...

I see. Well, let's review!

Your teacher gives you a quick lesson on the wolves' language. Write the word "Lair" in the Notes area of your Quest Tracker, and then head to 60 to decide how you'll find John.

083

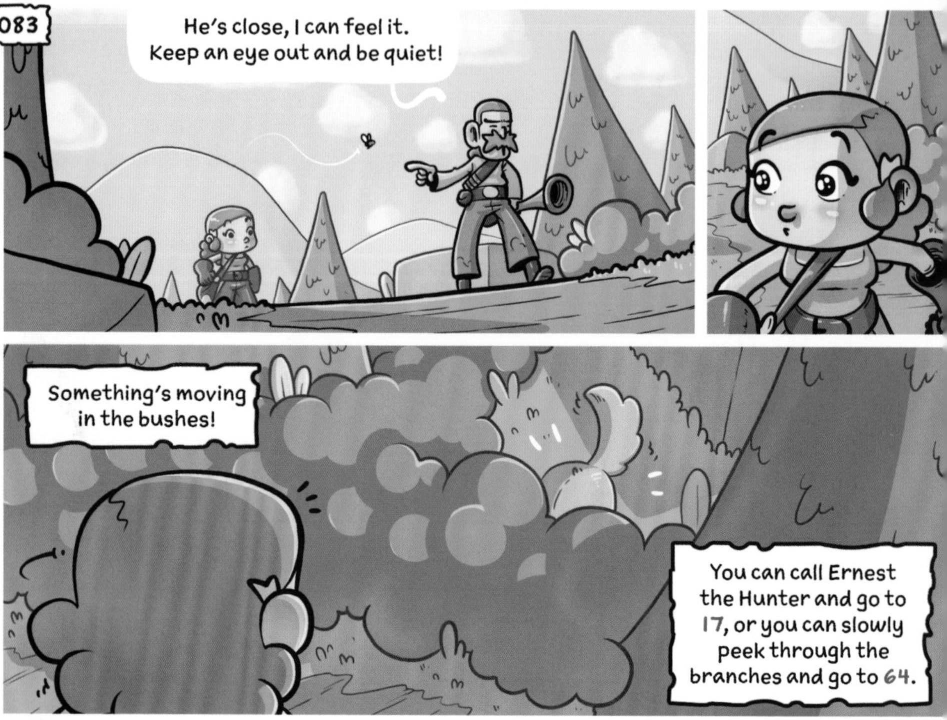
He's close, I can feel it.
Keep an eye out and be quiet!
Something's moving in the bushes!
You can call Ernest the Hunter and go to 17, or you can slowly peek through the branches and go to 64.

084

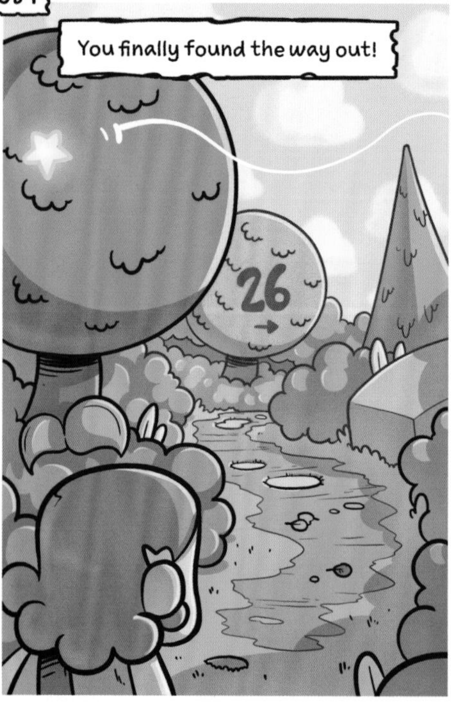
You finally found the way out!
26

085

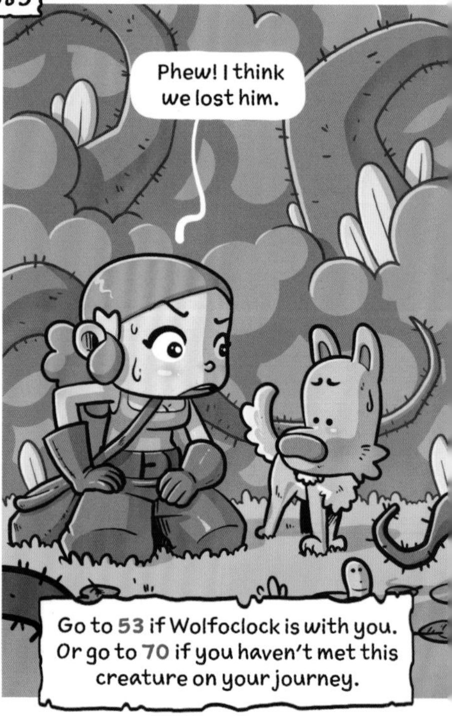
Phew! I think we lost him.
Go to 53 if Wolfoclock is with you. Or go to 70 if you haven't met this creature on your journey.

086

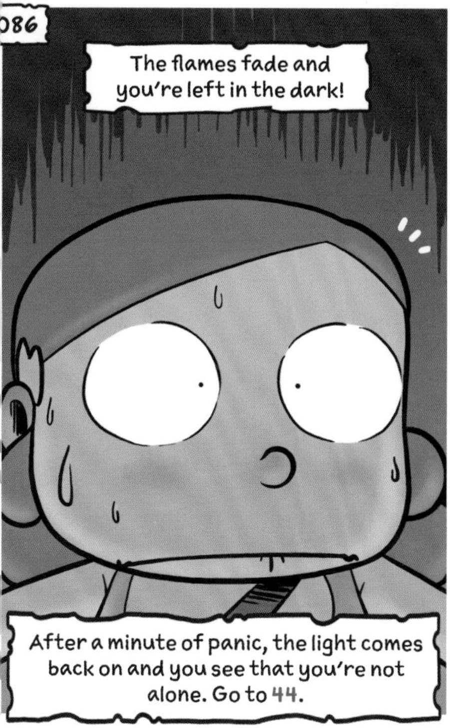
The flames fade and you're left in the dark!
After a minute of panic, the light comes back on and you see that you're not alone. Go to 44.

087

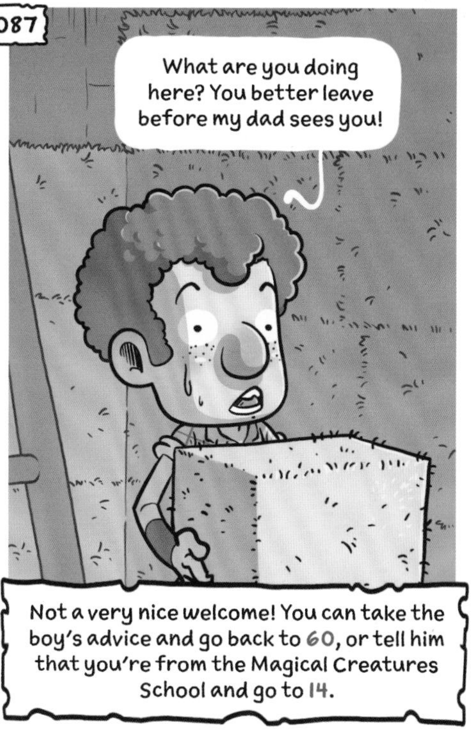
What are you doing here? You better leave before my dad sees you!
Not a very nice welcome! You can take the boy's advice and go back to 60, or tell him that you're from the Magical Creatures School and go to 14.

088

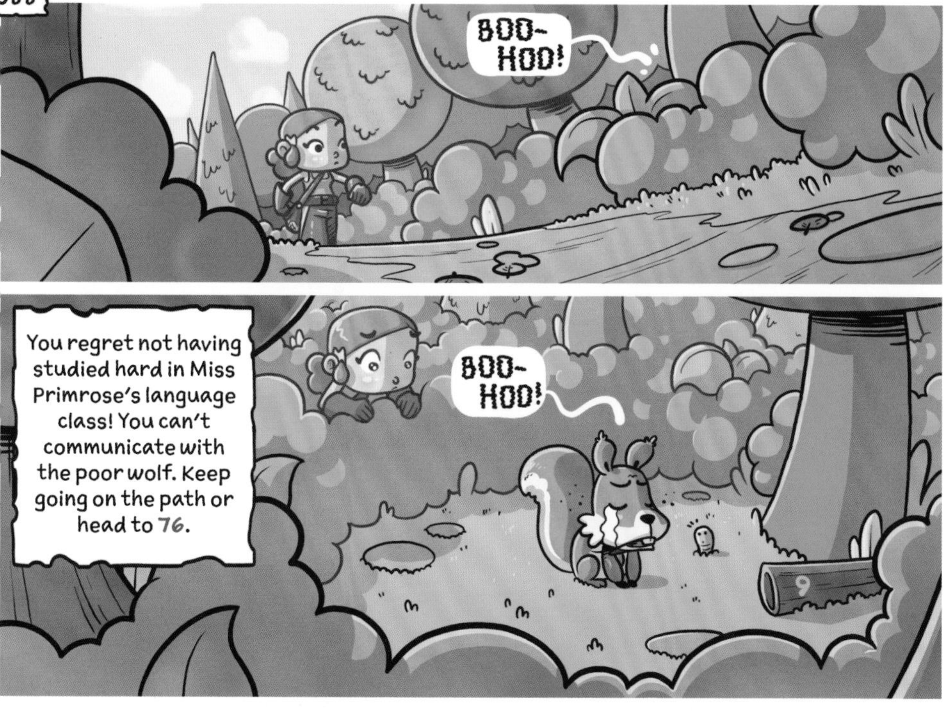
BOO-HOO!
You regret not having studied hard in Miss Primrose's language class! You can't communicate with the poor wolf. Keep going on the path or head to 76.
BOO-HOO!

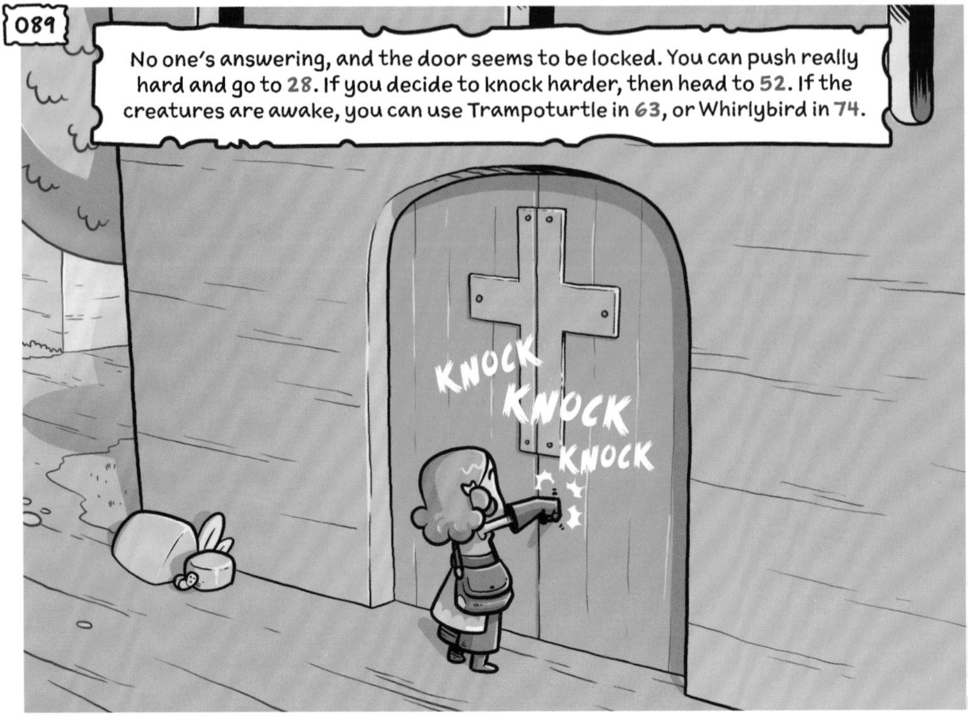
089
No one's answering, and the door seems to be locked. You can push really hard and go to 28. If you decide to knock harder, then head to 52. If the creatures are awake, you can use Trampoturtle in 63, or Whirlybird in 74.
KNOCK
KNOCK
KNOCK

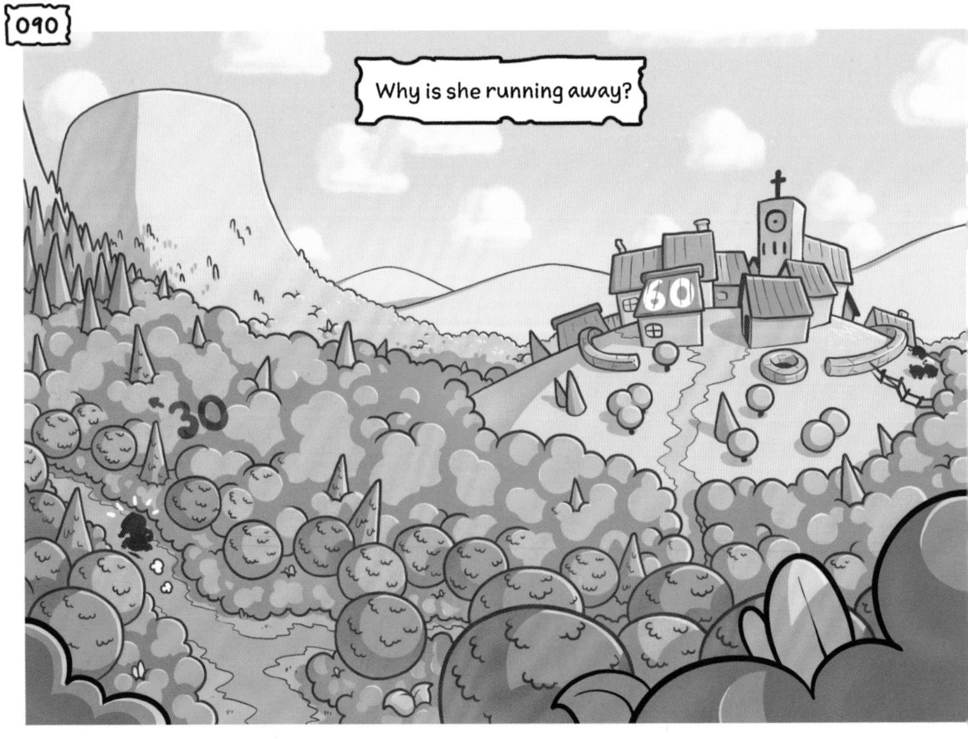
090
Why is she running away?
60
30

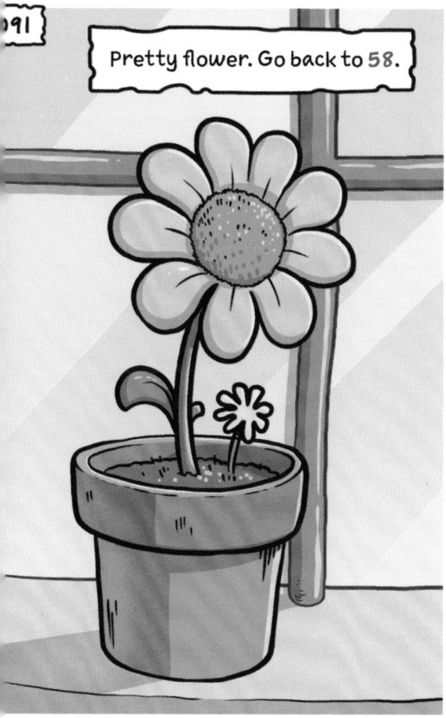
91
Pretty flower. Go back to 58.

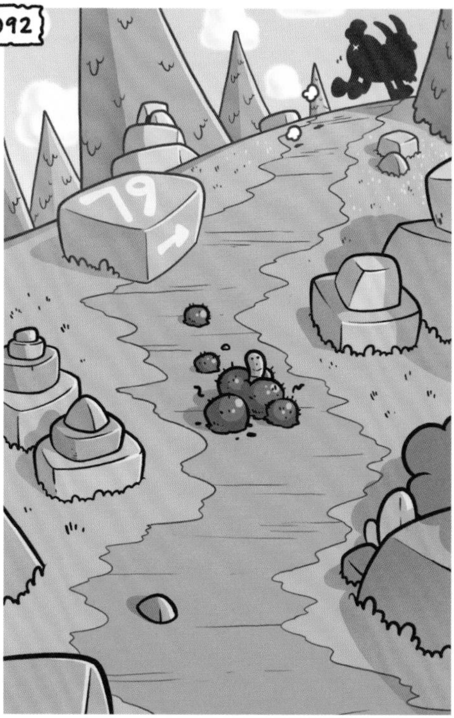
092
79

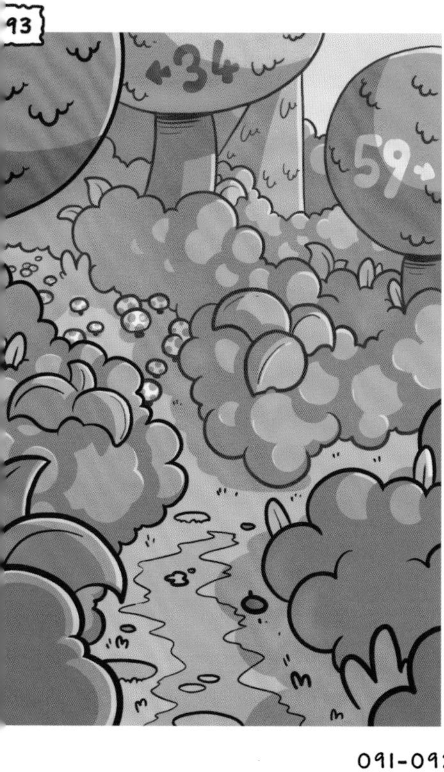
93
34
59

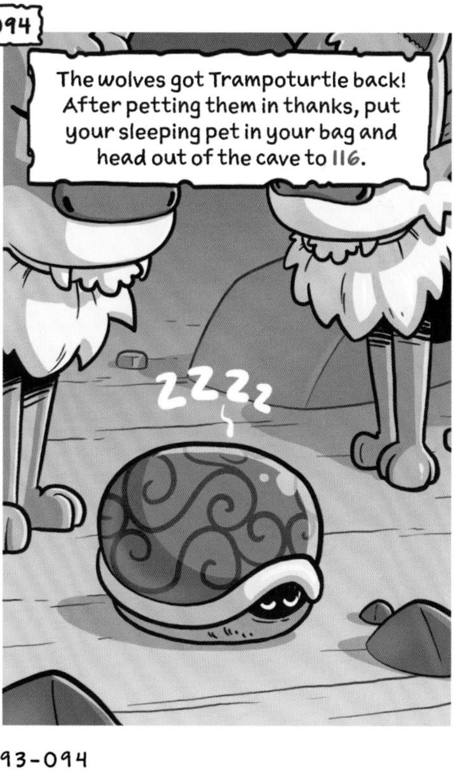
094
The wolves got Trampoturtle back! After petting them in thanks, put your sleeping pet in your bag and head out of the cave to 116.
ZZZz

Let's play Pass the Dragon!

You will need:

- a die
- 6 pennies (dragons)
- a dime (you)

Place the dime in your choice of white square on the bottom row.

Your goal is to reach one of the six white squares on the top row before one of the dragons reaches a white square on the bottom row. Move the dime (you) and the pennies (one for each dragon) according to the die.

The dragons start the game. Throw the die for them. Move the dragons according to the number on the die:

1: All dragons go down two rows.
2: The blue dragons go down one row.
3: The black dragons go down one row.
4: The red dragons go down one row.
5 or 6: All the dragons go down one row.

Your turn: Move one box in whatever direction you wish: up, down, sideways, or diagonally.

Then it's the dragons' turn again, then yours, and so on.

You win if you reach one of the white squares at the top.

You lose if you land on a square with a dragon, if a dragon crosses your square, or if the dragon reaches one of the white squares at the bottom.

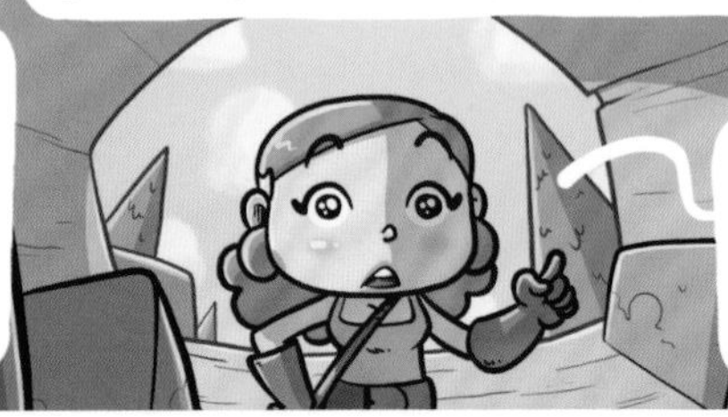

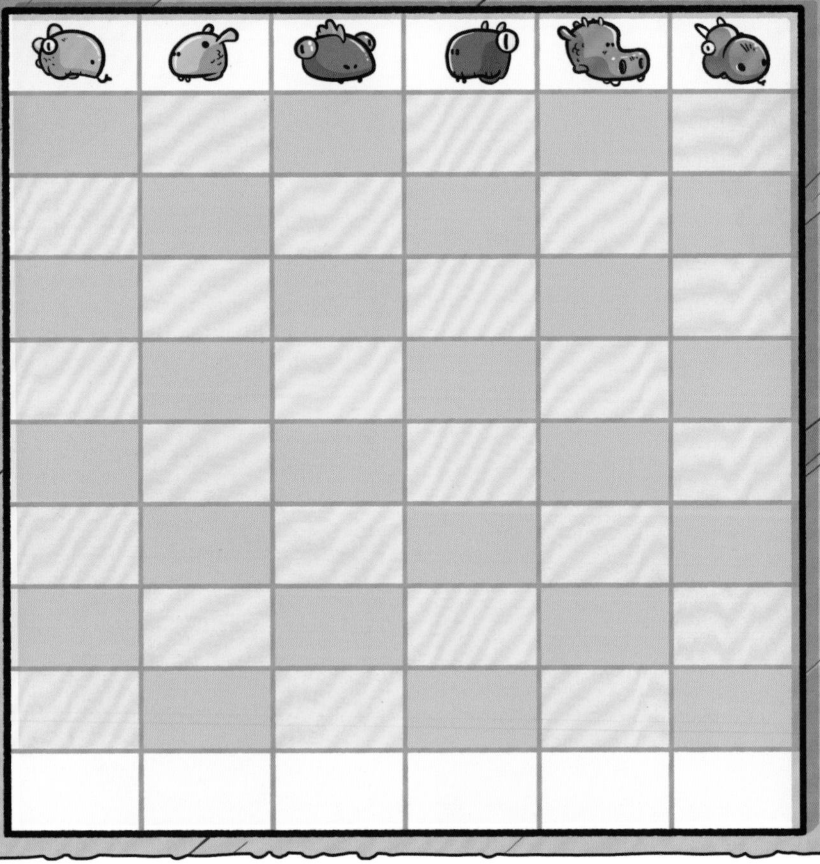

Add a star to your Quest Tracker for each game you win. After playing three times, go to **22**.

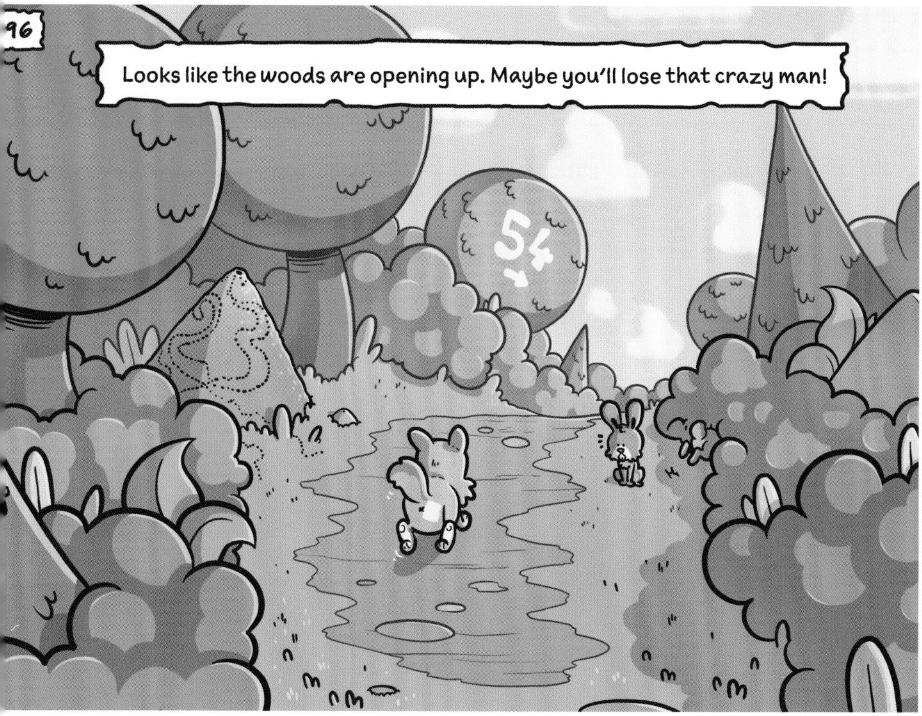
96
Looks like the woods are opening up. Maybe you'll lose that crazy man!
54

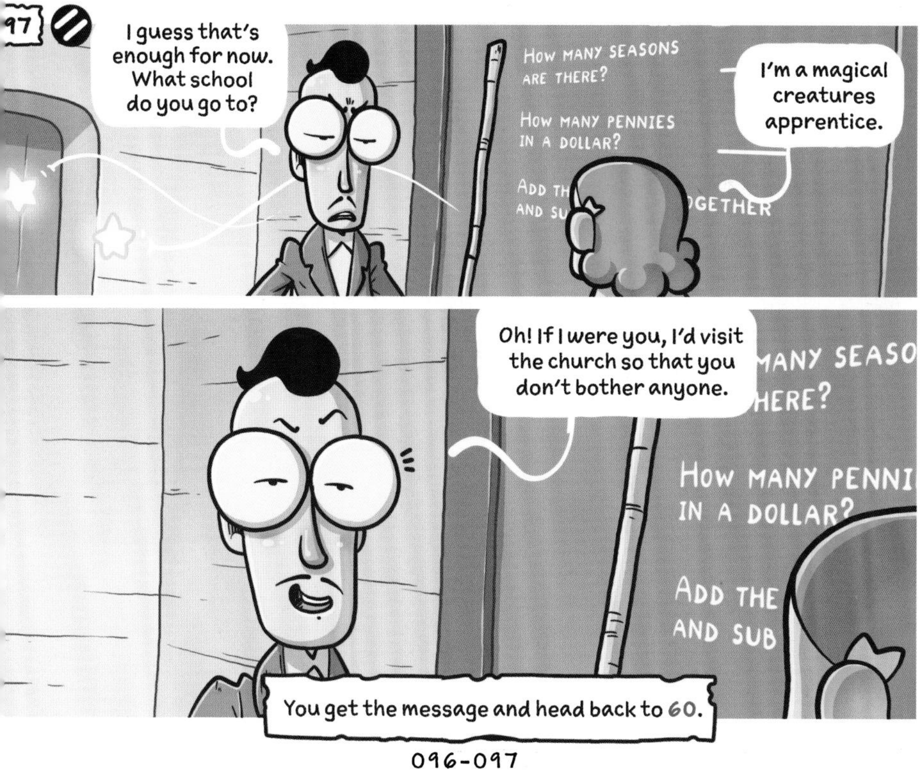
97
I guess that's enough for now. What school do you go to?
HOW MANY SEASONS ARE THERE?
HOW MANY PENNIES IN A DOLLAR?
I'm a magical creatures apprentice.
Oh! If I were you, I'd visit the church so that you don't bother anyone.
You get the message and head back to 60.

098

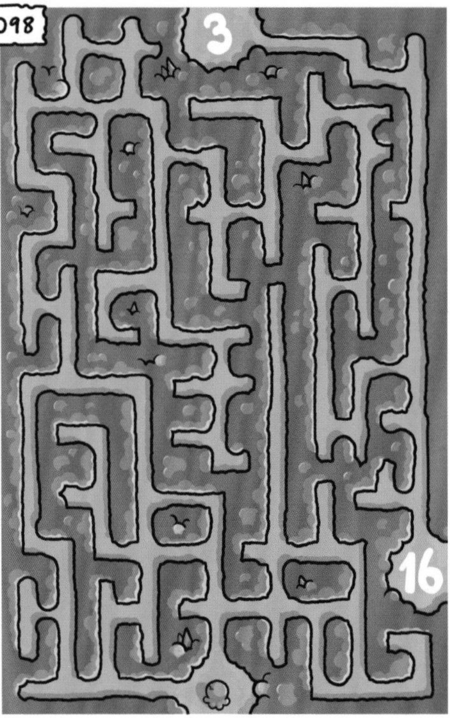
3
16

099

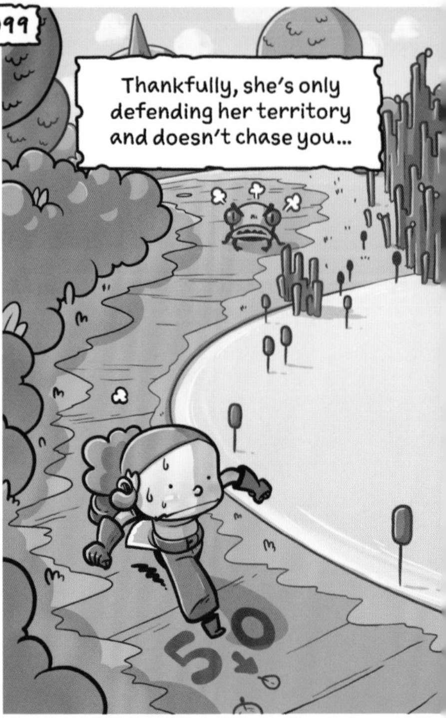
Thankfully, she's only defending her territory and doesn't chase you...
50

100

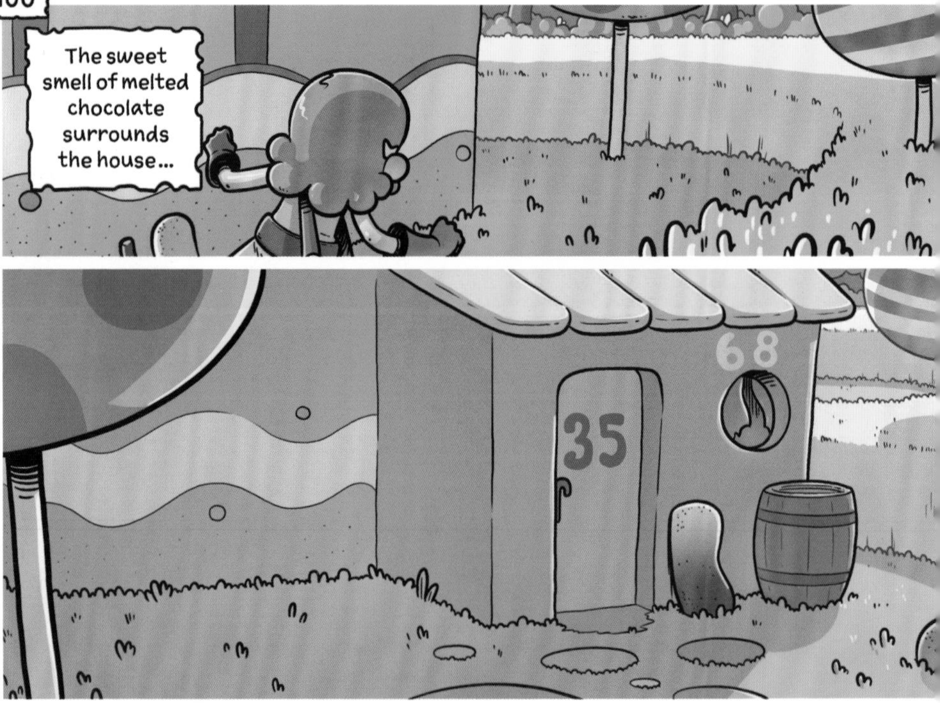
The sweet smell of melted chocolate surrounds the house...
68
35

101

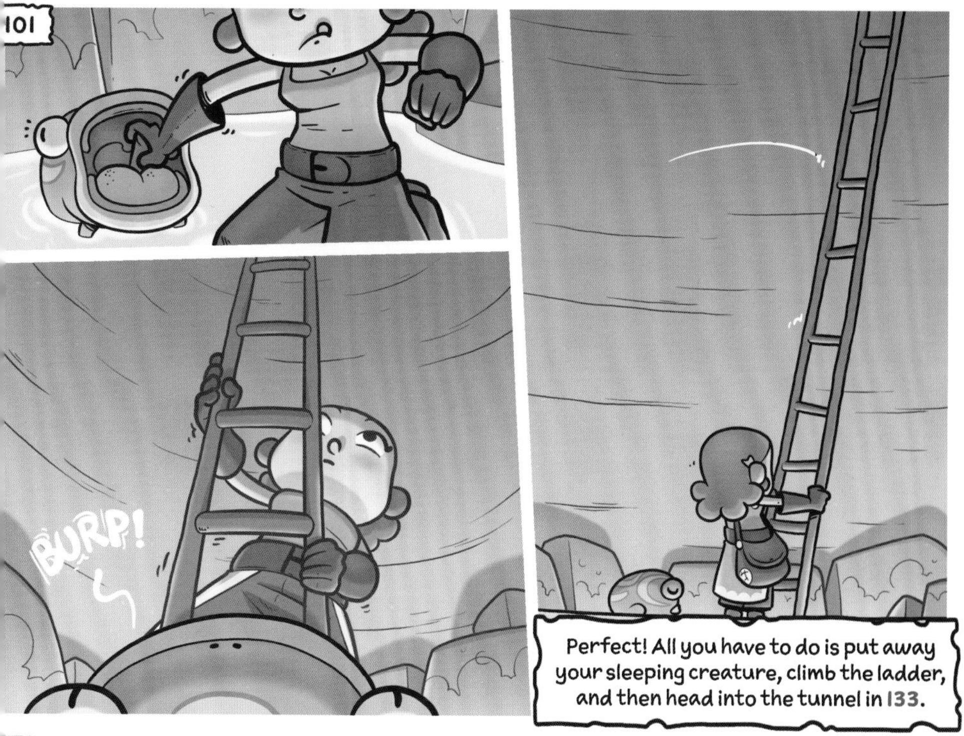
BURP!
Perfect! All you have to do is put away your sleeping creature, climb the ladder, and then head into the tunnel in 133.

02

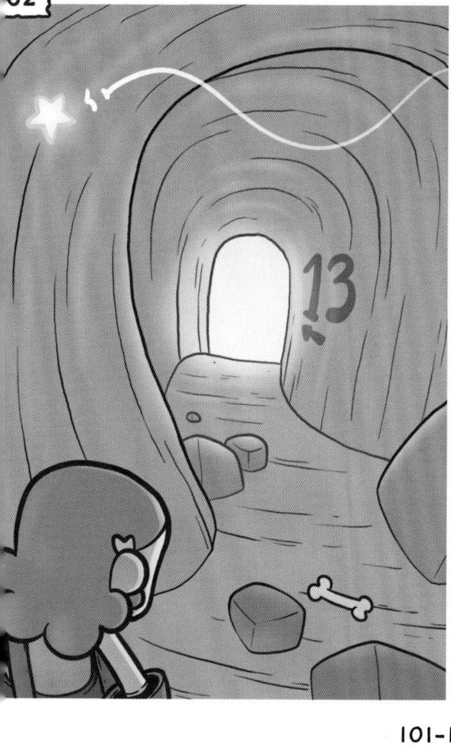
13

103

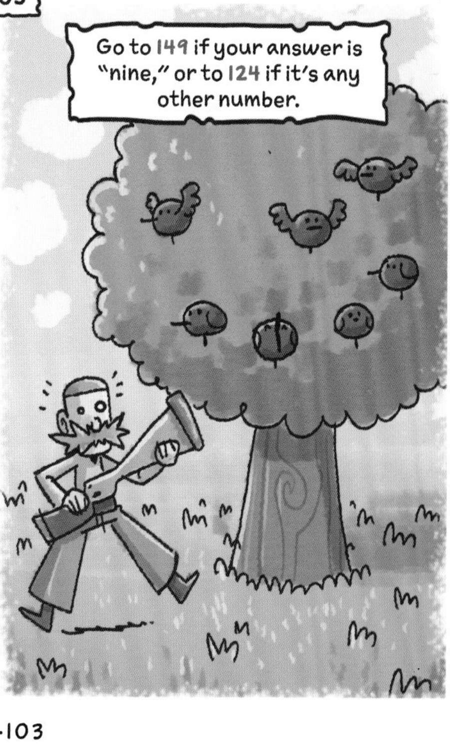
Go to 149 if your answer is "nine," or to 124 if it's any other number.

104

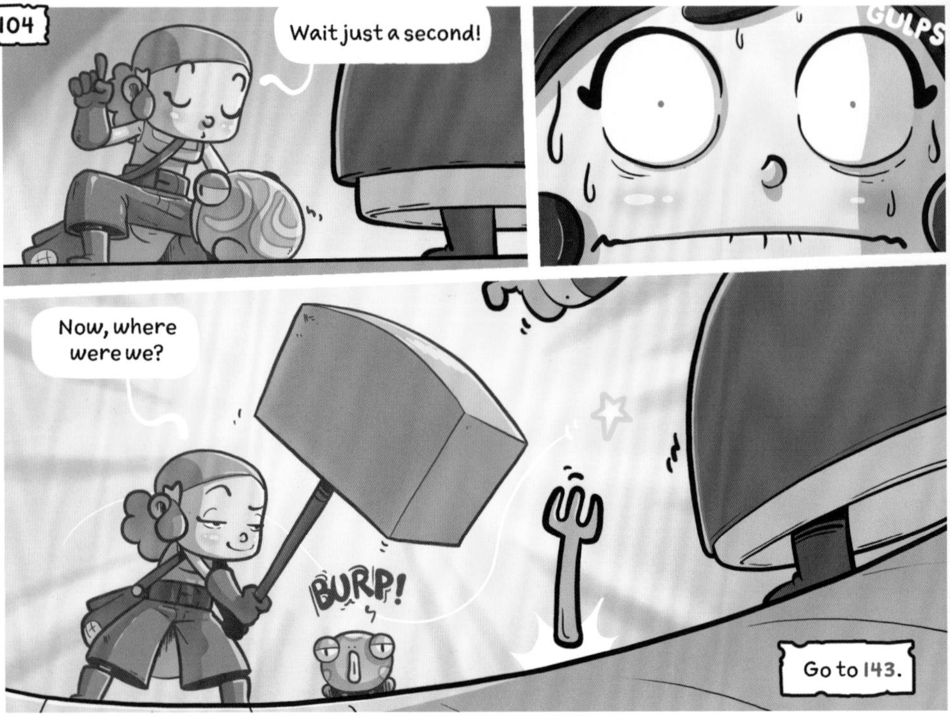
Wait just a second!
GULPS
Now, where were we?
BURP!
Go to 143.

105

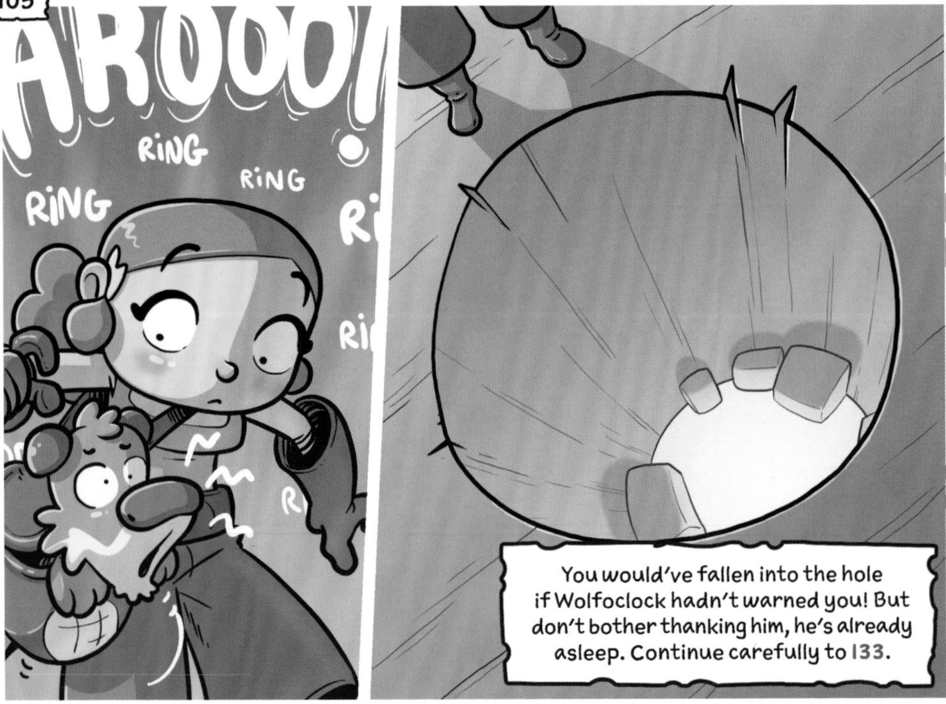
AROOO
RING
RING
RING
You would've fallen into the hole if Wolfoclock hadn't warned you! But don't bother thanking him, he's already asleep. Continue carefully to 133.

06

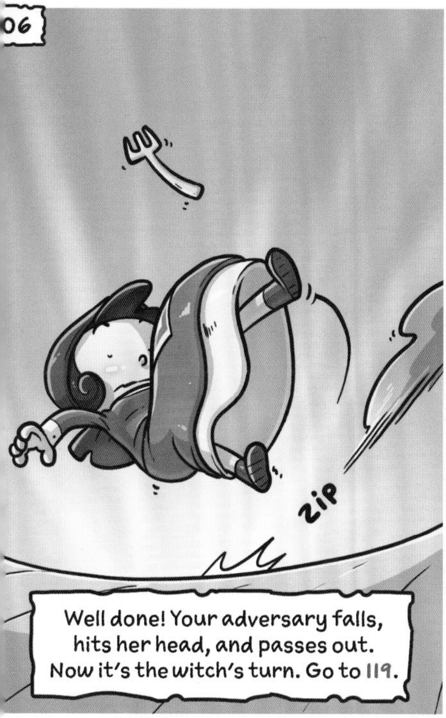
ZIP
Well done! Your adversary falls, hits her head, and passes out. Now it's the witch's turn. Go to 119.

107

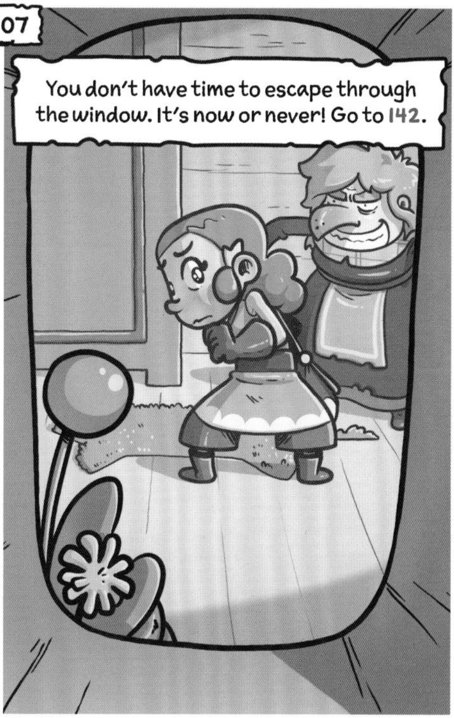
You don't have time to escape through the window. It's now or never! Go to 142.

08

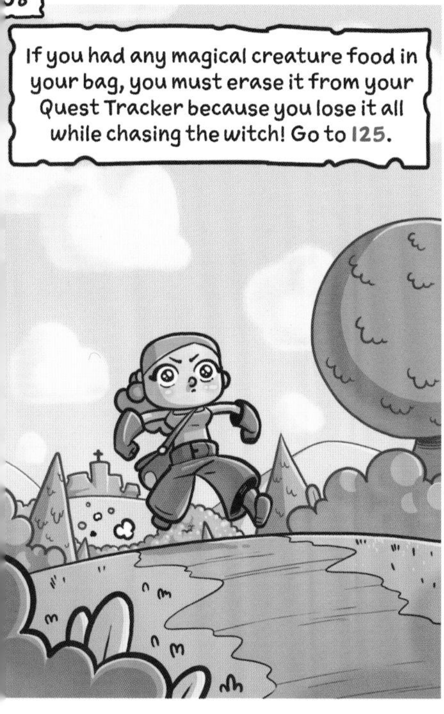
If you had any magical creature food in your bag, you must erase it from your Quest Tracker because you lose it all while chasing the witch! Go to 125.

109

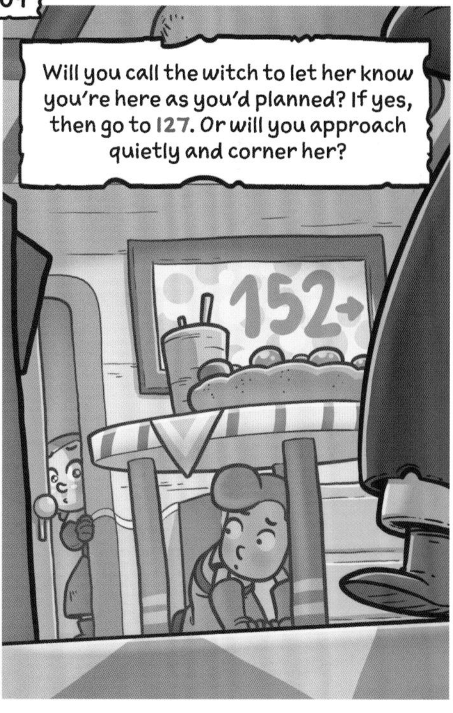
Will you call the witch to let her know you're here as you'd planned? If yes, then go to 127. Or will you approach quietly and corner her?
152→

110

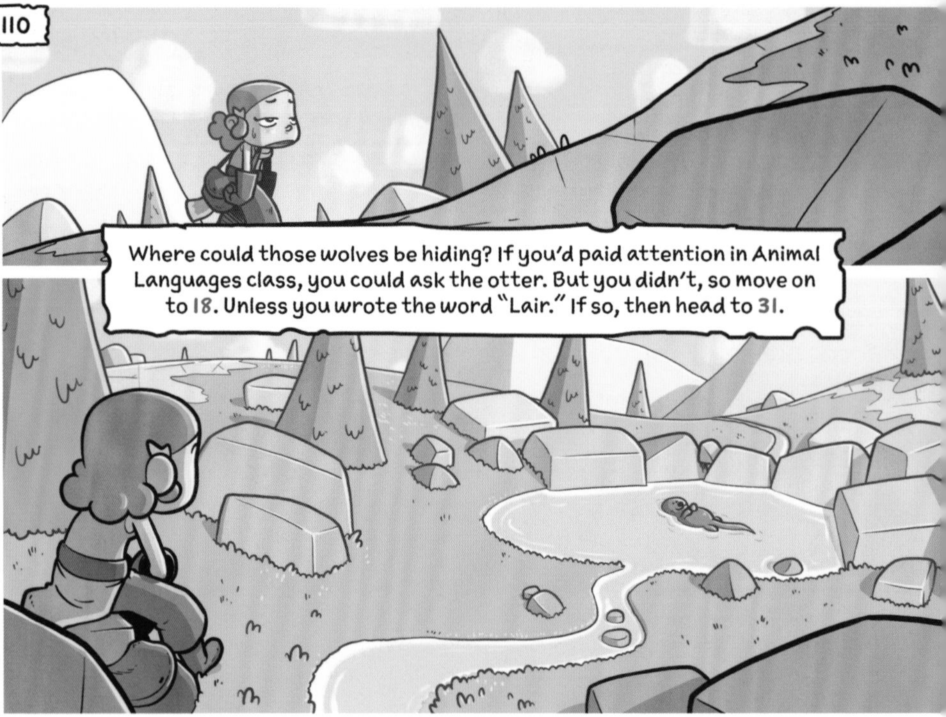
Where could those wolves be hiding? If you'd paid attention in Animal Languages class, you could ask the otter. But you didn't, so move on to 18. Unless you wrote the word "Lair." If so, then head to 31.

111

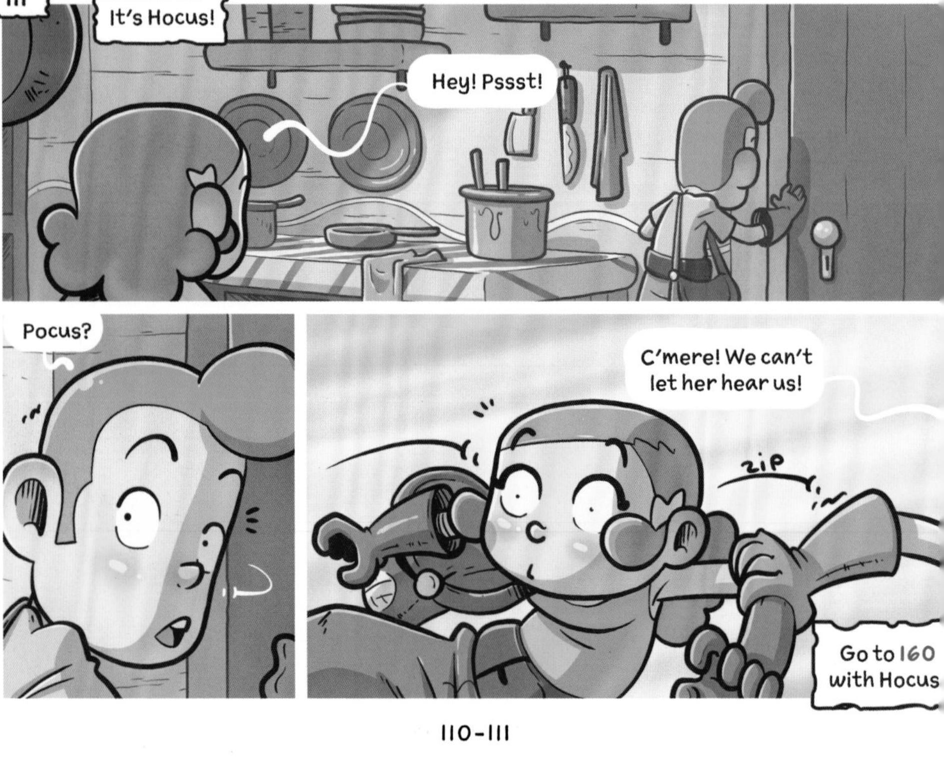
It's Hocus!
Hey! Pssst!
Pocus?
C'mere! We can't let her hear us!
ZIP
Go to 160 with Hocus

112

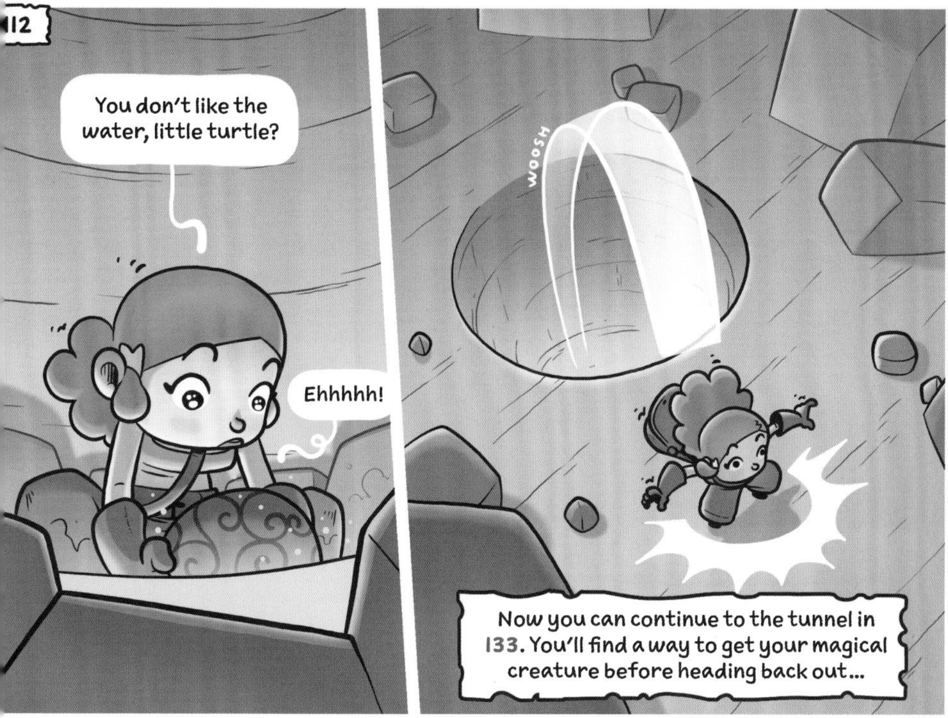
You don't like the water, little turtle?
Ehhhhh!
WOOSH
Now you can continue to the tunnel in 133. You'll find a way to get your magical creature before heading back out...

113

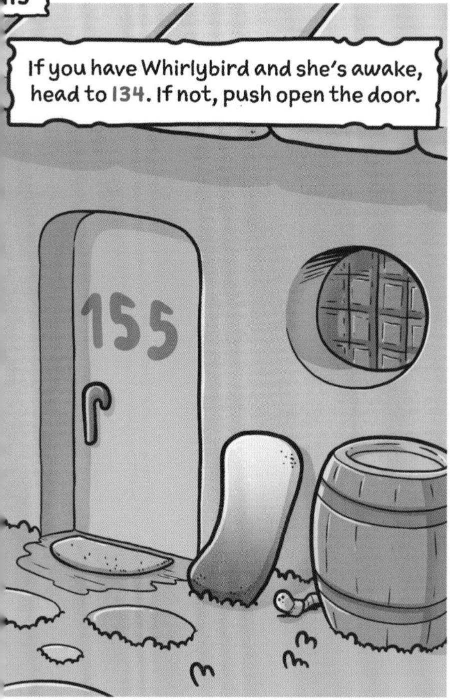
If you have Whirlybird and she's awake, head to 134. If not, push open the door.
155

114

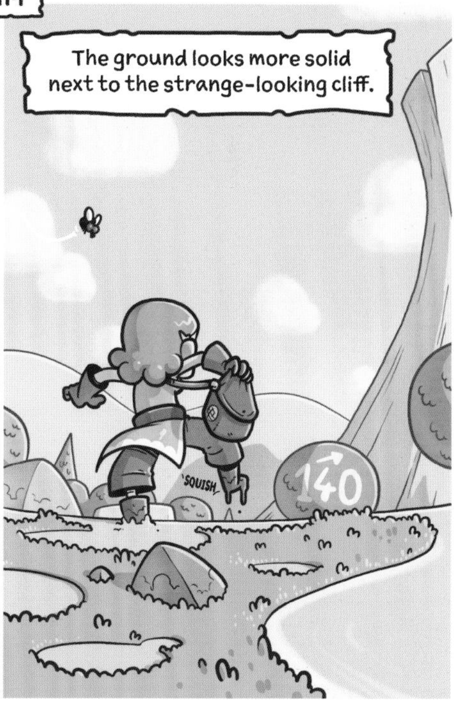
The ground looks more solid next to the strange-looking cliff.
SQUISH
140

115

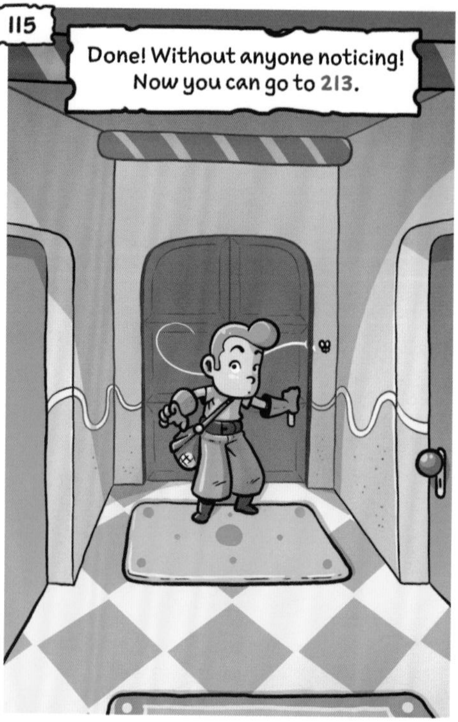
Done! Without anyone noticing!
Now you can go to 213.

116

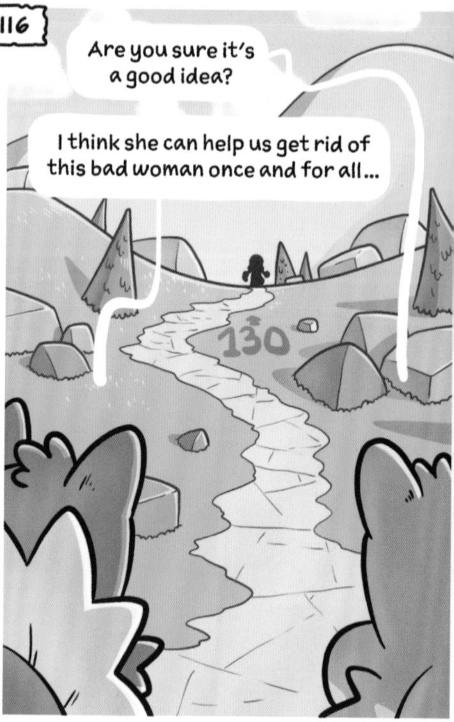
Are you sure it's a good idea?
I think she can help us get rid of this bad woman once and for all...
130

117

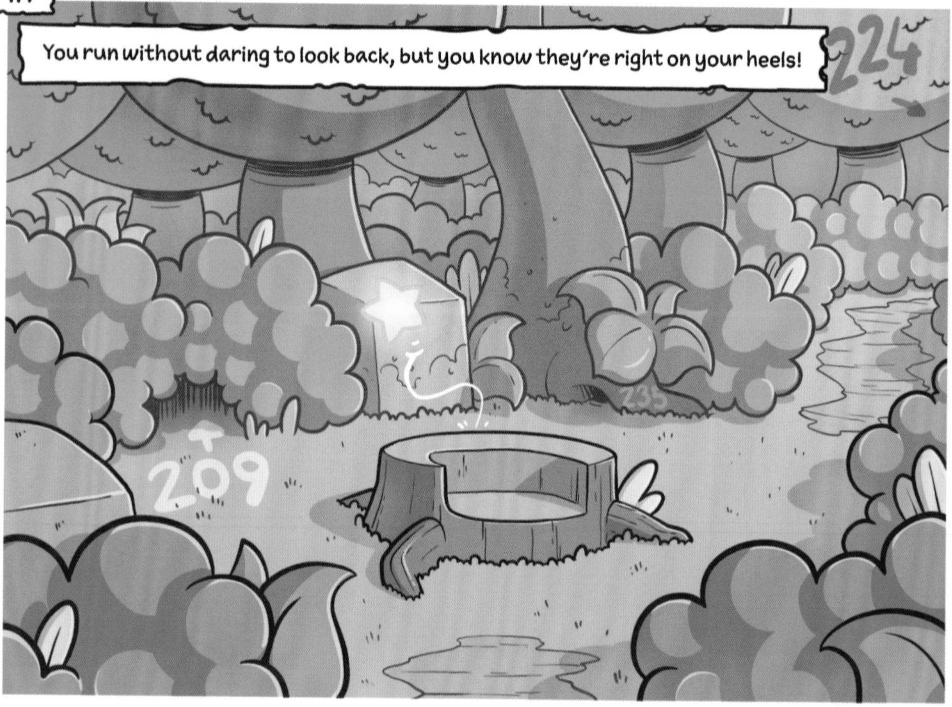
You run without daring to look back, but you know they're right on your heels!
224
235
209

118

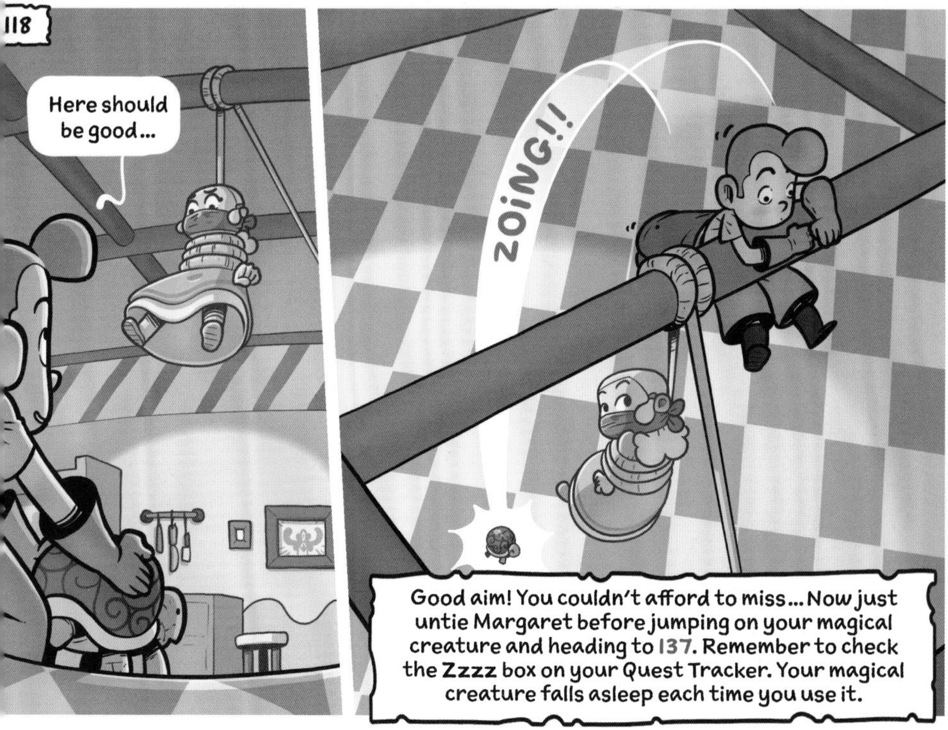
Here should be good...
ZOiNG!!
Good aim! You couldn't afford to miss... Now just untie Margaret before jumping on your magical creature and heading to 137. Remember to check the Zzzz box on your Quest Tracker. Your magical creature falls asleep each time you use it.

119

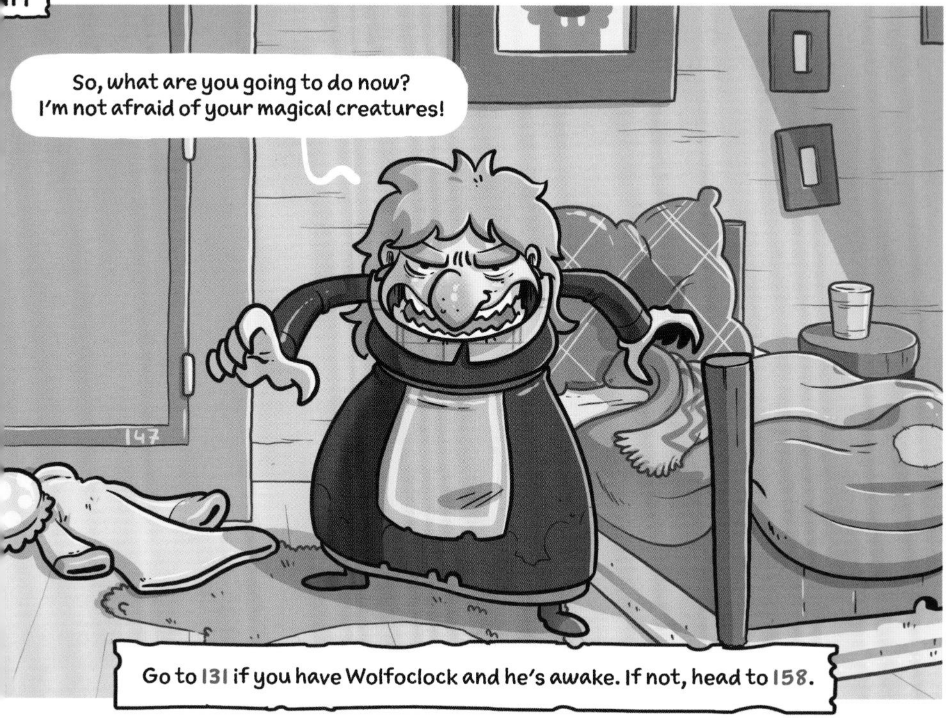
So, what are you going to do now? I'm not afraid of your magical creatures!
147
Go to 131 if you have Wolfoclock and he's awake. If not, head to 158.

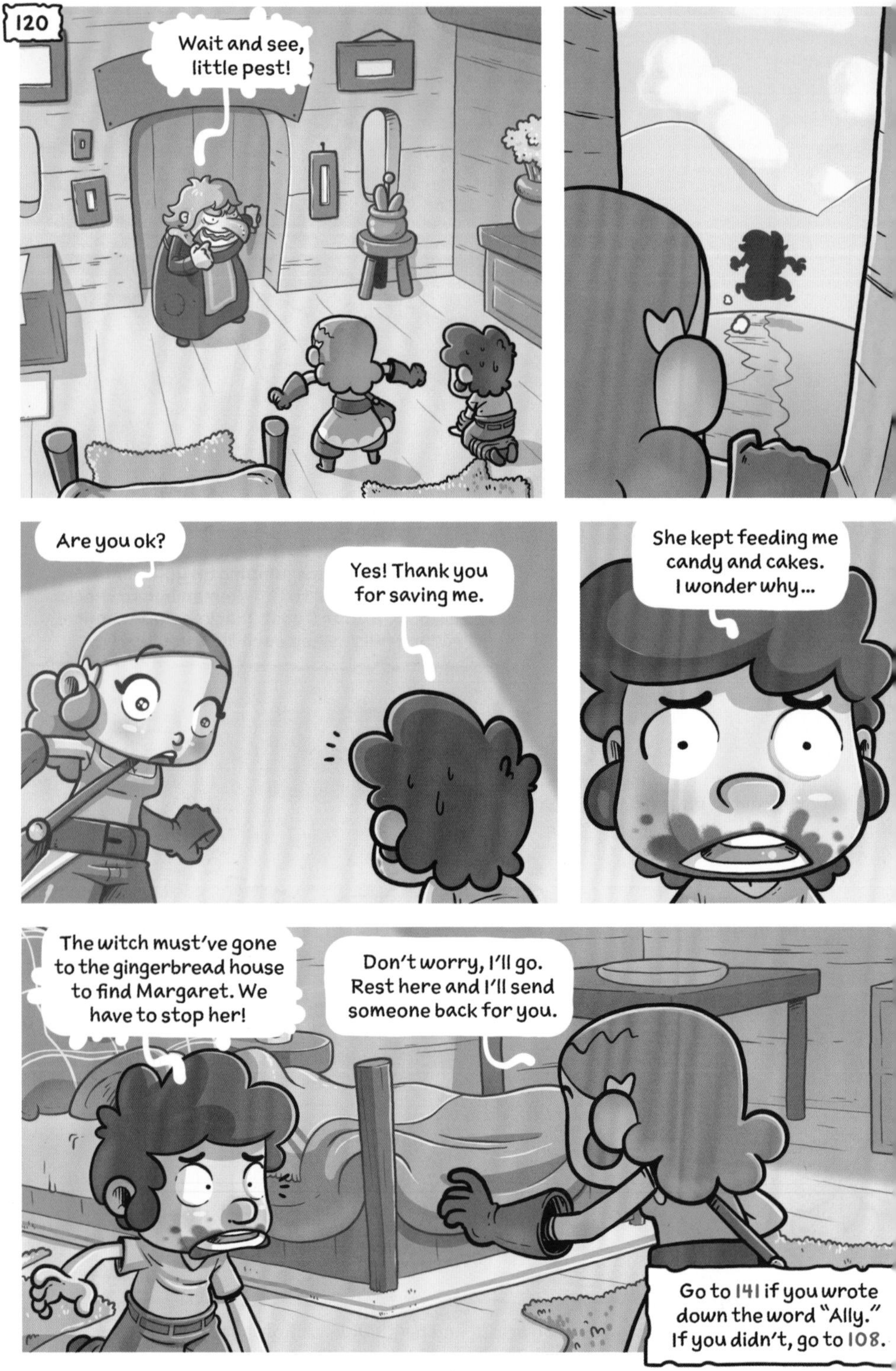
120
Wait and see, little pest!
Are you ok?
Yes! Thank you for saving me.
She kept feeding me candy and cakes. I wonder why...
The witch must've gone to the gingerbread house to find Margaret. We have to stop her!
Don't worry, I'll go. Rest here and I'll send someone back for you.

Go to 141 if you wrote down the word "Ally."
If you didn't, go to 108.

21

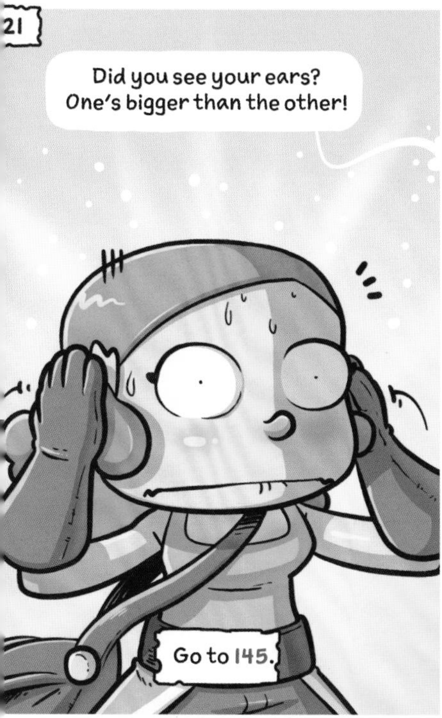
Did you see your ears?
One's bigger than the other!
Go to 145.

122

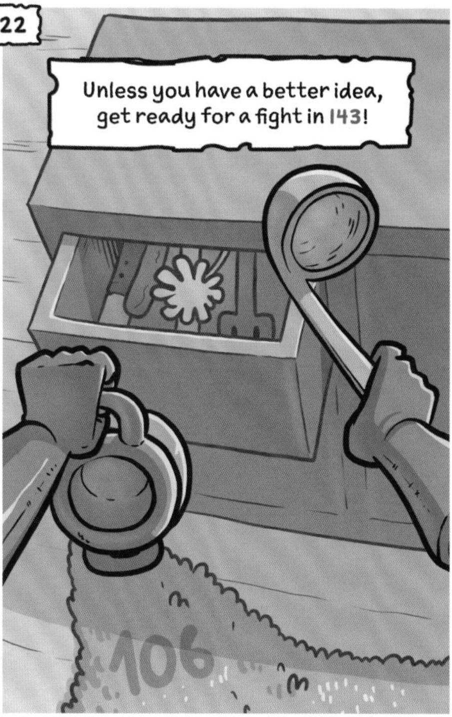
Unless you have a better idea, get ready for a fight in 143!
106

23

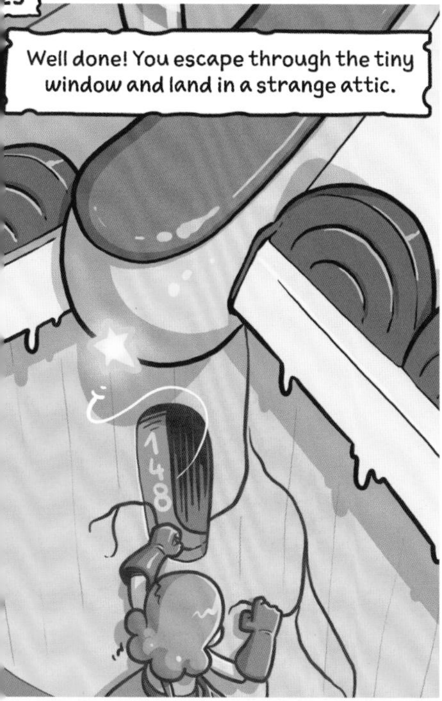
Well done! You escape through the tiny window and land in a strange attic.
148

124

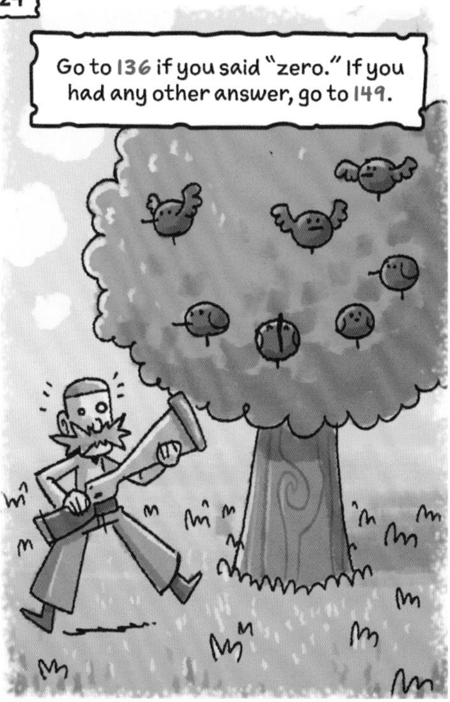
Go to 136 if you said "zero." If you had any other answer, go to 149.

125

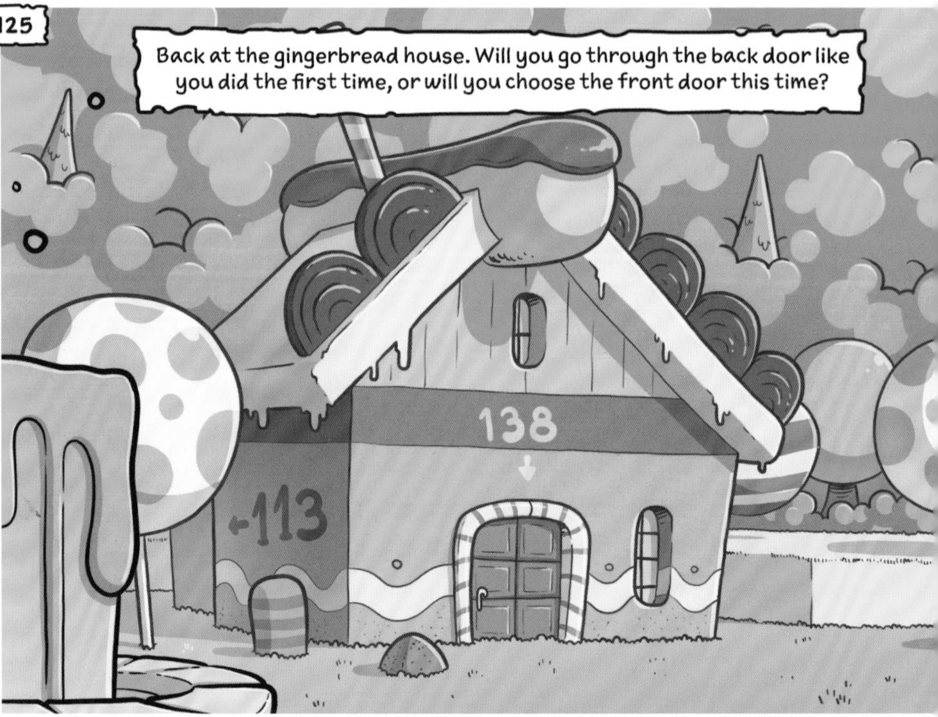

Back at the gingerbread house. Will you go through the back door like you did the first time, or will you choose the front door this time?
138
←113

126

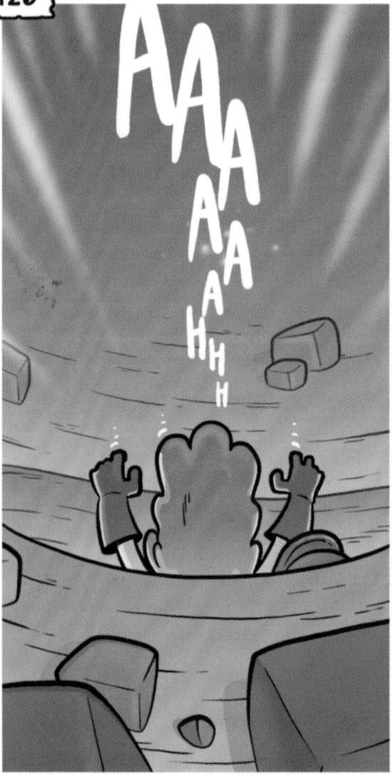

AAAAAAHHH

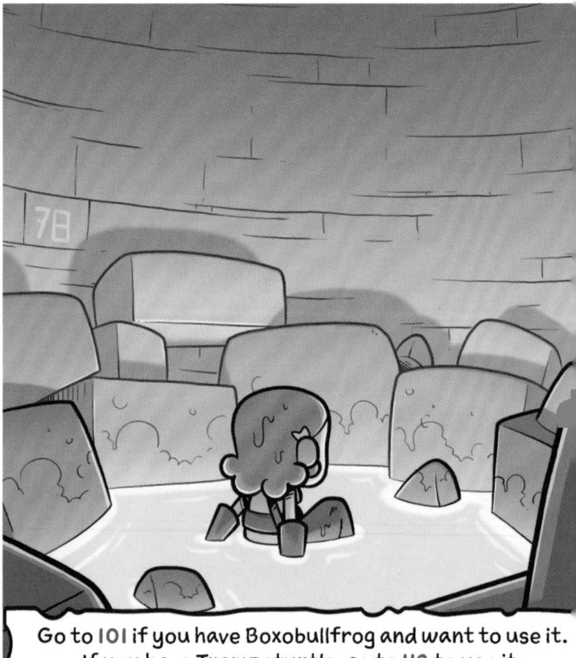

78
Go to 101 if you have Boxobullfrog and want to use it.
If you have Trampoturtle, go to 112 to use it.
You can also call for help in 44.

127

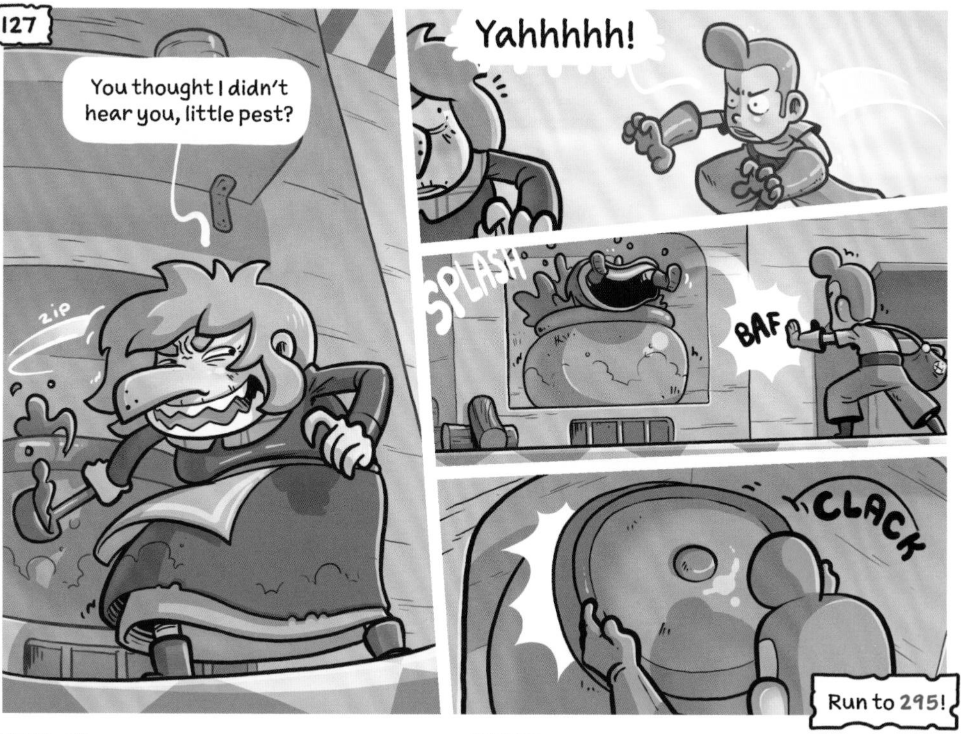
You thought I didn't hear you, little pest?
zip
Yahhhhh!
SPLASH
BAF
CLACK
Run to 295!

128

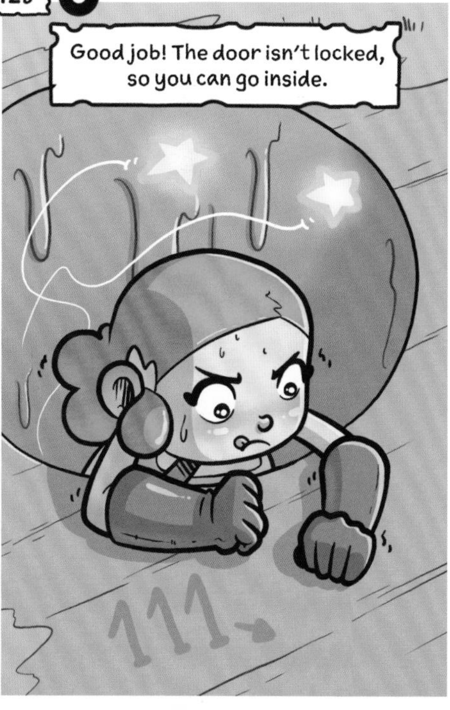
Good job! The door isn't locked, so you can go inside.
111

129

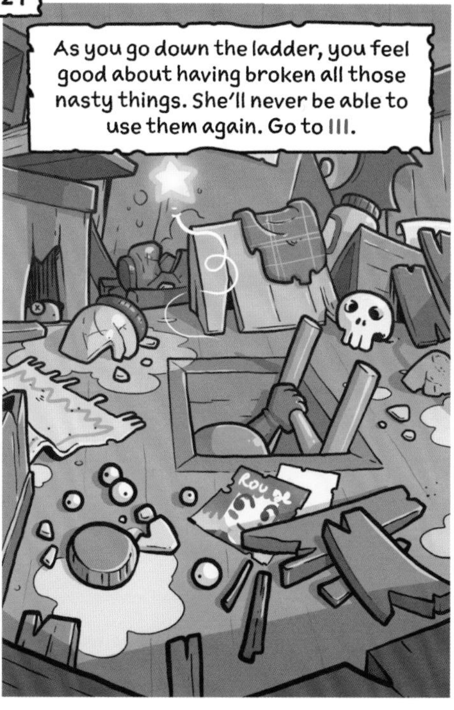
As you go down the ladder, you feel good about having broken all those nasty things. She'll never be able to use them again. Go to 111.

Even if the place looks super cute, stay on alert because the witch can't be far...

If you're selling something, I already have it!

No, I'm looking for a little boy...

Ah, well then come in, my dear. Pull on the bobbin and open sesame!

Huh? I don't understand...

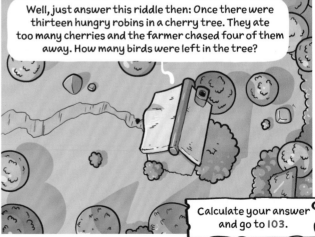

Well, just answer this riddle then: Once there were thirteen hungry robins in a cherry tree. They ate too many cherries and the farmer chased four of them away. How many birds were left in the tree?

Calculate your answer and go to 103.

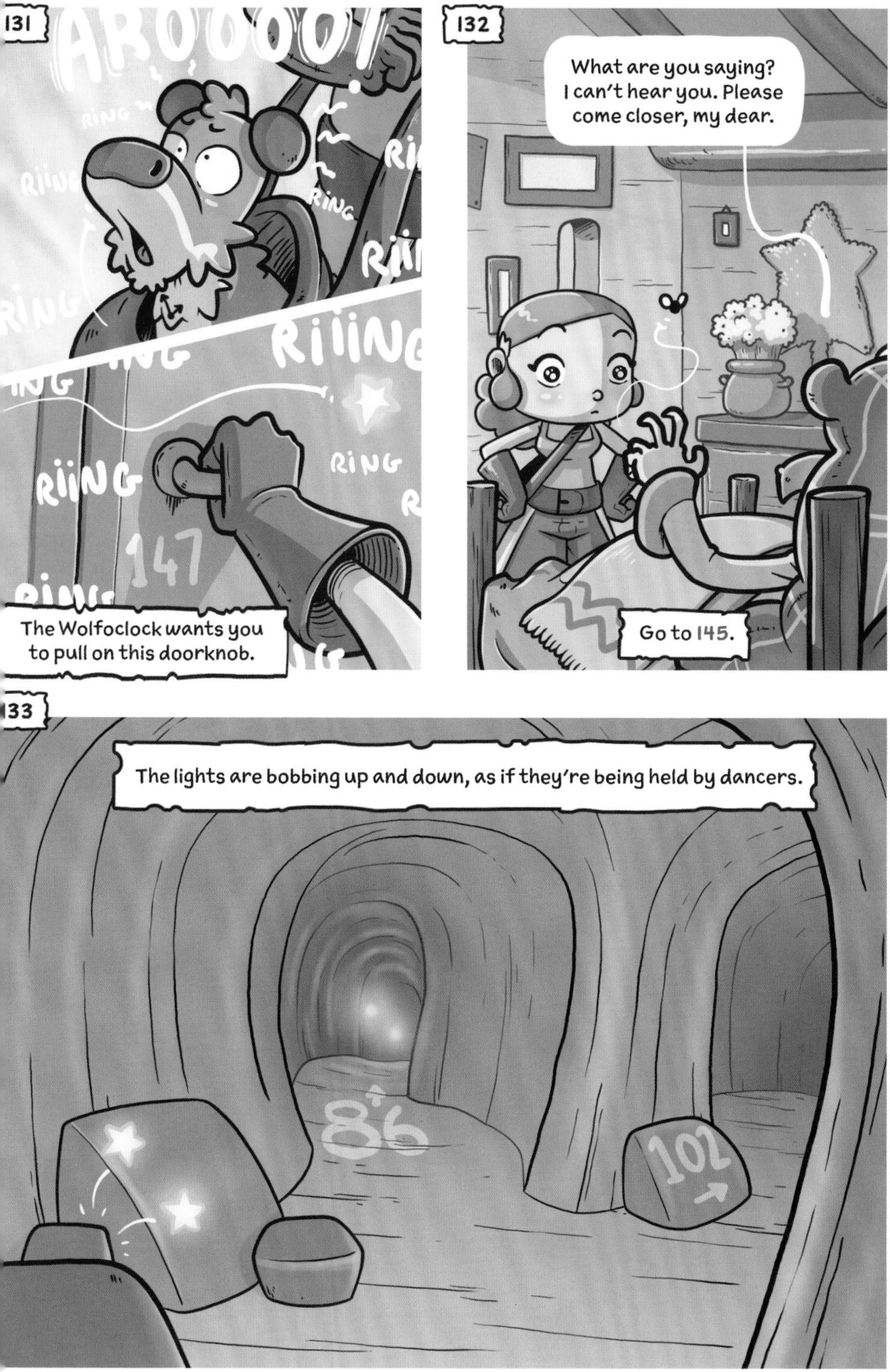
131
AROOOO!
RING
RIING
RING
RIING
RIING
RING
RIING
RING
RIING
147
The Wolfoclock wants you to pull on this doorknob.
132
What are you saying? I can't hear you. Please come closer, my dear.
Go to 145.
133
The lights are bobbing up and down, as if they're being held by dancers.
86
102

134

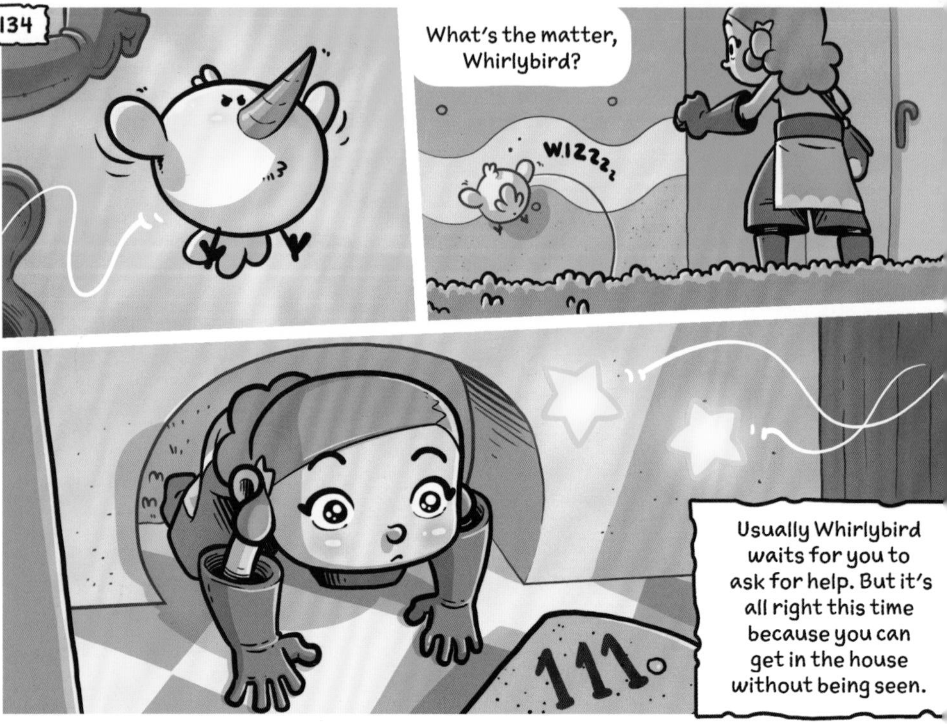
What's the matter, Whirlybird?
WIZZZZ
Usually Whirlybird waits for you to ask for help. But it's all right this time because you can get in the house without being seen.
111

135

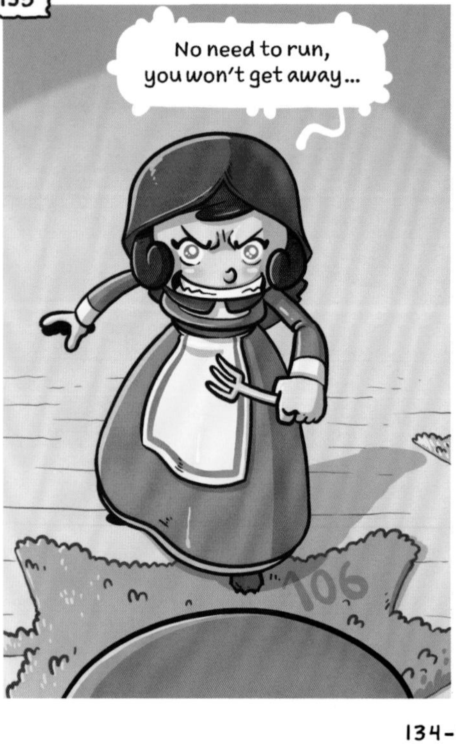
No need to run, you won't get away...
106

136

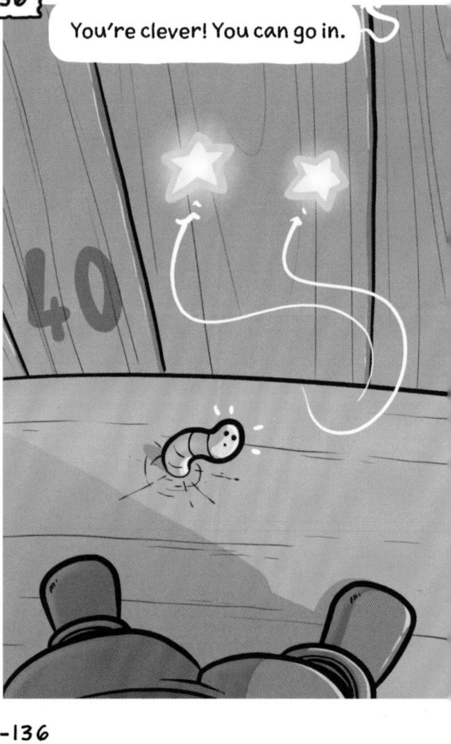
You're clever! You can go in.
40

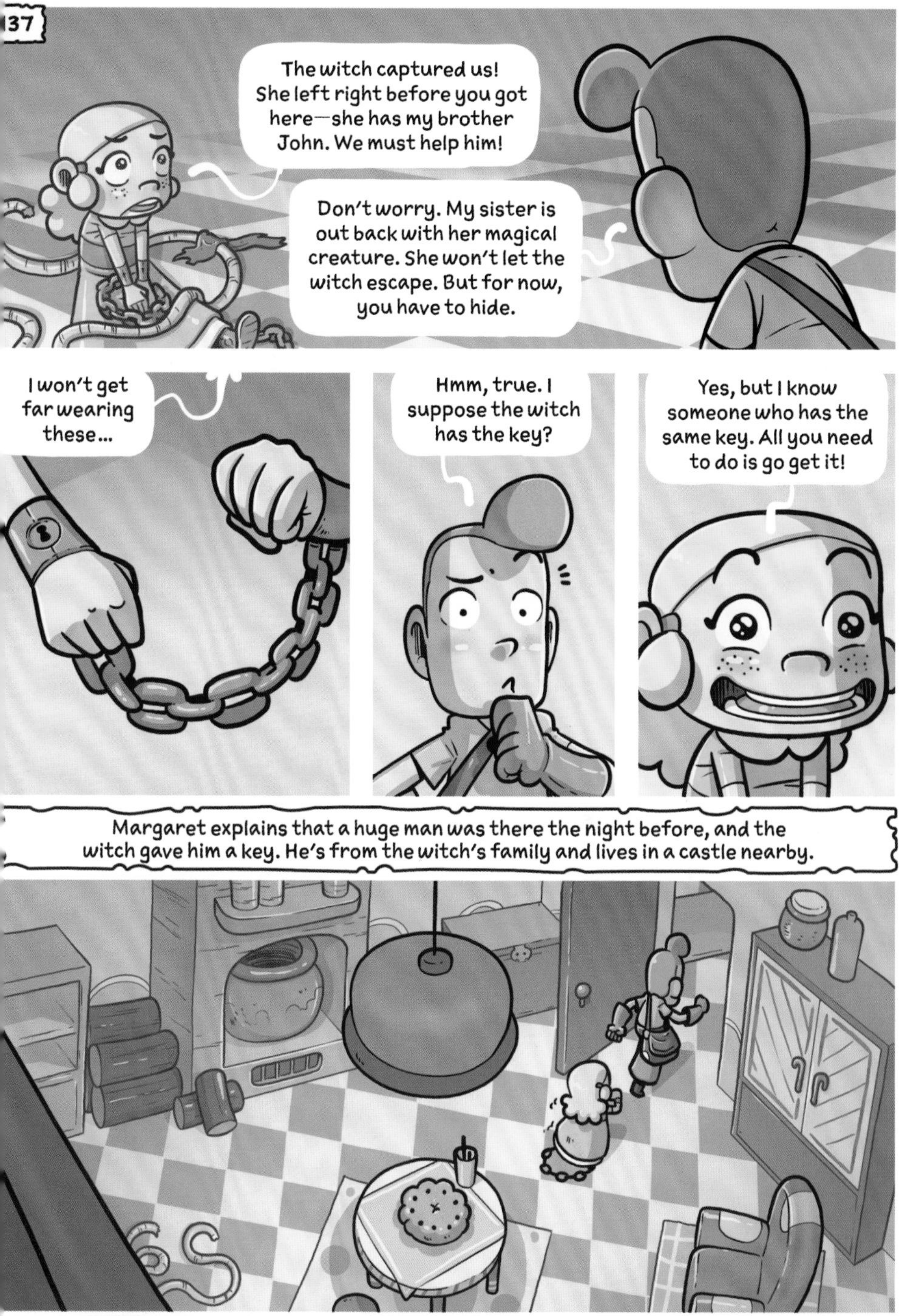
137
The witch captured us! She left right before you got here—she has my brother John. We must help him!
Don't worry. My sister is out back with her magical creature. She won't let the witch escape. But for now, you have to hide.
I won't get far wearing these...
Hmm, true. I suppose the witch has the key?
Yes, but I know someone who has the same key. All you need to do is go get it!
Margaret explains that a huge man was there the night before, and the witch gave him a key. He's from the witch's family and lives in a castle nearby.
You and Margaret decide that she should hide in the basement in case the witch comes back before you do... Once that's done, go to 220.

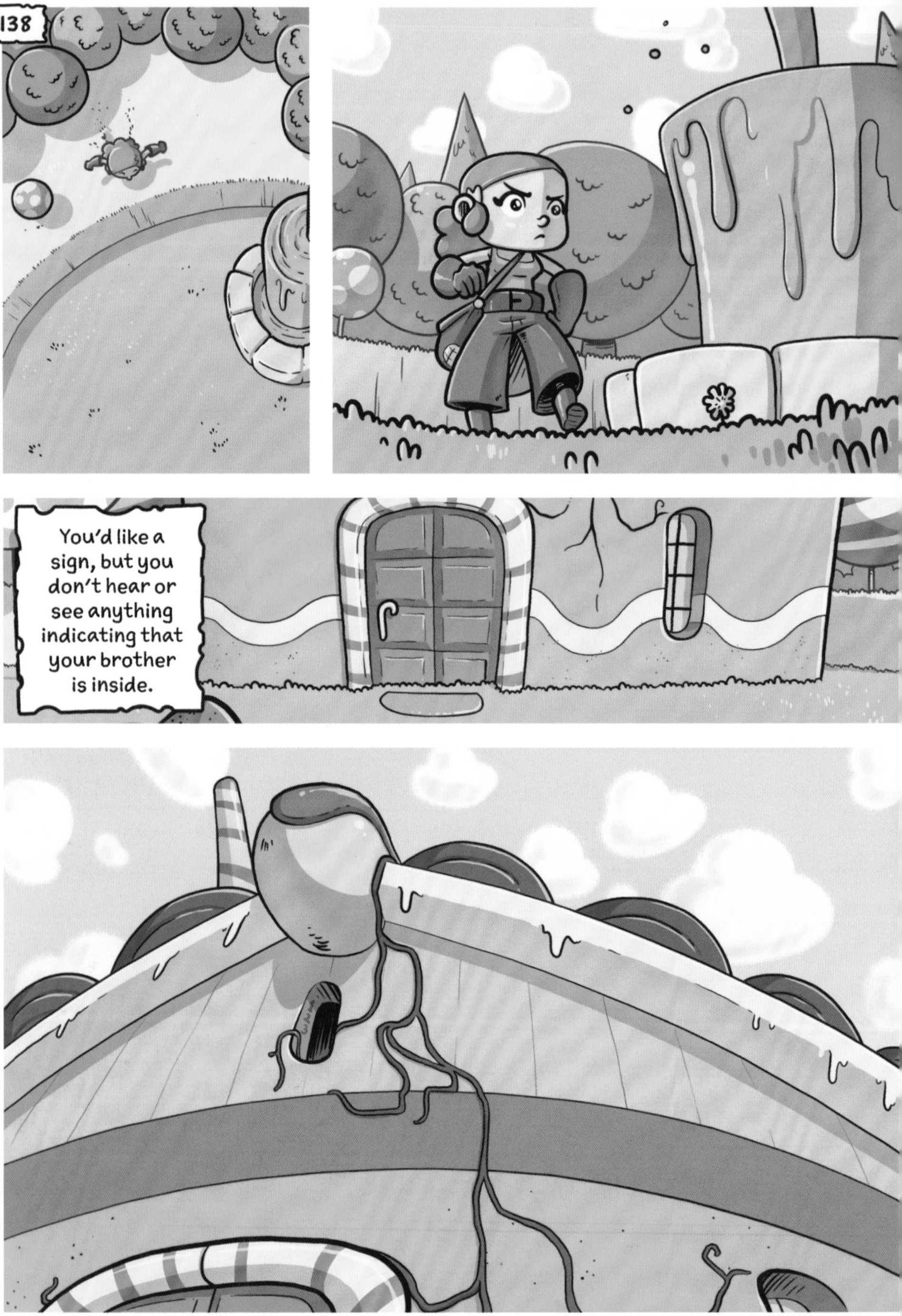
138
You'd like a sign, but you don't hear or see anything indicating that your brother is inside.

You'd love to go through the little window, but it's too high. If you have Trampoturtle and it's awake, then go to 166. If not, you'll have to enter through the door in 155.

139

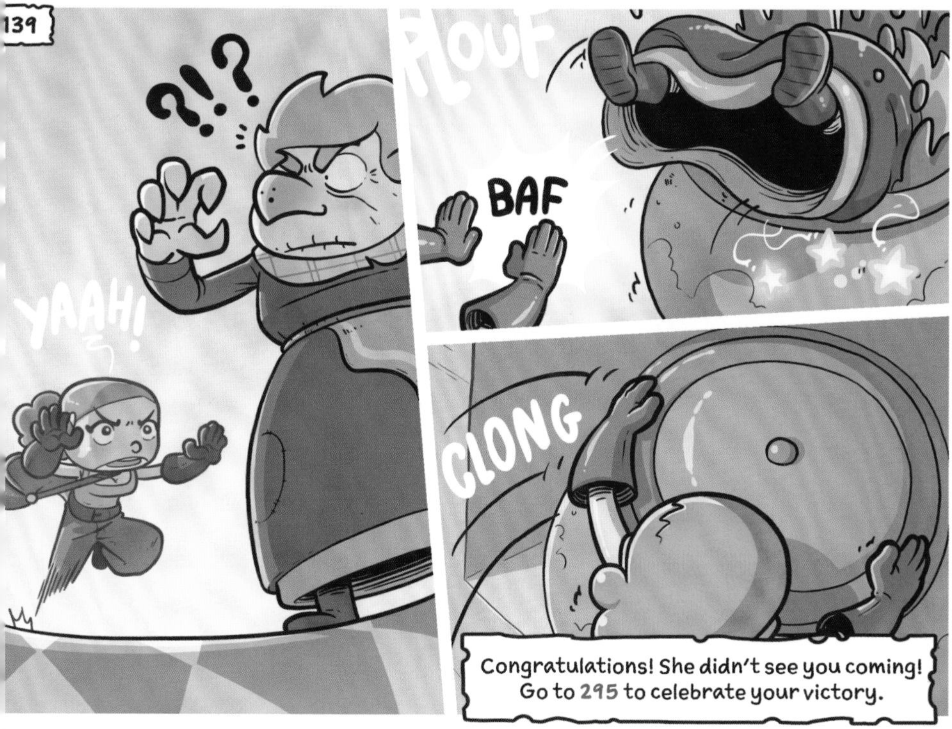
?!?
YAAAH!
PLOUF
BAF
CLONG
Congratulations! She didn't see you coming! Go to 295 to celebrate your victory.

140

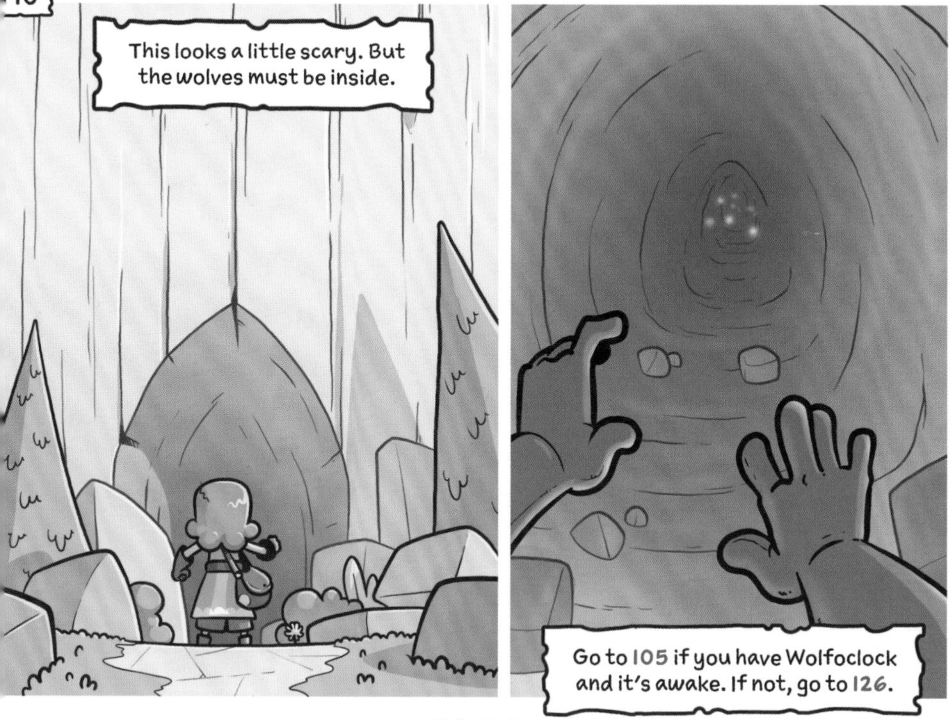
This looks a little scary. But the wolves must be inside.
Go to 105 if you have Wolfoclock and it's awake. If not, go to 126.

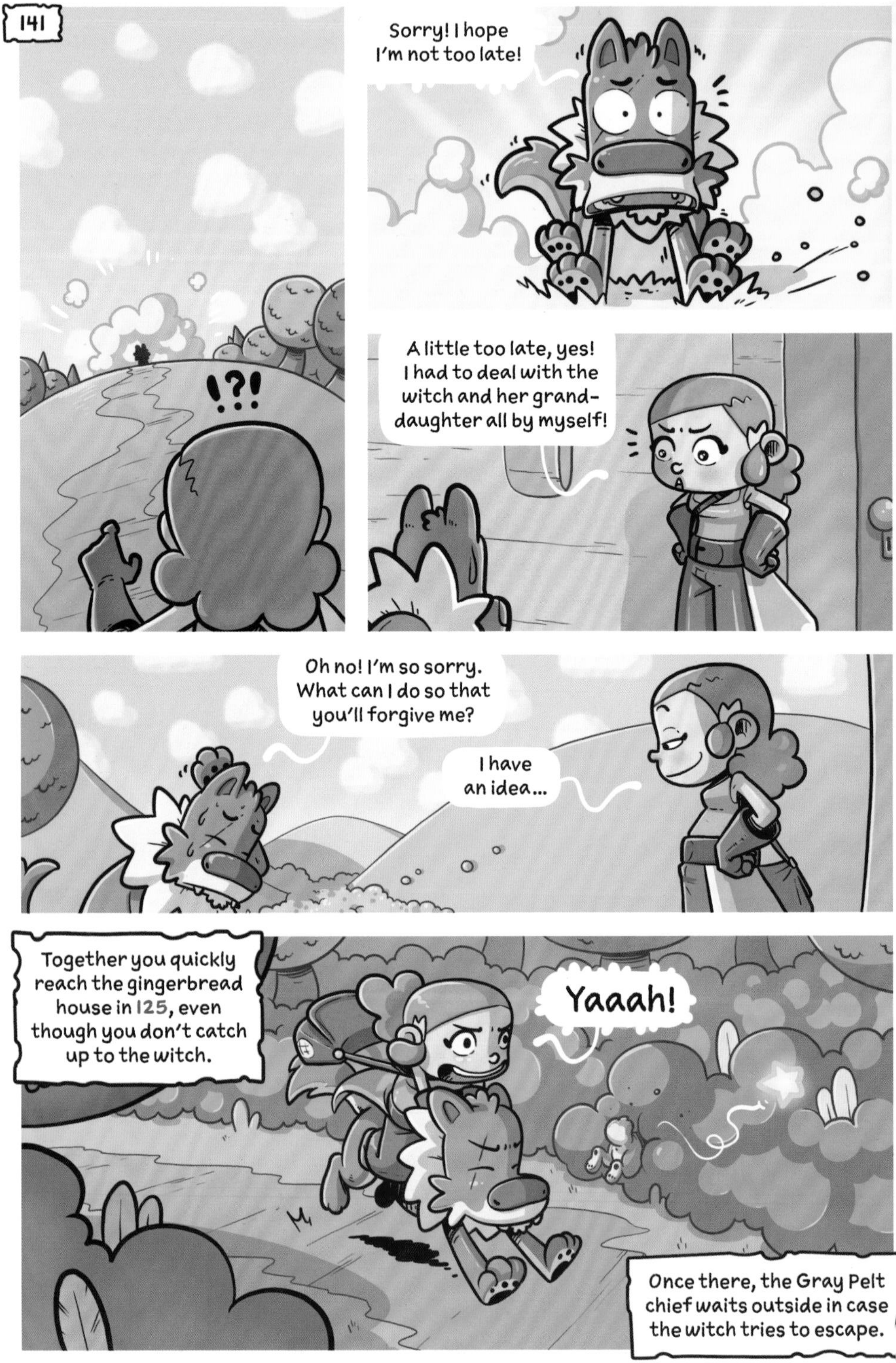
141
Sorry! I hope I'm not too late!
!?!
A little too late, yes! I had to deal with the witch and her grand-daughter all by myself!
Oh no! I'm so sorry. What can I do so that you'll forgive me?
I have an idea...
Together you quickly reach the gingerbread house in 125, even though you don't catch up to the witch.
Yaaah!
Once there, the Gray Pelt chief waits outside in case the witch tries to escape.

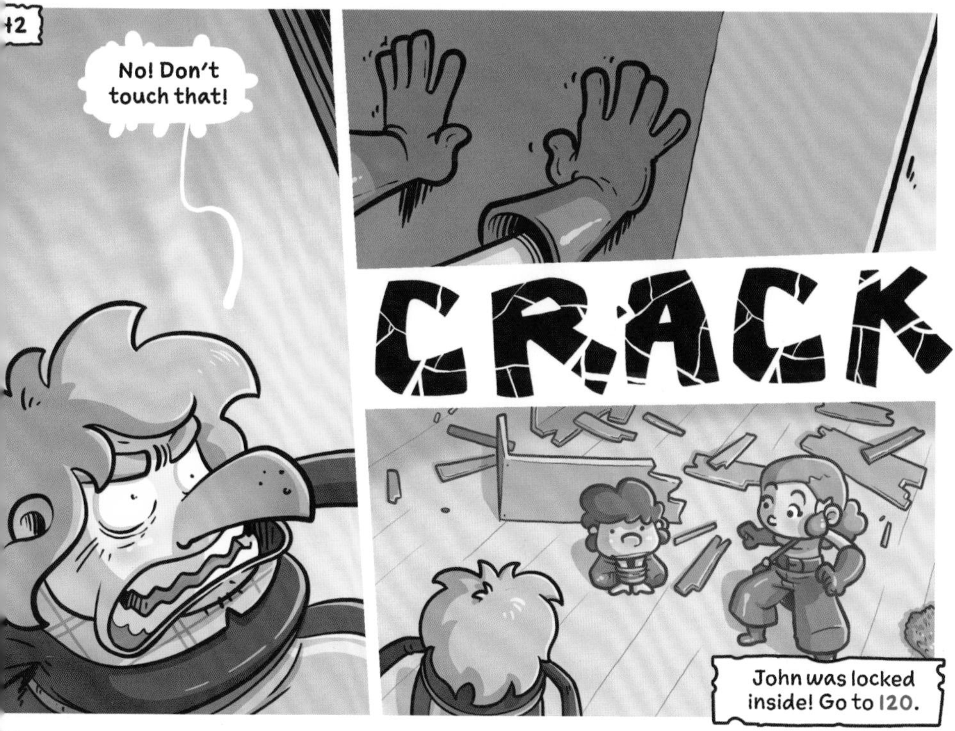
42
No! Don't touch that!
CRACK
John was locked inside! Go to 120.

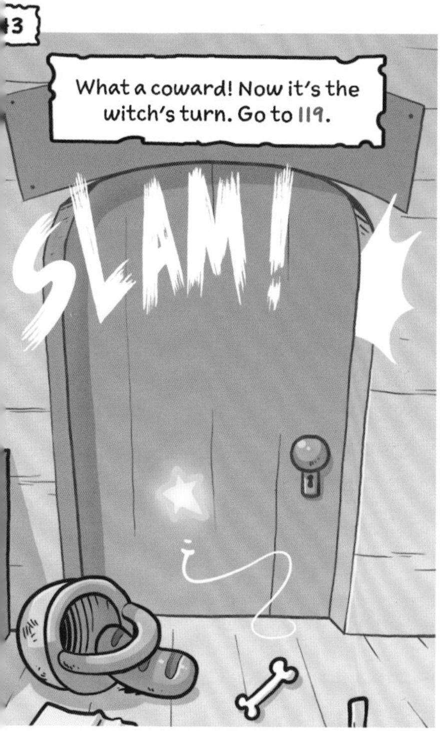
3
What a coward! Now it's the witch's turn. Go to 119.
SLAM!

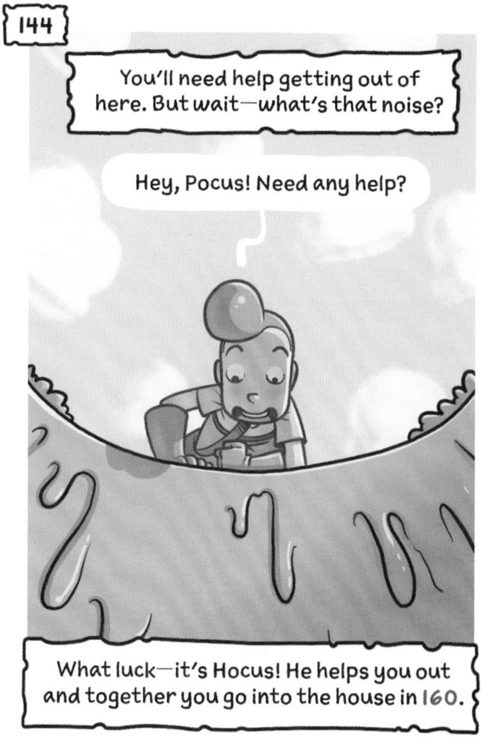
144
You'll need help getting out of here. But wait—what's that noise?
Hey, Pocus! Need any help?
What luck—it's Hocus! He helps you out and together you go into the house in 160.

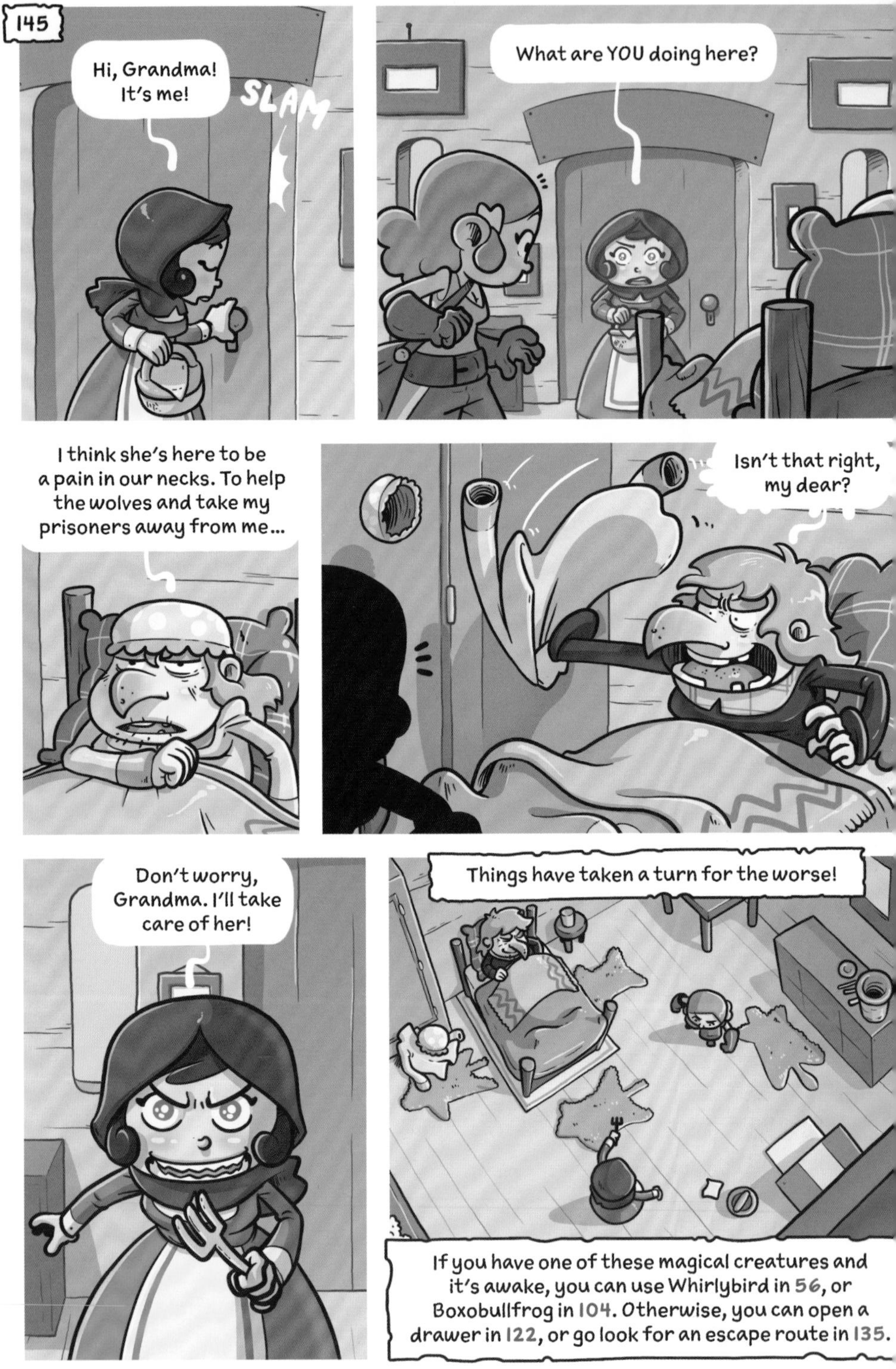
145
Hi, Grandma! It's me!
SLAM
What are YOU doing here?
I think she's here to be a pain in our necks. To help the wolves and take my prisoners away from me...
Isn't that right, my dear?
Don't worry, Grandma. I'll take care of her!
Things have taken a turn for the worse!
If you have one of these magical creatures and it's awake, you can use Whirlybird in 56, or Boxobullfrog in 104. Otherwise, you can open a drawer in 122, or go look for an escape route in 135.

46

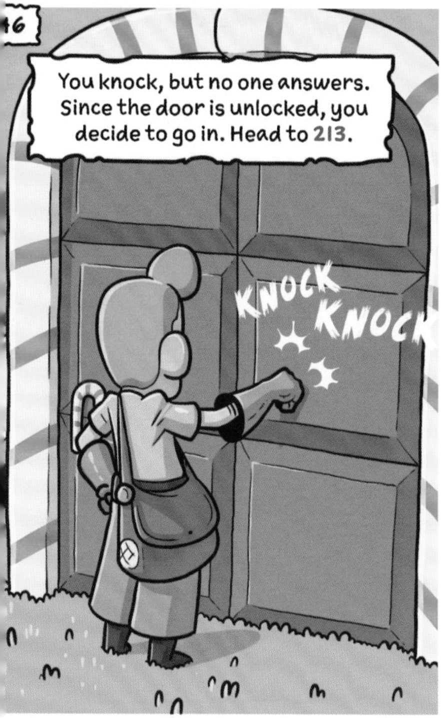
You knock, but no one answers. Since the door is unlocked, you decide to go in. Head to 213.
KNOCK
KNOCK

147

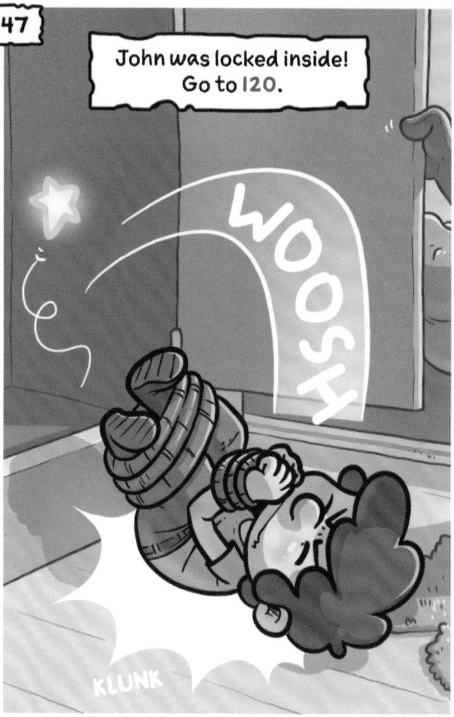
John was locked inside! Go to 120.
WOOSH
KLUNK

48

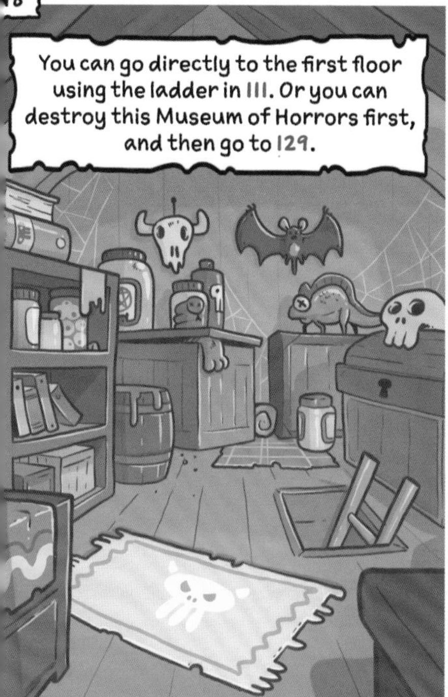
You can go directly to the first floor using the ladder in 111. Or you can destroy this Museum of Horrors first, and then go to 129.

149

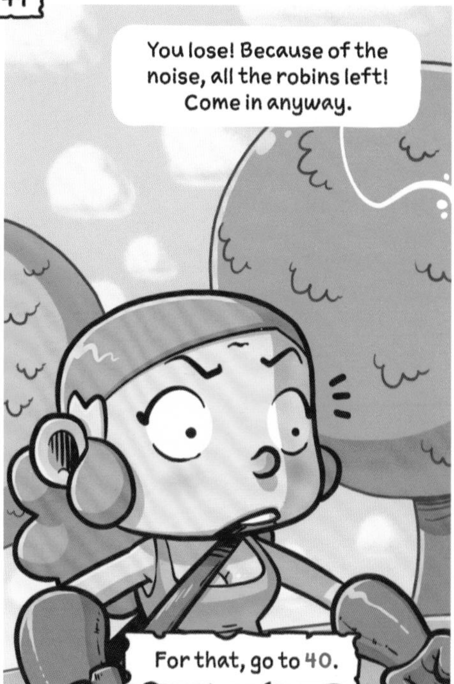
You lose! Because of the noise, all the robins left! Come in anyway.
For that, go to 40.

150

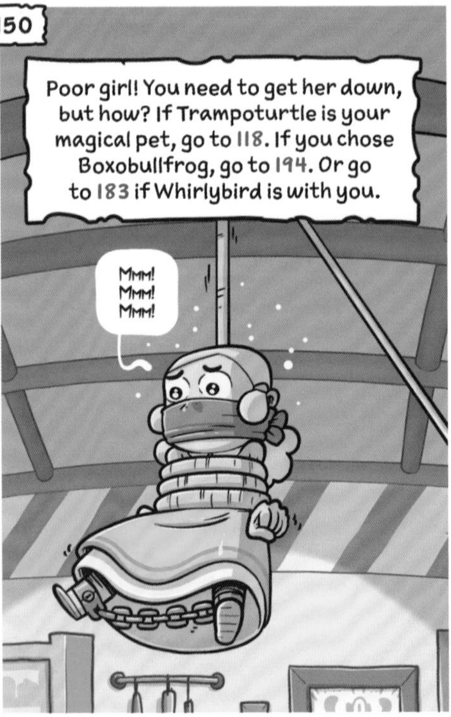
Poor girl! You need to get her down, but how? If Trampoturtle is your magical pet, go to 118. If you chose Boxobullfrog, go to 194. Or go to 183 if Whirlybird is with you.
Mmm! Mmm! Mmm!

151

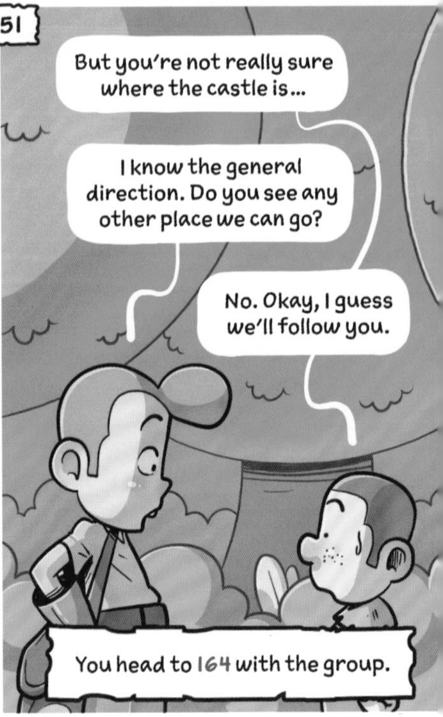
But you're not really sure where the castle is...
I know the general direction. Do you see any other place we can go?
No. Okay, I guess we'll follow you.
You head to 164 with the group.

152

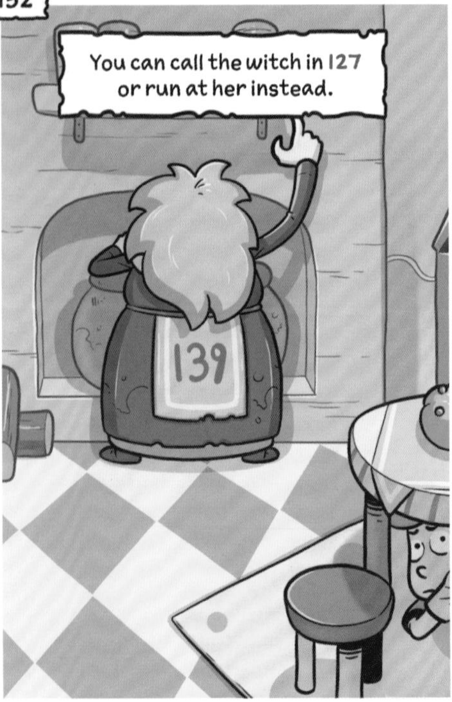
You can call the witch in 127 or run at her instead.
139

153

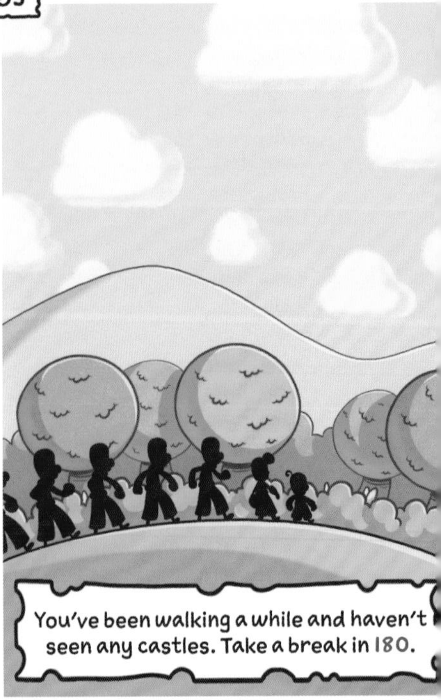
You've been walking a while and haven't seen any castles. Take a break in 180.

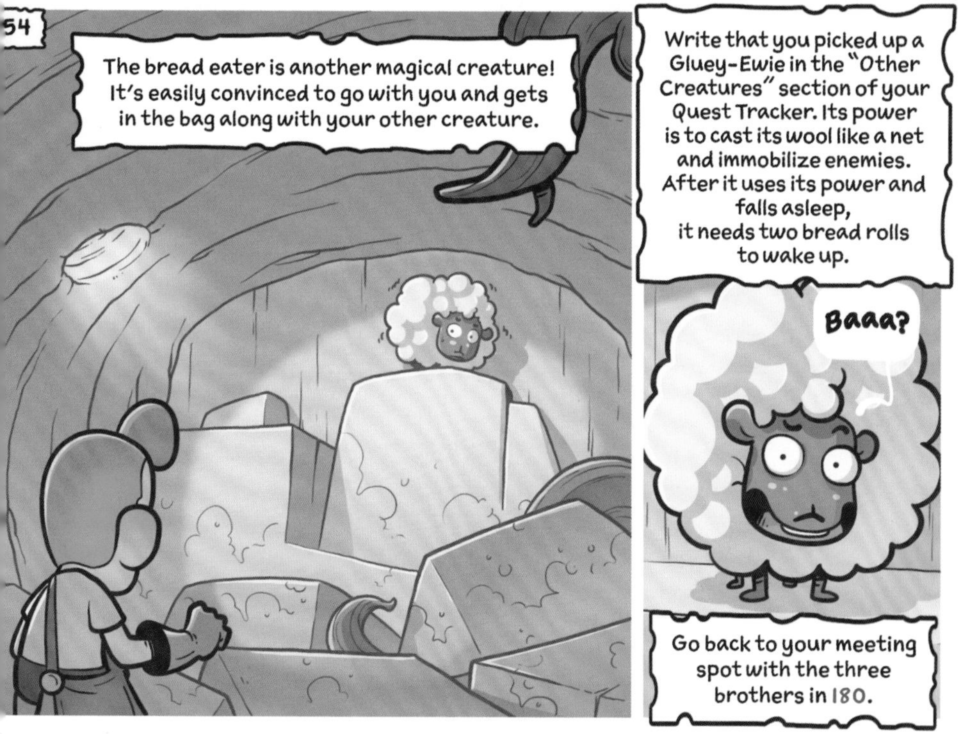
54
The bread eater is another magical creature! It's easily convinced to go with you and gets in the bag along with your other creature.
Write that you picked up a Gluey-Ewie in the "Other Creatures" section of your Quest Tracker. Its power is to cast its wool like a net and immobilize enemies. After it uses its power and falls asleep, it needs two bread rolls to wake up.
Baaa?
Go back to your meeting spot with the three brothers in 180.

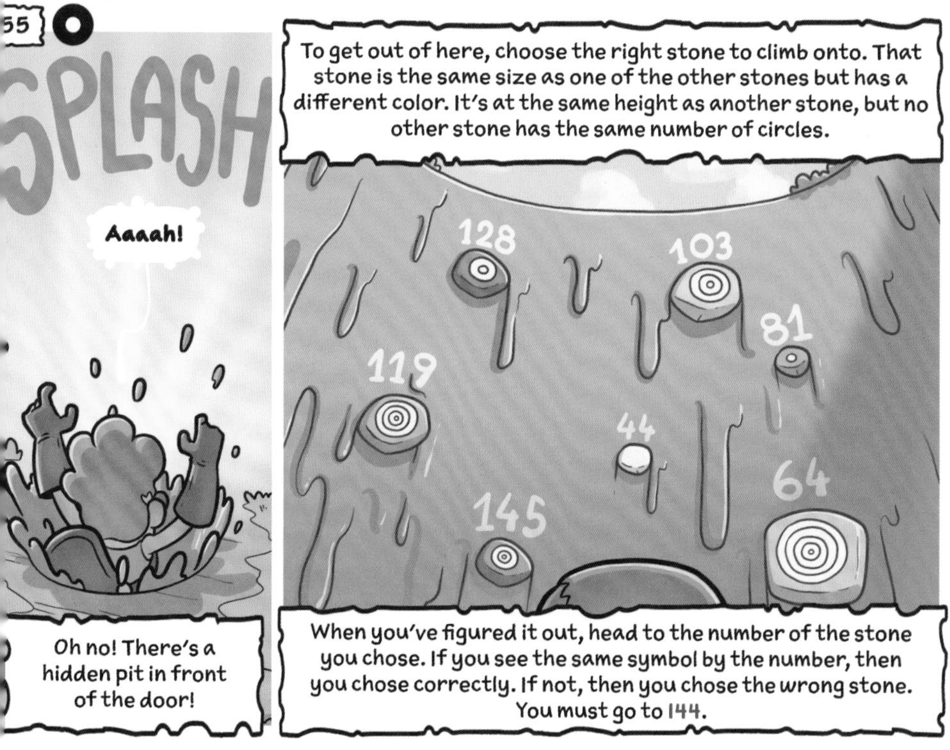
55
SPLASH
Aaaah!
Oh no! There's a hidden pit in front of the door!
To get out of here, choose the right stone to climb onto. That stone is the same size as one of the other stones but has a different color. It's at the same height as another stone, but no other stone has the same number of circles.
128
103
81
119
44
64
145
When you've figured it out, head to the number of the stone you chose. If you see the same symbol by the number, then you chose correctly. If not, then you chose the wrong stone. You must go to 144.

156

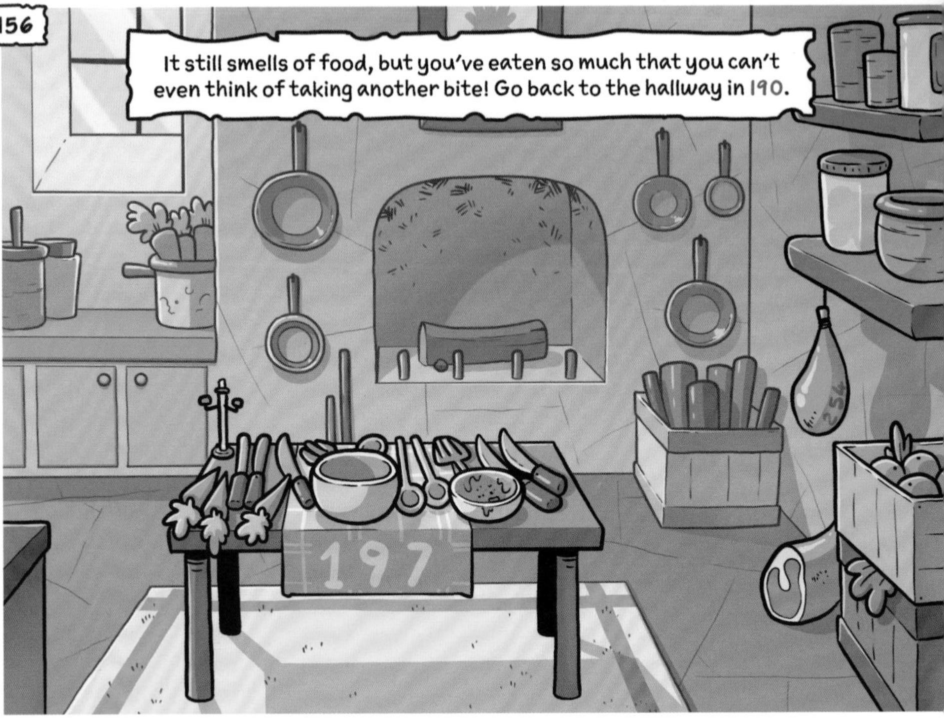
It still smells of food, but you've eaten so much that you can't even think of taking another bite! Go back to the hallway in 190.
197
254

157

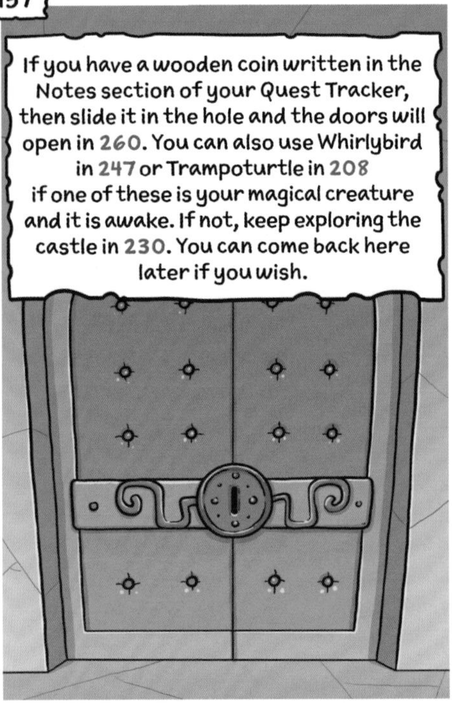
If you have a wooden coin written in the Notes section of your Quest Tracker, then slide it in the hole and the doors will open in 260. You can also use Whirlybird in 247 or Trampoturtle in 208 if one of these is your magical creature and it is awake. If not, keep exploring the castle in 230. You can come back here later if you wish.

158

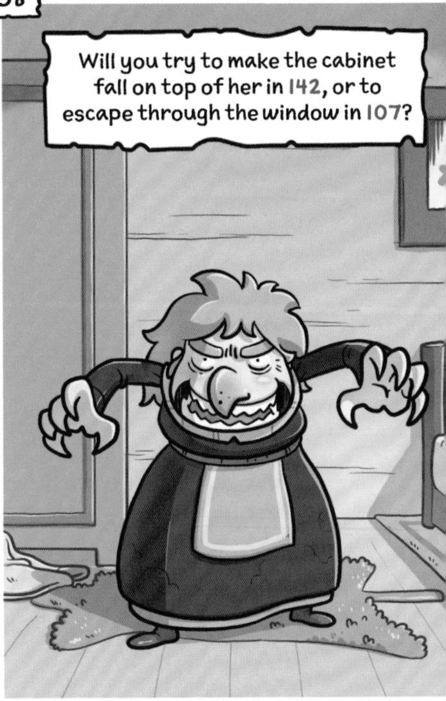
Will you try to make the cabinet fall on top of her in 142, or to escape through the window in 107?

Let's play Jump the Wall!

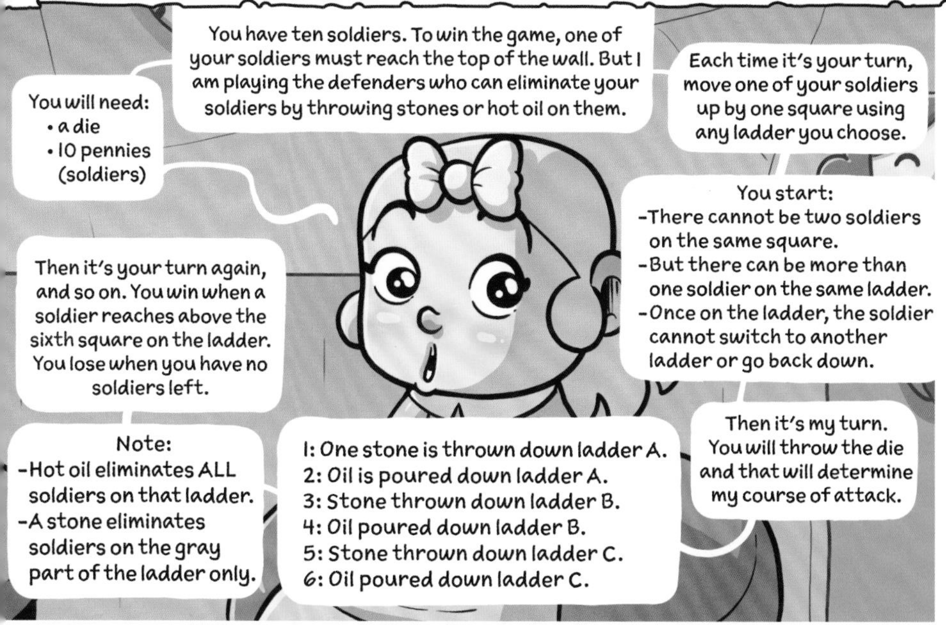
You have ten soldiers. To win the game, one of your soldiers must reach the top of the wall. But I am playing the defenders who can eliminate your soldiers by throwing stones or hot oil on them.
You will need:
• a die
• 10 pennies (soldiers)
Each time it's your turn, move one of your soldiers up by one square using any ladder you choose.
You start:
-There cannot be two soldiers on the same square.
-But there can be more than one soldier on the same ladder.
-Once on the ladder, the soldier cannot switch to another ladder or go back down.
Then it's your turn again, and so on. You win when a soldier reaches above the sixth square on the ladder. You lose when you have no soldiers left.
Then it's my turn. You will throw the die and that will determine my course of attack.
1: One stone is thrown down ladder A.
2: Oil is poured down ladder A.
3: Stone thrown down ladder B.
4: Oil poured down ladder B.
5: Stone thrown down ladder C.
6: Oil poured down ladder C.
Note:
-Hot oil eliminates ALL soldiers on that ladder.
-A stone eliminates soldiers on the gray part of the ladder only.

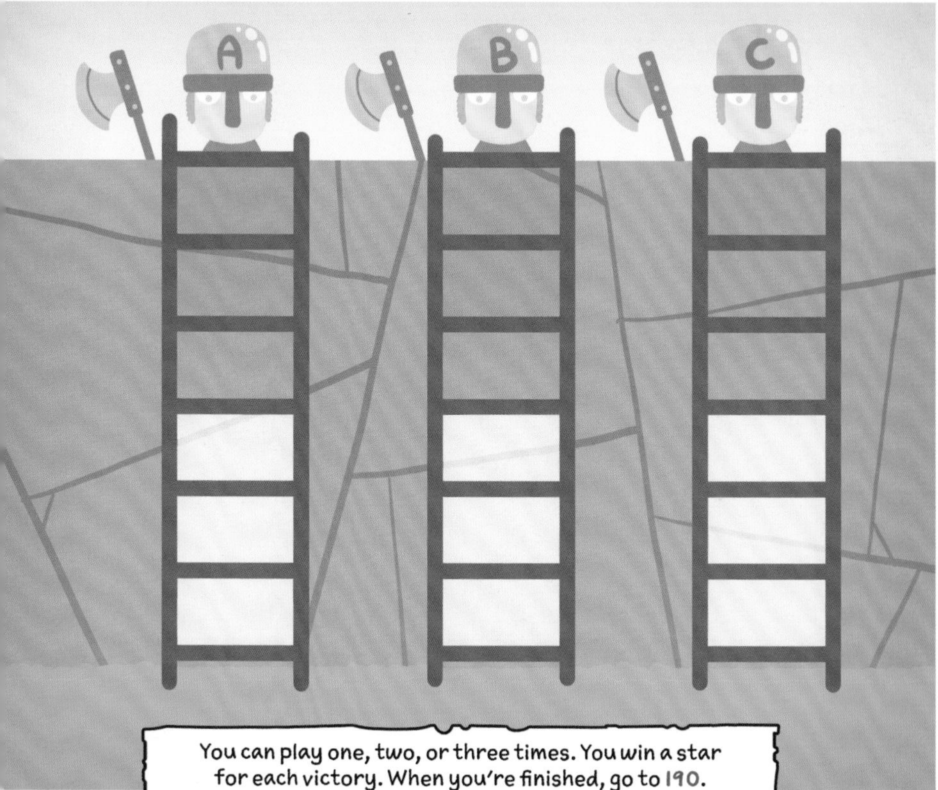
A
B
C

You can play one, two, or three times. You win a star for each victory. When you're finished, go to 190.

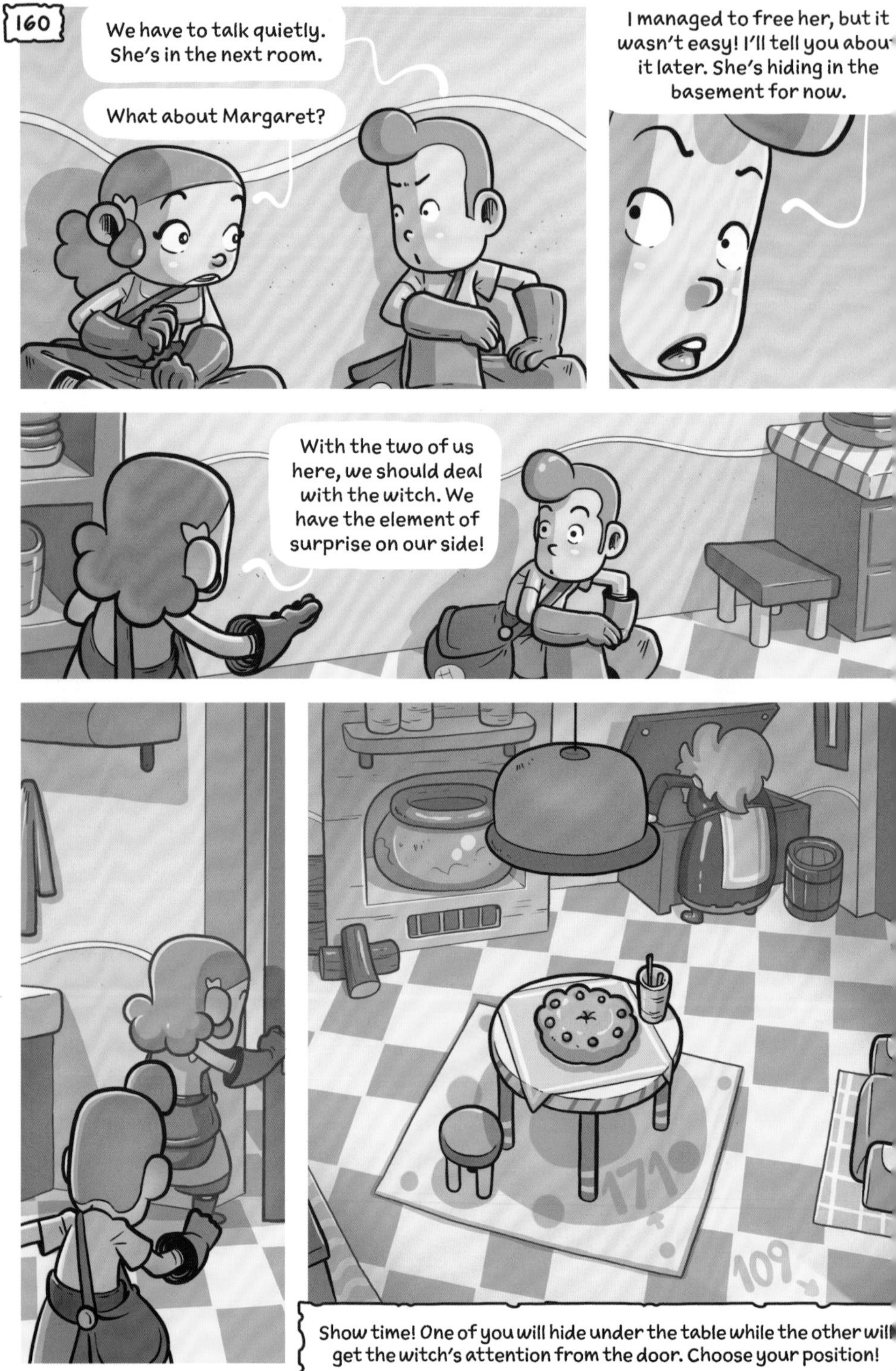
160
We have to talk quietly. She's in the next room.
What about Margaret?
I managed to free her, but it wasn't easy! I'll tell you about it later. She's hiding in the basement for now.
With the two of us here, we should deal with the witch. We have the element of surprise on our side!
171
109
Show time! One of you will hide under the table while the other will get the witch's attention from the door. Choose your position!

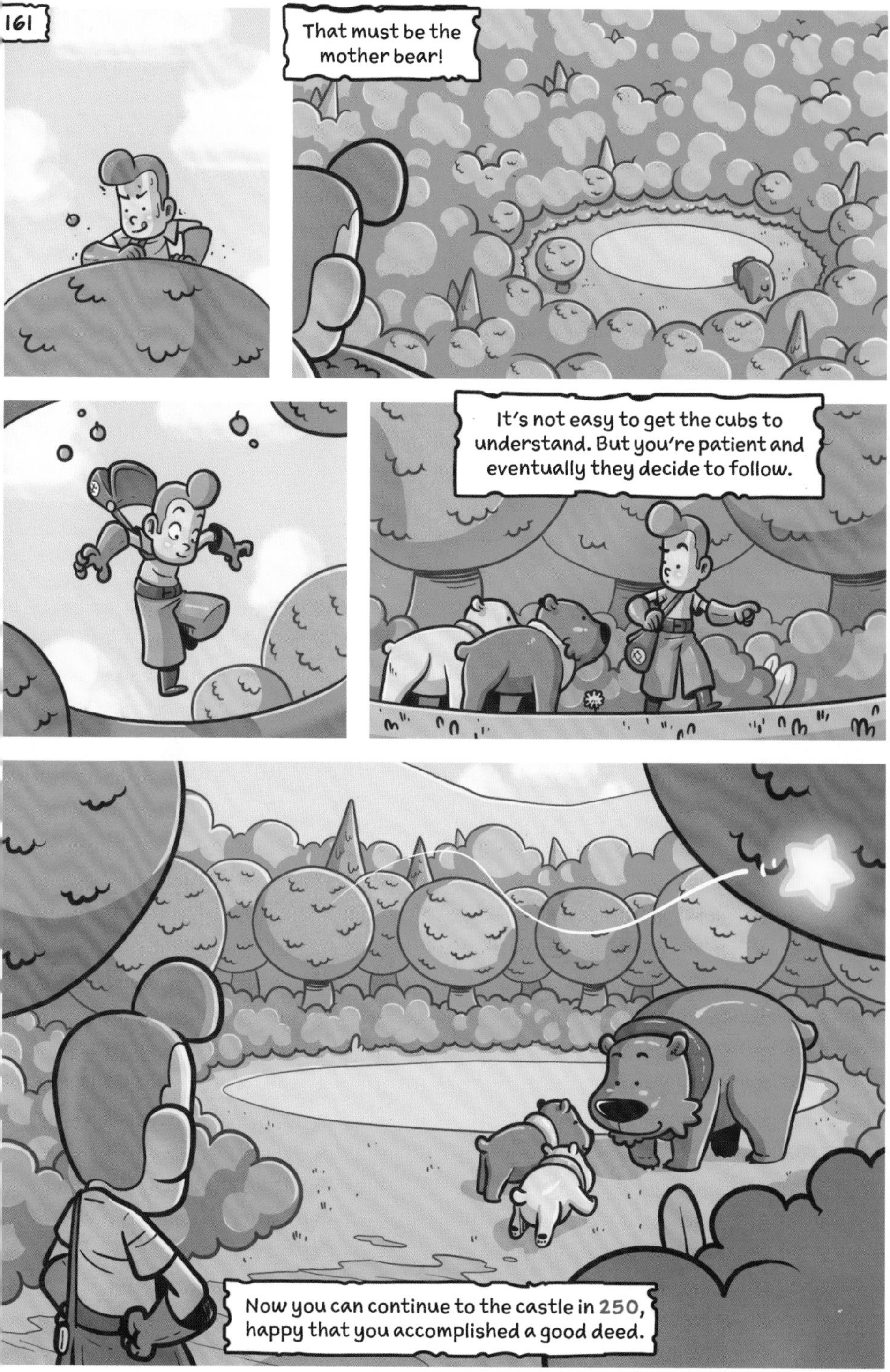
161
That must be the mother bear!
It's not easy to get the cubs to understand. But you're patient and eventually they decide to follow.
Now you can continue to the castle in 250, happy that you accomplished a good deed.

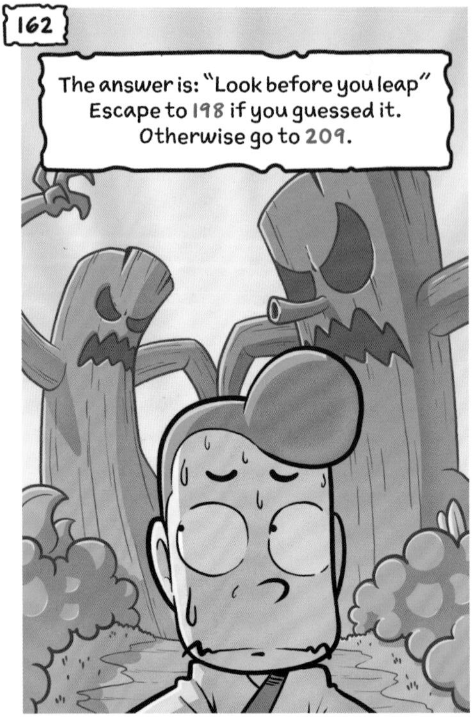
162
The answer is: "Look before you leap"
Escape to 198 if you guessed it.
Otherwise go to 209.

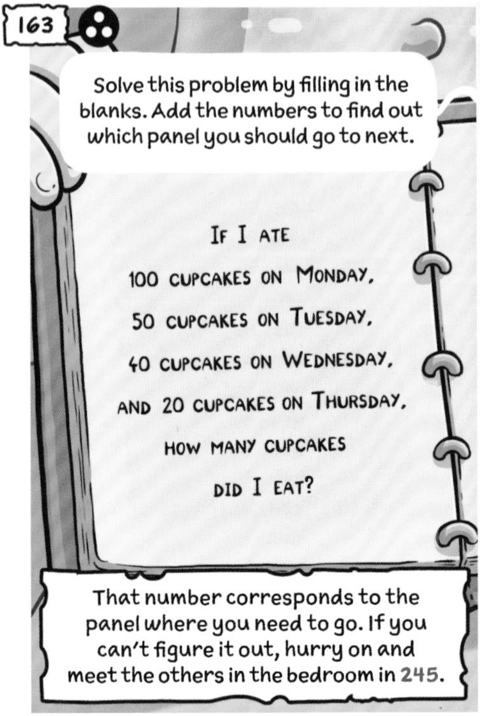
163
Solve this problem by filling in the blanks. Add the numbers to find out which panel you should go to next.
IF I ATE
100 CUPCAKES ON MONDAY,
50 CUPCAKES ON TUESDAY,
40 CUPCAKES ON WEDNESDAY,
AND 20 CUPCAKES ON THURSDAY,
HOW MANY CUPCAKES
DID I EAT?
That number corresponds to the panel where you need to go. If you can't figure it out, hurry on and meet the others in the bedroom in 245.

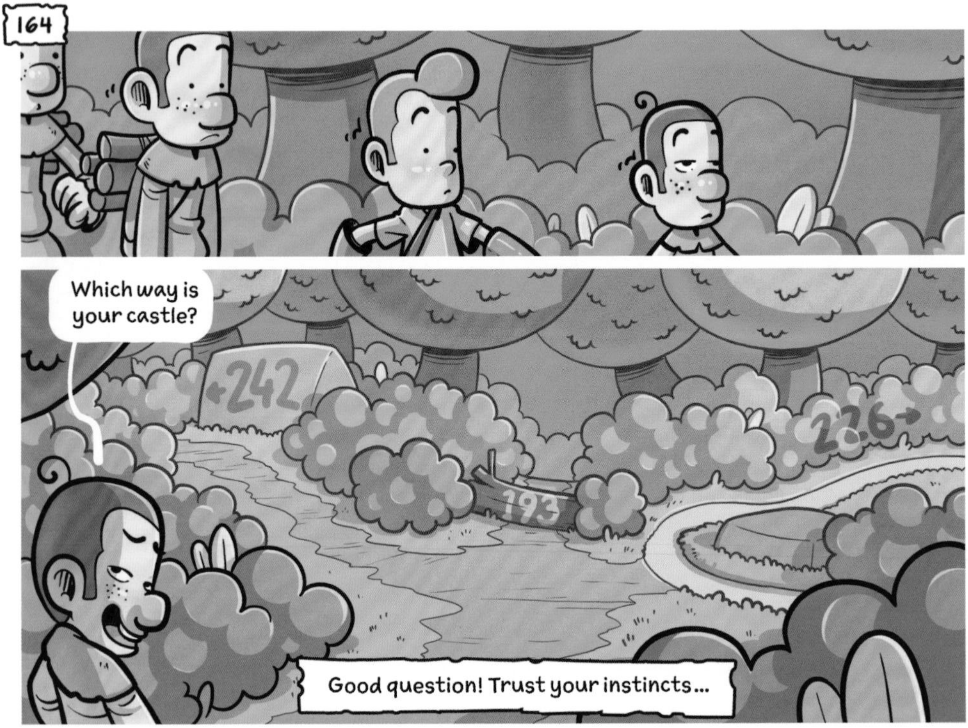
164
Which way is your castle?
242
226
193
Good question! Trust your instincts...

65

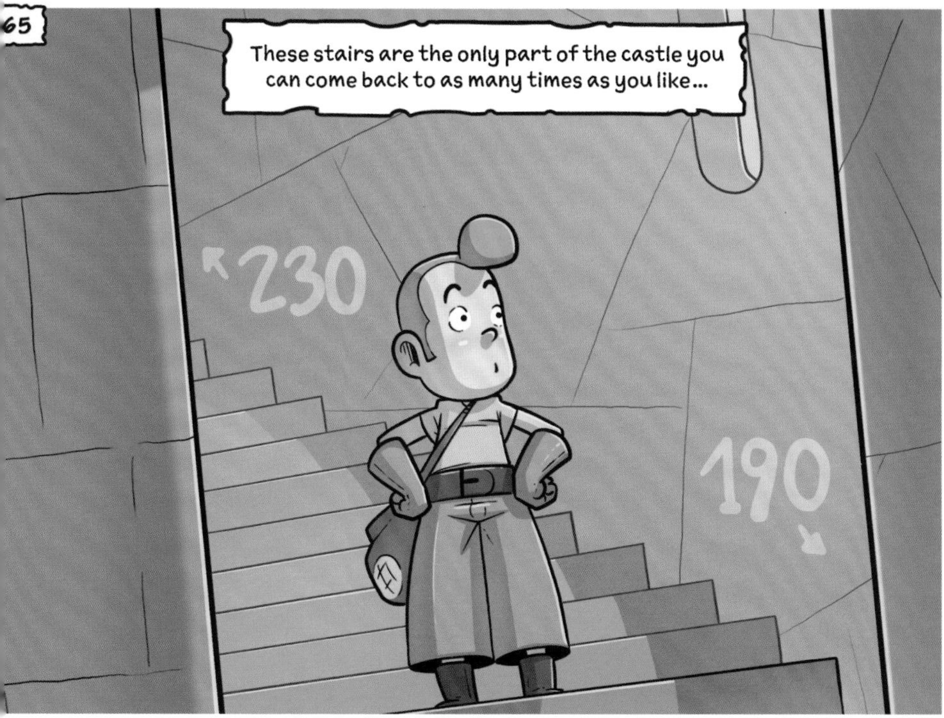
These stairs are the only part of the castle you can come back to as many times as you like...
230
190

66

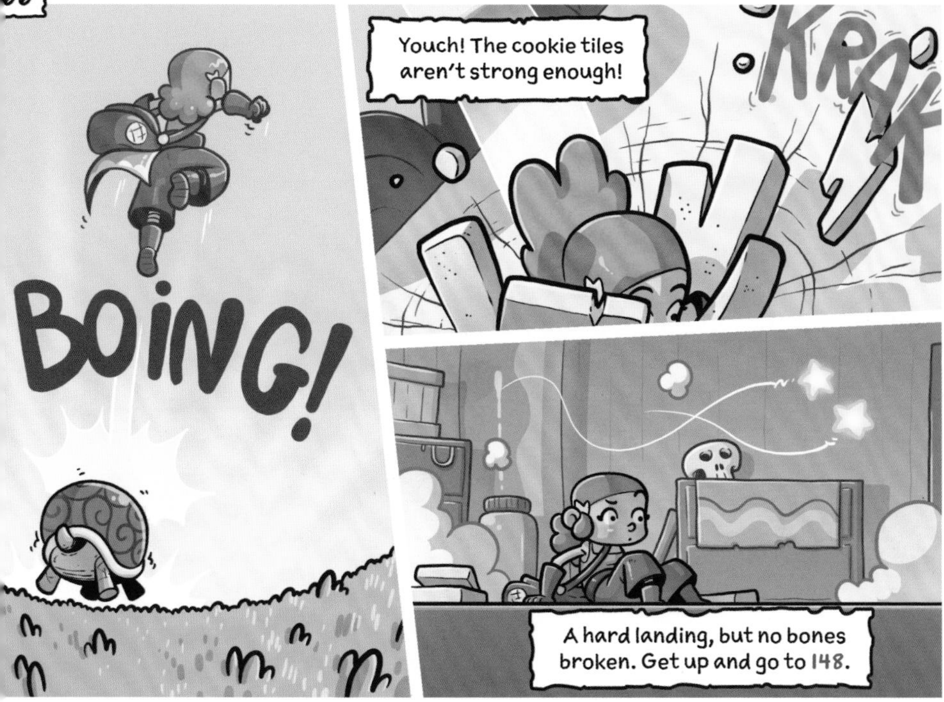
BOING!
Youch! The cookie tiles aren't strong enough!
KRAK
A hard landing, but no bones broken. Get up and go to 148.

We can escape through here but...

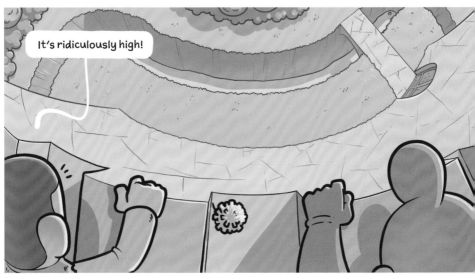

It's ridiculously high!

What if we use this rope? It looks long enough.

Will it hold both of us? Let's take turns, just to be safe.

Good idea!

We'll use a coin to play heads or tails to see who goes first.

Choose heads or tails and then flip your coin. Don't cheat! Go to 202 if you win or 255 if you lose.

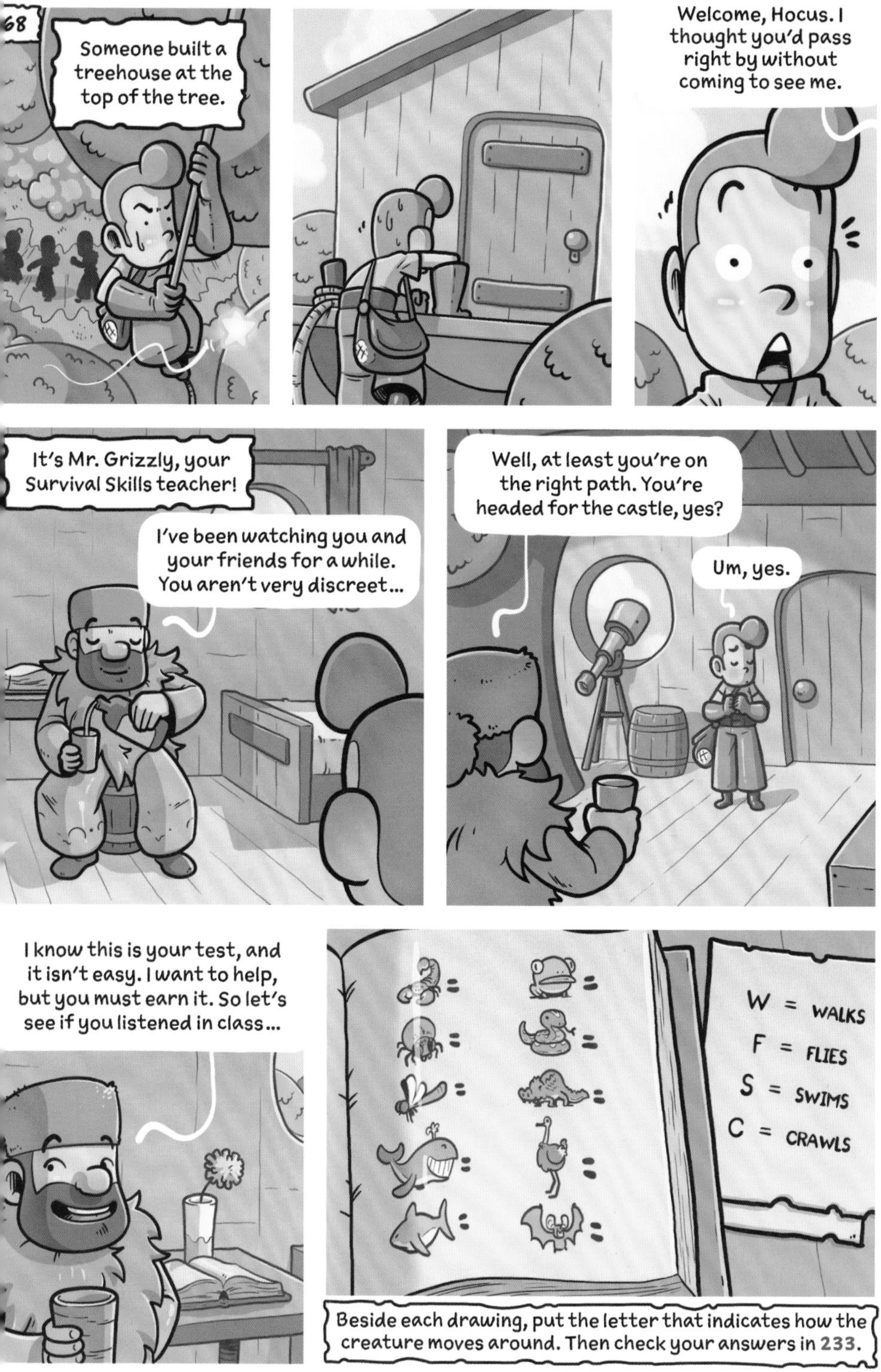
168
Someone built a treehouse at the top of the tree.
Welcome, Hocus. I thought you'd pass right by without coming to see me.
It's Mr. Grizzly, your Survival Skills teacher!
I've been watching you and your friends for a while. You aren't very discreet...
Well, at least you're on the right path. You're headed for the castle, yes?
Um, yes.
I know this is your test, and it isn't easy. I want to help, but you must earn it. So let's see if you listened in class...
W = WALKS
F = FLIES
S = SWIMS
C = CRAWLS
Beside each drawing, put the letter that indicates how the creature moves around. Then check your answers in 233.

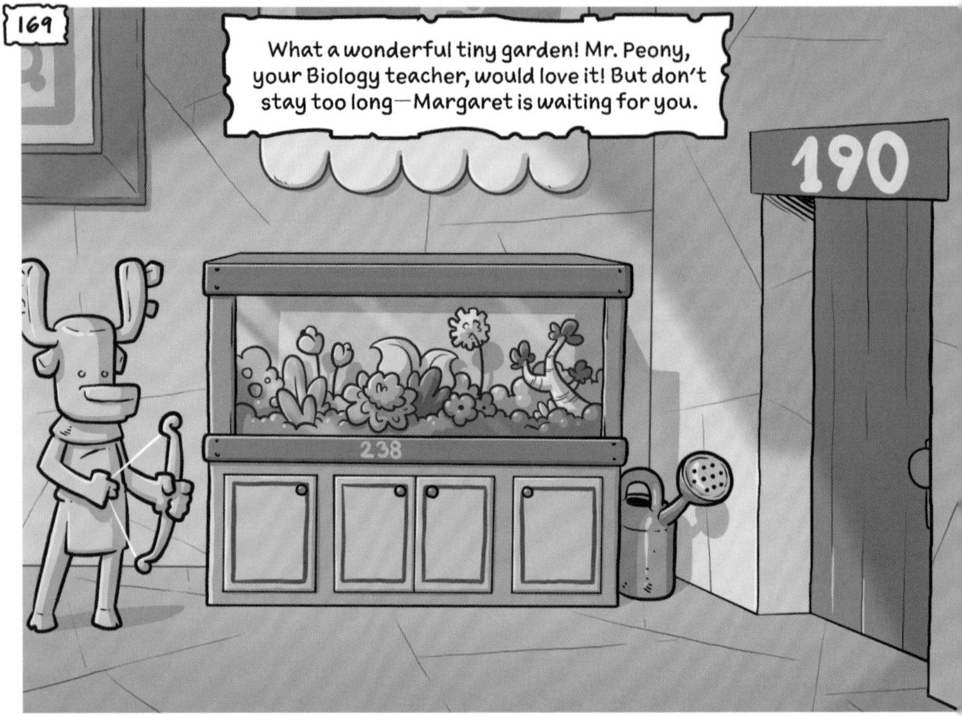
169
What a wonderful tiny garden! Mr. Peony, your Biology teacher, would love it! But don't stay too long—Margaret is waiting for you.
190
238

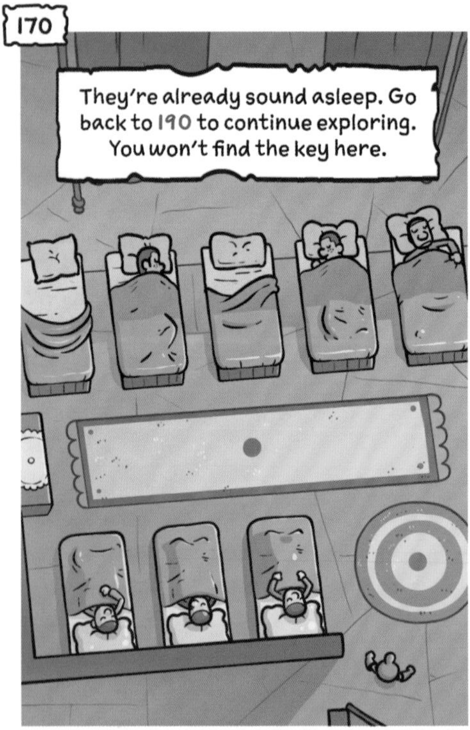
170
They're already sound asleep. Go back to 190 to continue exploring. You won't find the key here.

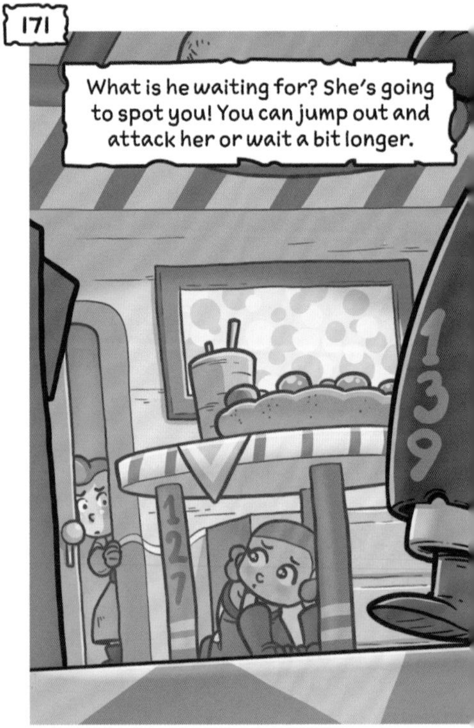
171
What is he waiting for? She's going to spot you! You can jump out and attack her or wait a bit longer.
127
139

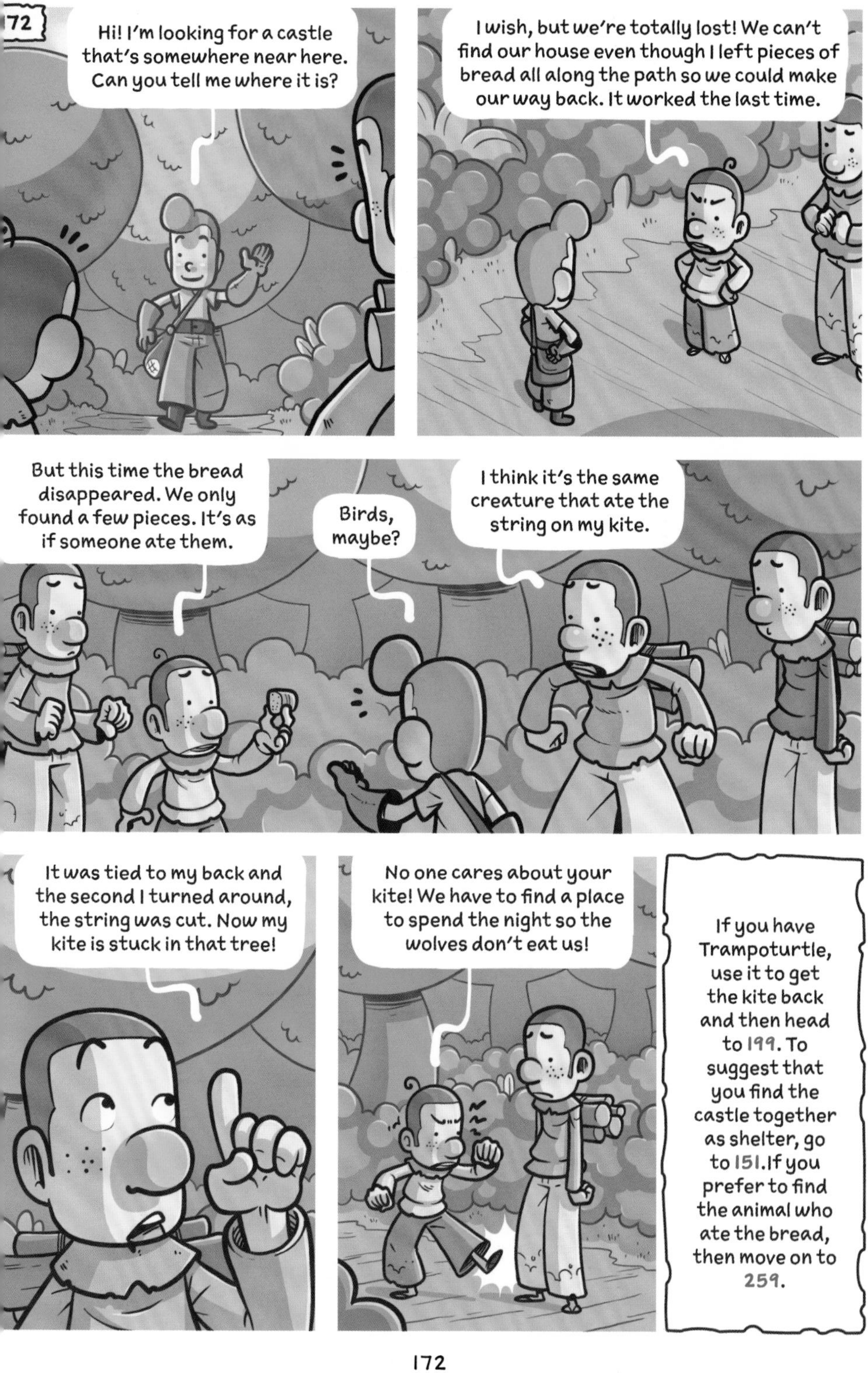
172
Hi! I'm looking for a castle that's somewhere near here. Can you tell me where it is?
I wish, but we're totally lost! We can't find our house even though I left pieces of bread all along the path so we could make our way back. It worked the last time.
But this time the bread disappeared. We only found a few pieces. It's as if someone ate them.
Birds, maybe?
I think it's the same creature that ate the string on my kite.
It was tied to my back and the second I turned around, the string was cut. Now my kite is stuck in that tree!
No one cares about your kite! We have to find a place to spend the night so the wolves don't eat us!
If you have Trampoturtle, use it to get the kite back and then head to 199. To suggest that you find the castle together as shelter, go to 151. If you prefer to find the animal who ate the bread, then move on to 259.

173

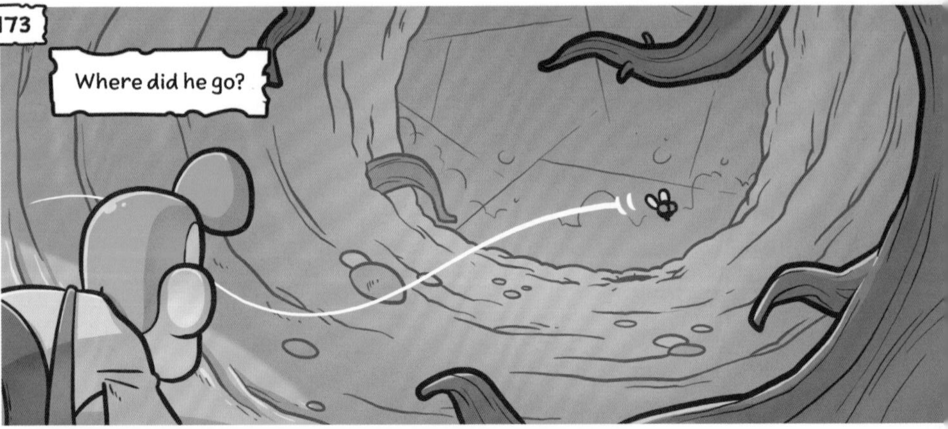
Where did he go?

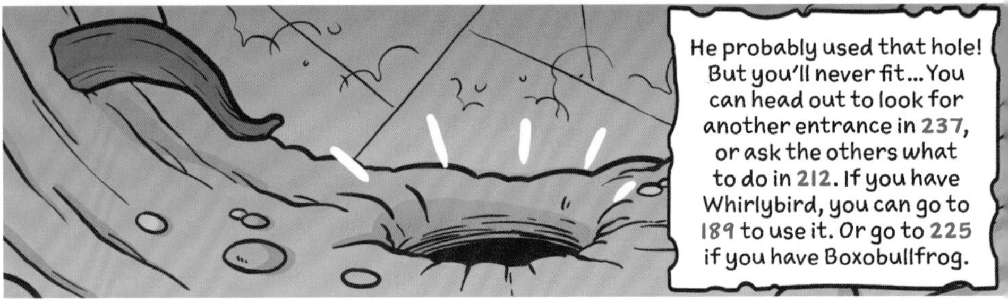
He probably used that hole! But you'll never fit... You can head out to look for another entrance in 237, or ask the others what to do in 212. If you have Whirlybird, you can go to 189 to use it. Or go to 225 if you have Boxobullfrog.

174

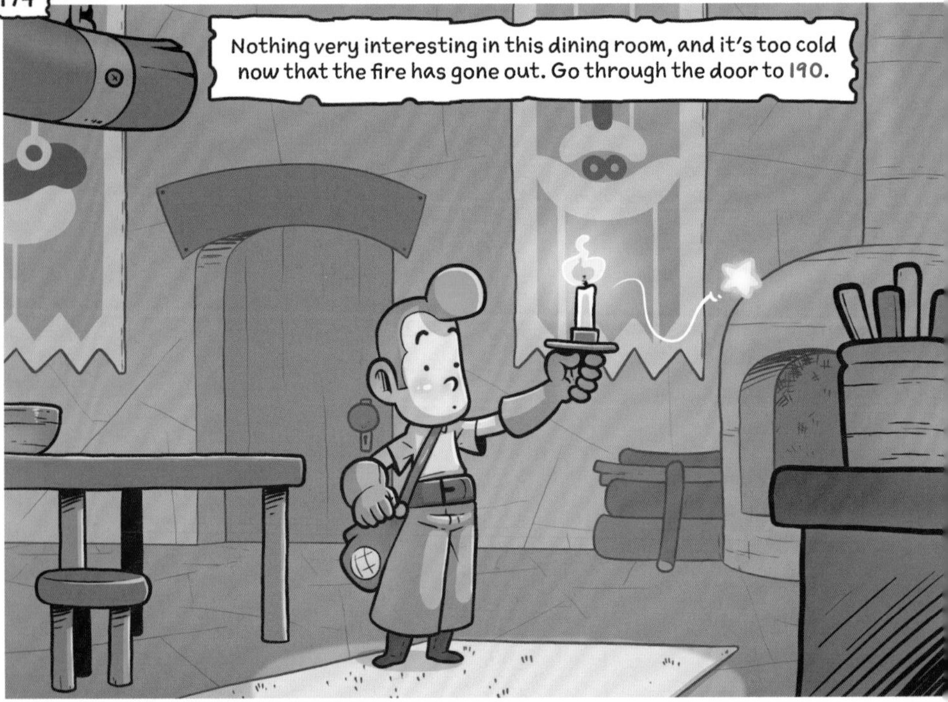
Nothing very interesting in this dining room, and it's too cold now that the fire has gone out. Go through the door to 190.

75

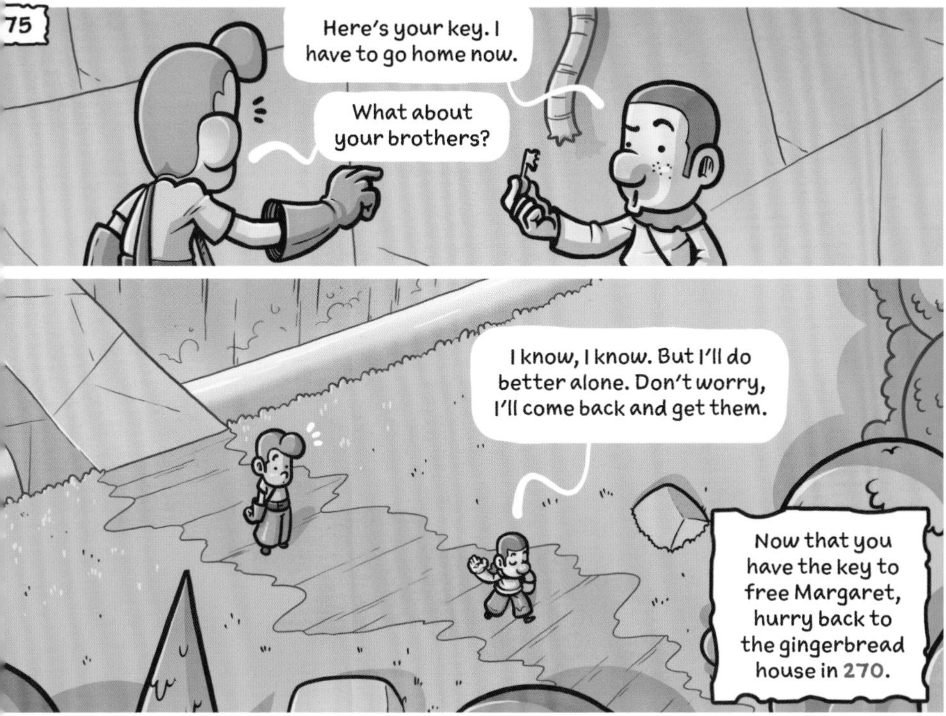
Here's your key. I have to go home now.
What about your brothers?
I know, I know. But I'll do better alone. Don't worry, I'll come back and get them.
Now that you have the key to free Margaret, hurry back to the gingerbread house in 270.

76

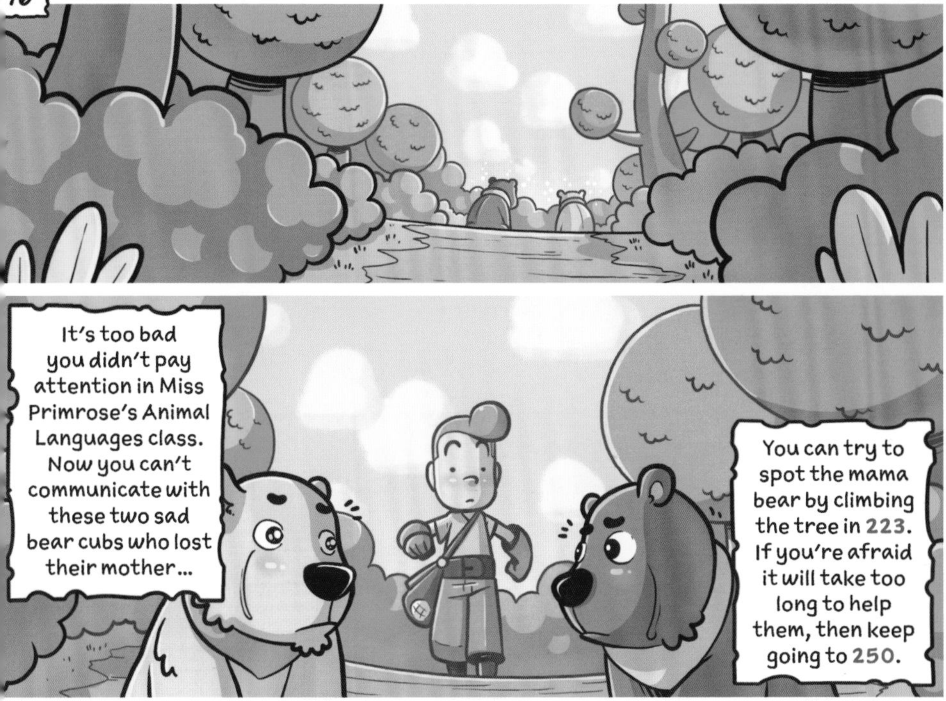
It's too bad you didn't pay attention in Miss Primrose's Animal Languages class. Now you can't communicate with these two sad bear cubs who lost their mother...
You can try to spot the mama bear by climbing the tree in 223. If you're afraid it will take too long to help them, then keep going to 250.

177

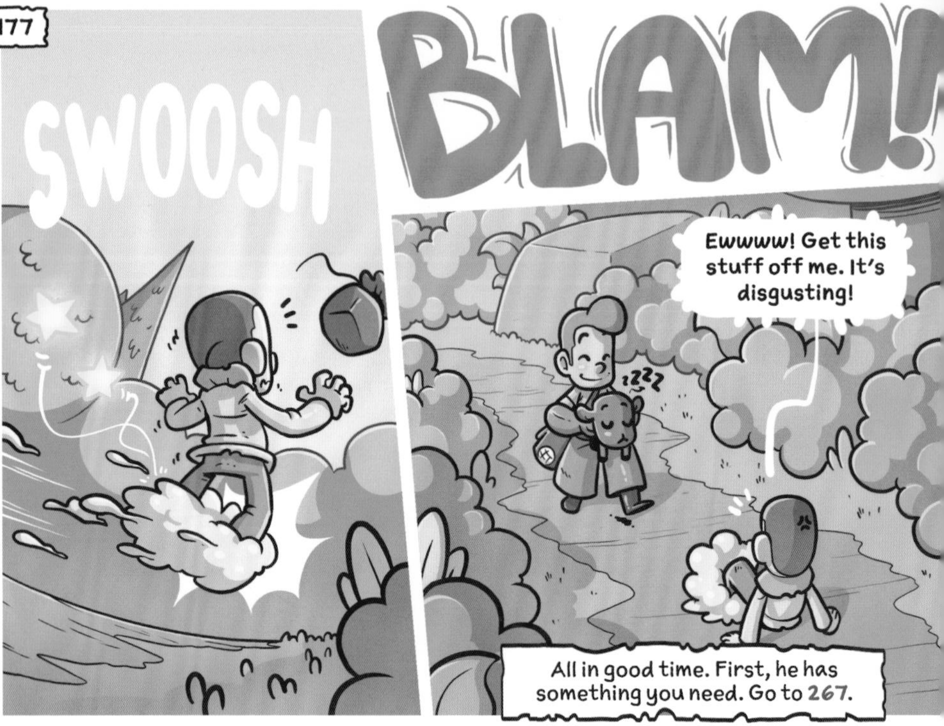
SWOOSH
BLAM!
Ewwww! Get this stuff off me. It's disgusting!
zZZ
All in good time. First, he has something you need. Go to 267.

178

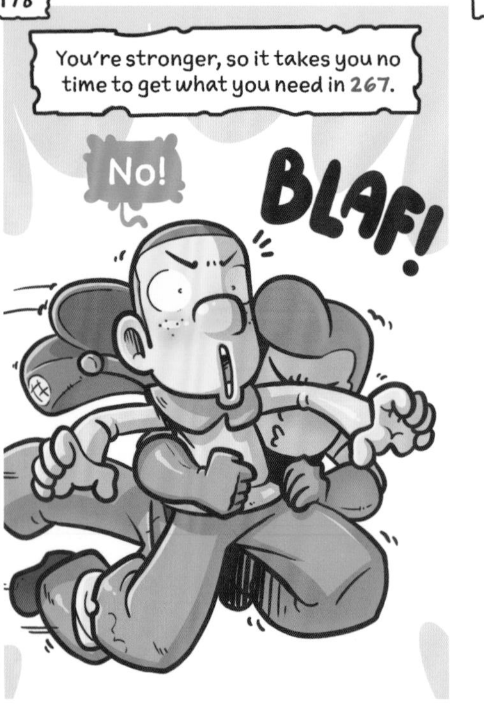
You're stronger, so it takes you no time to get what you need in 267.
No!
BLAF!

179

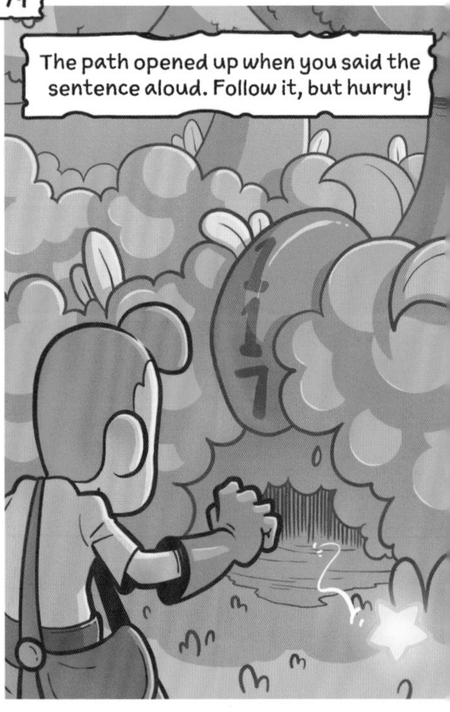
The path opened up when you said the sentence aloud. Follow it, but hurry!

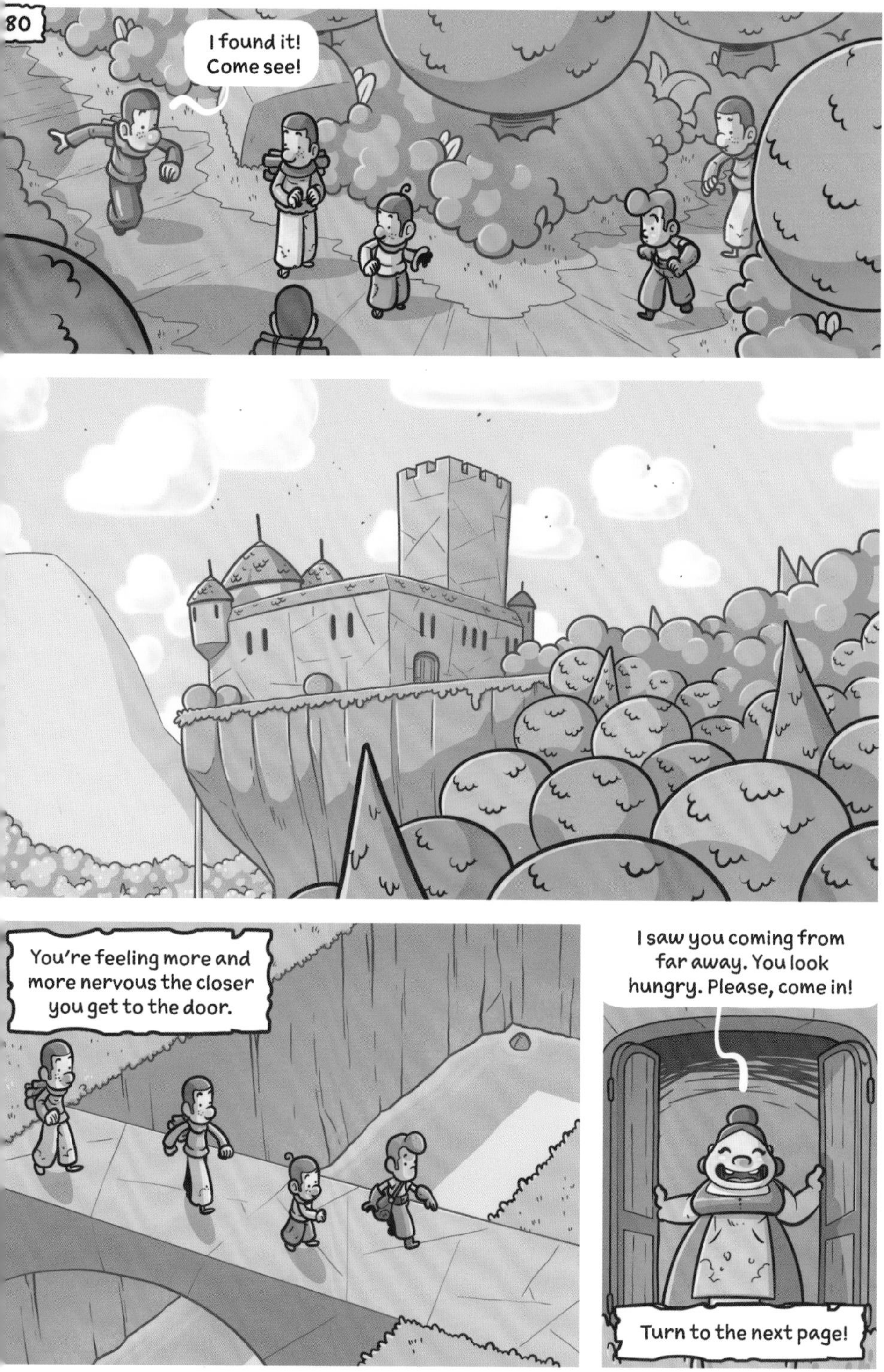
80
I found it! Come see!
You're feeling more and more nervous the closer you get to the door.
I saw you coming from far away. You look hungry. Please, come in!
Turn to the next page!

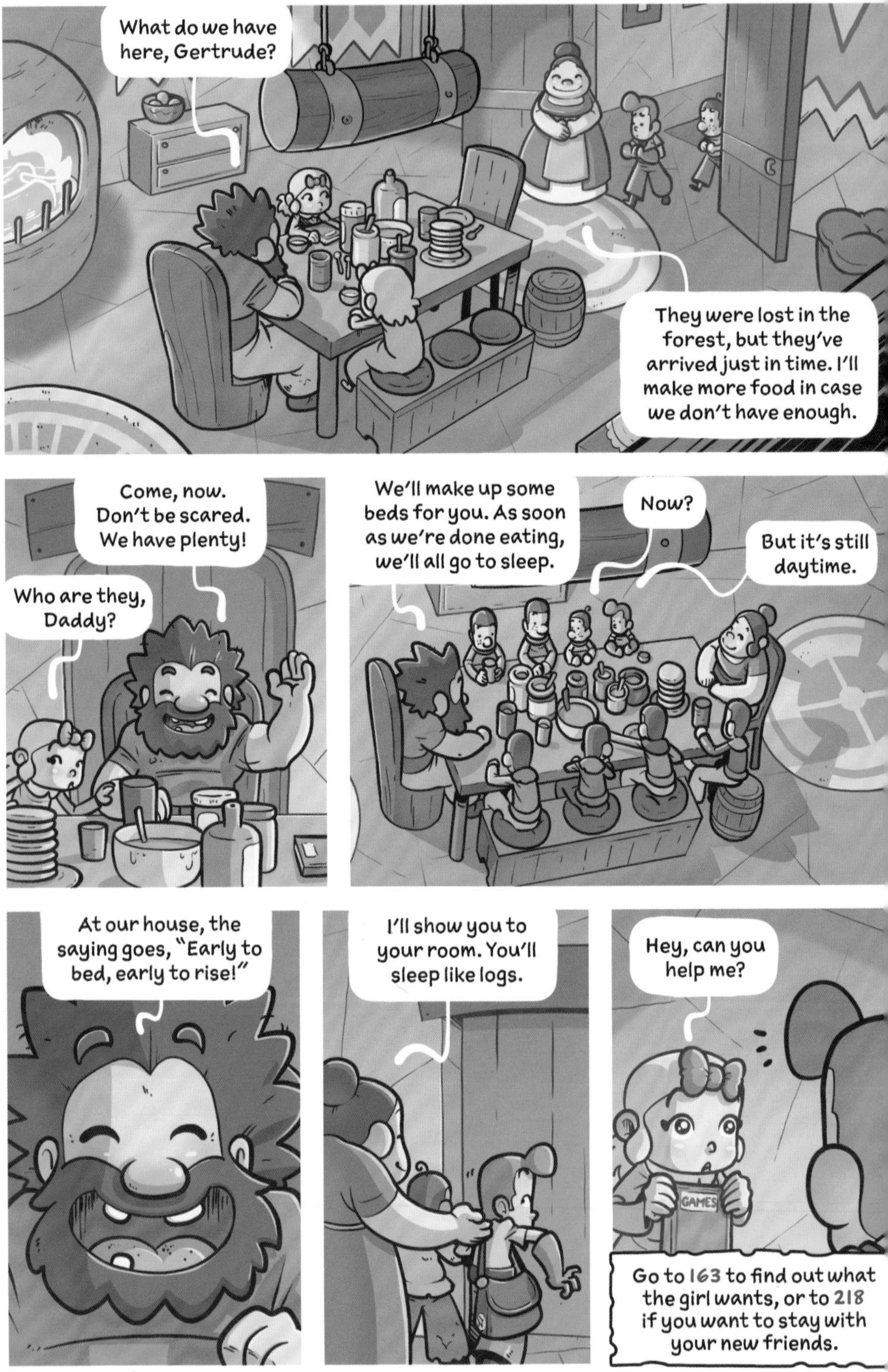
What do we have here, Gertrude?
They were lost in the forest, but they've arrived just in time. I'll make more food in case we don't have enough.
Come, now. Don't be scared. We have plenty!
Who are they, Daddy?
We'll make up some beds for you. As soon as we're done eating, we'll all go to sleep.
Now?
But it's still daytime.
At our house, the saying goes, "Early to bed, early to rise!"
I'll show you to your room. You'll sleep like logs.
Hey, can you help me?
GAMES
Go to 163 to find out what the girl wants, or to 218 if you want to stay with your new friends.

81

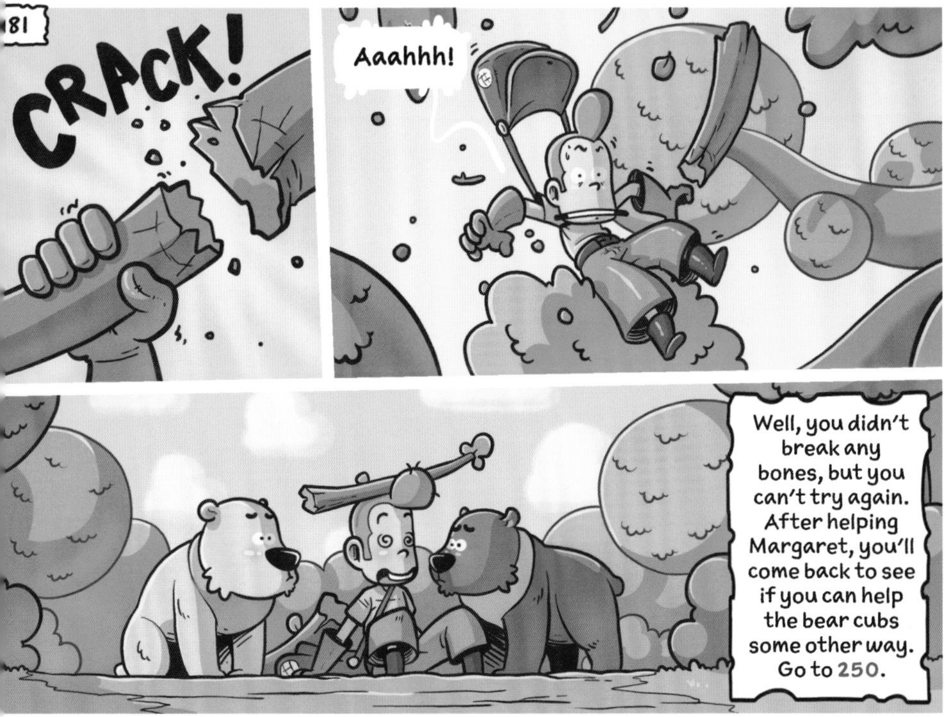
CRACK!
Aaahhh!
Well, you didn't break any bones, but you can't try again. After helping Margaret, you'll come back to see if you can help the bear cubs some other way. Go to 250.

82

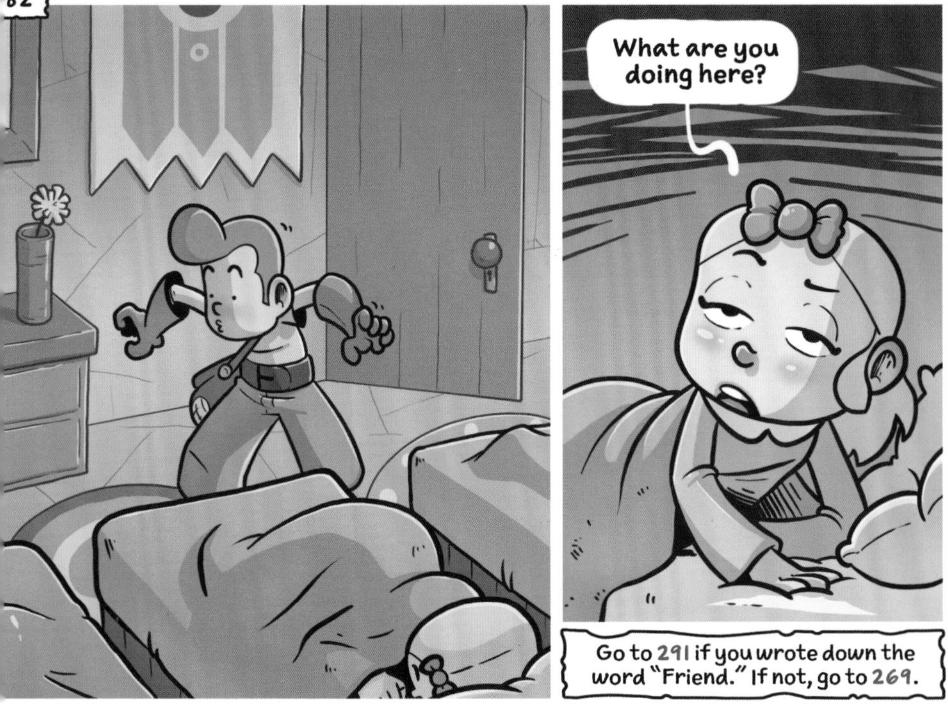
What are you doing here?
Go to 291 if you wrote down the word "Friend." If not, go to 269.

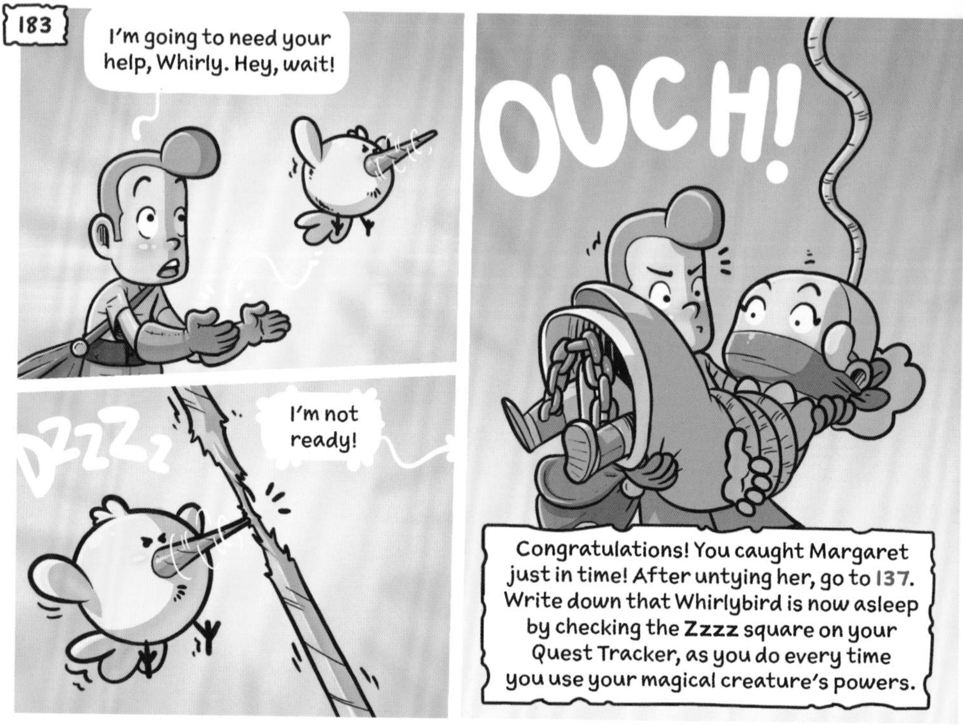
183
I'm going to need your help, Whirly. Hey, wait!
ZZZZZ
I'm not ready!
OUCH!
Congratulations! You caught Margaret just in time! After untying her, go to 137. Write down that Whirlybird is now asleep by checking the **Zzzz** square on your Quest Tracker, as you do every time you use your magical creature's powers.

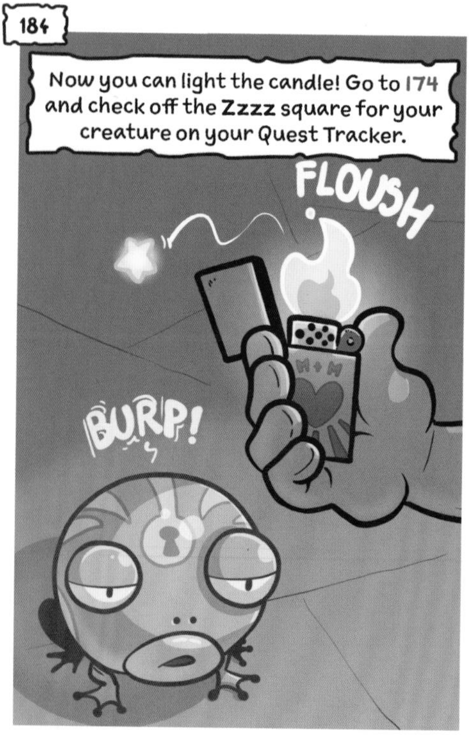
184
Now you can light the candle! Go to 174 and check off the **Zzzz** square for your creature on your Quest Tracker.
FLOUSH
M + M
BURP!

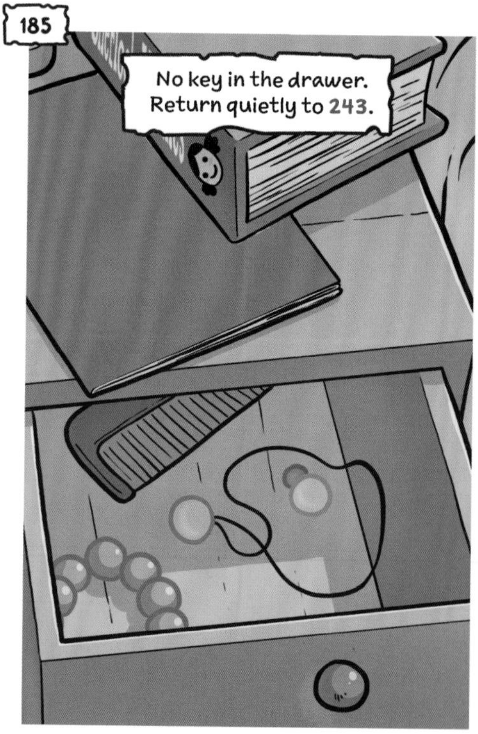
185
No key in the drawer. Return quietly to 243.

86

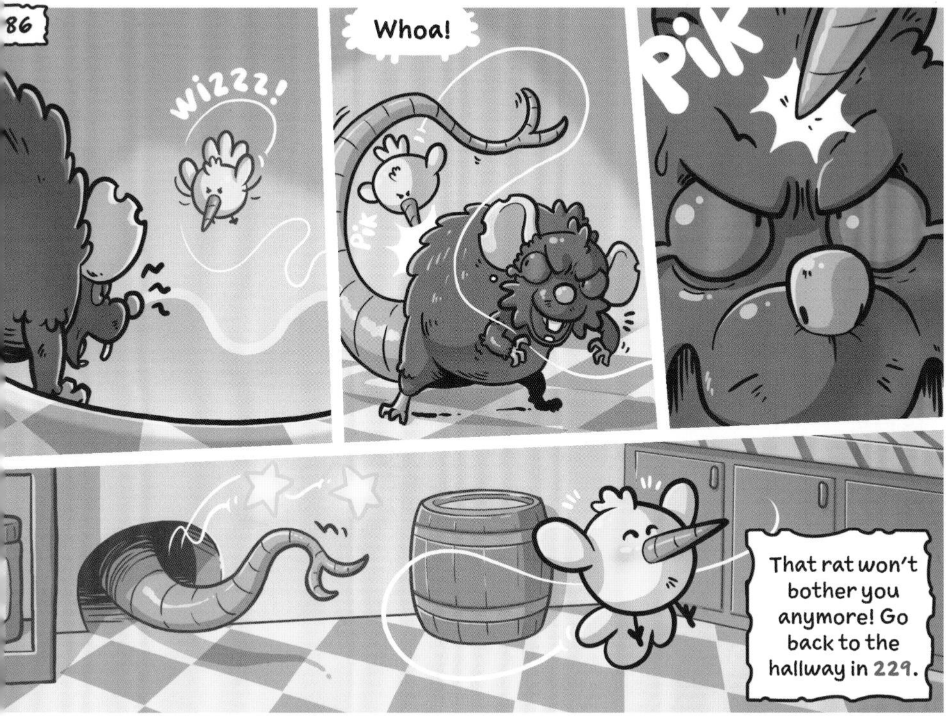
WIZZZ!
Whoa!
PIK
PIK
That rat won't bother you anymore! Go back to the hallway in 229.

87

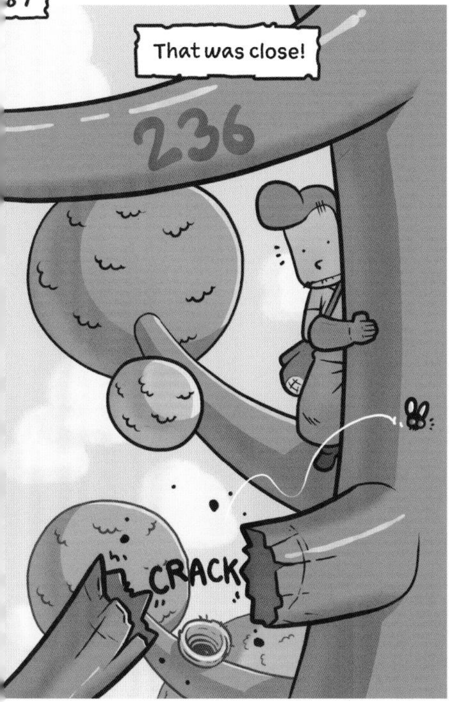
That was close!
236
CRACK

188

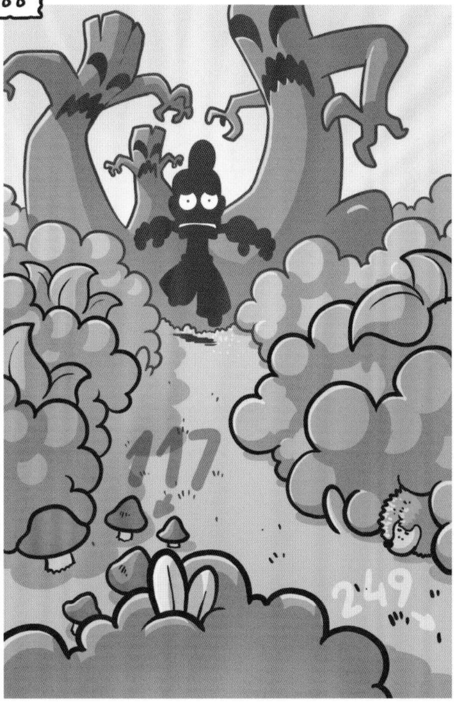
117
249

189

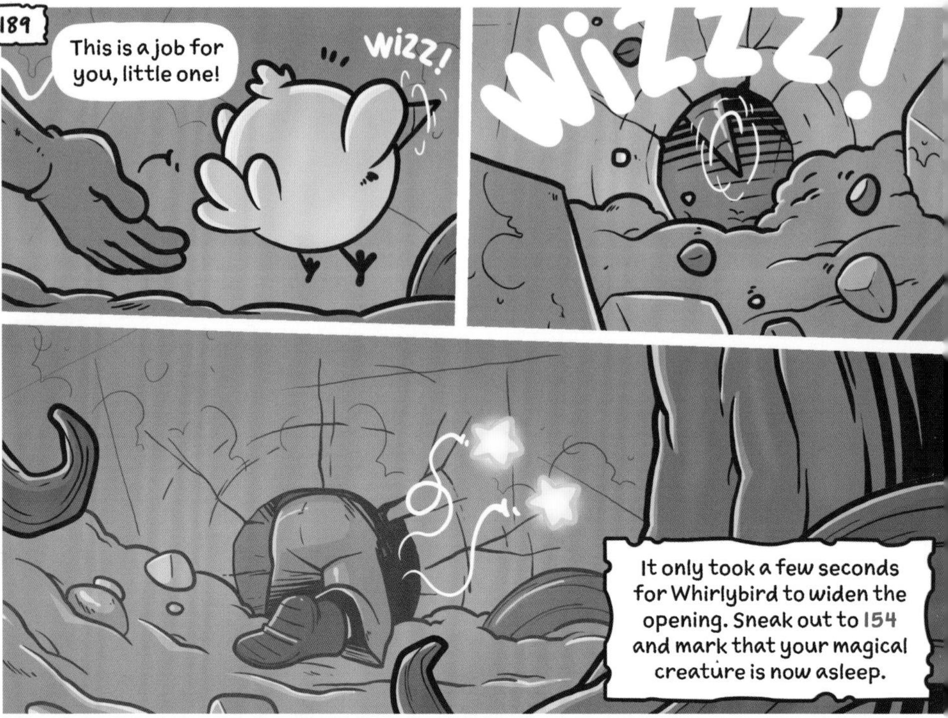
This is a job for you, little one!
WIZZ!
WIZZZZ!
It only took a few seconds for Whirlybird to widen the opening. Sneak out to 154 and mark that your magical creature is now asleep.

190

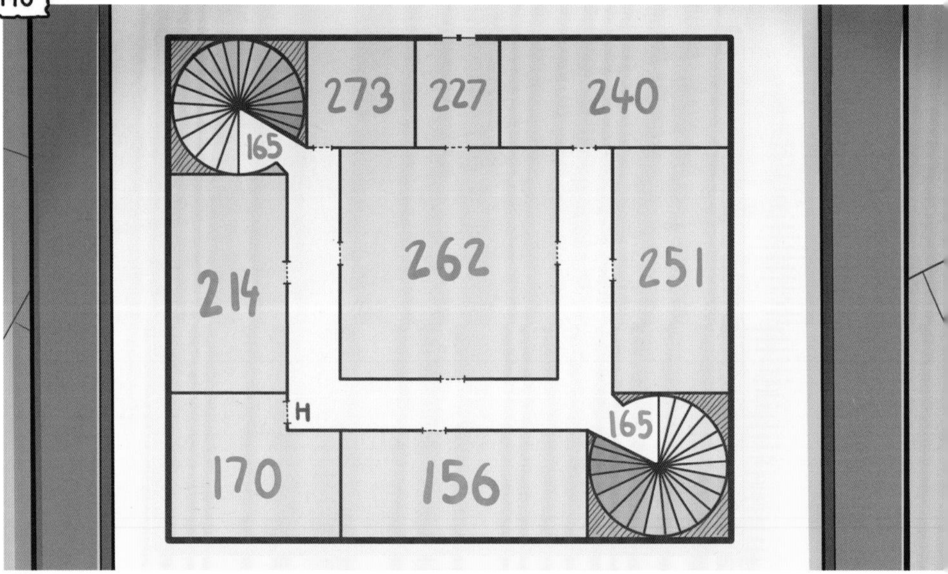
273
227
240
165
262
214
251
H
165
170
156

This is a map of the castle's ground floor. Start exploring at "H." When you come to a room with a number, go to the corresponding number in the book and read the text. Time is of the essence, be quick—you can't go back to a room you've already been in. Good luck!

191

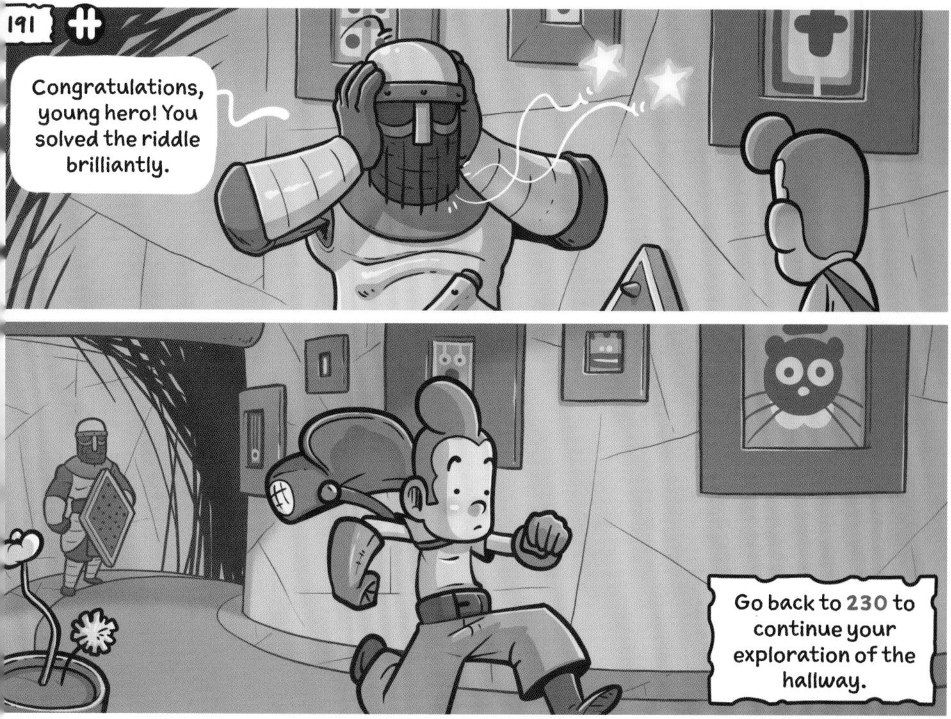
Congratulations, young hero! You solved the riddle brilliantly.
Go back to 230 to continue your exploration of the hallway.

192

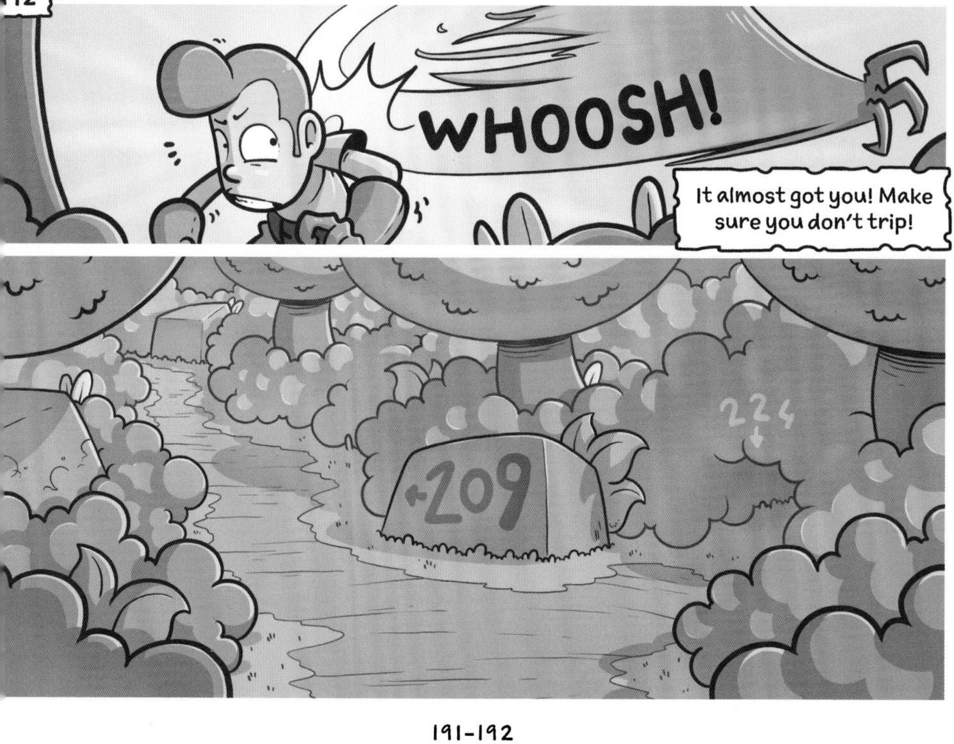
WHOOSH!
It almost got you! Make sure you don't trip!
←209
224

193

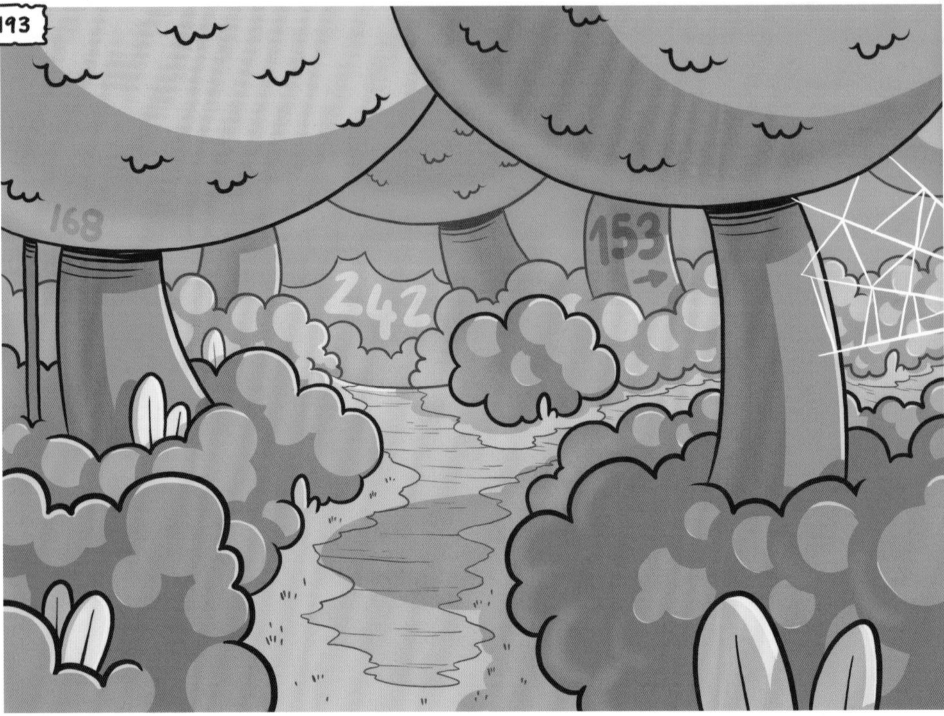
168
242
153

194

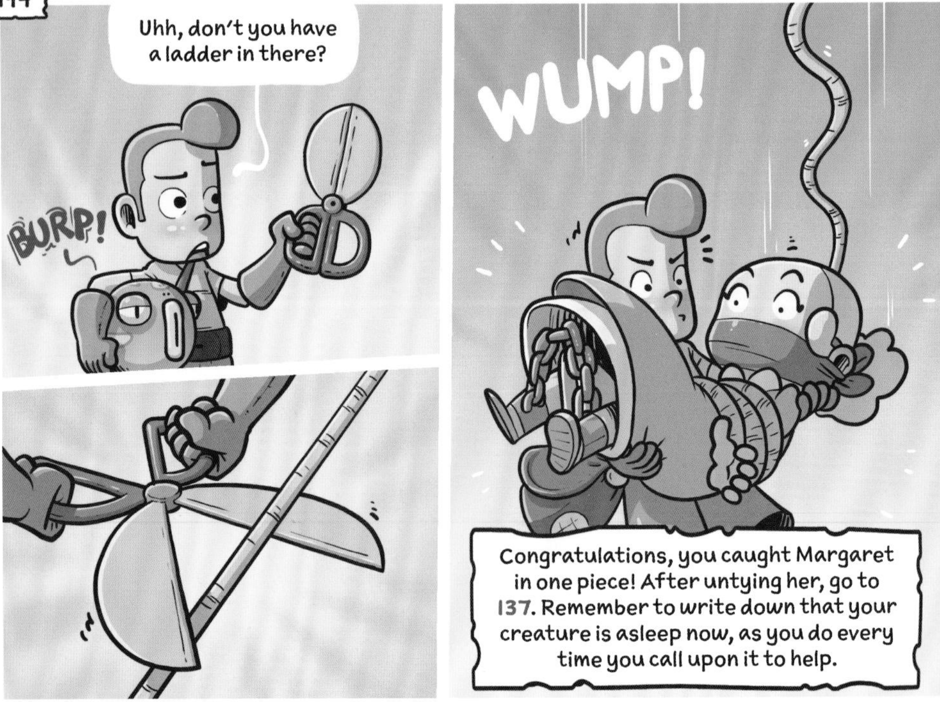
Uhh, don't you have a ladder in there?
BURP!
WUMP!
Congratulations, you caught Margaret in one piece! After untying her, go to 137. Remember to write down that your creature is asleep now, as you do every time you call upon it to help.

95

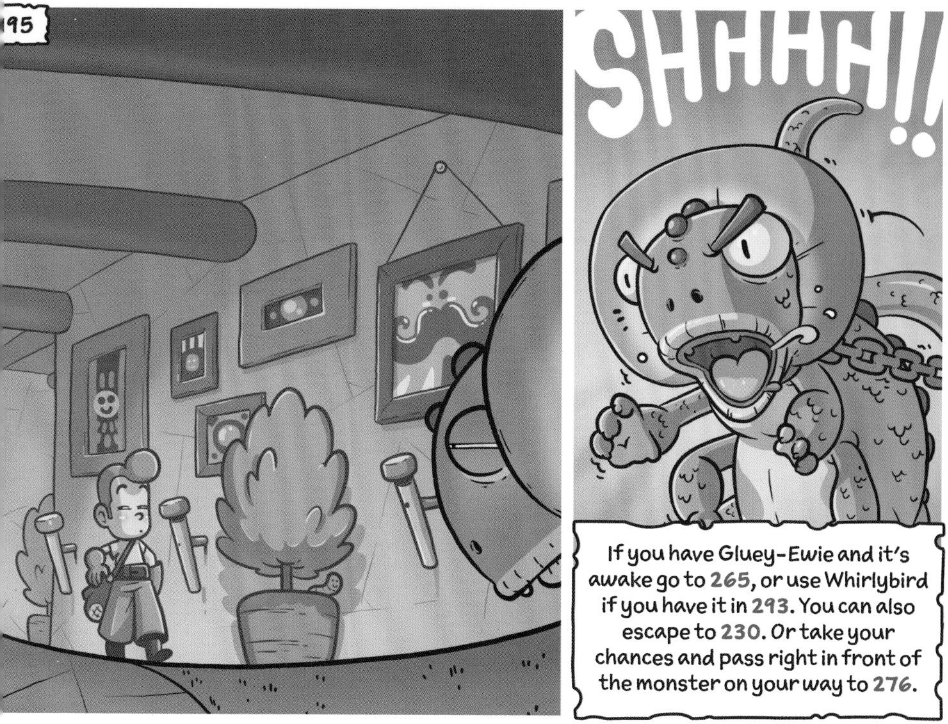
SHHHH!!
If you have Gluey-Ewie and it's awake go to 265, or use Whirlybird if you have it in 293. You can also escape to 230. Or take your chances and pass right in front of the monster on your way to 276.

96

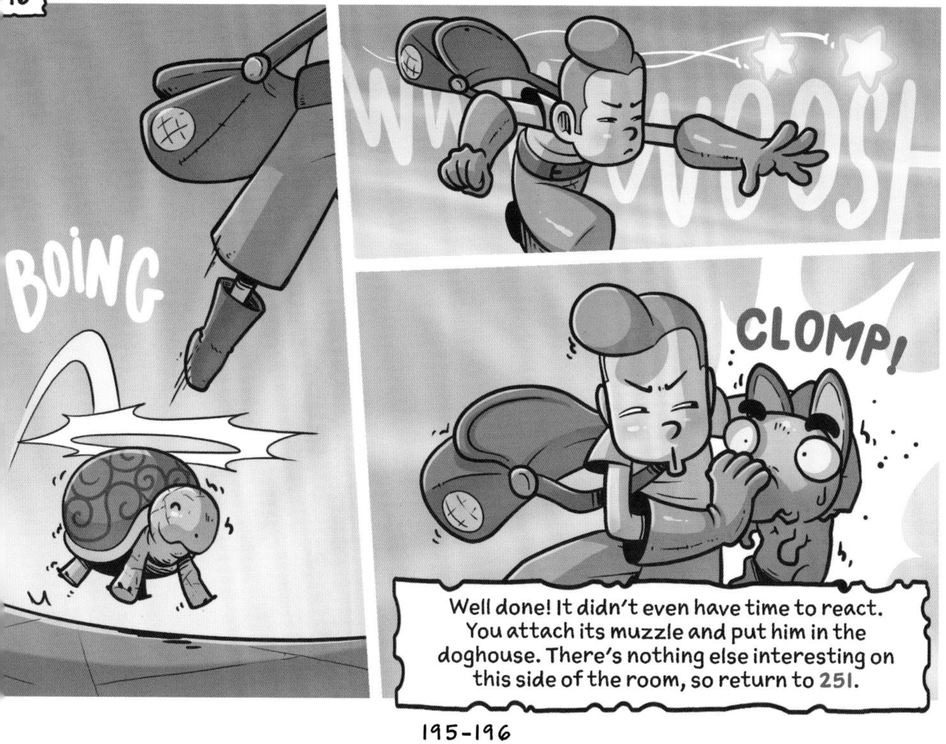
BOING
CLOMP!
Well done! It didn't even have time to react. You attach its muzzle and put him in the doghouse. There's nothing else interesting on this side of the room, so return to 251.

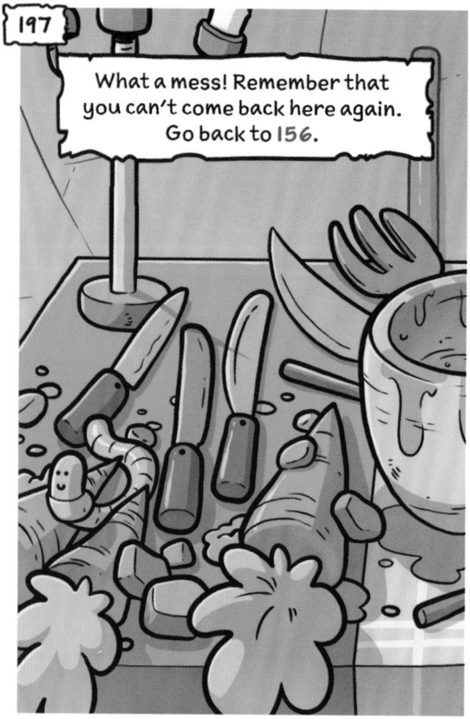
197
What a mess! Remember that you can't come back here again. Go back to 156.

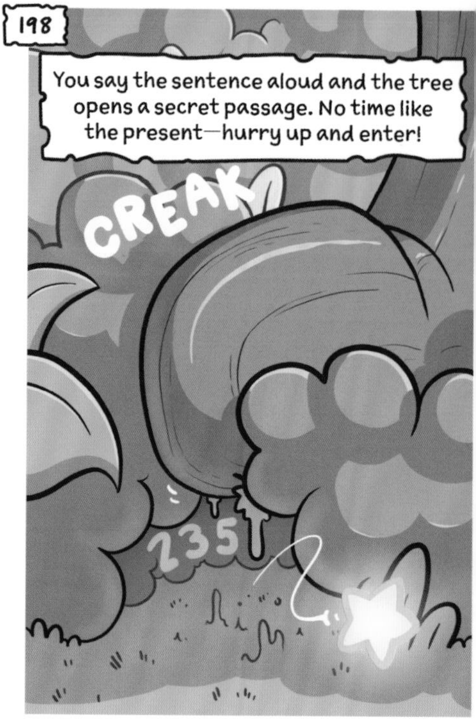
198
You say the sentence aloud and the tree opens a secret passage. No time like the present—hurry up and enter!
CREAK
235

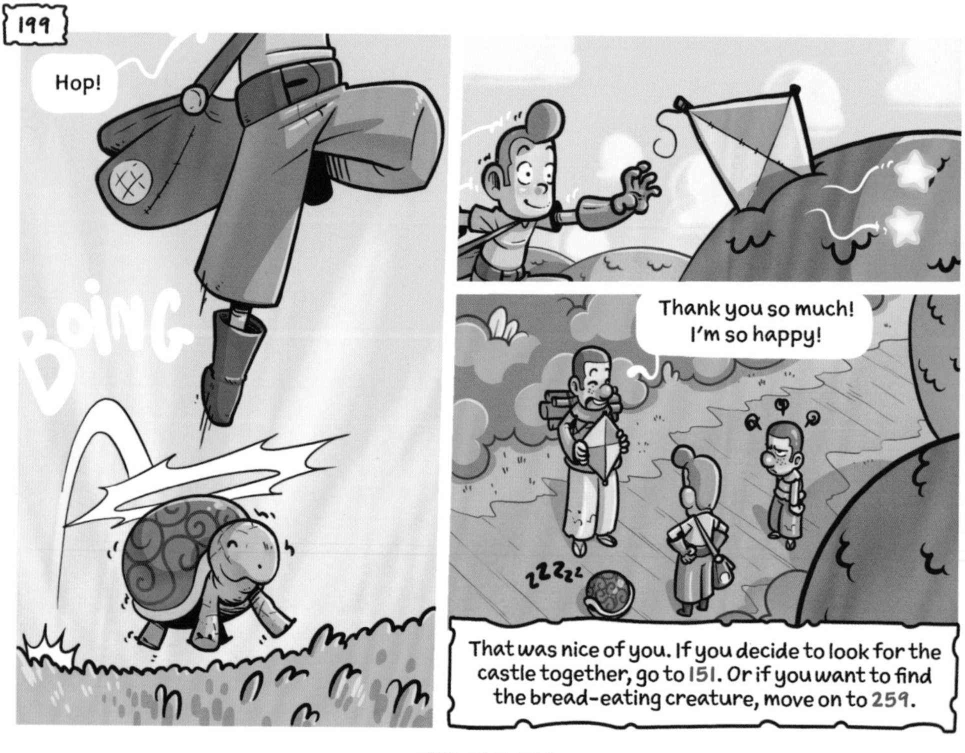
199
Hop!
BOING
Thank you so much! I'm so happy!
ZZZZZ
That was nice of you. If you decide to look for the castle together, go to 151. Or if you want to find the bread-eating creature, move on to 259.

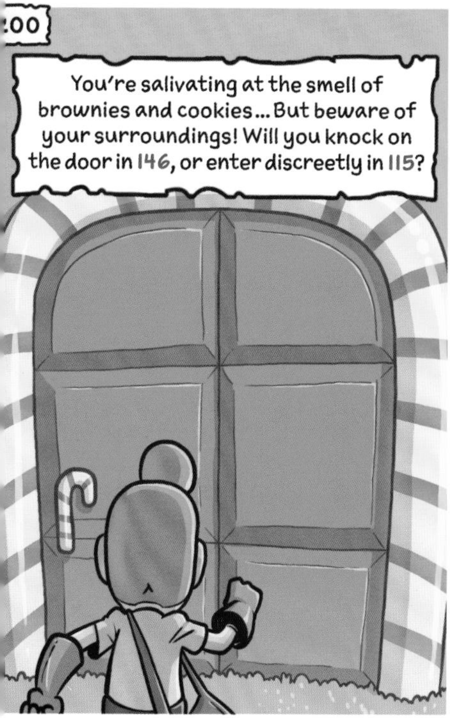
200
You're salivating at the smell of brownies and cookies... But beware of your surroundings! Will you knock on the door in 146, or enter discreetly in 115?

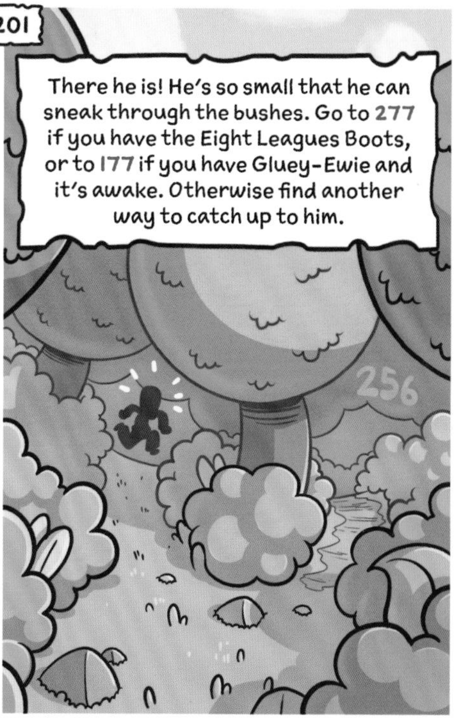
201
There he is! He's so small that he can sneak through the bushes. Go to 277 if you have the Eight Leagues Boots, or to 177 if you have Gluey-Ewie and it's awake. Otherwise find another way to catch up to him.
256

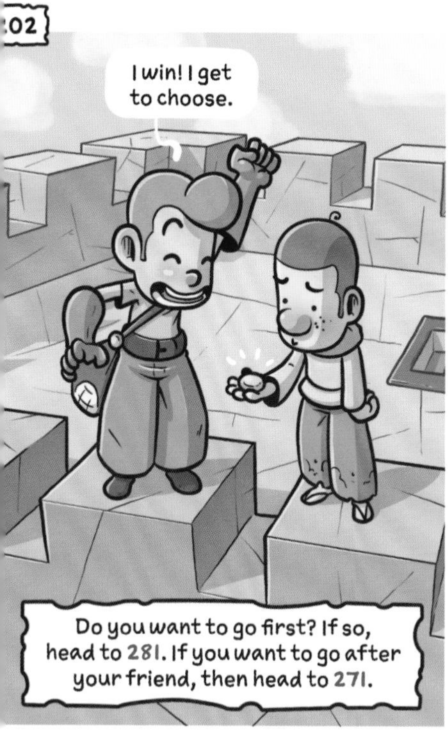
202
I win! I get to choose.
Do you want to go first? If so, head to 281. If you want to go after your friend, then head to 271.

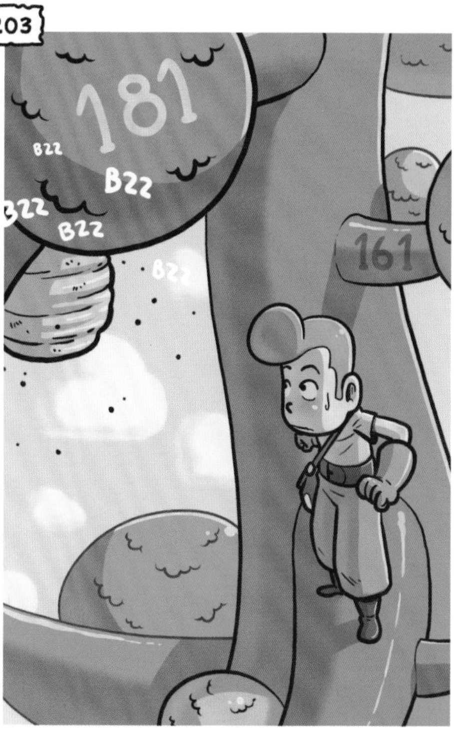
203
181
BZZ
BZZ
BZZ
BZZ
BZZ
161

204

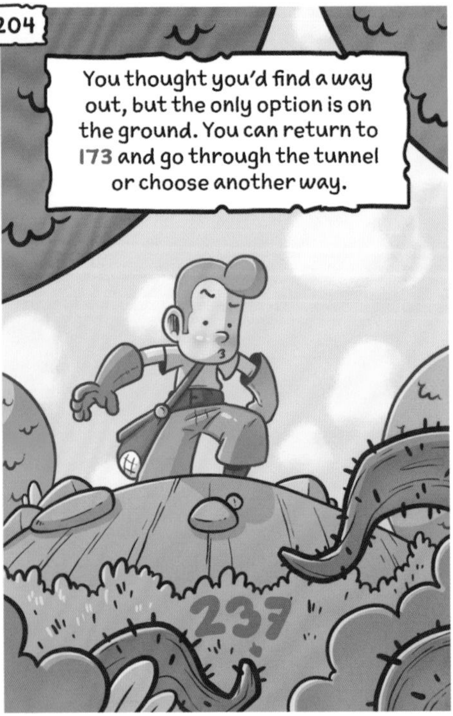
You thought you'd find a way out, but the only option is on the ground. You can return to 173 and go through the tunnel or choose another way.
237

205

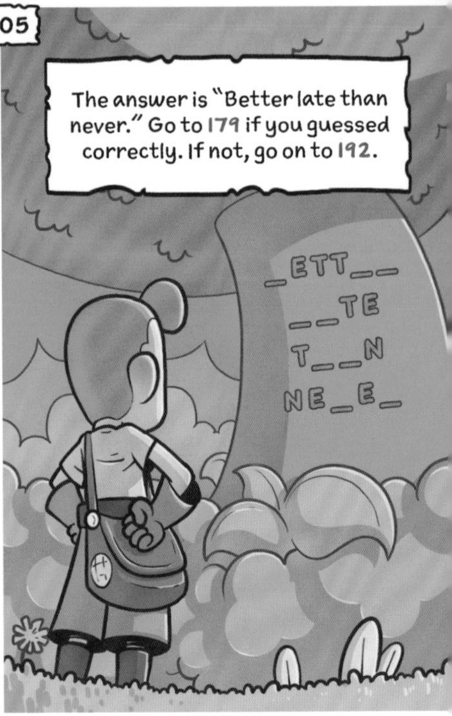
The answer is "Better late than never." Go to 179 if you guessed correctly. If not, go on to 192.
_ETT__
__TE
T__N
NE_E_

206

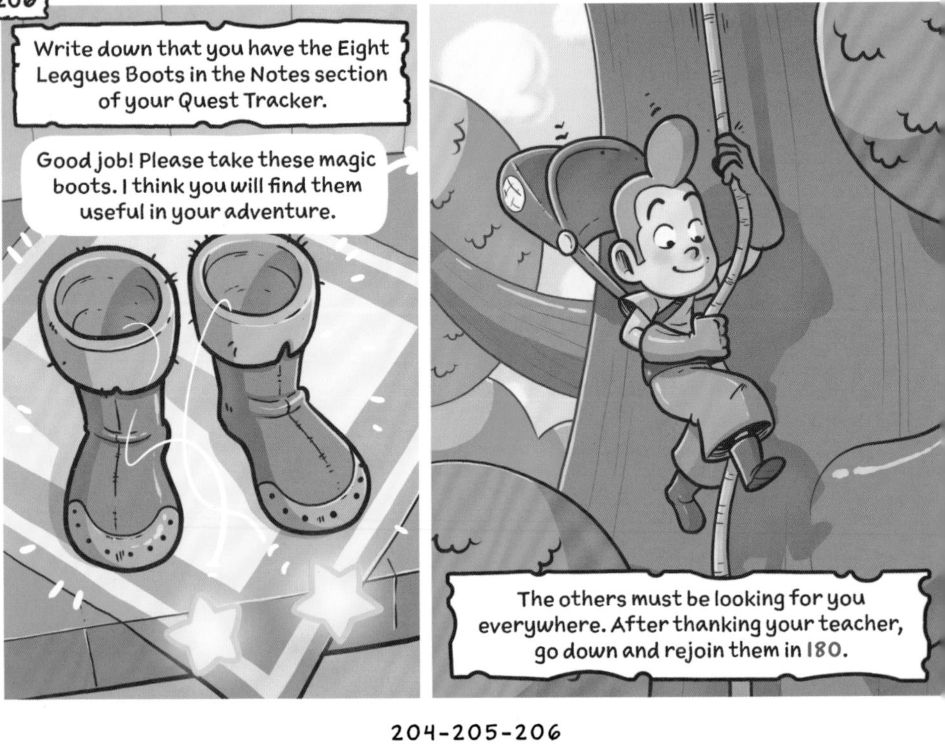
Write down that you have the Eight Leagues Boots in the Notes section of your Quest Tracker.
Good job! Please take these magic boots. I think you will find them useful in your adventure.
The others must be looking for you everywhere. After thanking your teacher, go down and rejoin them in 180.

07

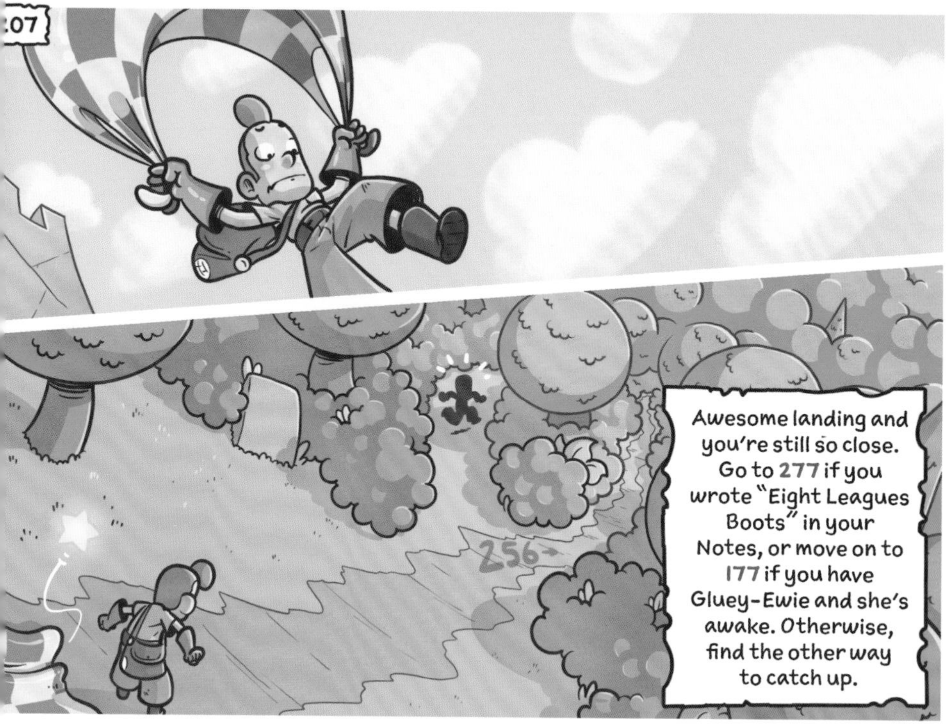
256→
Awesome landing and you're still so close. Go to 277 if you wrote "Eight Leagues Boots" in your Notes, or move on to 177 if you have Gluey-Ewie and she's awake. Otherwise, find the other way to catch up.

08

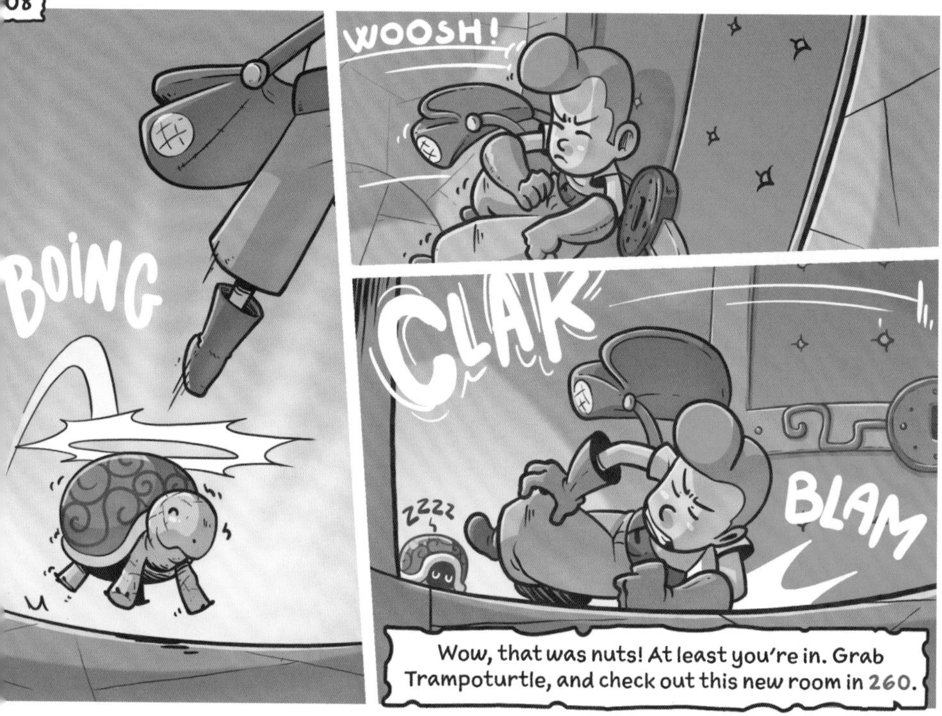
BOING
WOOSH!
CLAK
BLAM
ZZZZ
Wow, that was nuts! At least you're in. Grab Trampoturtle, and check out this new room in 260.

209

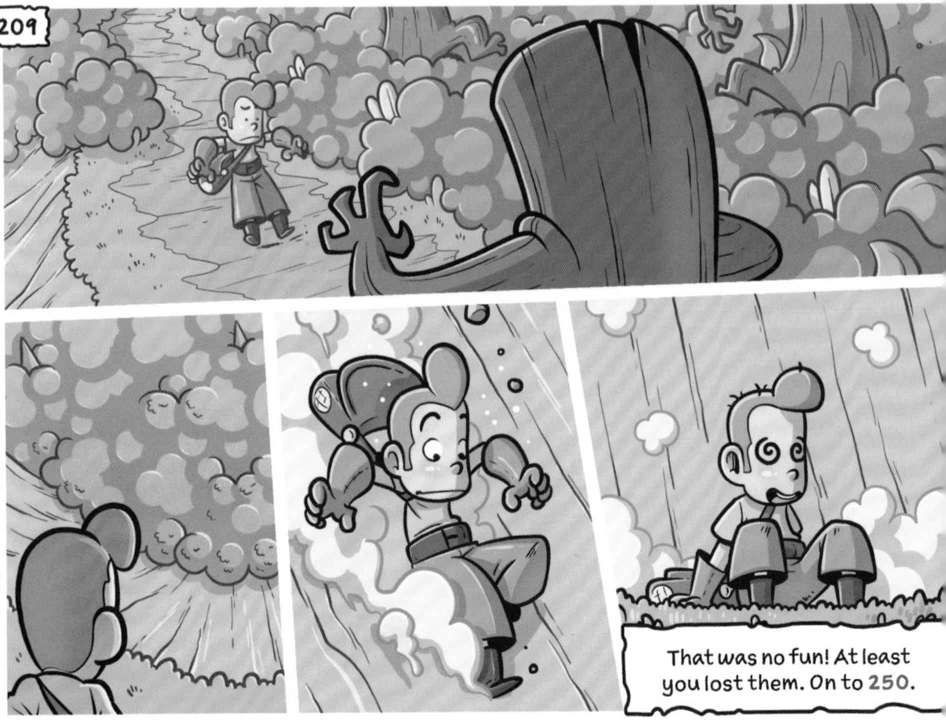
That was no fun! At least you lost them. On to 250.

210

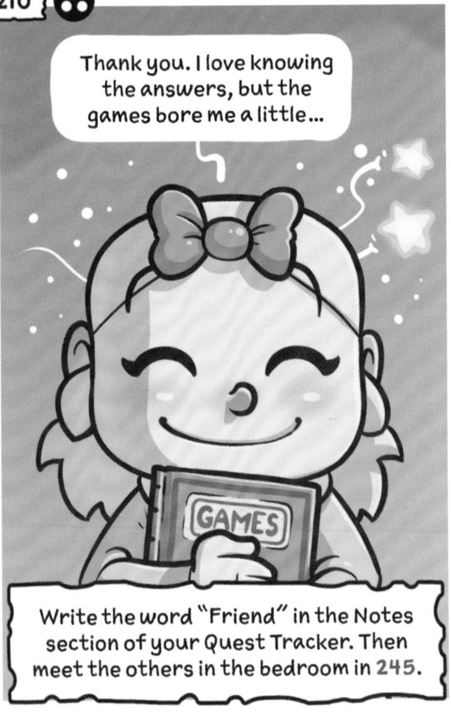
Thank you. I love knowing the answers, but the games bore me a little...
GAMES
Write the word "Friend" in the Notes section of your Quest Tracker. Then meet the others in the bedroom in 245.

211

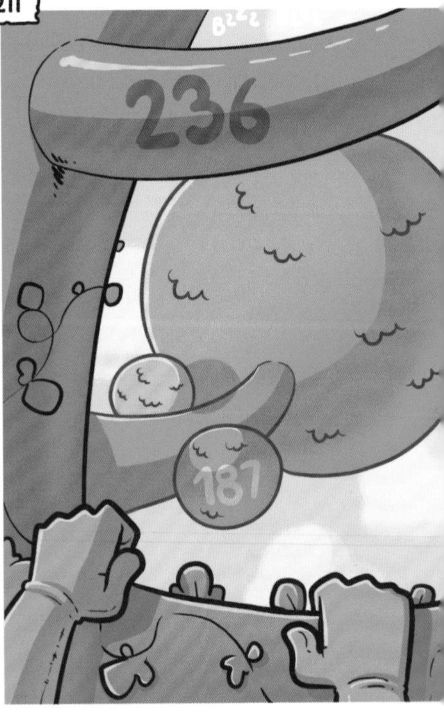
236
187

212

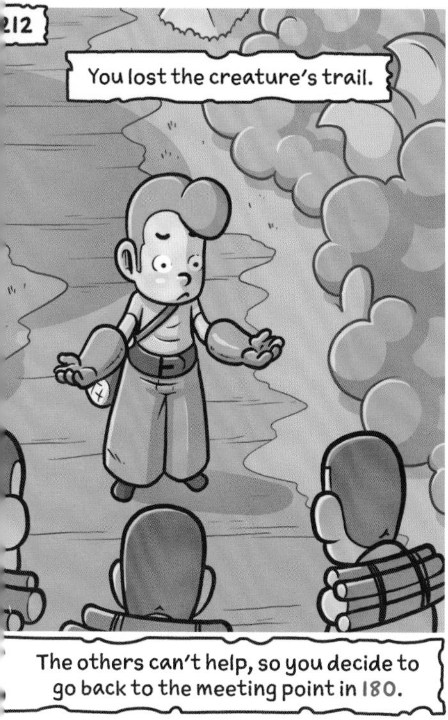
You lost the creature's trail.
The others can't help, so you decide to go back to the meeting point in 180.

213

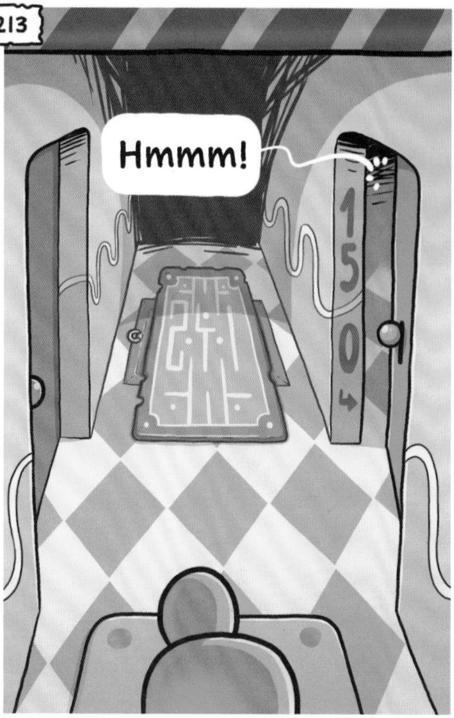
Hmmm!
150

214

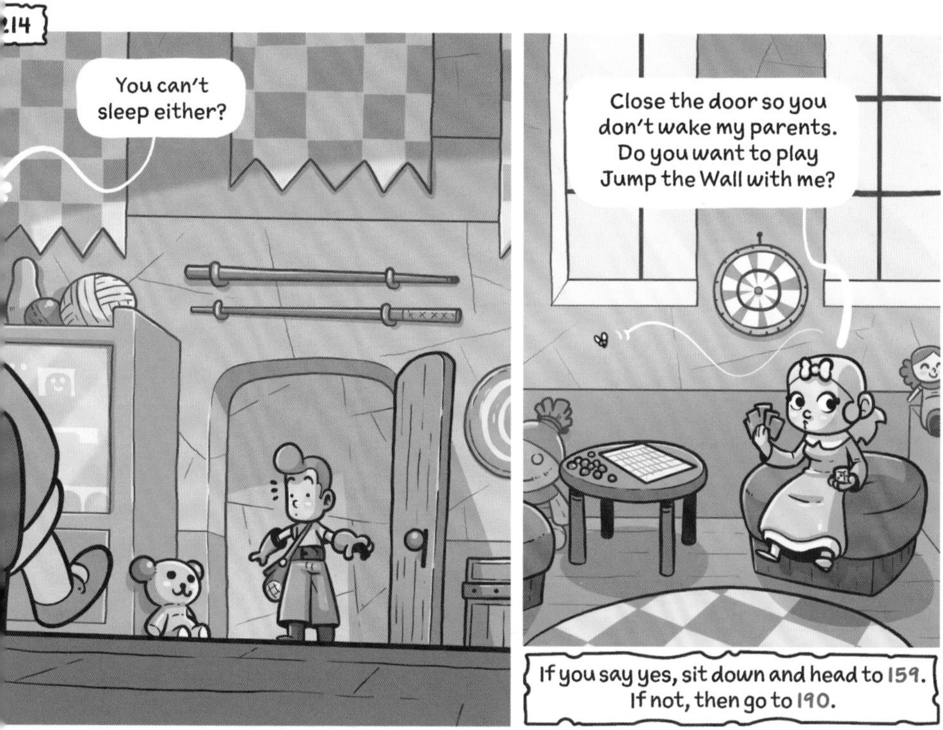
You can't sleep either?
Close the door so you don't wake my parents. Do you want to play Jump the Wall with me?
If you say yes, sit down and head to 159. If not, then go to 190.

215

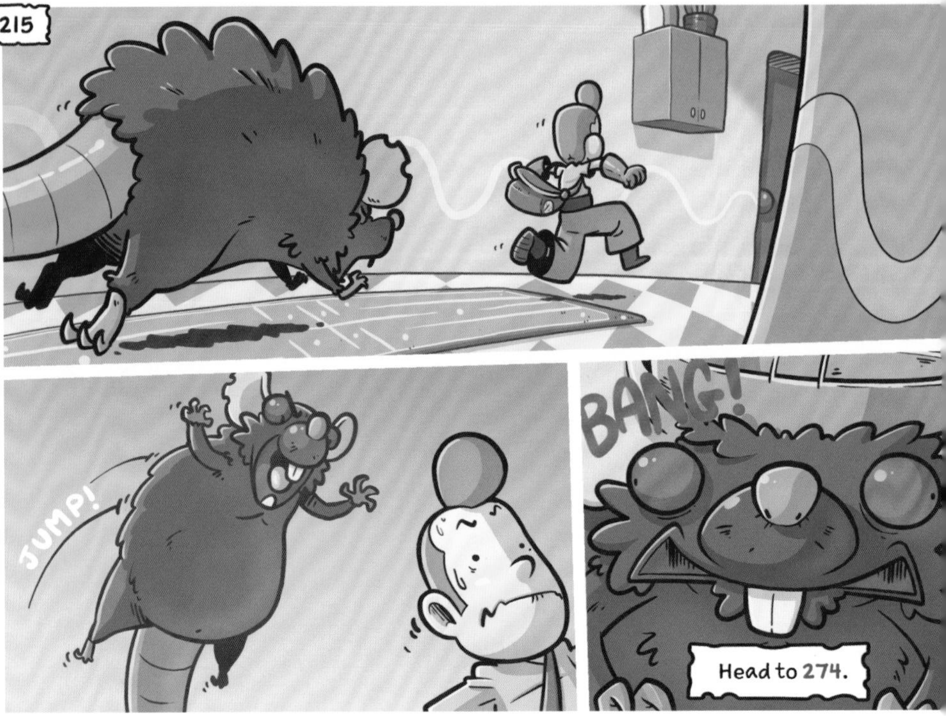
JUMP!
BANG!
Head to 274.

216

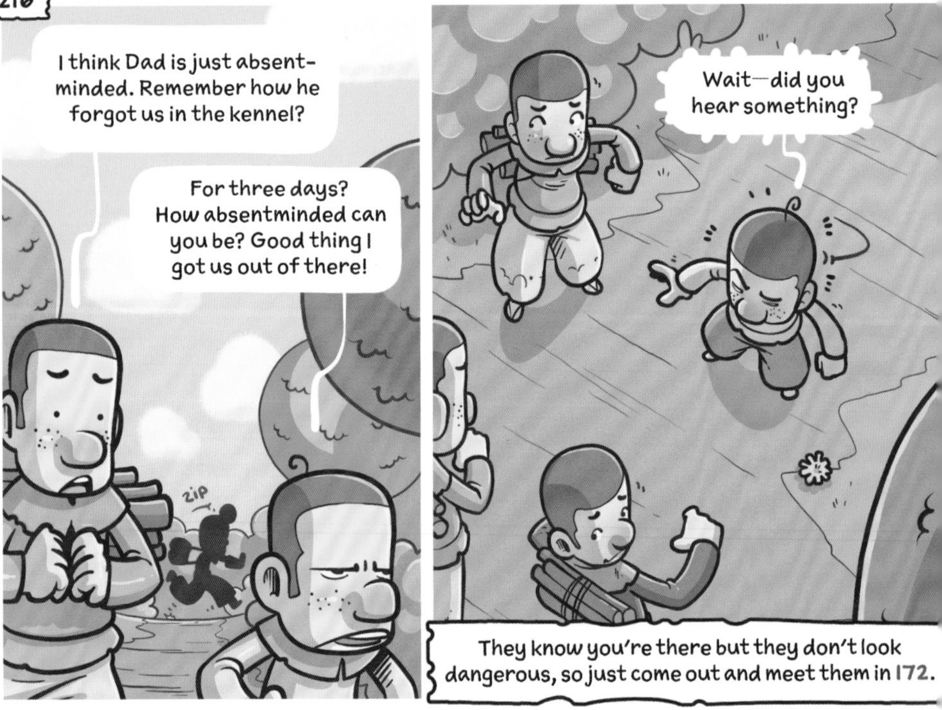
I think Dad is just absent-minded. Remember how he forgot us in the kennel?
For three days? How absentminded can you be? Good thing I got us out of there!
ZIP
Wait—did you hear something?
They know you're there but they don't look dangerous, so just come out and meet them in 172.

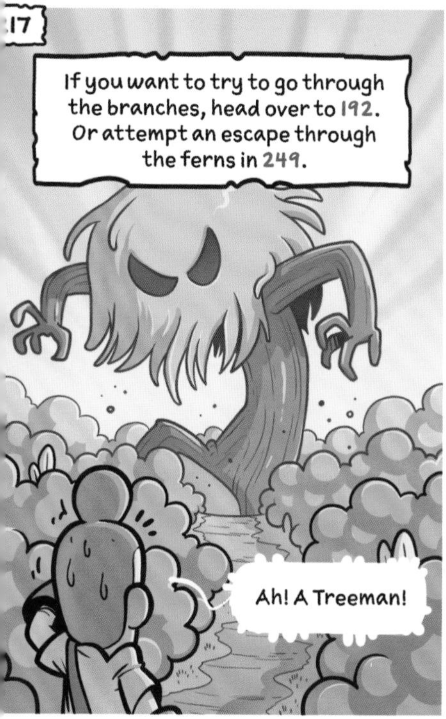
17
If you want to try to go through the branches, head over to 192. Or attempt an escape through the ferns in 249.
Ah! A Treeman!

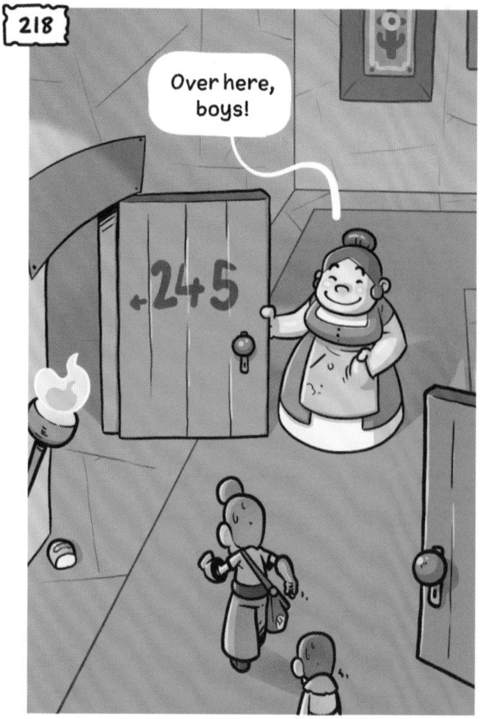
218
Over here, boys!
245

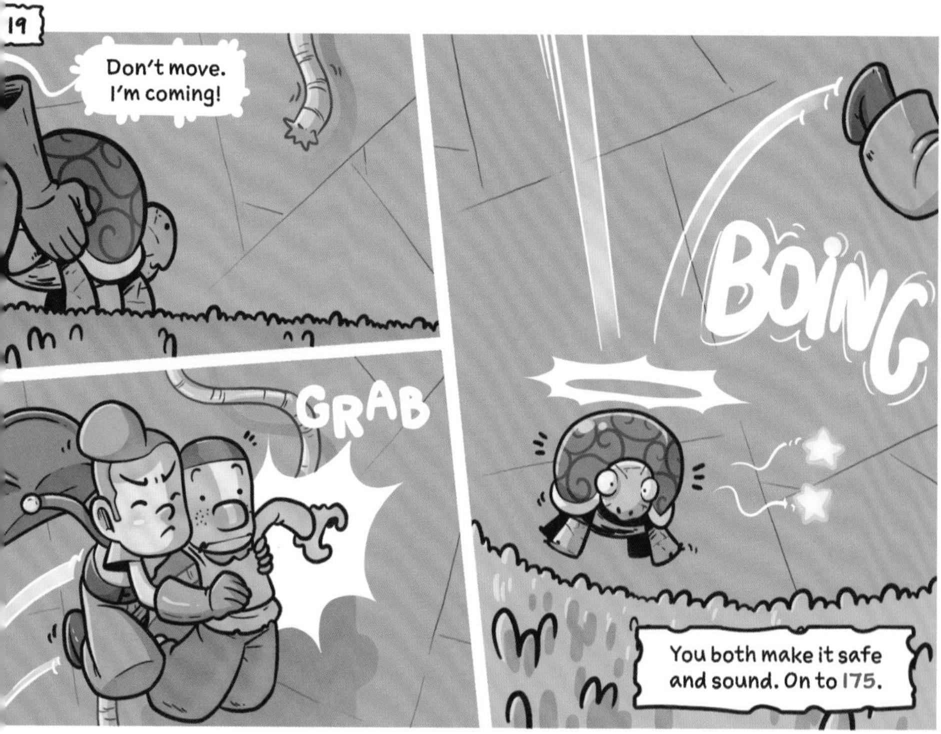
19
Don't move. I'm coming!
GRAB
BOING
You both make it safe and sound. On to 175.

220

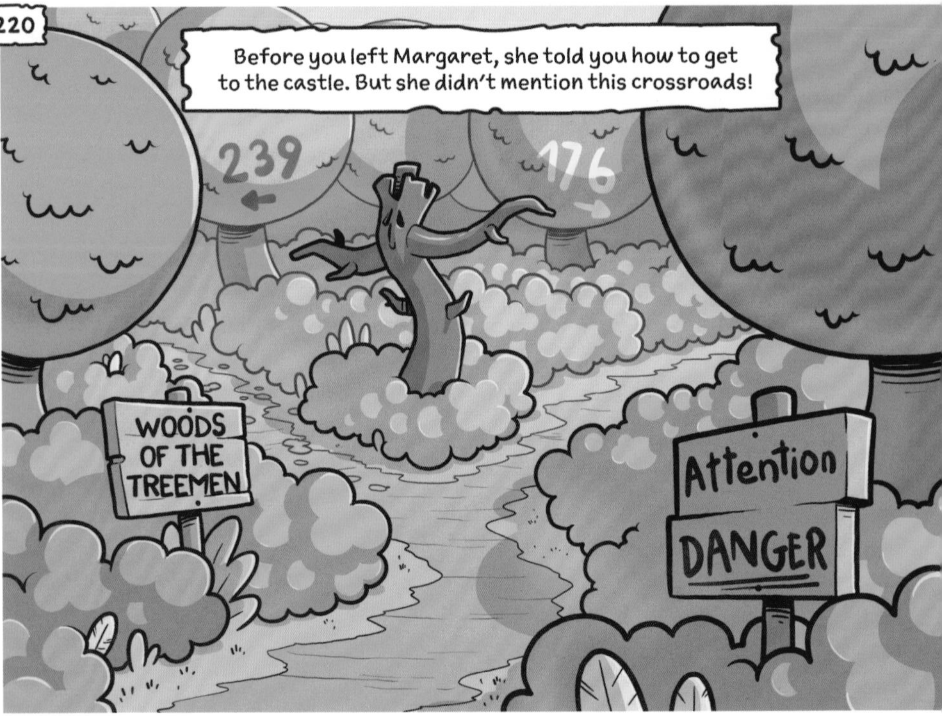
Before you left Margaret, she told you how to get to the castle. But she didn't mention this crossroads!
239
176
WOODS OF THE TREEMEN
Attention
DANGER

221

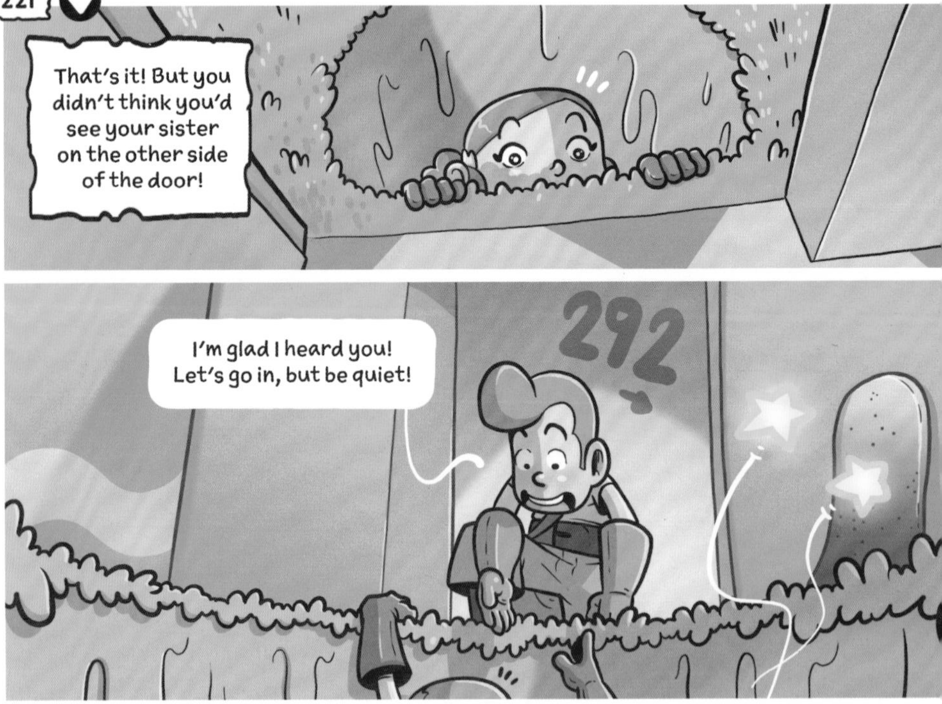
That's it! But you didn't think you'd see your sister on the other side of the door!
I'm glad I heard you! Let's go in, but be quiet!
292

22

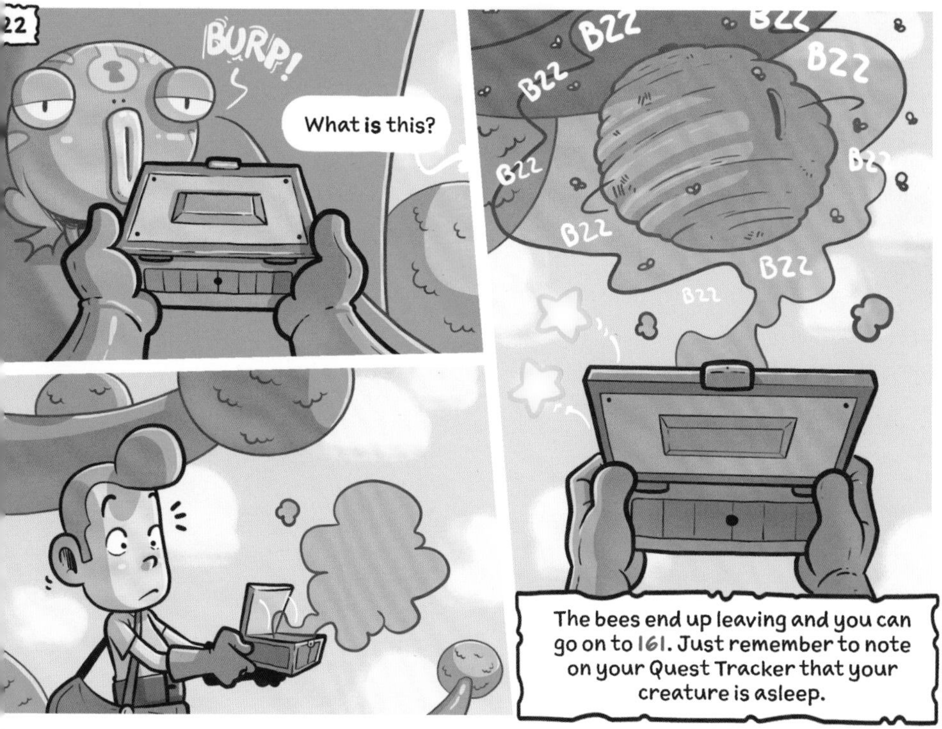
BURP!
What is this?
BZZ
BZZ
BZZ
BZZ
BZZ
BZZ
BZZ
The bees end up leaving and you can go on to 161. Just remember to note on your Quest Tracker that your creature is asleep.

23

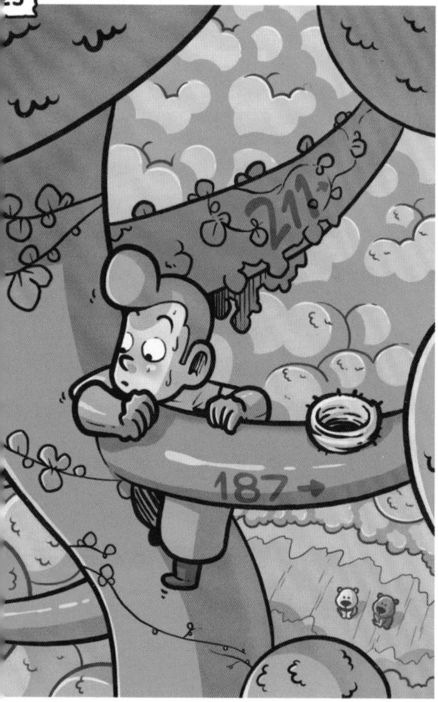
211
187 →

224

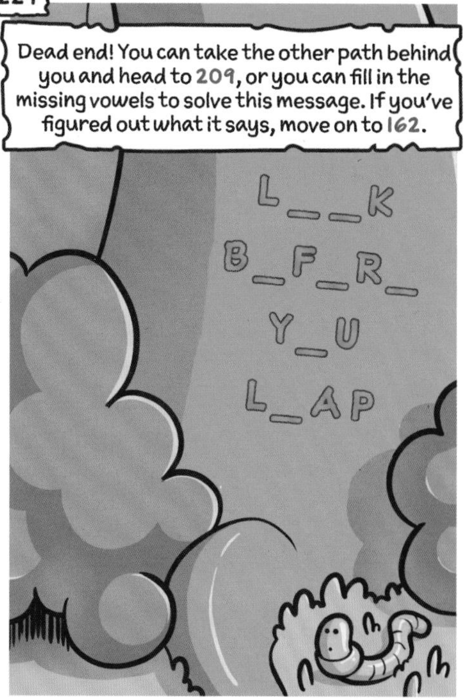
Dead end! You can take the other path behind you and head to 209, or you can fill in the missing vowels to solve this message. If you've figured out what it says, move on to 162.
L__K
B_F_R_
Y_U
L_AP

225

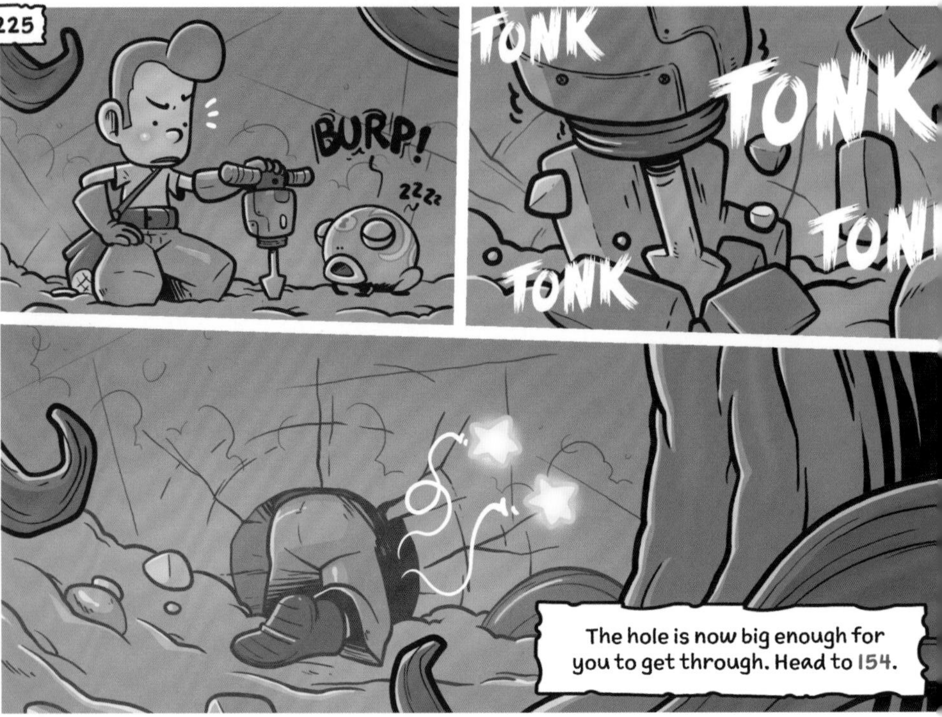
BURP!
zzzz
TONK
TONK
TONK
TONK
The hole is now big enough for you to get through. Head to 154.

226

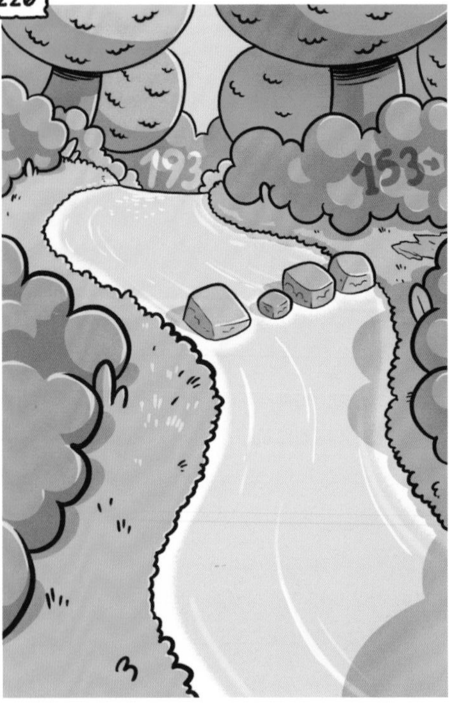
193
153→

227

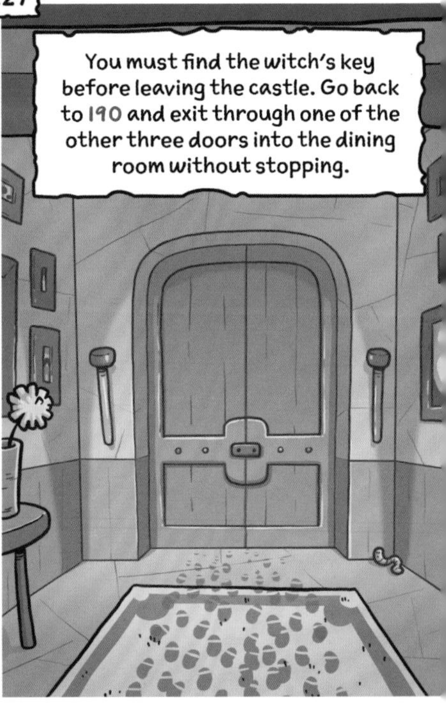
You must find the witch's key before leaving the castle. Go back to 190 and exit through one of the other three doors into the dining room without stopping.

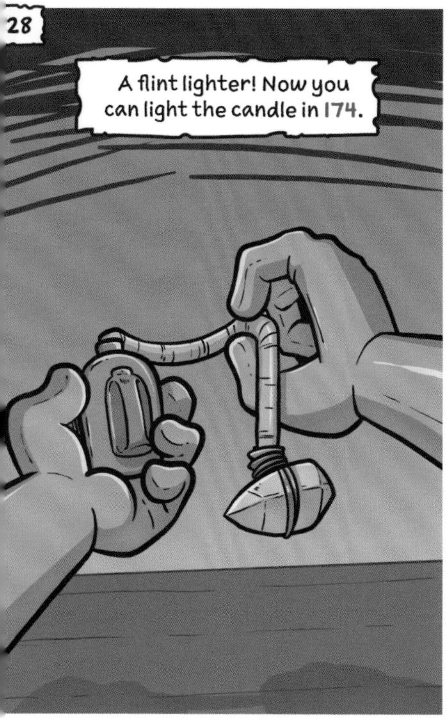
228
A flint lighter! Now you can light the candle in 174.

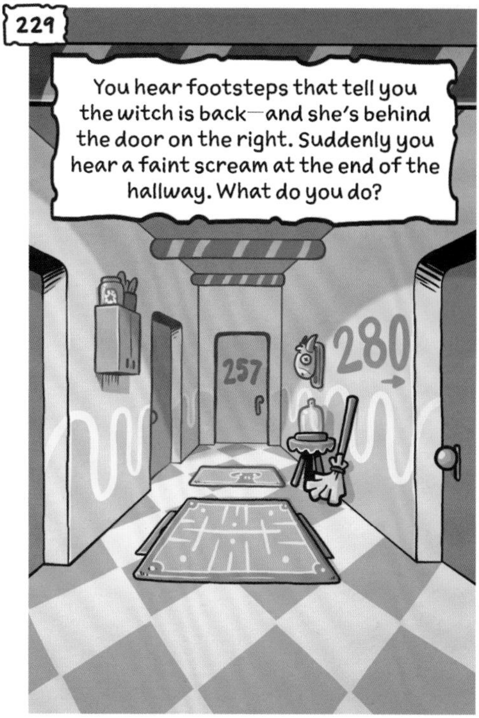
229
You hear footsteps that tell you the witch is back—and she's behind the door on the right. Suddenly you hear a faint scream at the end of the hallway. What do you do?
257
280

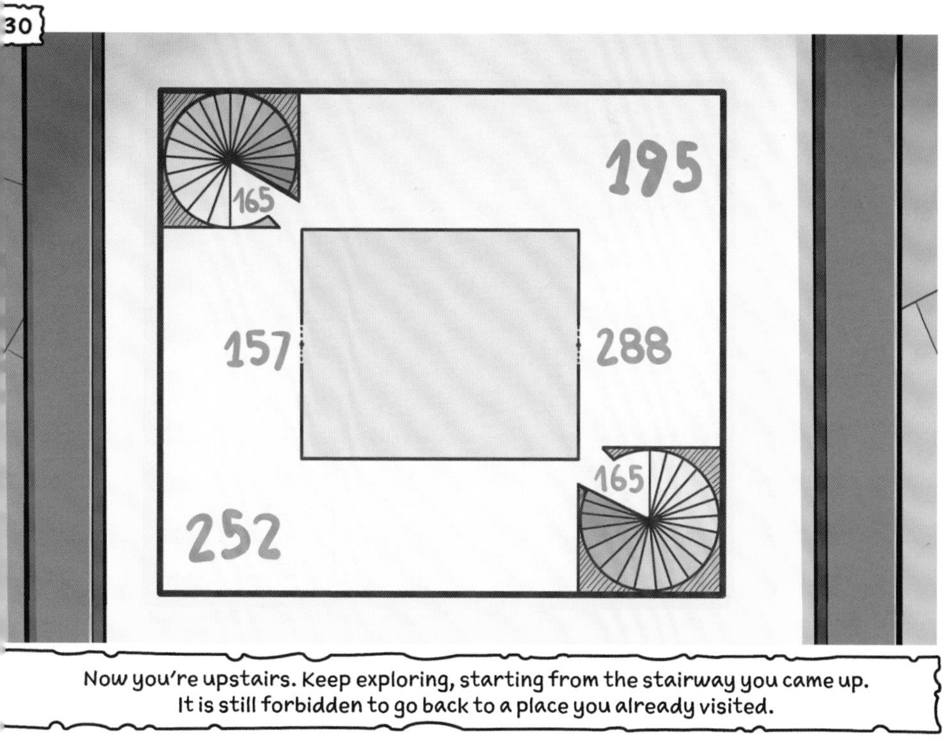
230
195
165
157
288
165
252
Now you're upstairs. Keep exploring, starting from the stairway you came up. It is still forbidden to go back to a place you already visited.

231

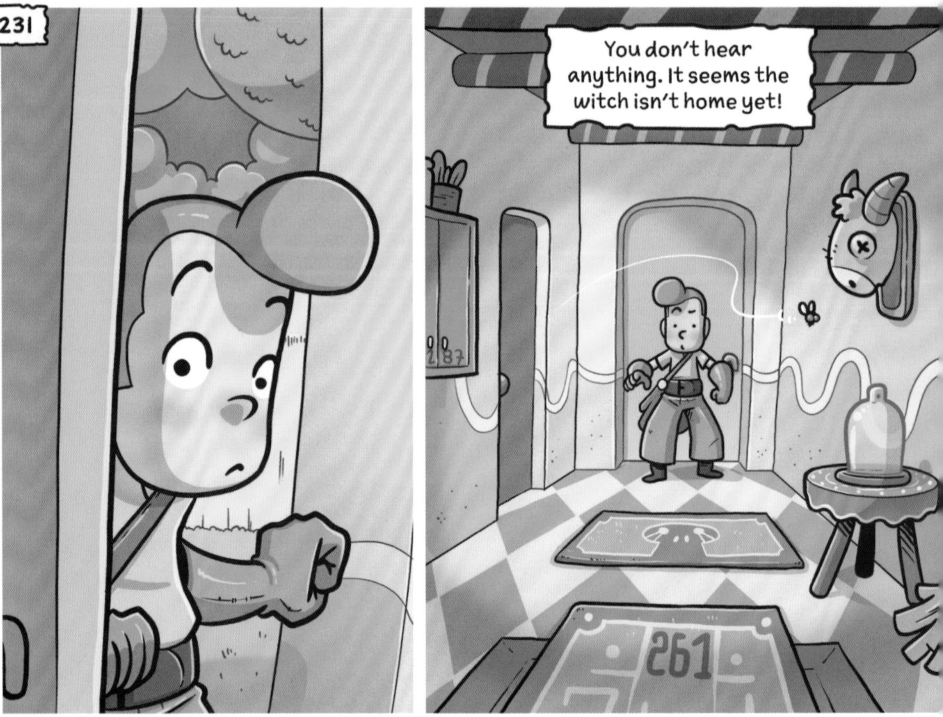
You don't hear anything. It seems the witch isn't home yet!
287
261

232

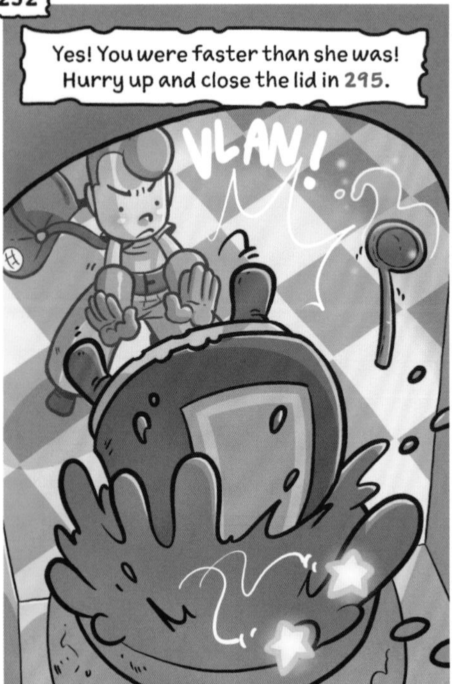
Yes! You were faster than she was! Hurry up and close the lid in 295.
VLAN!

233

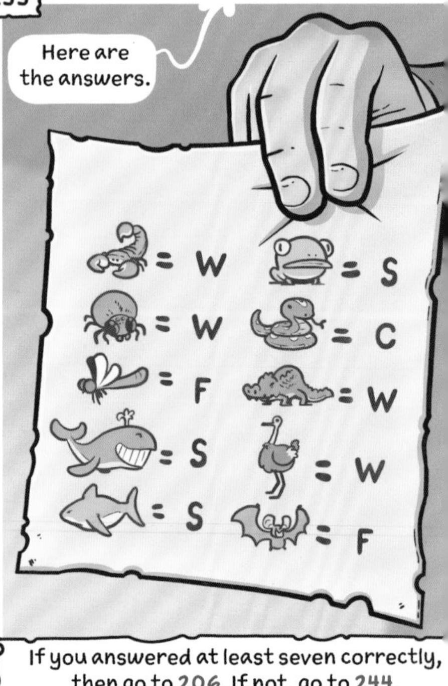
Here are the answers.
= W
= S
= W
= C
= F
= W
= S
= W
= S
= F
If you answered at least seven correctly, then go to 206. If not, go to 244.

34

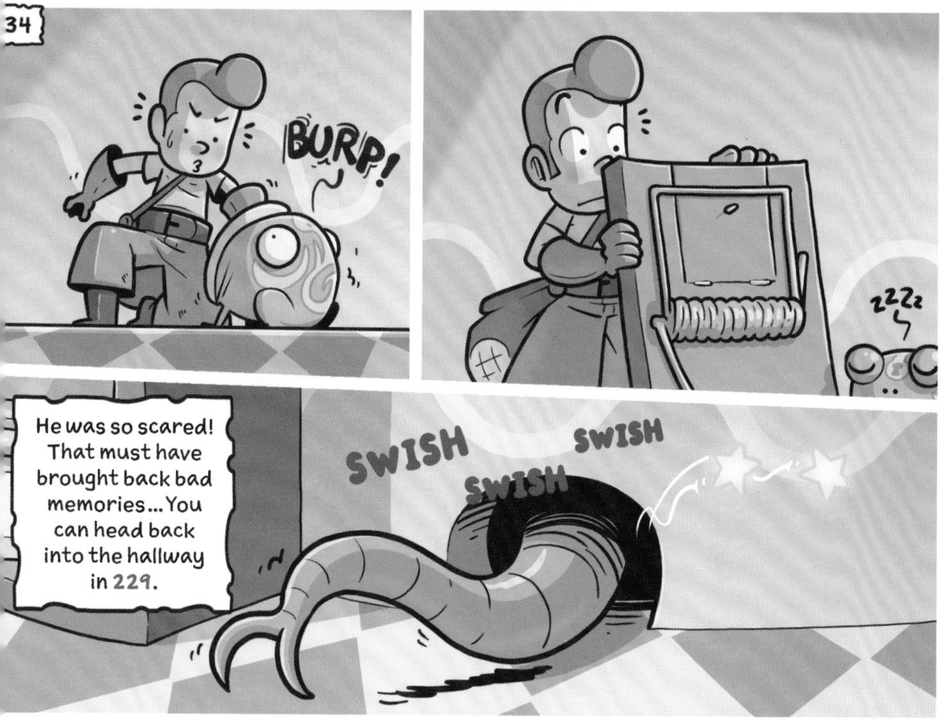
BURP!
zzzz
He was so scared! That must have brought back bad memories... You can head back into the hallway in 229.
SWISH
SWISH
SWISH

35

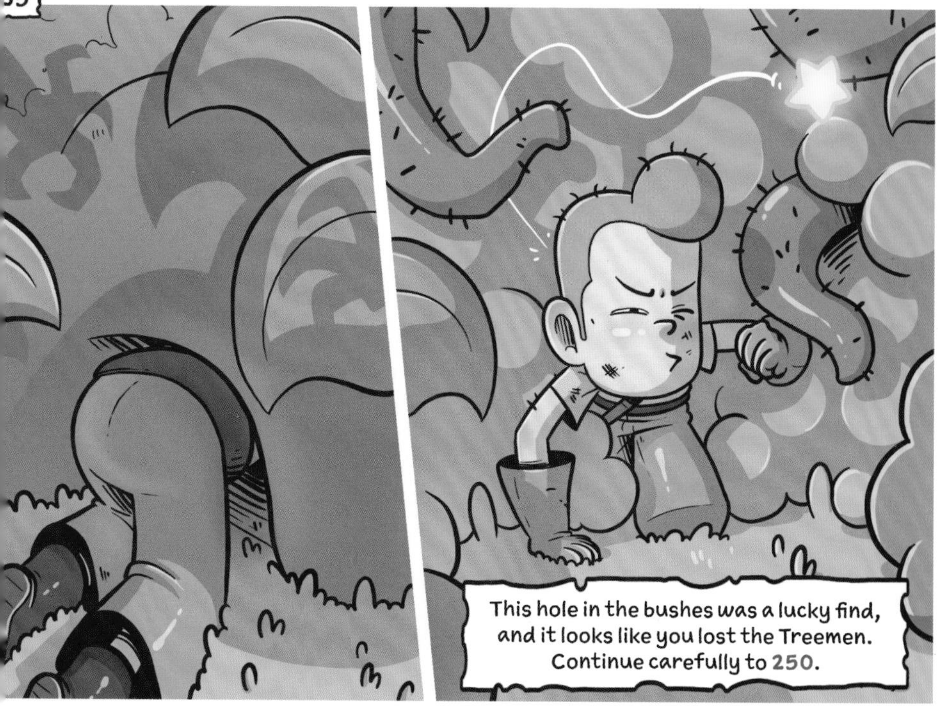
This hole in the bushes was a lucky find, and it looks like you lost the Treemen. Continue carefully to 250.

236

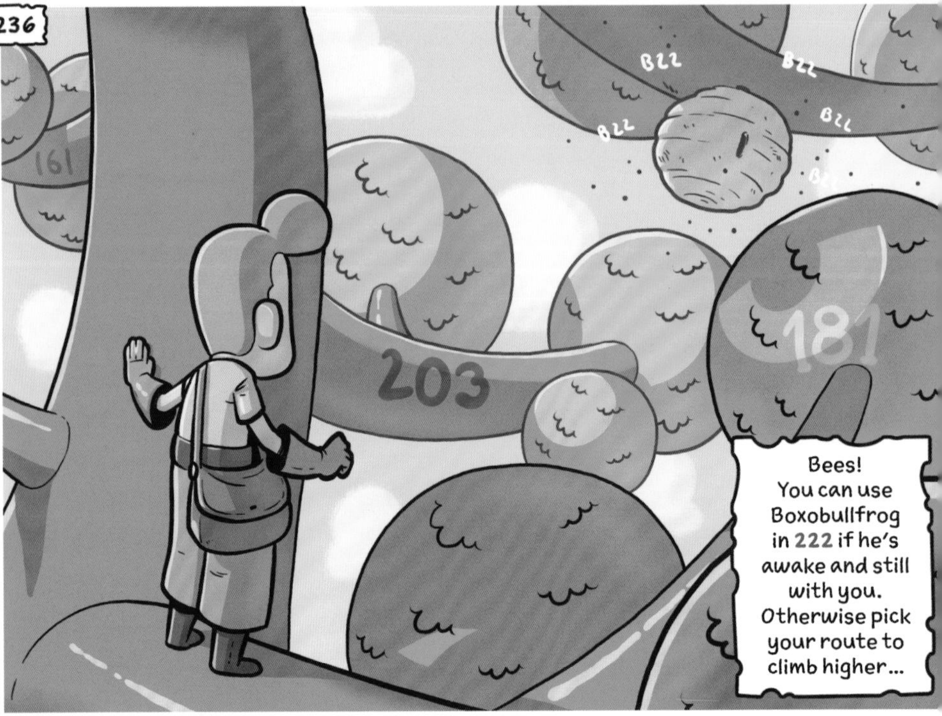
BZZ
BZZ
BZZ
BZZ
161
203
181
Bees!
You can use Boxobullfrog in 222 if he's awake and still with you. Otherwise pick your route to climb higher...

237

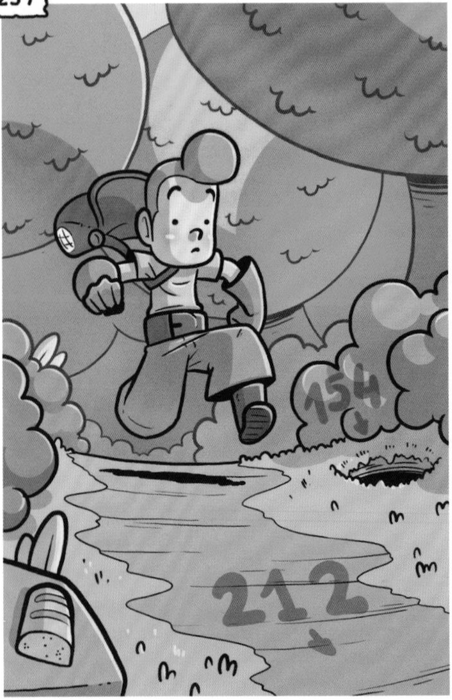
154
212

238

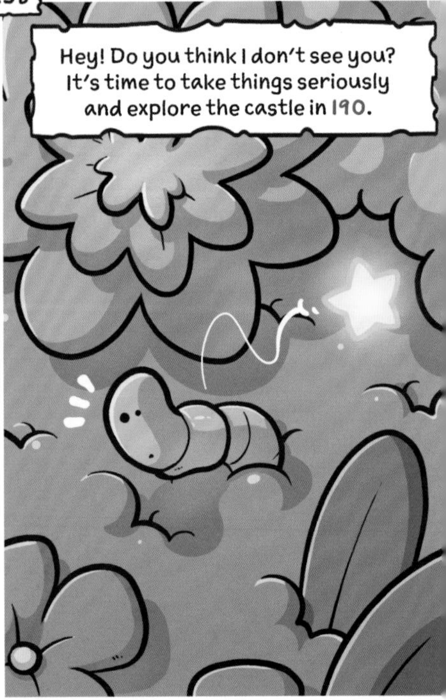
Hey! Do you think I don't see you? It's time to take things seriously and explore the castle in 190.

239

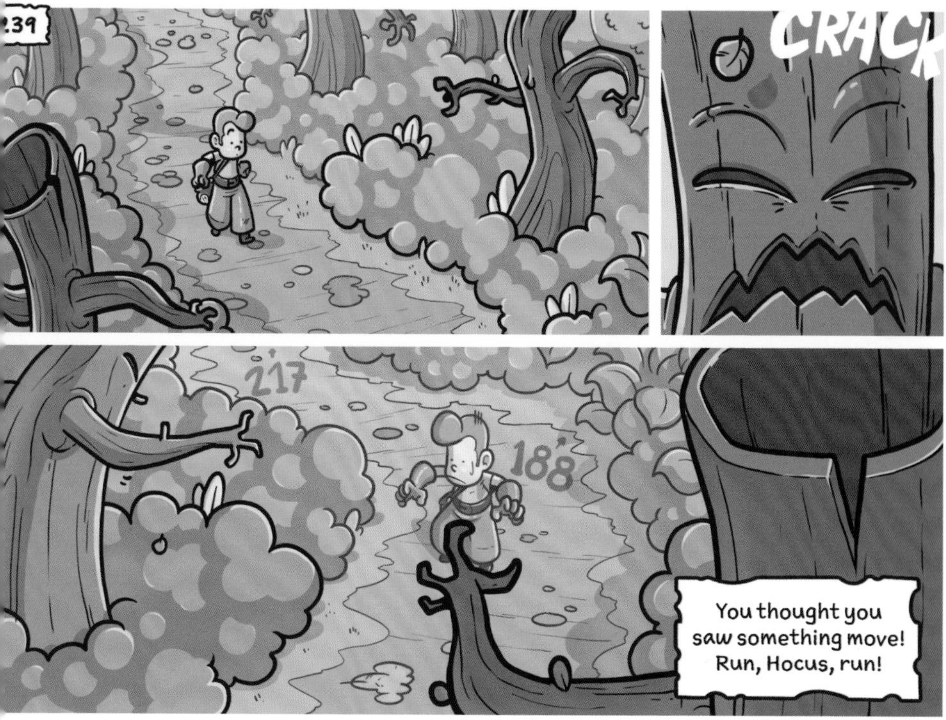
CRACK
217
188
You thought you saw something move! Run, Hocus, run!

240

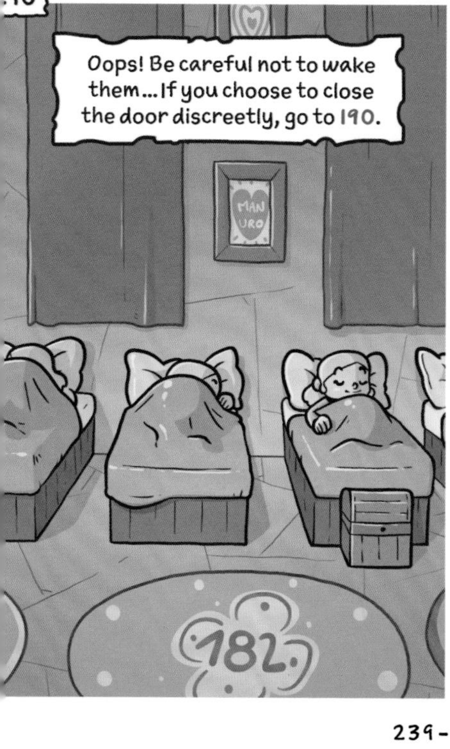
Oops! Be careful not to wake them... If you choose to close the door discreetly, go to 190.
MAN URO
182

241

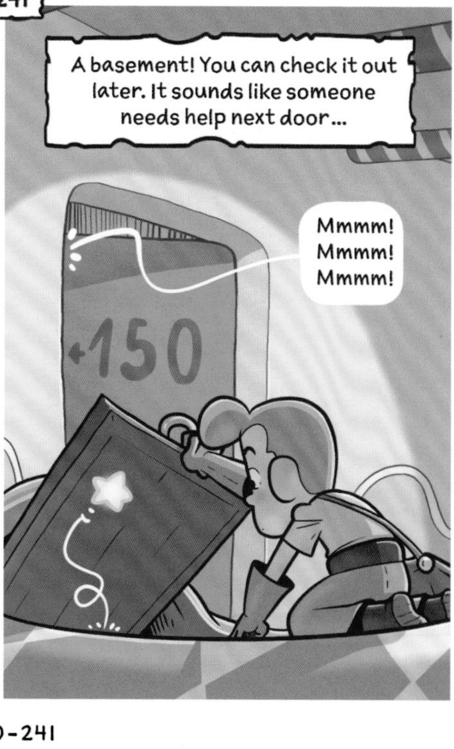
A basement! You can check it out later. It sounds like someone needs help next door...
Mmmm! Mmmm! Mmmm!
150

242

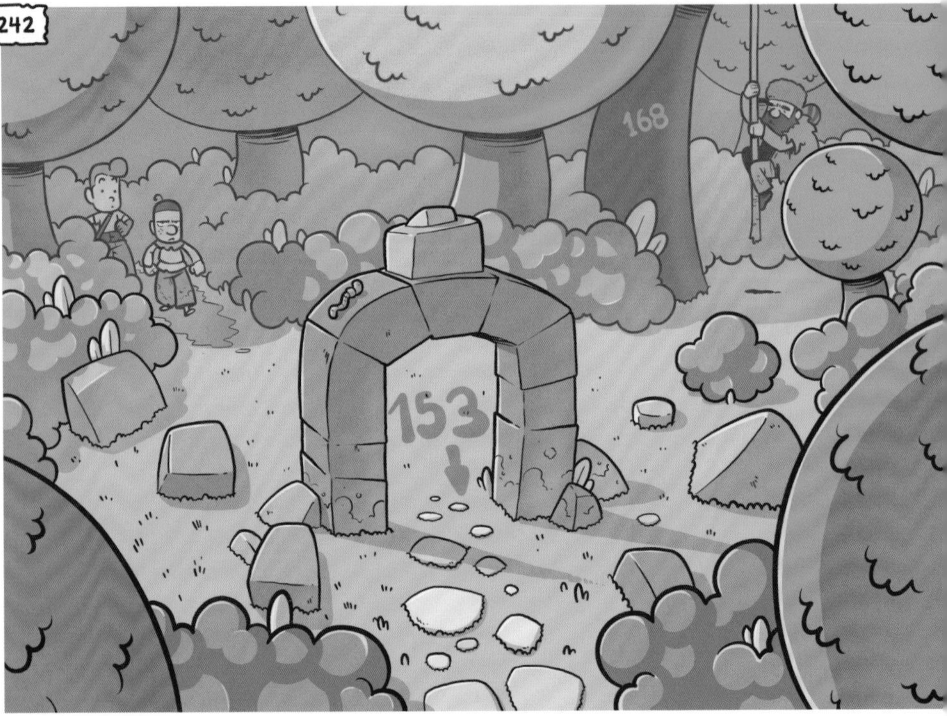
168
153

243

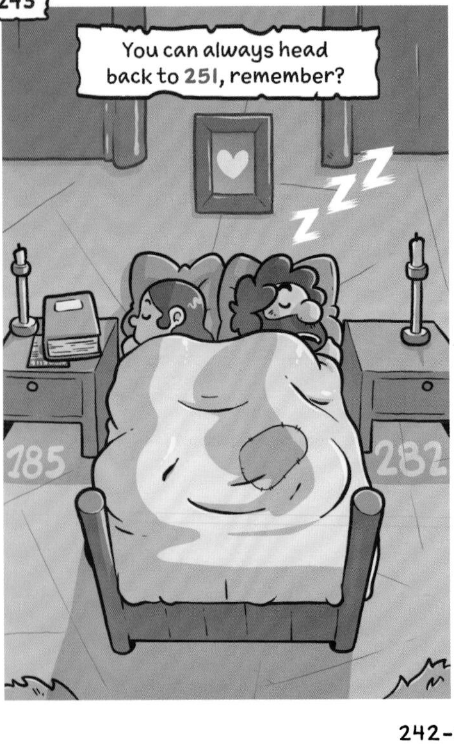
You can always head back to 251, remember?
ZZZ
185
282

244

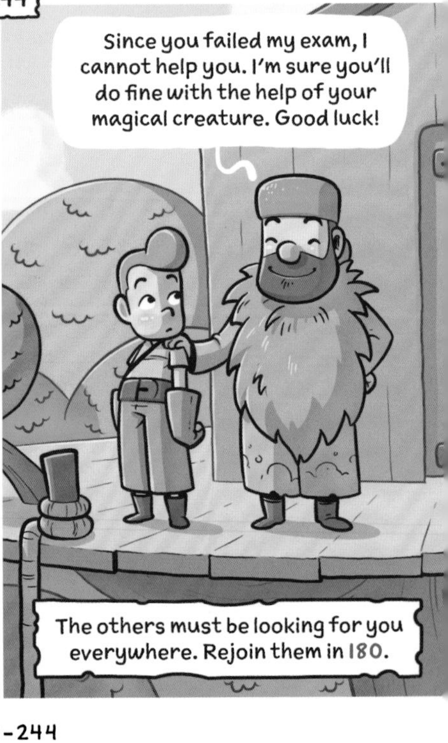
Since you failed my exam, I cannot help you. I'm sure you'll do fine with the help of your magical creature. Good luck!
The others must be looking for you everywhere. Rejoin them in 180.

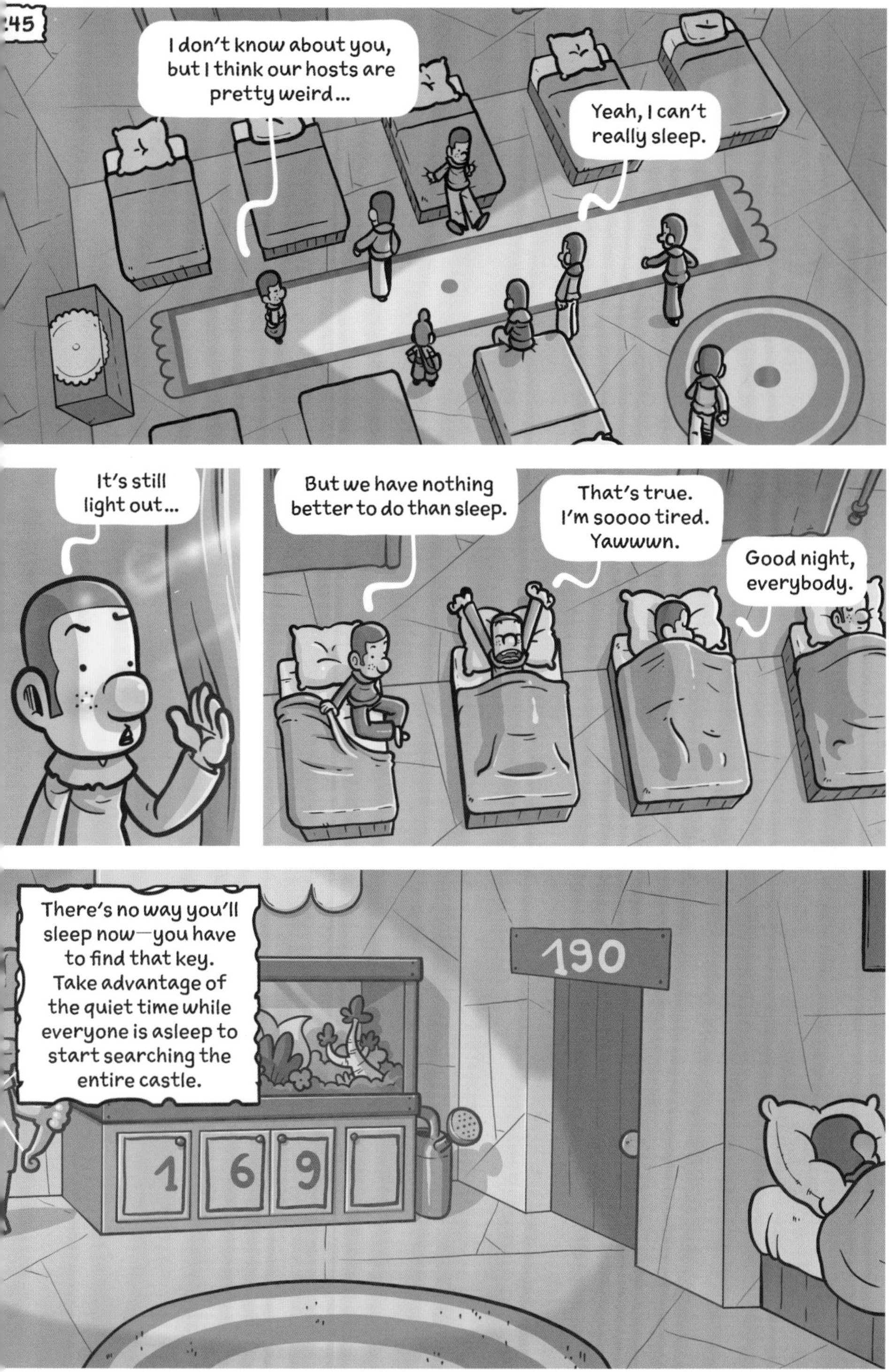
245
I don't know about you, but I think our hosts are pretty weird...
Yeah, I can't really sleep.
It's still light out...
But we have nothing better to do than sleep.
That's true. I'm soooo tired. Yawwwn.
Good night, everybody.
There's no way you'll sleep now—you have to find that key. Take advantage of the quiet time while everyone is asleep to start searching the entire castle.
190
1 6 9

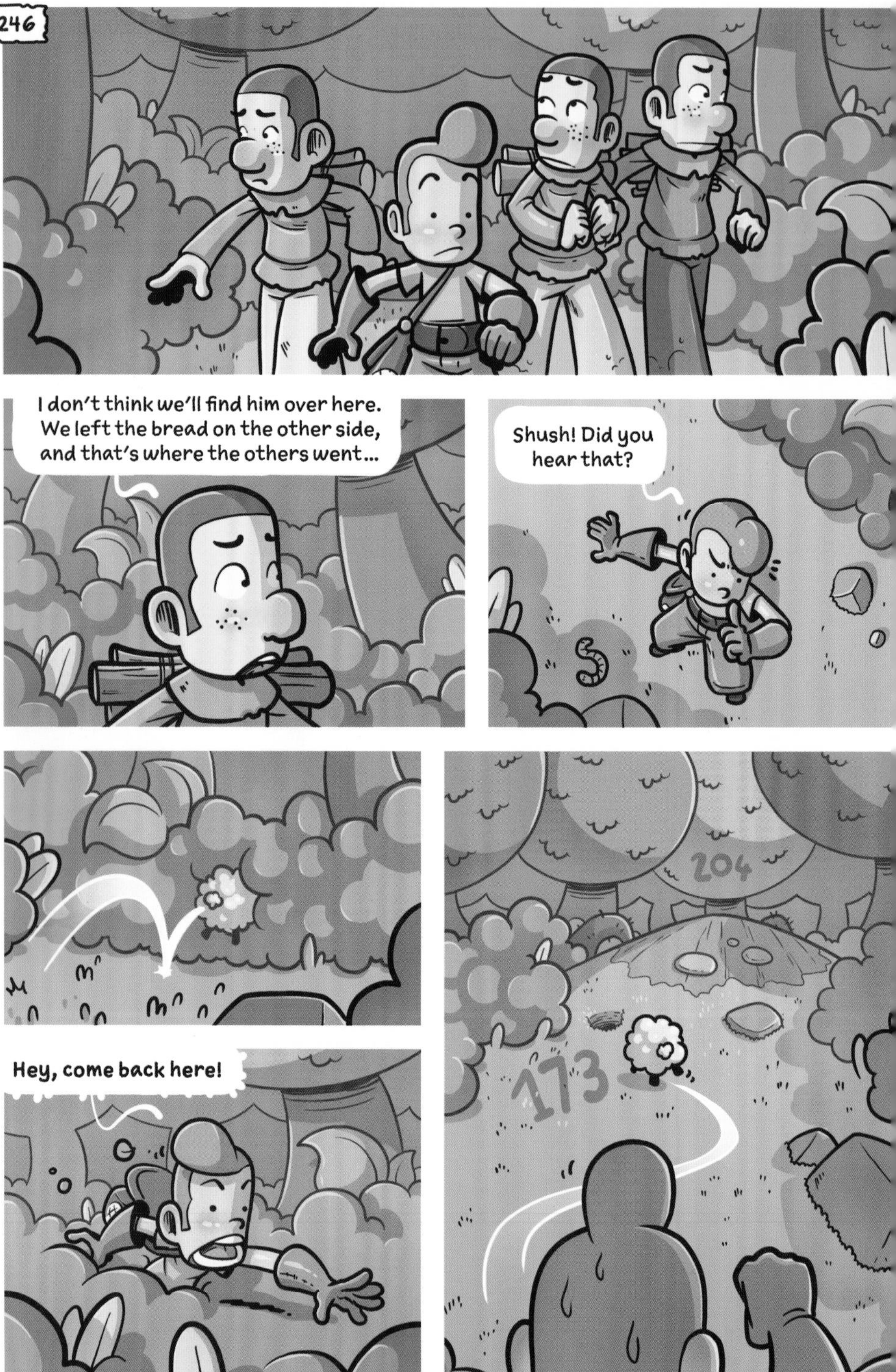
I don't think we'll find him over here. We left the bread on the other side, and that's where the others went...
Shush! Did you hear that?
Hey, come back here!
204
173

47

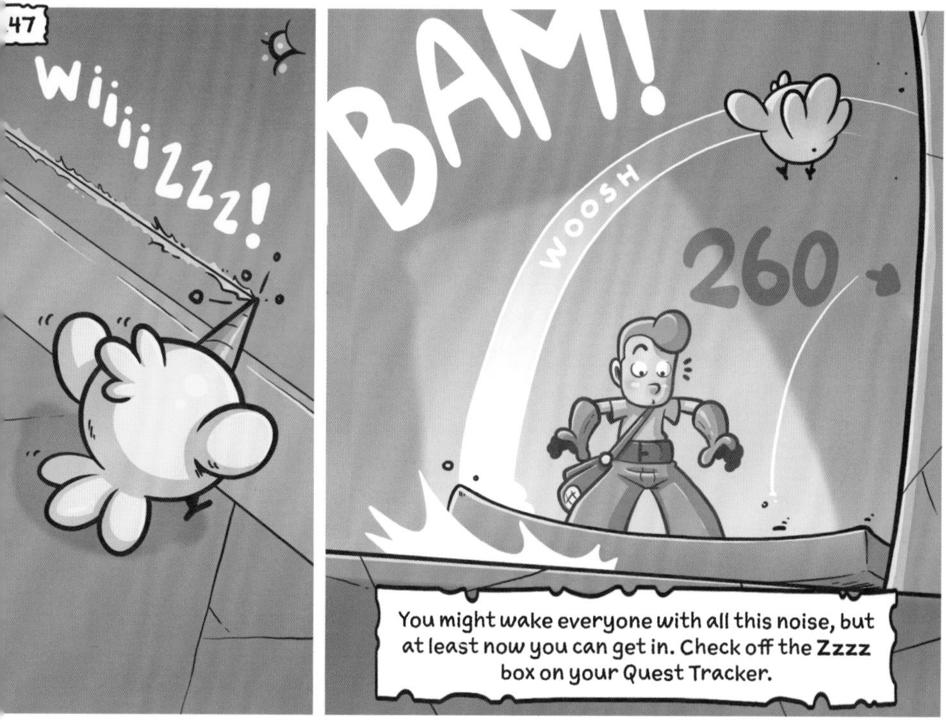
WiiiiZZZZ!
BAM!
WOOSH
260
You might wake everyone with all this noise, but at least now you can get in. Check off the **Zzzz** box on your Quest Tracker.

48

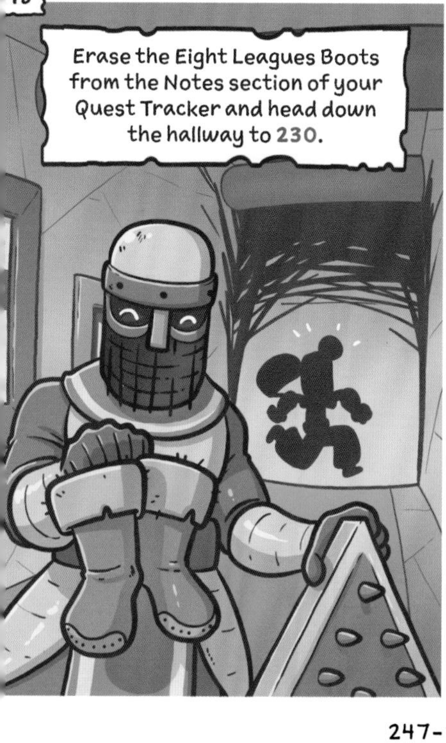
Erase the Eight Leagues Boots from the Notes section of your Quest Tracker and head down the hallway to 230.

249

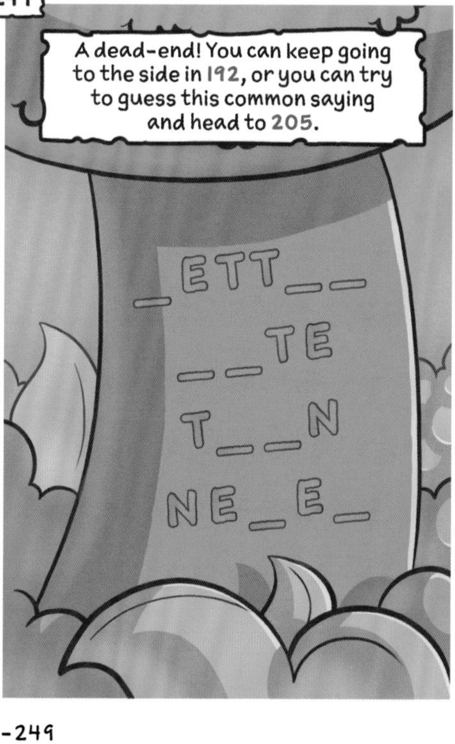
A dead-end! You can keep going to the side in 192, or you can try to guess this common saying and head to 205.
_ETT__
__TE
T__N
NE_E_

250

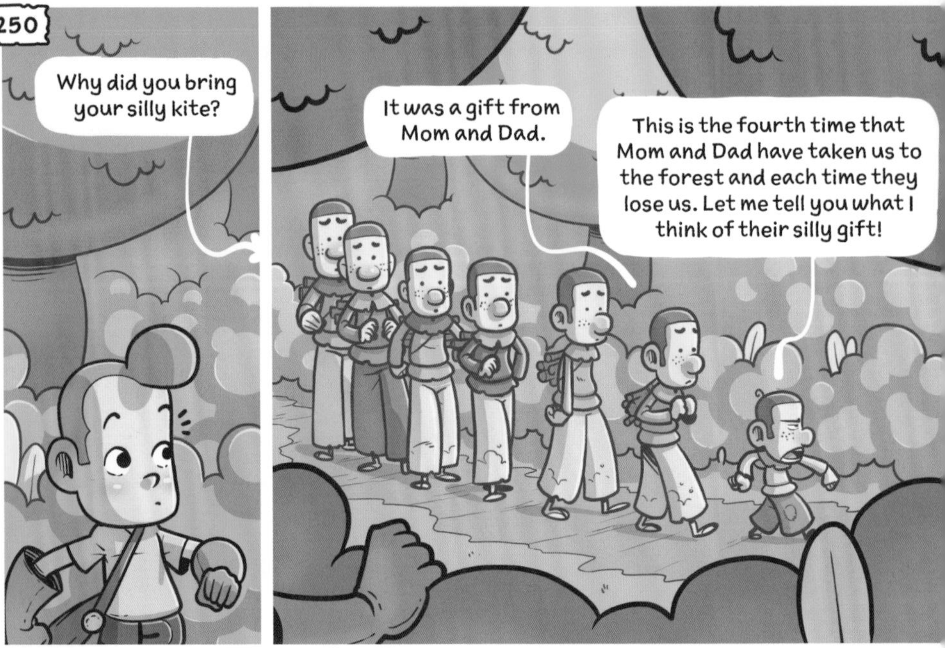
Why did you bring your silly kite?
It was a gift from Mom and Dad.
This is the fourth time that Mom and Dad have taken us to the forest and each time they lose us. Let me tell you what I think of their silly gift!

You can come out of the bushes in 172 or follow the boys secretly to 216.

251

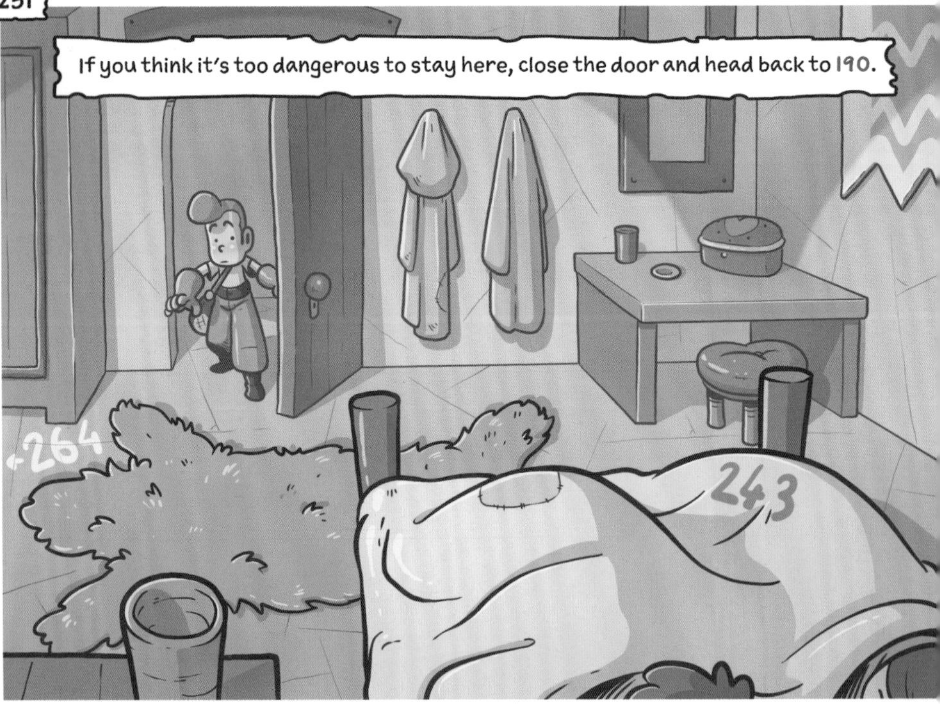
If you think it's too dangerous to stay here, close the door and head back to 190.
264
243

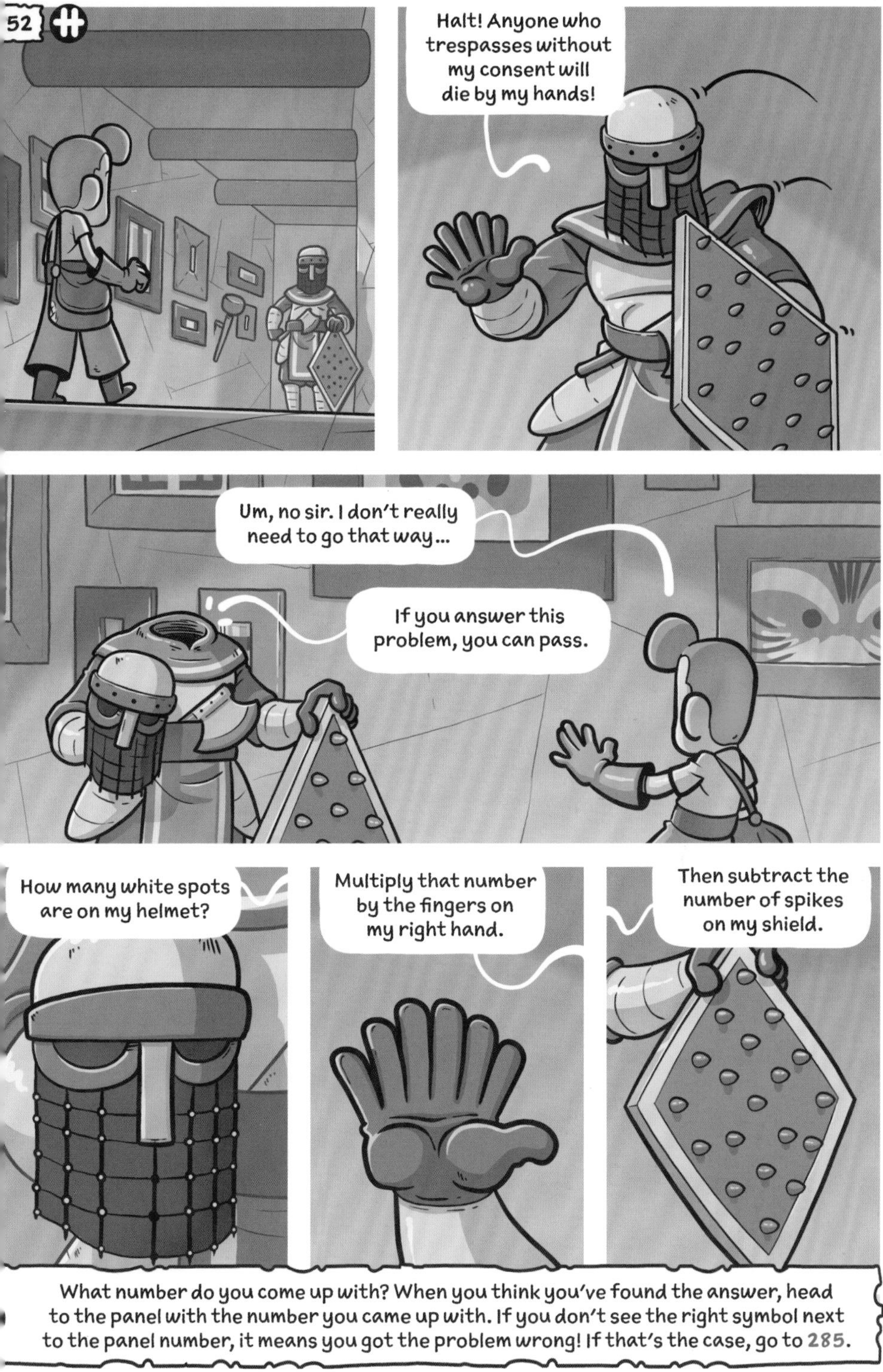
52
Halt! Anyone who trespasses without my consent will die by my hands!
Um, no sir. I don't really need to go that way...
If you answer this problem, you can pass.
How many white spots are on my helmet?
Multiply that number by the fingers on my right hand.
Then subtract the number of spikes on my shield.

What number do you come up with? When you think you've found the answer, head to the panel with the number you came up with. If you don't see the right symbol next to the panel number, it means you got the problem wrong! If that's the case, go to 285.

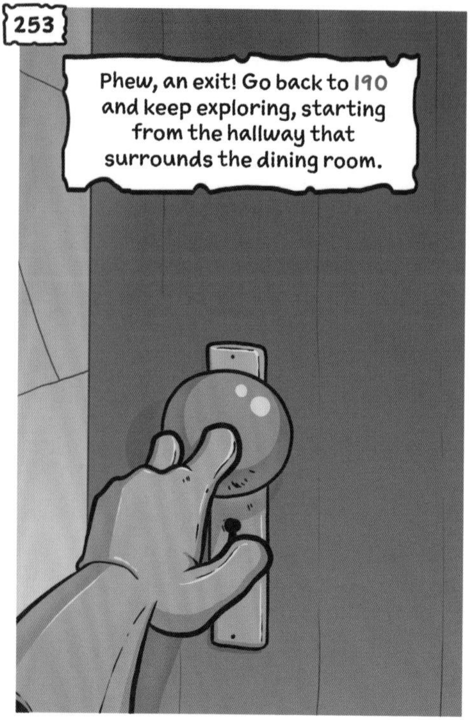
253
Phew, an exit! Go back to 190 and keep exploring, starting from the hallway that surrounds the dining room.

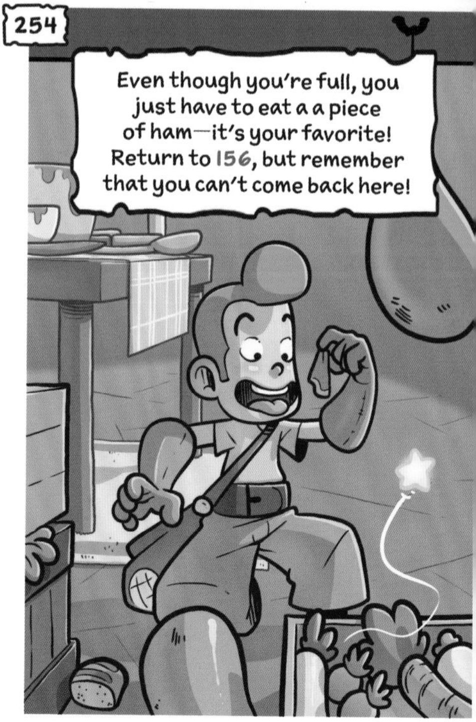
254
Even though you're full, you just have to eat a a piece of ham—it's your favorite! Return to 156, but remember that you can't come back here!

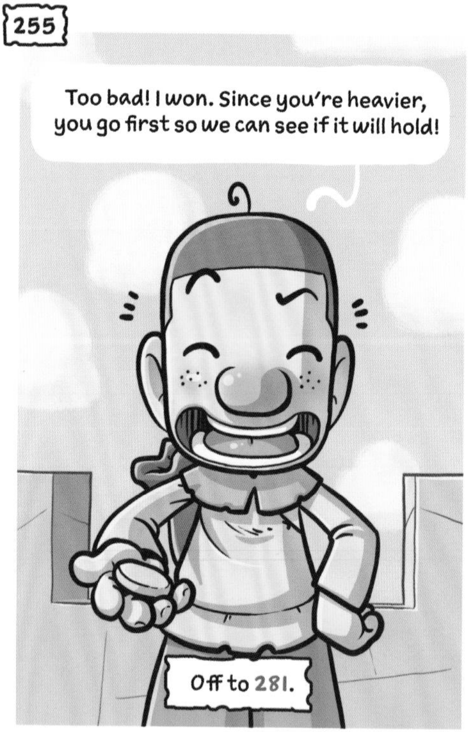
255
Too bad! I won. Since you're heavier, you go first so we can see if it will hold!
Off to 281.

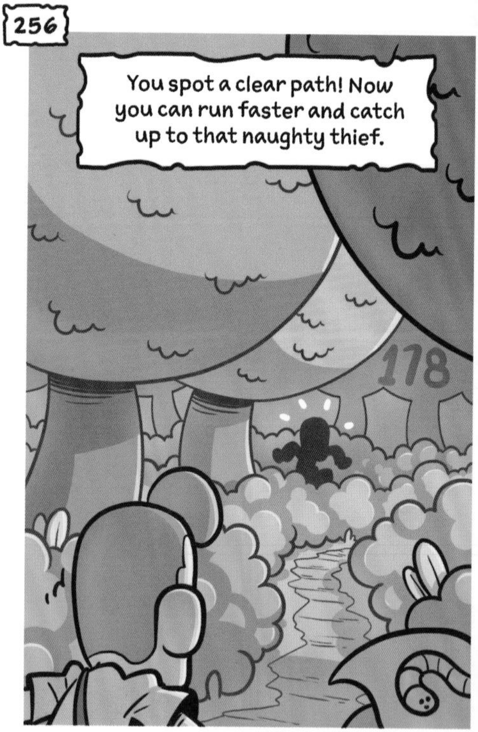
256
You spot a clear path! Now you can run faster and catch up to that naughty thief.
178

57

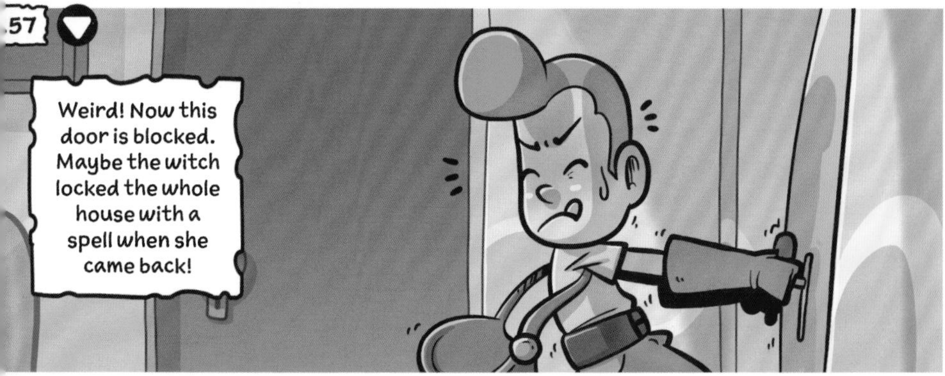
Weird! Now this door is blocked. Maybe the witch locked the whole house with a spell when she came back!

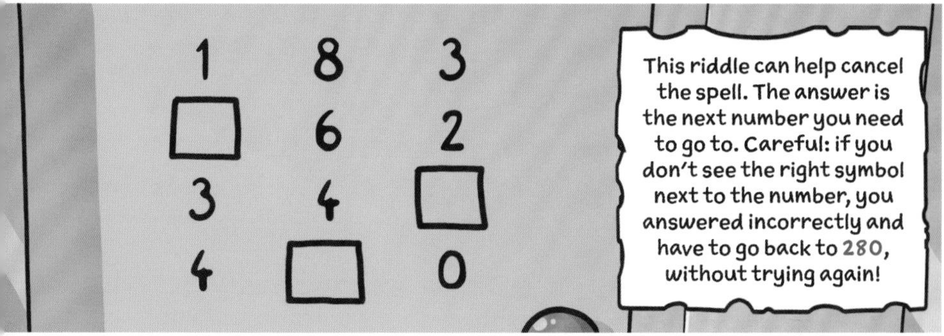
1 8 3
6 2
3 4
4 0
This riddle can help cancel the spell. The answer is the next number you need to go to. Careful: if you don't see the right symbol next to the number, you answered incorrectly and have to go back to 280, without trying again!

58

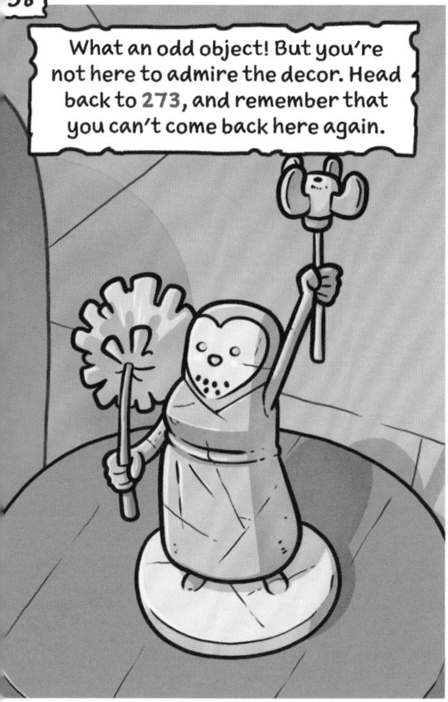
What an odd object! But you're not here to admire the decor. Head back to 273, and remember that you can't come back here again.

259

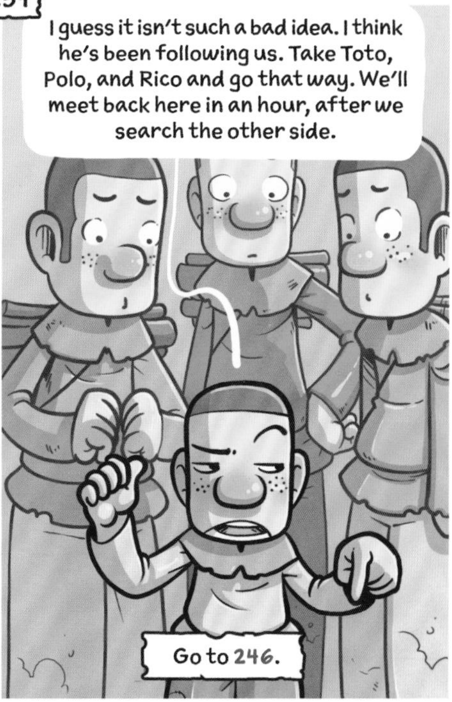
I guess it isn't such a bad idea. I think he's been following us. Take Toto, Polo, and Rico and go that way. We'll meet back here in an hour, after we search the other side.
Go to 246.

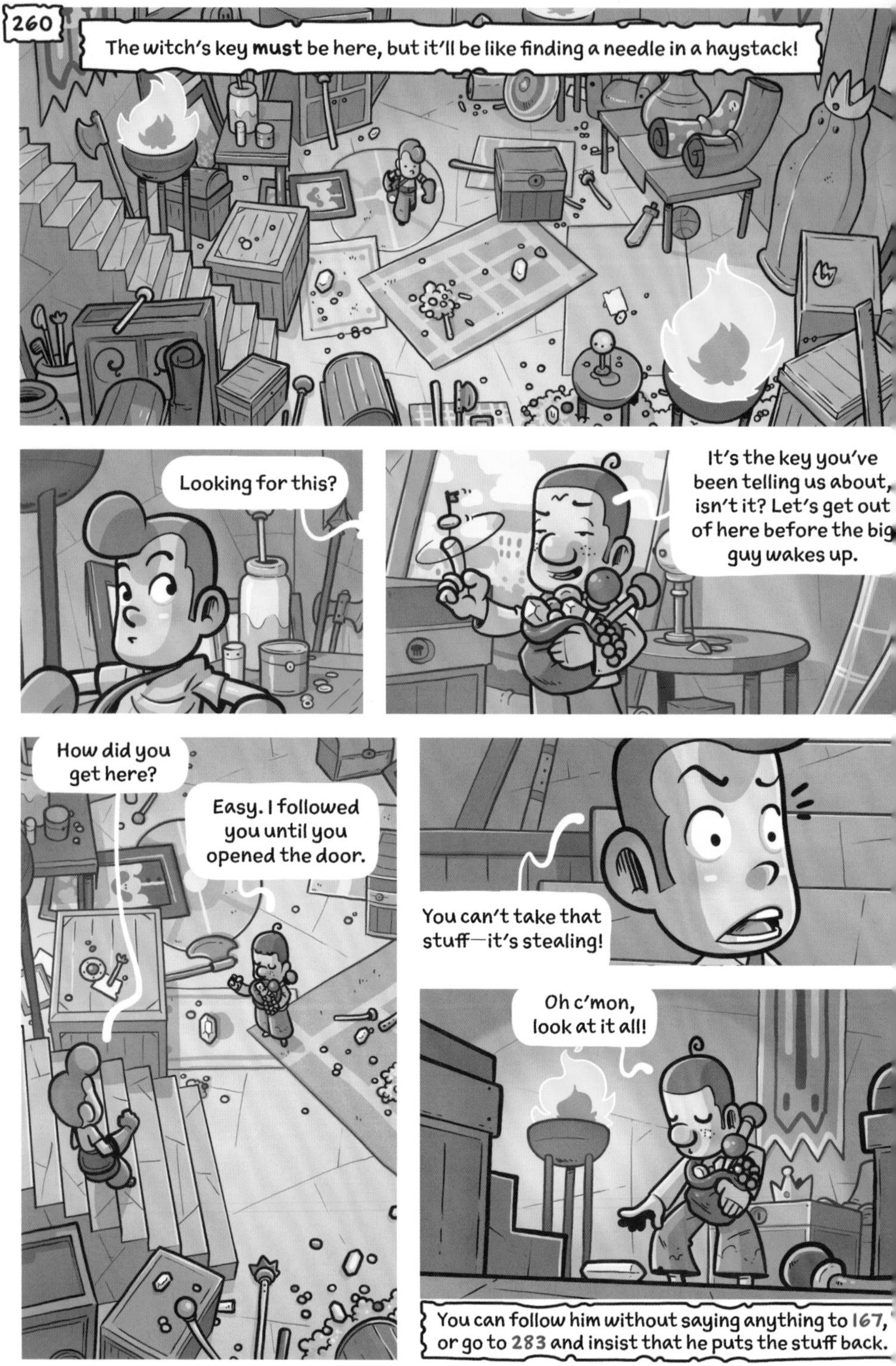
260
The witch's key **must** be here, but it'll be like finding a needle in a haystack!
Looking for this?
It's the key you've been telling us about, isn't it? Let's get out of here before the big guy wakes up.
How did you get here?
Easy. I followed you until you opened the door.
You can't take that stuff—it's stealing!
Oh c'mon, look at it all!
You can follow him without saying anything to 167, or go to 283 and insist that he puts the stuff back.

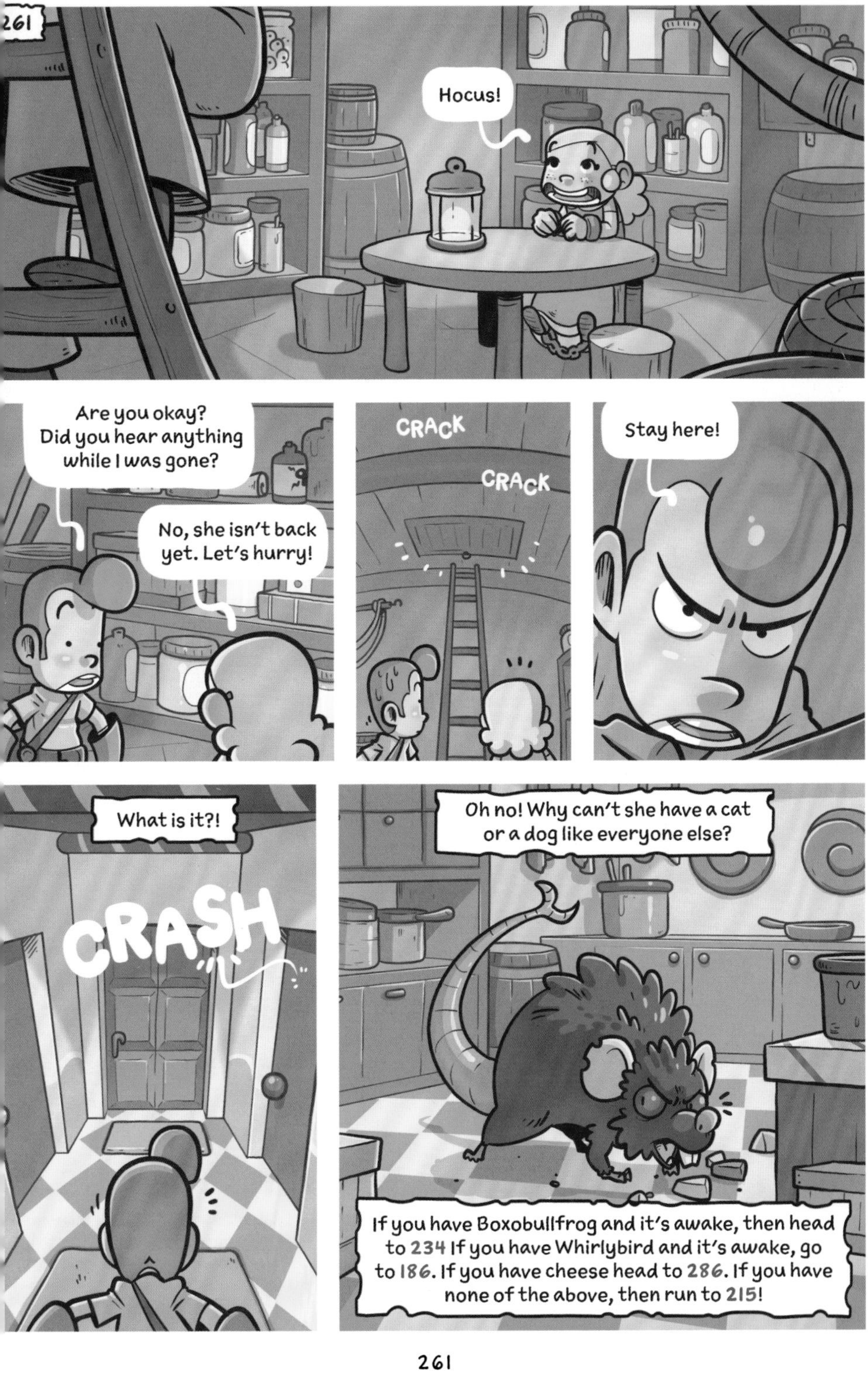
Hocus!
Are you okay? Did you hear anything while I was gone?
No, she isn't back yet. Let's hurry!
CRACK
CRACK
Stay here!
What is it?!
CRASH
Oh no! Why can't she have a cat or a dog like everyone else?
If you have Boxobullfrog and it's awake, then head to 234 If you have Whirlybird and it's awake, go to 186. If you have cheese head to 286. If you have none of the above, then run to 215!

262

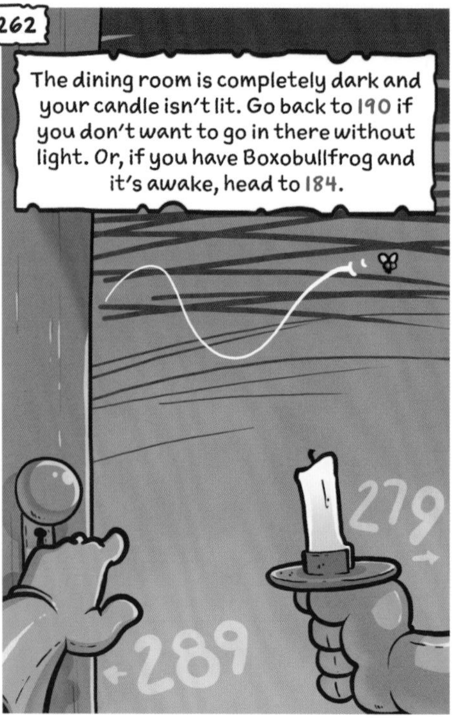
The dining room is completely dark and your candle isn't lit. Go back to 190 if you don't want to go in there without light. Or, if you have Boxobullfrog and it's awake, head to 184.
279
289

263

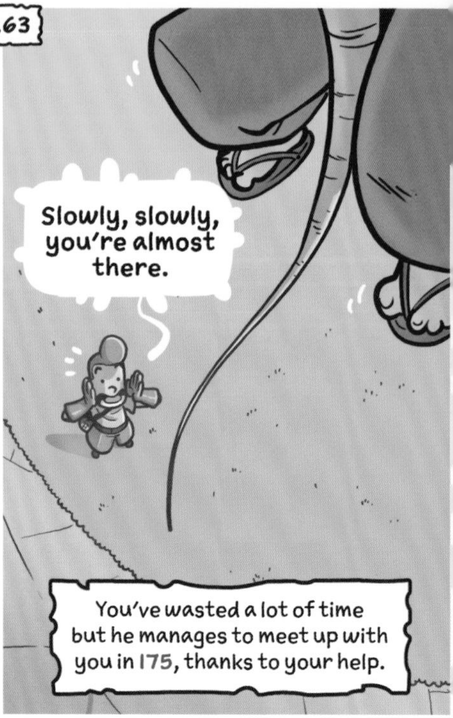
Slowly, slowly, you're almost there.
You've wasted a lot of time but he manages to meet up with you in 175, thanks to your help.

264

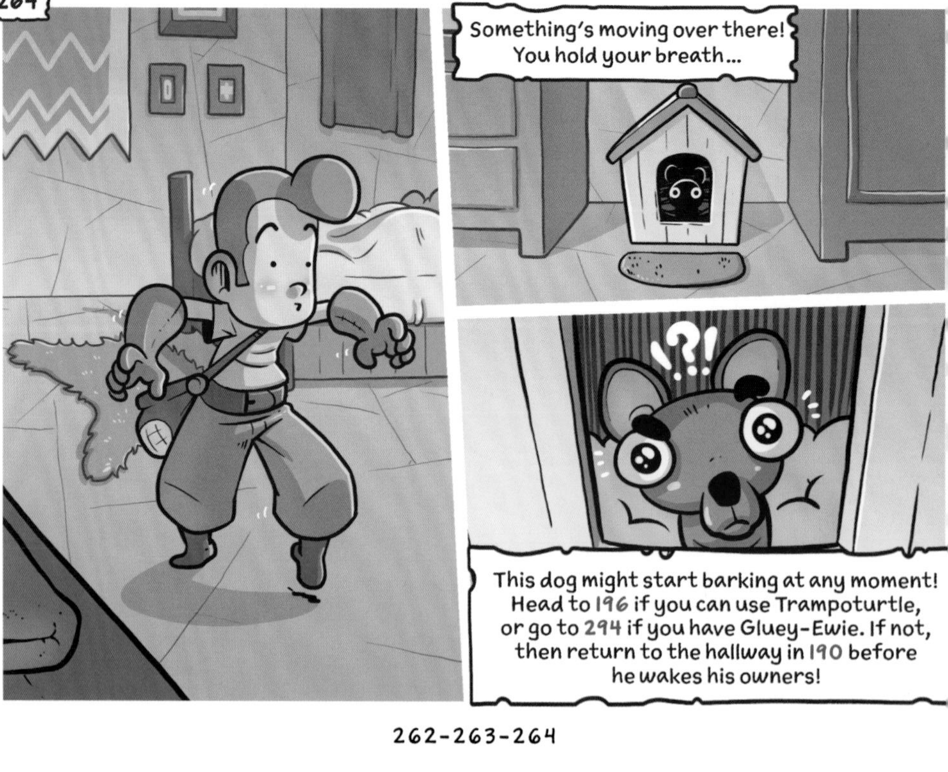
Something's moving over there! You hold your breath...
!?!
This dog might start barking at any moment! Head to 196 if you can use Trampoturtle, or go to 294 if you have Gluey-Ewie. If not, then return to the hallway in 190 before he wakes his owners!

65

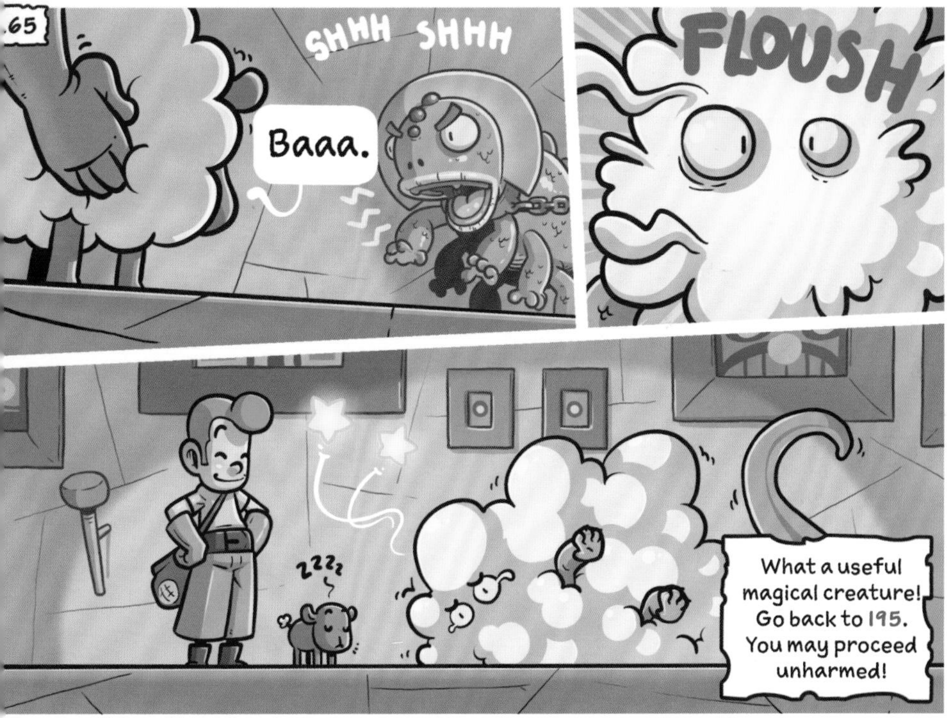
SHHH SHHH
Baaa.
FLOUSH
What a useful magical creature! Go back to 195. You may proceed unharmed!

66

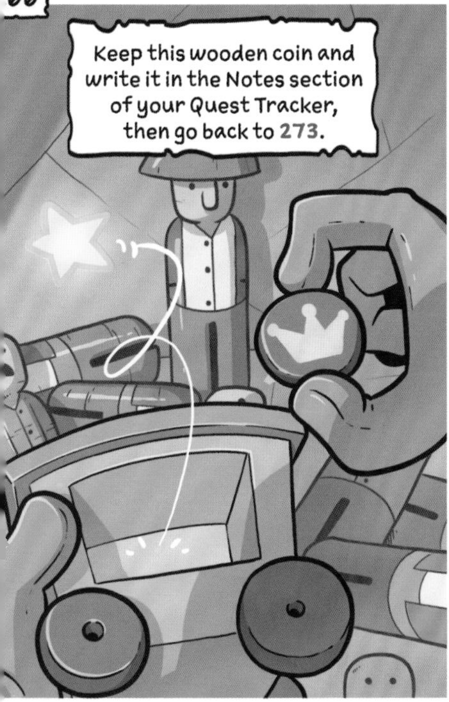
Keep this wooden coin and write it in the Notes section of your Quest Tracker, then go back to 273.

267

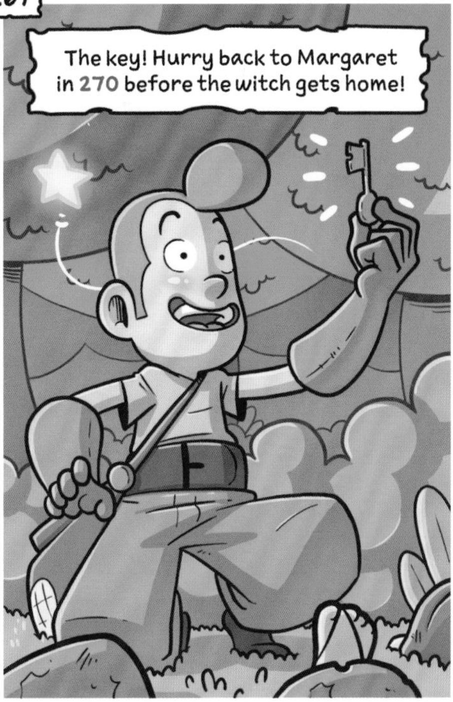
The key! Hurry back to Margaret in 270 before the witch gets home!

268

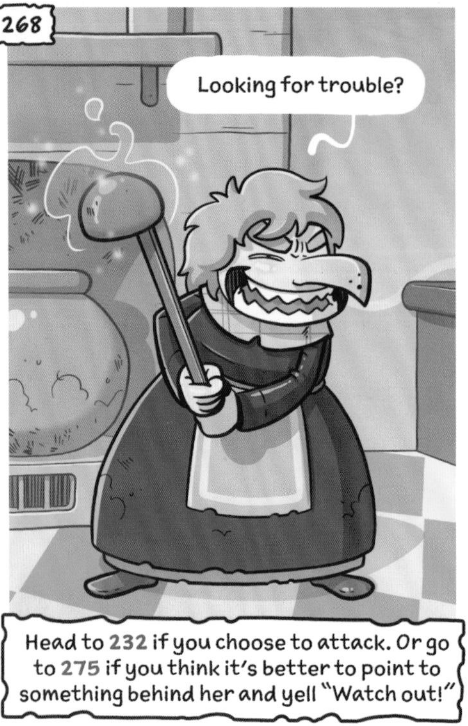
Looking for trouble?
Head to 232 if you choose to attack. Or go to 275 if you think it's better to point to something behind her and yell "Watch out!"

269

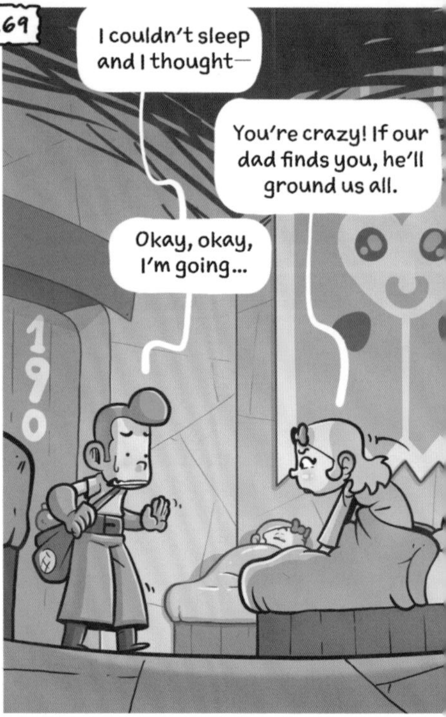
I couldn't sleep and I thought—
You're crazy! If our dad finds you, he'll ground us all.
Okay, okay, I'm going...
190

270

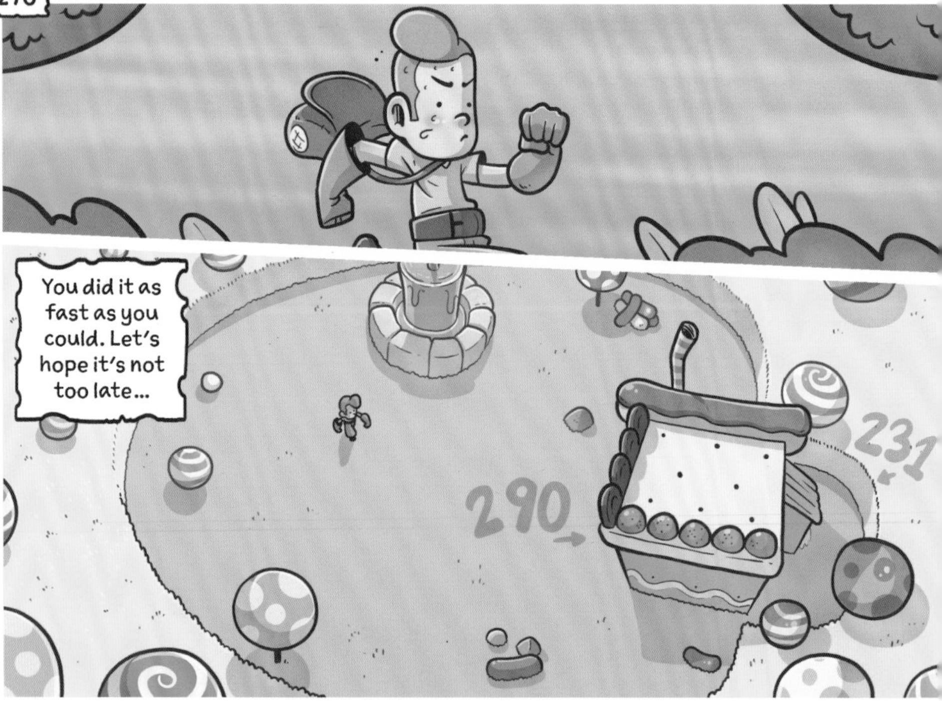
You did it as fast as you could. Let's hope it's not too late...
231
290

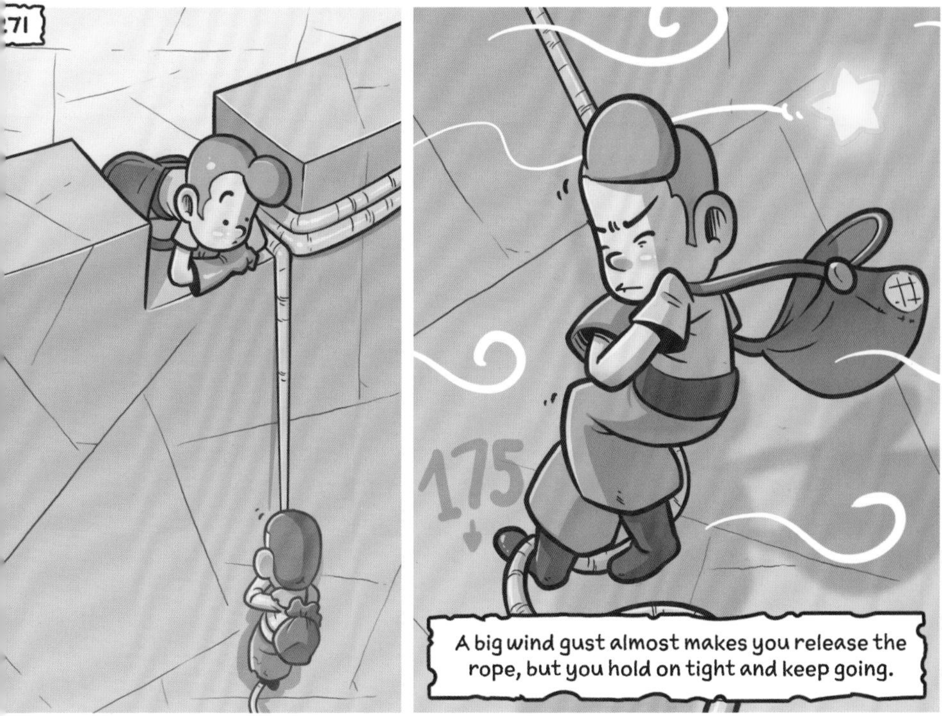
271
175
A big wind gust almost makes you release the rope, but you hold on tight and keep going.

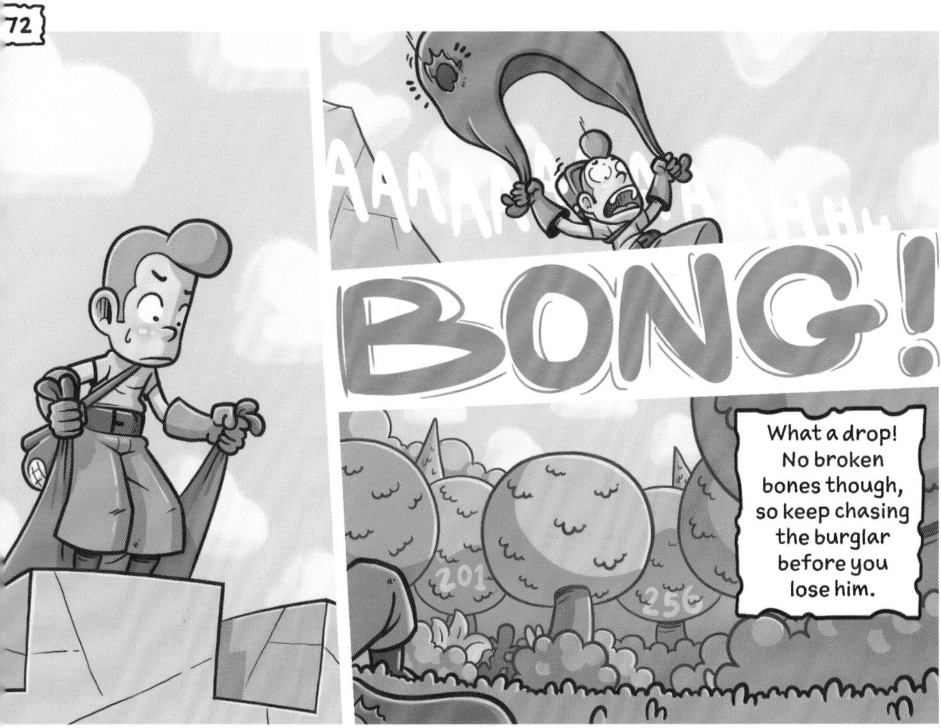
272
BONG!
What a drop! No broken bones though, so keep chasing the burglar before you lose him.
201
256

273

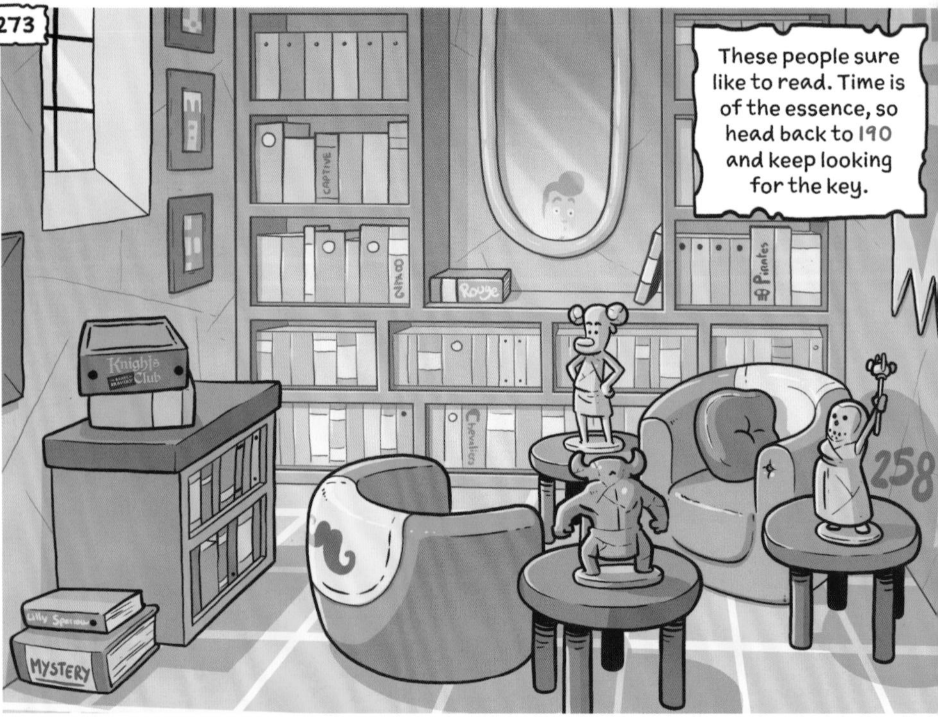
These people sure like to read. Time is of the essence, so head back to 190 and keep looking for the key.
CAPTIVE
Rouge
Pirates
Knights Club
Chevaliers
MYSTERY
258

274

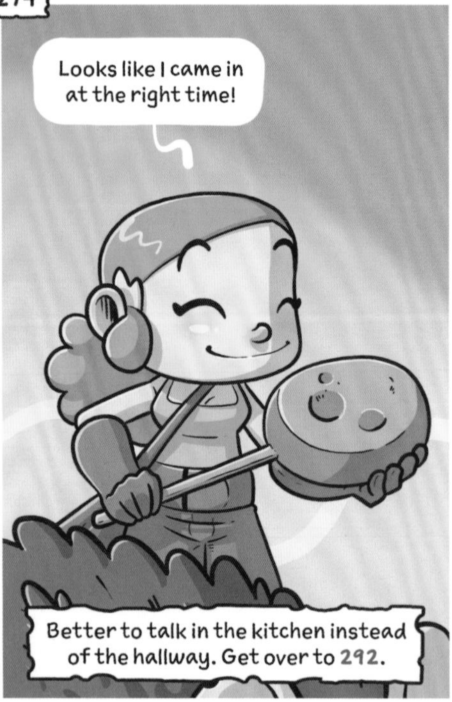
Looks like I came in at the right time!
Better to talk in the kitchen instead of the hallway. Get over to 292.

275

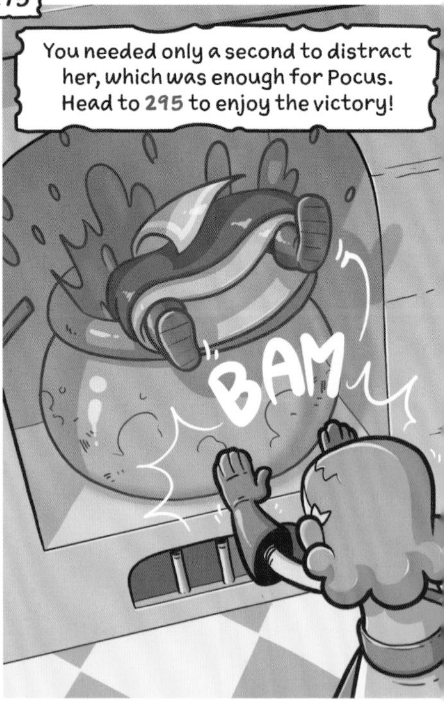
You needed only a second to distract her, which was enough for Pocus. Head to 295 to enjoy the victory!
BAM

76

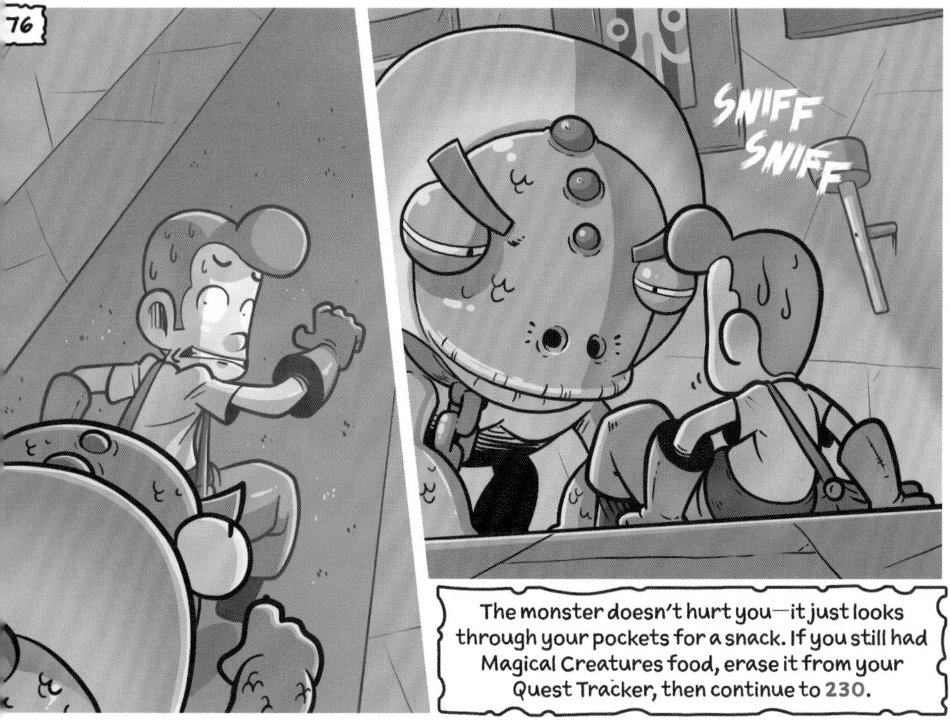
SNIFF
SNIFF
The monster doesn't hurt you—it just looks through your pockets for a snack. If you still had Magical Creatures food, erase it from your Quest Tracker, then continue to 230.

77

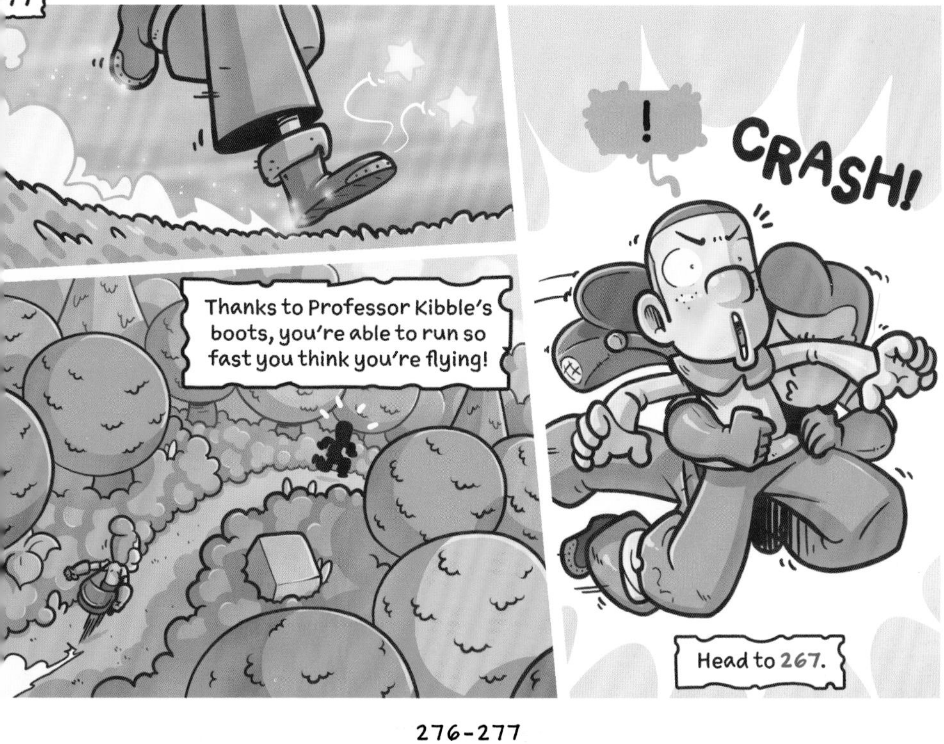
Thanks to Professor Kibble's boots, you're able to run so fast you think you're flying!
!
CRASH!
Head to 267.

278

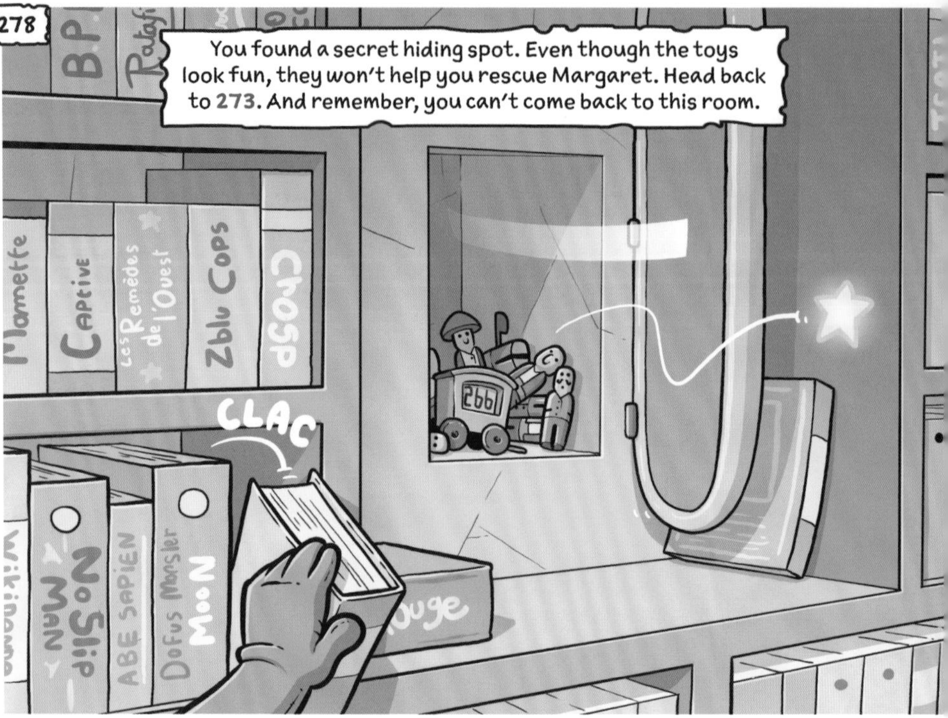
You found a secret hiding spot. Even though the toys look fun, they won't help you rescue Margaret. Head back to 273. And remember, you can't come back to this room.
Captive
Zblu Cops
CLAC
No Slip Man
ABE SAPIEN
MooN

279

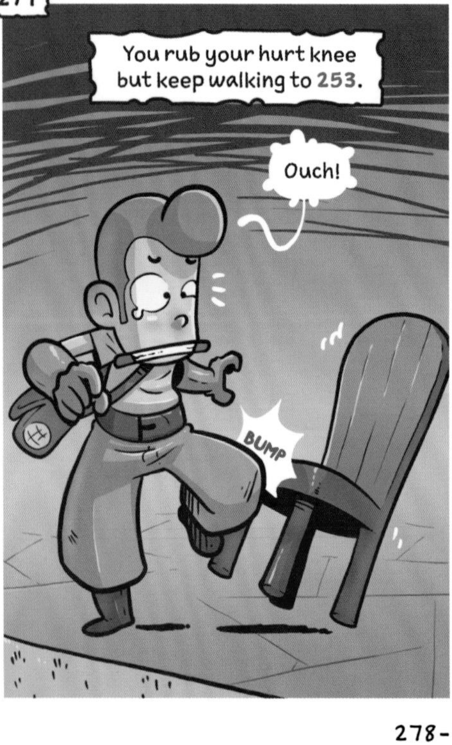
You rub your hurt knee but keep walking to 253.
Ouch!
BUMP

280

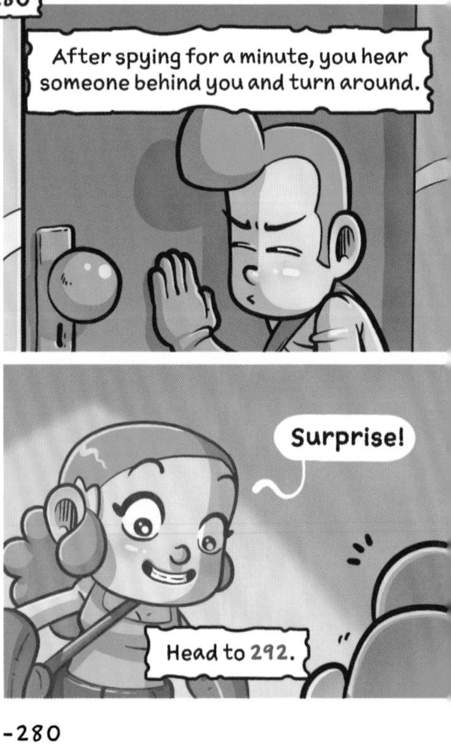
After spying for a minute, you hear someone behind you and turn around.
Surprise!
Head to 292.

281

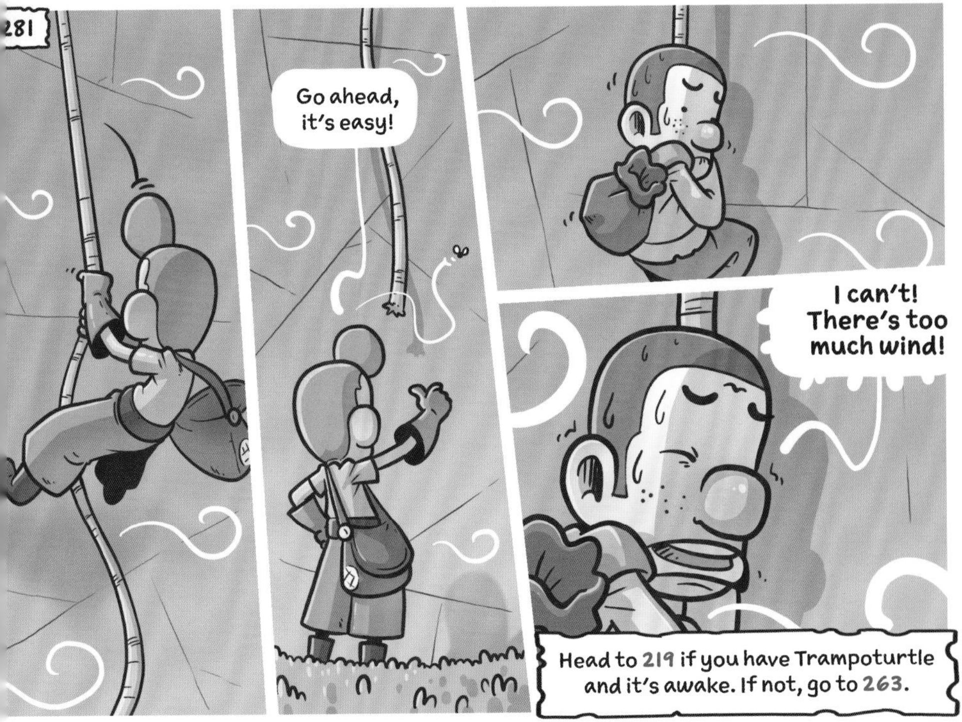
Go ahead, it's easy!
I can't! There's too much wind!
Head to 219 if you have Trampoturtle and it's awake. If not, go to 263.

282

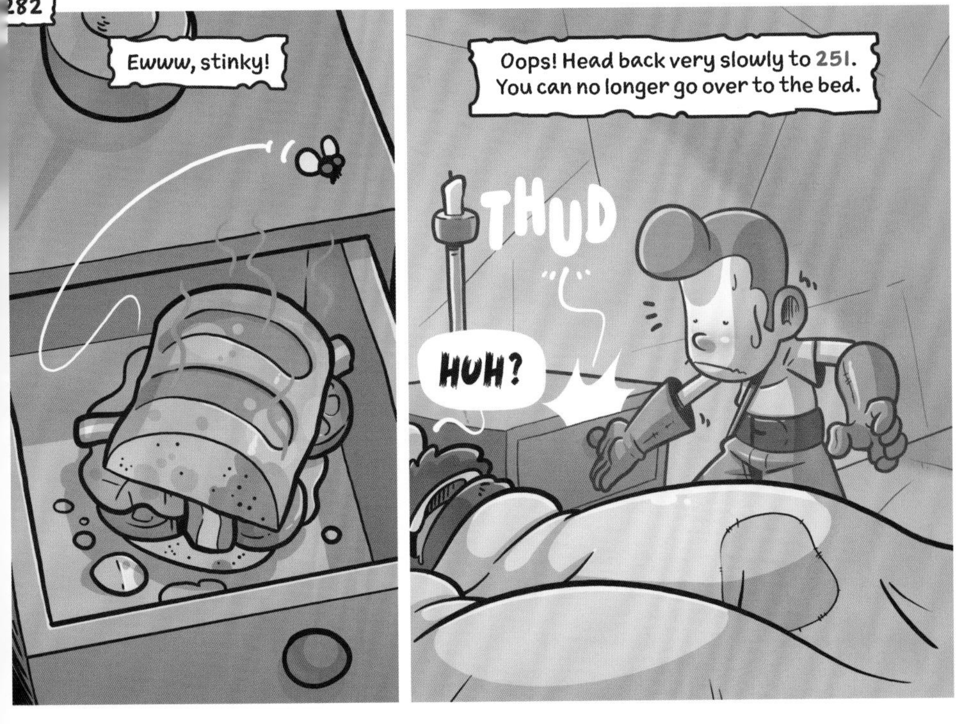
Ewww, stinky!
Oops! Head back very slowly to 251. You can no longer go over to the bed.
THUD
HUH?

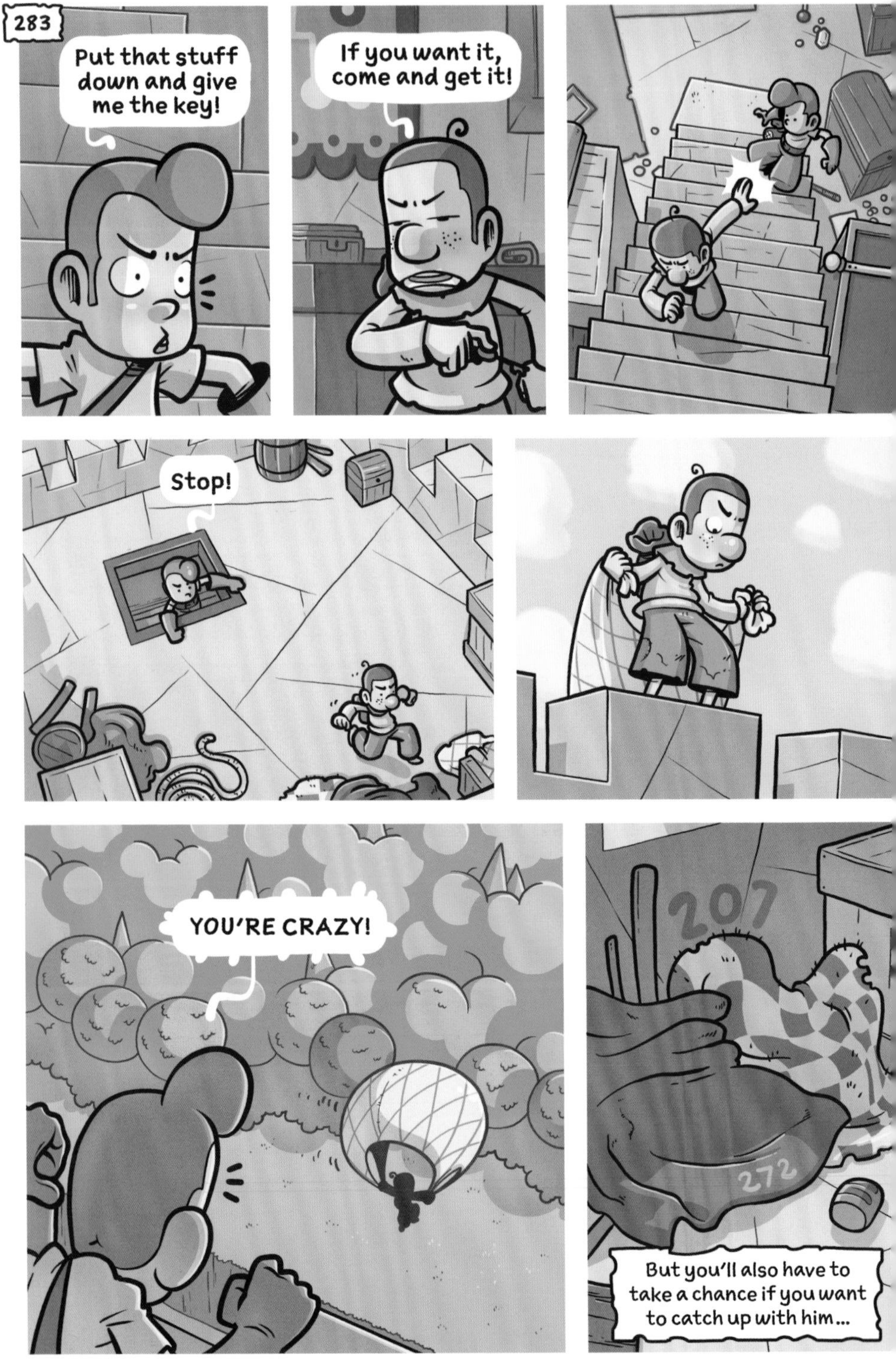
283
Put that stuff down and give me the key!
If you want it, come and get it!
Stop!
YOU'RE CRAZY!
207
272
But you'll also have to take a chance if you want to catch up with him...

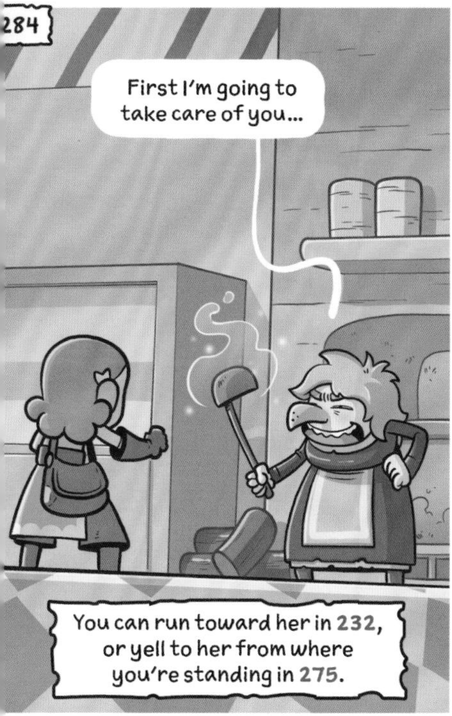
284
First I'm going to take care of you...
You can run toward her in 232, or yell to her from where you're standing in 275.

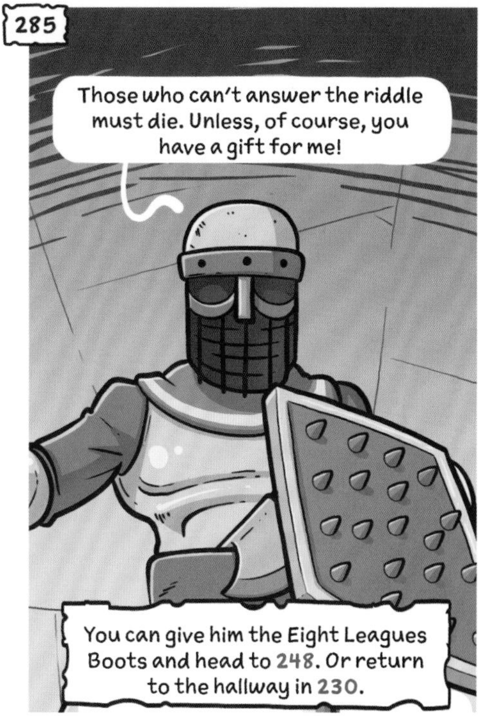
285
Those who can't answer the riddle must die. Unless, of course, you have a gift for me!
You can give him the Eight Leagues Boots and head to 248. Or return to the hallway in 230.

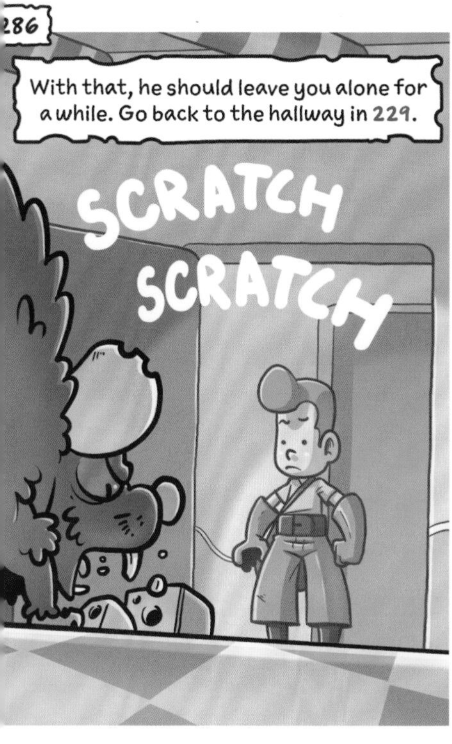
286
With that, he should leave you alone for a while. Go back to the hallway in 229.
SCRATCH
SCRATCH

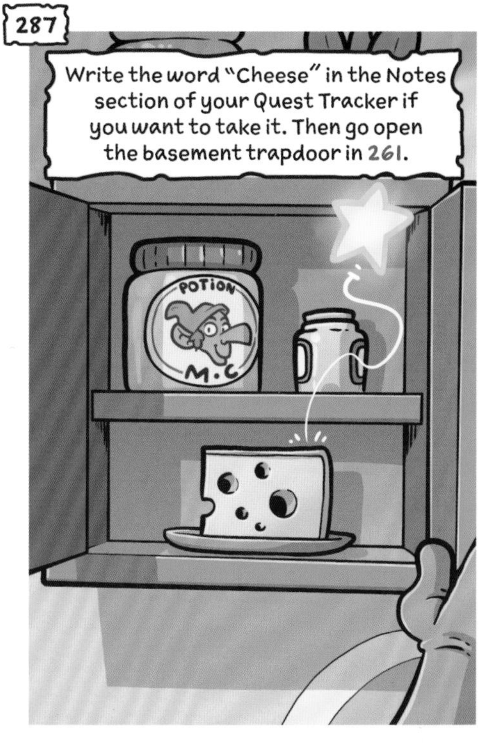
287
Write the word "Cheese" in the Notes section of your Quest Tracker if you want to take it. Then go open the basement trapdoor in 261.
POTION
M.C

288

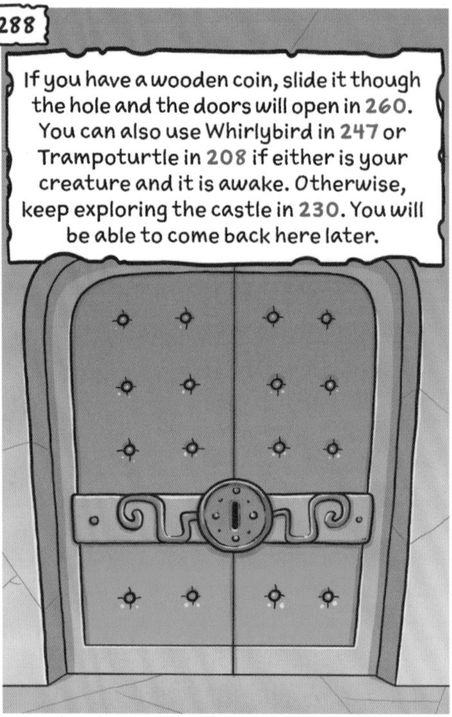
If you have a wooden coin, slide it though the hole and the doors will open in 260. You can also use Whirlybird in 247 or Trampoturtle in 208 if either is your creature and it is awake. Otherwise, keep exploring the castle in 230. You will be able to come back here later.

289

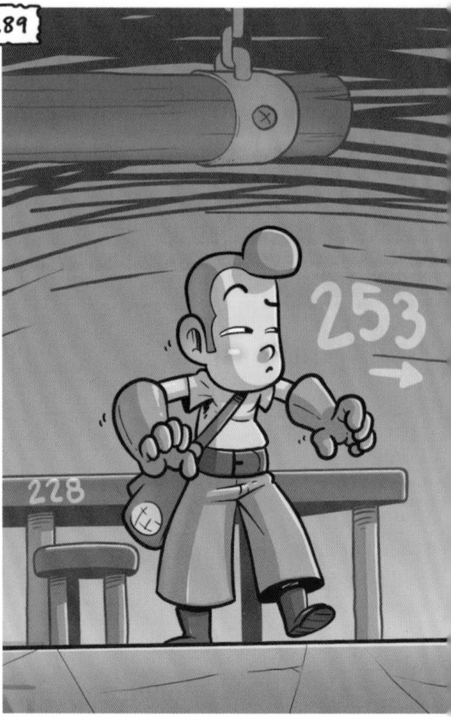
253
228

290

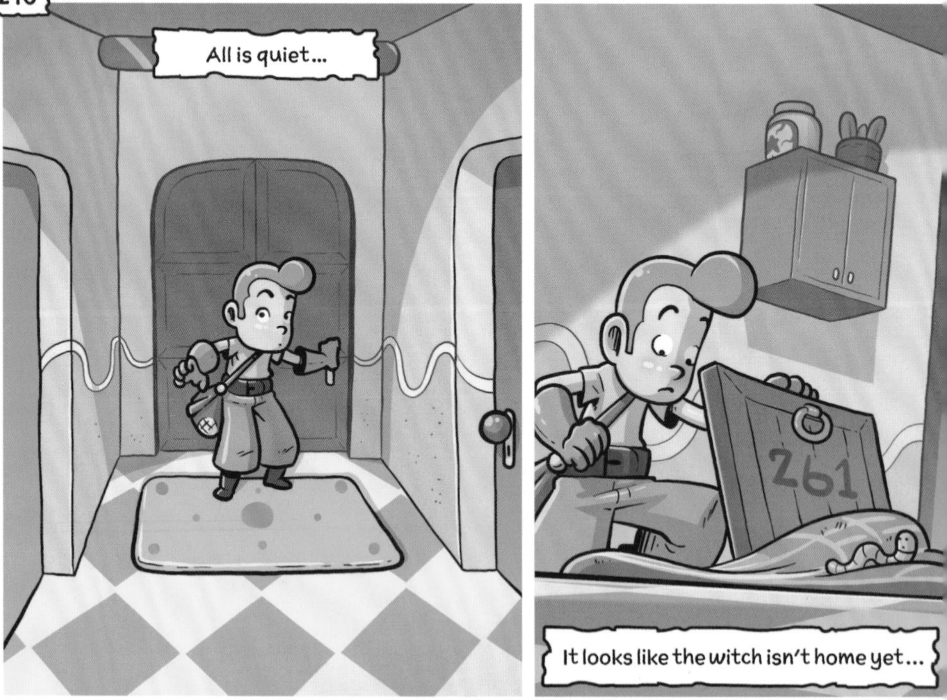
All is quiet...
261
It looks like the witch isn't home yet...

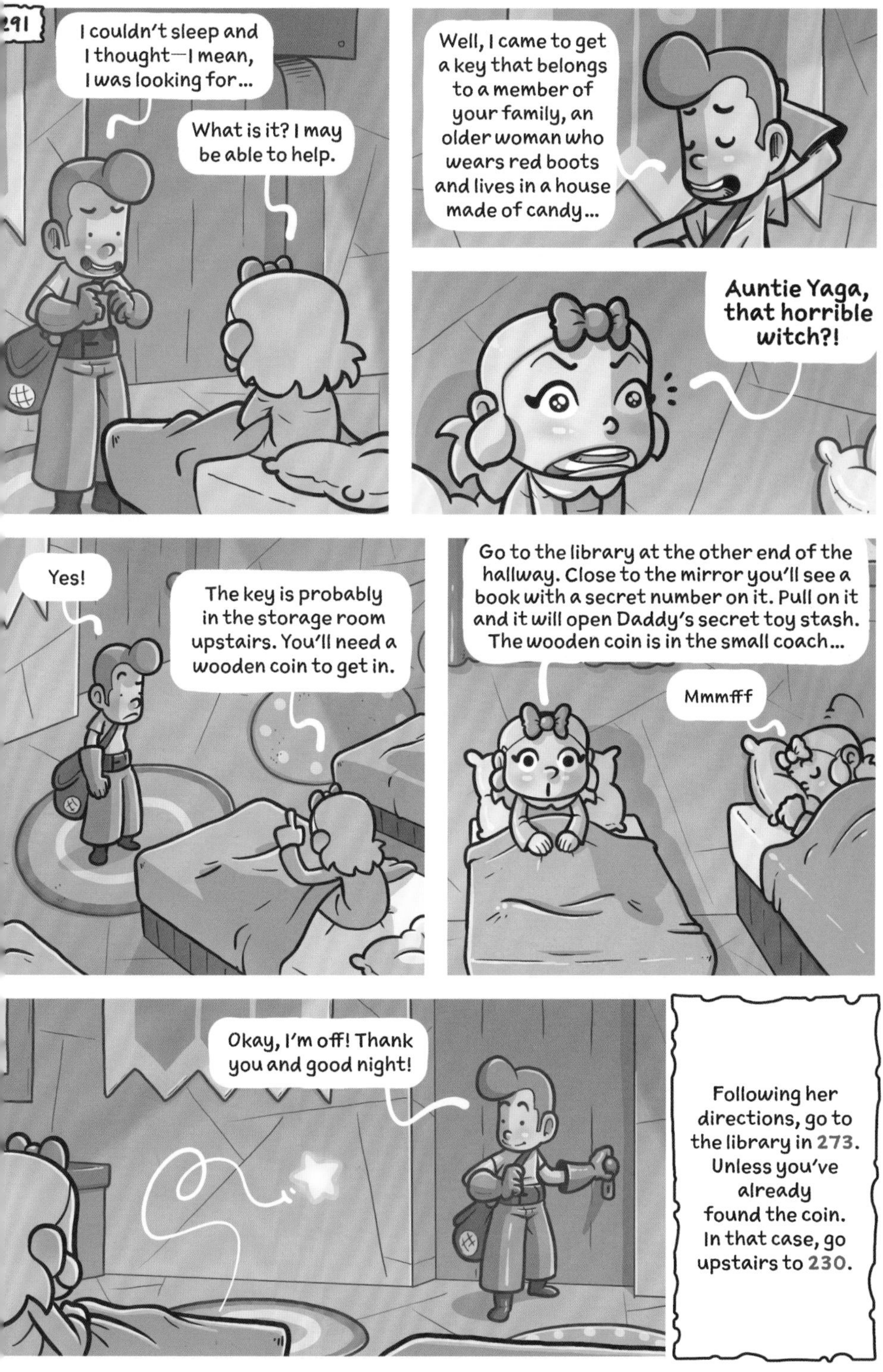
291
I couldn't sleep and I thought—I mean, I was looking for...
What is it? I may be able to help.
Well, I came to get a key that belongs to a member of your family, an older woman who wears red boots and lives in a house made of candy...
Auntie Yaga, that horrible witch?!
Yes!
The key is probably in the storage room upstairs. You'll need a wooden coin to get in.
Go to the library at the other end of the hallway. Close to the mirror you'll see a book with a secret number on it. Pull on it and it will open Daddy's secret toy stash. The wooden coin is in the small coach...
Mmmfff
Okay, I'm off! Thank you and good night!
Following her directions, go to the library in 273. Unless you've already found the coin. In that case, go upstairs to 230.

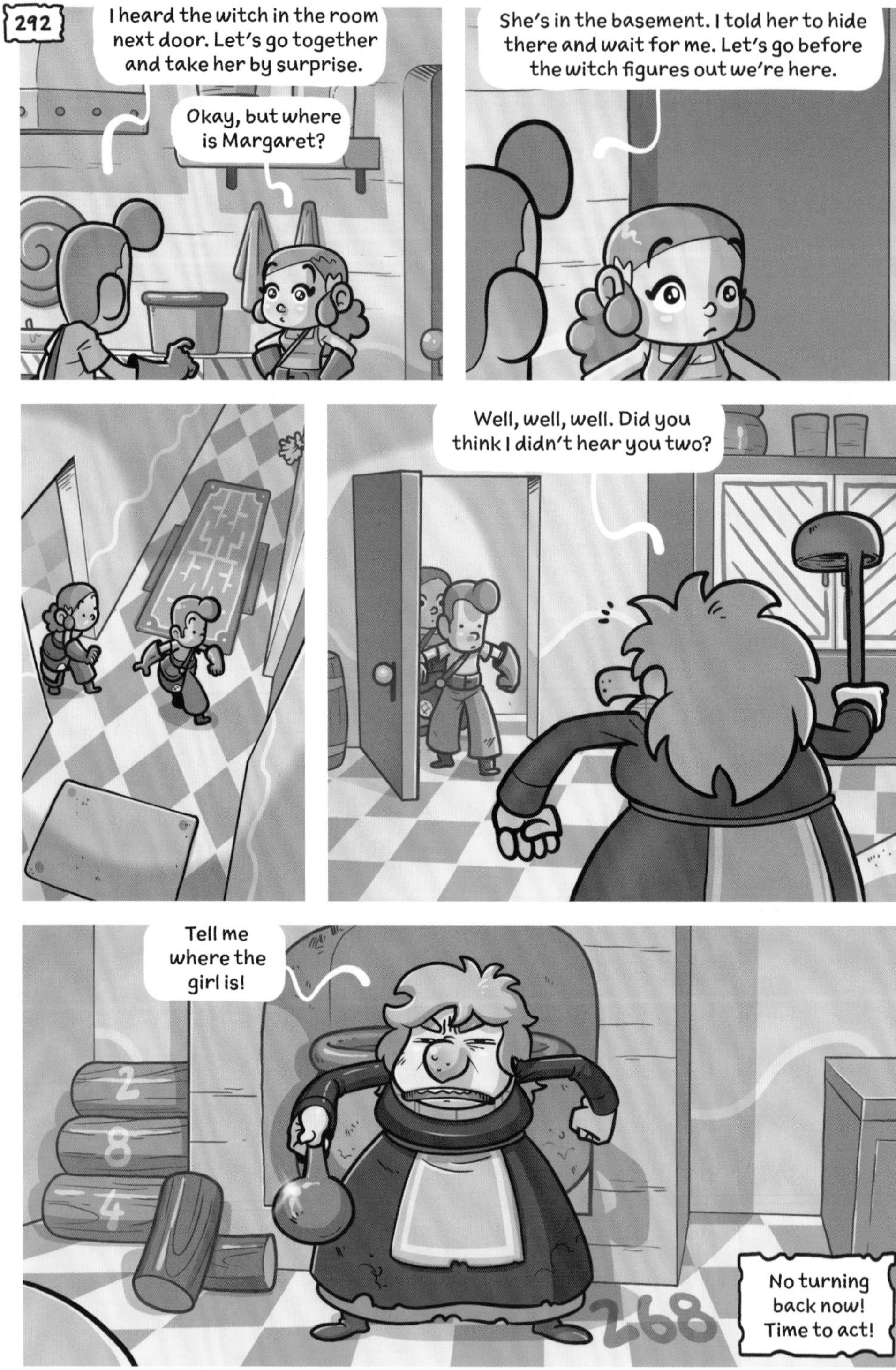
292
I heard the witch in the room next door. Let's go together and take her by surprise.
Okay, but where is Margaret?
She's in the basement. I told her to hide there and wait for me. Let's go before the witch figures out we're here.
Well, well, well. Did you think I didn't hear you two?
Tell me where the girl is!
2
8
4
268
No turning back now! Time to act!

293

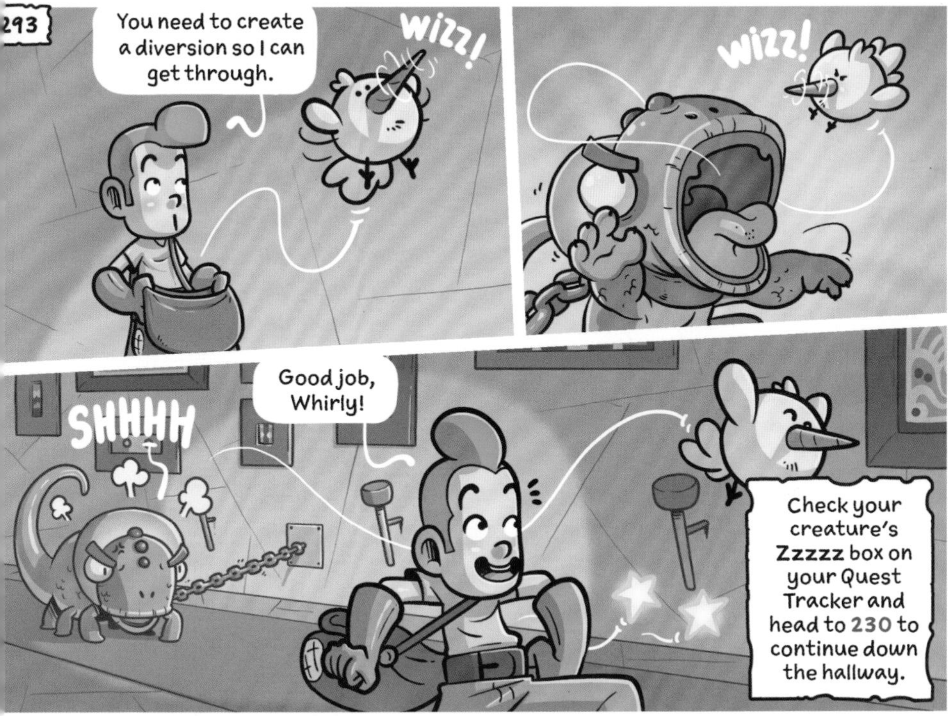
You need to create a diversion so I can get through.
WIZZ!
WIZZ!
SHHHH
Good job, Whirly!
Check your creature's **Zzzzz** box on your Quest Tracker and head to 230 to continue down the hallway.

294

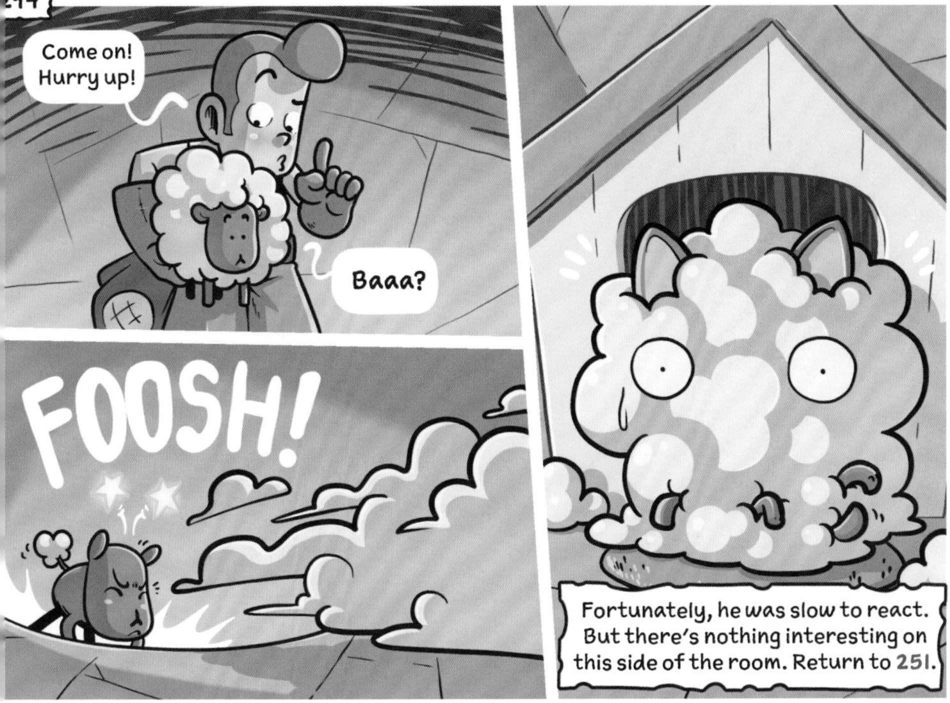
Come on! Hurry up!
Baaa?
FOOSH!
Fortunately, he was slow to react. But there's nothing interesting on this side of the room. Return to 251.

295

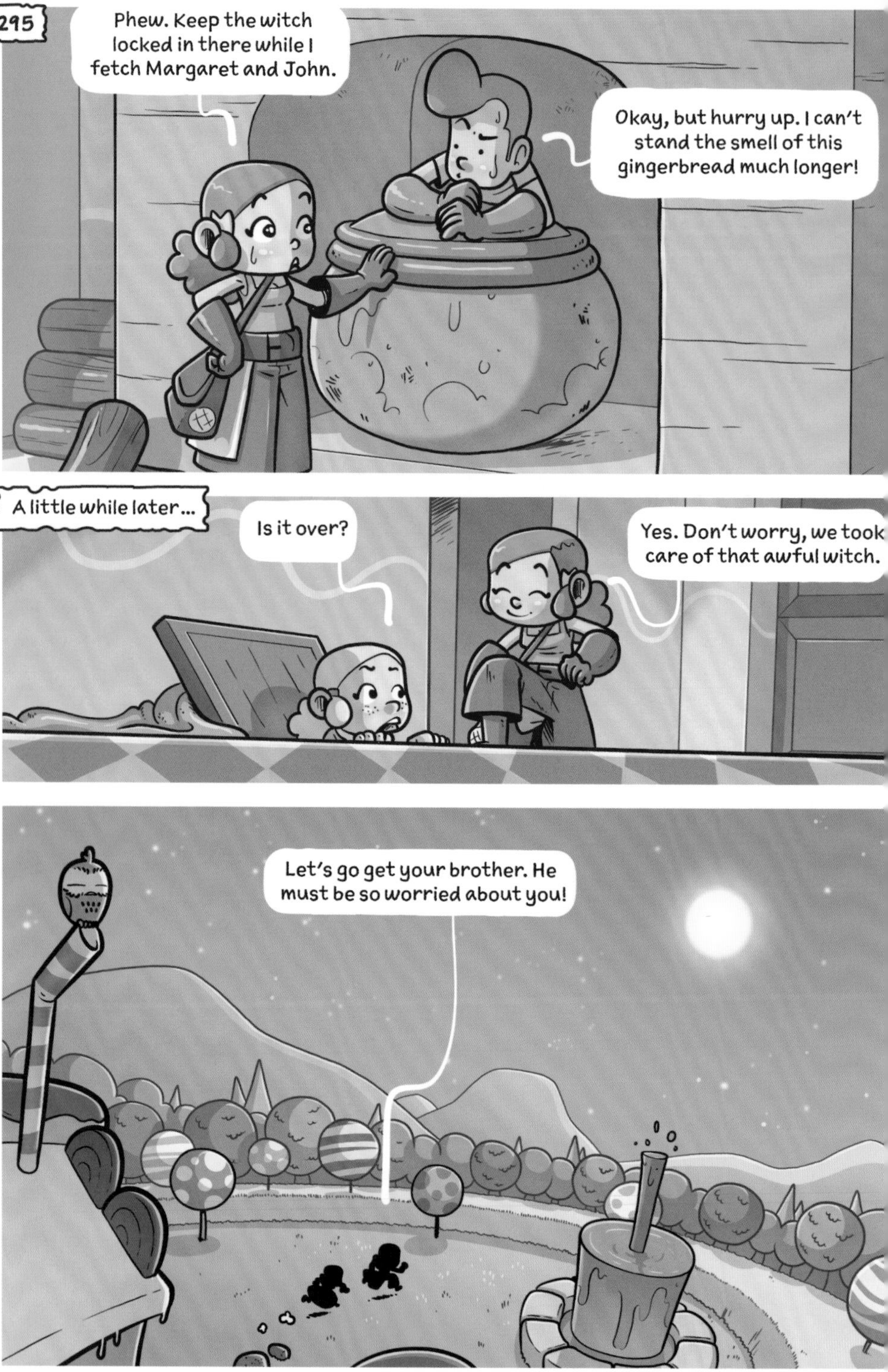
Phew. Keep the witch locked in there while I fetch Margaret and John.
Okay, but hurry up. I can't stand the smell of this gingerbread much longer!
A little while later...
Is it over?
Yes. Don't worry, we took care of that awful witch.
Let's go get your brother. He must be so worried about you!

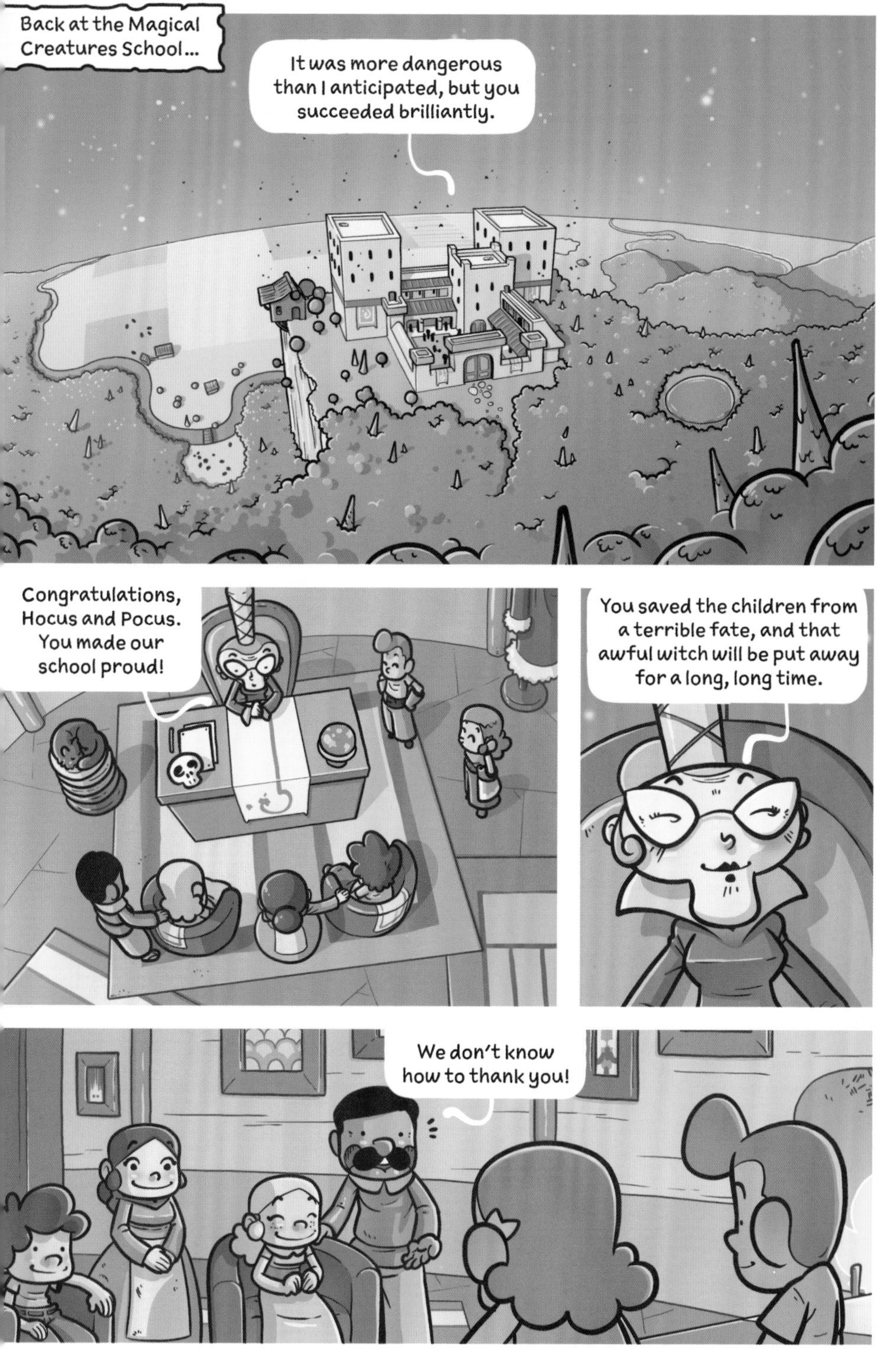
Back at the Magical Creatures School...
It was more dangerous than I anticipated, but you succeeded brilliantly.
Congratulations, Hocus and Pocus. You made our school proud!
You saved the children from a terrible fate, and that awful witch will be put away for a long, long time.
We don't know how to thank you!

I think I know how...

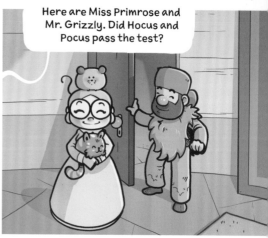

Here are Miss Primrose and Mr. Grizzly. Did Hocus and Pocus pass the test?

Impressively so! These two are very talented.

And they're not scared of anything. I've seen much less dangerous tests in the past...

In that case, all we need to do is organize the graduation ceremony for our two new Masters of Magical Creatures.

YAHOO!

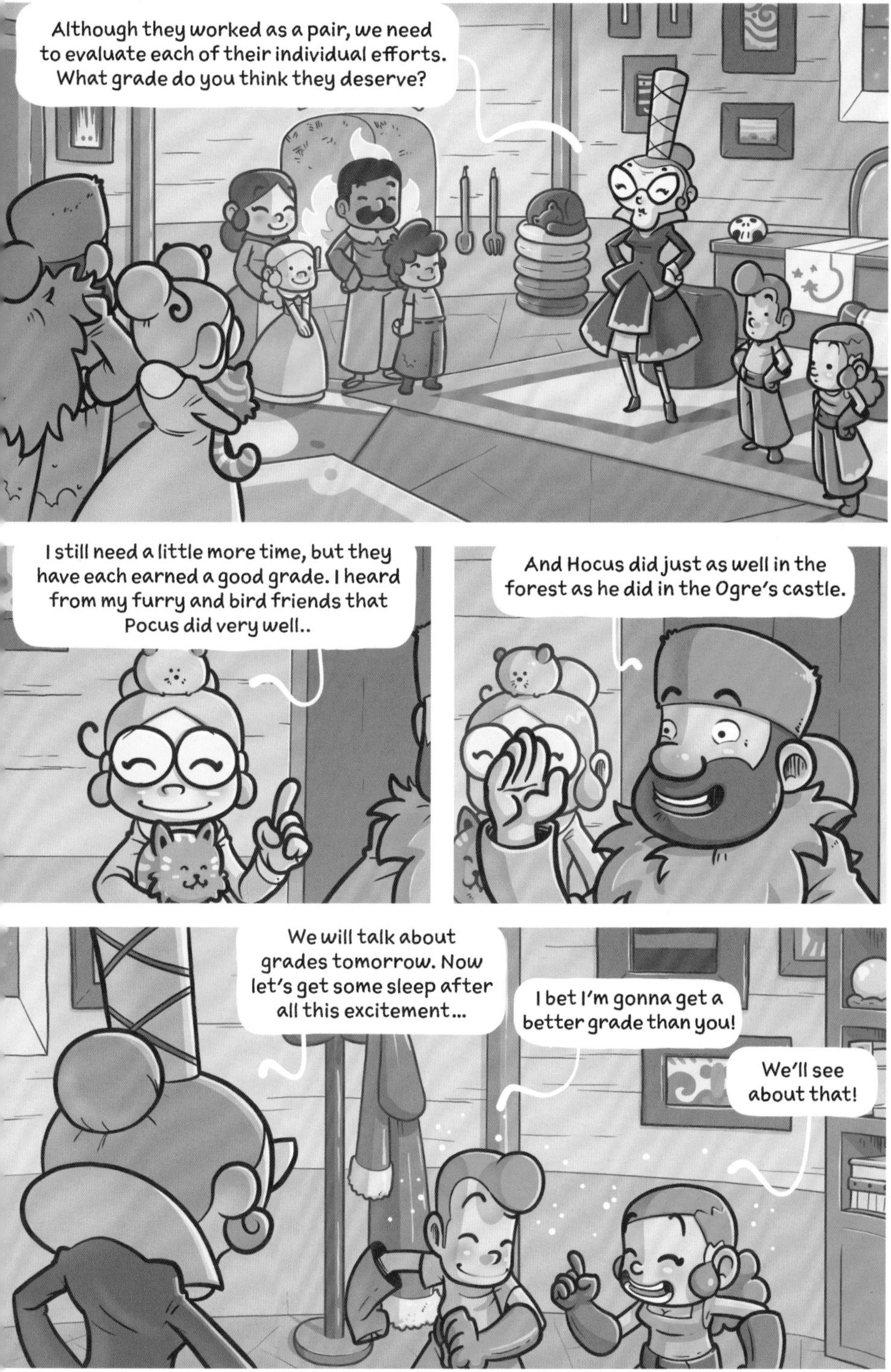
Although they worked as a pair, we need to evaluate each of their individual efforts. What grade do you think they deserve?
I still need a little more time, but they have each earned a good grade. I heard from my furry and bird friends that Pocus did very well..
And Hocus did just as well in the forest as he did in the Ogre's castle.
We will talk about grades tomorrow. Now let's get some sleep after all this excitement...
I bet I'm gonna get a better grade than you!
We'll see about that!

YOU DID IT!
YOU ARE NOW A MASTER OF THE MAGICAL CREATURES

Let's figure out your grade. Count the number of stars you found during your journey. Depending on whether you played **Hocus** or **Pocus**, your brother or sister will get a grade as well. To know their grade, throw the die, add 12 to the result, and see if you scored higher than your sibling. For example: You were Pocus. The die says 3, so Hocus had 15 stars (12 + 3). You win if you earned 16 stars or more.

If you didn't win, start over and play a different character or choose a different magical creature for your second trip!

Have a great adventure!